READER BEWARE

This novel MAY CONTAIN depictions of sex, assault, murder, blood, gore, horrors from the deep, multiple phobias, and other questionable acts.

A MESSAGE FROM APEX ACADEMY

Welcome to Apex Academy. Here we strive to give our students the best opportunities to survive in the ever changing world. While we understand that our methods may be questionable to some, but our results speak for themselves. If you choose to join us, your invitation will be found in the pages below. We hope that you enjoy and take advantage of everything this school of higher learning has to offer.

Sincerely,

C.C.

CHAPTER 1

The smell of sweat and the oil used to coat the hardwood floor filled the air of the gymnasium at St. Leon's high school, where the girls' volleyball team were in the final days of practice before the summer. One side of the court wore red jerseys and the other side wore blue. In the mist of blonde, brown, black ponytails, the sound of the girls' tennis shoes screeched on the floor, providing an odd sort of musical rhythm to which they all seemed to follow.

One of the blonde-haired girls in red served the ball across the net, only for it to be saved by another girl who extended her arms outward. The ball bounced off her extended forearms into the air as her knees dropped to the floor for support. A nearby teammate ran after it, jumped into the air, spiking it back across the net in retaliation. This was a process that continued to repeat itself on both sides of the net as the girls beat themselves up, trying to one-up each other. The sounds of their *uh* and *oh's* echoing off the walls of the near-empty gymnasium as the ball smashed against their skin adding to the song their efforts.

From the side door of the gymnasium stepped in a middle-aged man in a black blazer who began looking around, his brows furrowing as he scanned over the gym. Amid his gaze, he seemed to find who he was looking for. Ahead of him, sitting on the wooden bleachers was a brown-haired girl in jeans with a notebook in her hand. She wore a worn down flannel shirt with sleeves too long for her arms. Gazing down at the athletic girls on the floor, her face gave off a notion that she wasn't impressed.

"Hey there, Safia," said the man as he made his way up to her on the bleachers, his tight dress pants revealing his mismatched socks with every step upwards towards her.

"Hey, Mr. Dalub, what're you doing here?" asked the girl, her nature cheering up a bit at the appearance of the blazered man.

"Looking for you. I heard that you were here. I wanted to talk to you about going to college."

Safia smiled back. "Don't worry, I already discussed it with my mom. She agreed on me going to Richmond community college in the fall. I promised that I'd be able to take classes online and help in our diner."

The coach's whistle blew as the blue team scored another point, and Safia marked down a line on her paper.

"Oh, really? It seems I was worried for nothing," said Mr. Dalub as he stretched out on the bleachers, almost slipping down before he caught himself. "Oh! Dang thing, did they just polish these?"

"Careful now," said Safia. "I'm not sure you'd survive

another fall."

"Hey, I'm still young enough that I can survive a small tumble."

"You sure about that? You've been moving slower since you fell in the hallway that day," said Safia as the girls' team coach blew her whistle again. She marked another line for the red team.

"Hey, I'm still recovering. The janitor forgot to put up the caution sign when he was mopping. And it's not like I'm the only one who fell. I was dragged down when Brandon grabbed onto me. He was the one that fell. I was just collateral damage." Mr. Dalub placed his hands behind his back and extended his chest until an audible popping sound could be heard.

"That was pretty funny," Safia giggled, looking up at the lights. "You might wanna get the school to give you hazard pay then, if you're going to start having back problems at your age."

"Hey, don't act as if you're all perfect. I remember when you were Safia the trouble maker; always fighting with the boys, trying to protect the other girls from bullies," said Mr. Dalub with a chuckle as he looked up. "The other kids saw your mother so often that they thought she was another teacher."

"I just don't like bullies."

"I don't think anyone does. I don't even think bullies like themselves. But having those meetings with your mother was never fun. Although I do see where you get your ways from. Both of you are quite demanding women. Your father must have had it rough."

Safia giggled, "My dad, he's used to mom and me. But I remember your face during all those parent teacher meetings. It looked like you just wanted to be anywhere else."

"Well, I'm happy you found it funny. I sure didn't," said Mr. Dalub as he turned back to Safia waving a finger at her.

"Just try not to keep playing the hero after you graduate. Your knack for getting into trouble won't always work out so well in the real world?"

"The real world? Really?" said Safia, looking at Mr. Dalub with twisted lips and a cynical expression on her face. "That's the term you're going to use?"

"What? Is that term too old now? We'll either way, you'll see soon enough. The life of an adult is probably far more depressing than you realize. Especially the part about paying bills and taxes. Those are the worst," said Mr. Dalub as he gazed back down towards the girls playing volleyball just at the moment the blue team scored another point. "If you like volleyball so much, I don't understand why you didn't play. Maybe you could have gotten some type of scholarship for it. You've got the physique for it; slim, got good arms, probably could have gotten something out of it."

"What? Have you been checking me out, Mr. Dalub?" asked Safia with a smirk as she marked another check for the blue team in her notebook. "And here I thought I could trust you with my innocence. Although since I'm graduating, it might be okay now." Safia raised a brow at her teacher.

"Hey don't start that with me. You know what I mean. The last thing I need is for rumors to start about me showing interest in my students."

"Former student," said Safia with a giggle. "And I don't think Mr. Frohal had a problem with it."

"Okay, one, Mr. Frohal is now in the custody of the state, awaiting trial. Two, I prefer to date women my own age, so if you've got an auntie with a love for old math teachers. Then give her my number. It's in the graduation book this year."

"Sorry, no aunties for you, unless you're going to be in Cuba anytime soon," said Safia, genuinely enjoying the witty banter as she twiddled the pen between her fingers.

"So tell me, why did you never try out?" asked Mr. Dalub, steering the conversation back to more wholesome topics.

"I don't like volleyball, exactly. It's just that my brother and I make bets for the chores at home based on the games we watch."

"What? Yago? And how does that work out?"

"About as well as you'd guess," said Safia with a sigh as she laid the pen down between the pages of her notebook.

"Yeah, I bet. That boy's too smart for his own good. His mouth always gets him into trouble."

"You say that, but he's the one looking at a full scholarship, not me."

"Then why play against him if you don't win?"

"He's my brother, and he's an ass. The few times that I do beat him, makes it all worth it."

"Ah yes, the classic case of sibling rivalry," said Mr. Dalub, leaning back against the bleachers, taking a breath, remembering his own youth. "That sounds like you've got quite the grudge there, Miss Famosa."

"Yes, I do, and it's gonna last until he admits I'm better than him."

"Well," said Mr. Dalub, leaning forward and standing up, rubbing at his knees. "By the sounds of things, it seems like you have a long wait. So, I wish you luck. I'm going to check on the other graduates. Some of them may actually still need my guidance. Best of luck to you, Miss Famosa." He then made his way down the steps, being sure to be careful on his way down, and walked towards the exit as the blue team scored another point. The sound of the whistle blew once more across the gymnasium.

"Alright girls, hit the showers. That'll be the end of it today," said the coach as the girls rounded up and headed back towards the locker room.

Safia marked down another line in her notebook for the blue team.

"Damn," she said as she stood up, walking down the bleachers towards the exit of the gymnasium. *How does he always know this stuff? He's always been the lucky one.*

Fresh spring air replaced the musty gym atmosphere the moment she stepped through the doors. The air was chilly per usual as school buses littered the front of the campus downhill from her. As the last bell of the day sounded, it didn't take long before a flood of people exited from every door of the school as if they had been freed from captivity. A motley crew of colored hair, backpacks, and jackets made their way towards the circular roadway ahead of her.

And it all finally ends. Off to a life of serving tables and having old men mistakenly touch my butt. Safia gazed out at the students before rubbing at her face to clear her mind, then making her way down into the mass of people to join them in loading up on the bus.

This would be the last day she would have to worry about being pushed, shoved, and squeezed while trying to make her way onto the bus, and for that she was thankful. Eventually, after fighting her way through the crowd, she made her way up the steps and into the cabin. Making her way forward down the aisle of worn fake leather love seats, she ended up taking a place in the middle of the bus. The cheap fabric was torn, cut, duct-taped, and cut again through the duct-tape.

Goodbye duct-tape seats. I shall never see you again.

She turned to look out the window, but the glass was foggy with the chill of the weather. It gave the world outside a blurry image, the student's faces looking more like moving dolls. Their teenage facial features were stripped away by the dew on the glass, giving them the look of fleshed skin tone mannequins that move of their own free will.

"What's up, Safia? You stopping by for the party this weekend?" asked a boy in a green sweater as he swung around in the seat behind her, his arms dangling over the back of the seat as he leaned forward, looking into her face.

"David, when do I ever go to those parties?"

"Since whenever I beg you and nag you, till you give in. You are my little alligator after all."

"You know I still hate that nickname. And that was only one time and I still regret doing it," she said as the bus pulled off, out of the school's grounds, giving her the final view of the dreaded place that they called a learning facility for the last four years of her life.

"Oh please, oh please pretty sugar momma dumpling special snowflake," said the boy, pouting and sticking out his bottom lip, making it quiver exaggeratedly as he stared at her.

Safia laughed, shaking her head. "Stop being a dumbass. You know I help my mother at the diner after school. So I don't have time."

"Safia, the good girl. Well, tell your mom that I said hello."

"Aren't guys supposed to distance themselves from their female friends after they get girlfriends?"

"Hey now, If I did that, who would you have to talk to? There's more than just your books, you know."

"And Sara doesn't mind you chasing behind me, even though we used to date?"

"Who's chasing?" said the boy in protest, shaking his head. "I'm just having a wonderful conversation with a friend that I occasionally used to sleep with from time to time."

Safia raised a brow.

"Okay, so I might have left that part out. And I'd appreciate it if you did the same. Now come on, cheer up. This is our last day on the banana bus. Let's talk about our fond memories together at St. Leon's. The school of the damned."

"How about, let's not? Have you picked a college yet?"

"Yeah, either I'll go somewhere or somewhere else. It was kinda hard to decide, but I'm sure it'll come to me sooner or later."

"Must be nice having options," said Safia, looking down at the floor of the bus.

"Your mom still asking you to help out at the diner?"

asked David, his tone changing from jovial to more sincere. "I thought you might have found a way out of it by now."

"Yeah, I promised I would. So I guess that's my fate, serving tables until I'm old and grey."

"Hey, don't worry. If you're not outta there by the time I finish college, then I'll swoop in like Superman and marry you. Whisking you off your feet to an exotic land," he said, placing his hands on Safia's shoulders.

Accepting the comfort of his touch, Safia still frowned at him with narrowed eyes. "And how does Sara feel about those plans? You keep saying things like that and you're going to end up in trouble."

"We've already decided to break up," said the boy, removing his hands as he placed them under his chin and folded his arms on the back of the seat. "She's gonna be headed off to California for college. And long-distance relationships aren't gonna work, not for me. I don't think any relationship survives hot beaches and alcohol."

"Nice to know I'm your number two," said Safia with a roll of her eyes. "You sure know how to talk to a girl.

"Number three, actually."

"Then who's two?"

"Marlena Palona."

"The porn star?"

"Correction," David, raising a finger in protest to her statement. "The Cuban porn star. I started watching her after we started dating. You inspired me and I needed to know what you Cuban ladies liked."

"It's Cuban and African. But it's nice to know I've gotten you so interested in my culture, you pervert."

"Now if only I could get you to start calling me Papi," said David before he was solidly whacked in the face with Safia's notebook.

"Stick to jacking off to your porn," said Safia as the bus stopped and she stood up, exiting her seat. "I'll tell Ma, you said hello." She then walked forward, but turned around at the door, giving a slight smirk to her ex-boyfriend. She did have to admit that talking to him, even though the conversation was stupid, it did make her feel a bit better.

He's such a dumbass.

Stepping down onto the concrete, the noise of the city filled her ears as cars honked their horns and people chatted away on their phones. Ahead and behind her was the housing district of a poor-looking neighborhood. Stone buildings, chalked sidewalks, children running the streets, and in the middle of it all, on a street corner where the signs had long since been taken down, stood a small diner with the name *Famosa's* written across the top.

Safia walked into the diner, spotting patrons in their chairs. The sight of the tiled gray floor and bar stools were an everyday sight for her as smiles and familiarity cascaded through the building as the TV blasted news anchors spouting the latest sports talk of the day. The many windows of the diner showed the thousands of people who would walk by outside on their way to wherever they were going. From men and women in business suits to the homeless people who often would be slumped against a concrete building nearby, it was all things she had grown accustomed to throughout the years. Coming down the steps of the diner from her family's home up above, she'd seen so much.

"Hey, Safia. How ya doing kiddo? Enjoyed your last day at school?" said an aged man with gray in his bread in a brown flat cap.

"Hey, Mr. Garcia. That depends. I slept through most of it," said Safia, as she walked by, the smell of the roasted coffee in the man's hand coming across her nose, mixing in smells of the diner.

"That sounds like Hector. Ya old man never was one for schooling. But at least ya made it farther than he did. He never even graduated."

"Hey, I think I did alright for myself," said a wavy-haired man with a thick mustache as he came down the steps wearing an apron. "But you, Jimmie, how far did you make it? Oh, that's right. You never went to school. Just started working the moment you were born." The man turned and smiled at Safia, "Hey, honey, welcome back."

"Hey Papa, you alright?"

"Just fine. Hey, grab an apron and serve a few tables for me before you head upstairs."

"Alright," said Safia, reaching across the counter to be greeted by the delicious smell of warm soup and burgers. "Hey, Martin," she said to another man behind the counter who also wore a dirty apron as he flipped over some eggs that were frying in front of him.

"What's up, Safia?" asked the man behind the counter as he began sprinkling some chopped onions on the grill. "Can you take number one to Maria and number twelve to Alvarez?"

"Sure thing. Just slide them up," said Safia as she walked over to the side of the counter and grabbed an apron that was hanging from a hook on the wall.

Martin then slid two warm plates of food across the counter. One was a simple fried ham sandwich and the other were some handmade empanadas.

Tying the apron around her waist, Safia reached back up for the plates, grabbing one in each hand and spun around, walking down the aisle of the restaurant to greet more patrons. Her smile was returned with well wishes as she spoke to the diners patrons as she passed their tables.

"Here ya go, Miss. Solana," said Safia as she placed one of the plates down in front of a mature woman in a blue two-piece suit who was looking down at her phone while sipping on a cup of tea.

"Thank you, dear. Hey, did you hear about this?" asked the woman, showing her phone to Safia.

"No, what happened?"

"Says the authorities made some big drug bust down in Florida. They even managed to get a few rappers and politicians wrapped up in this mess."

"They're always catching drugs down there. I wonder why it always happens in Florida."

"Don't know, but it's a big one this time. Apparently, the mayor down there is even making a fuss about it. Says they found like two hundred and fifty million in drugs on the boat."

"They can keep the drugs," said Mr. Famosa from behind the counter, catching wind of their conversation. "But it'd be nice if someone would just give me some of that money."

"Call me if you need anything Miss Solana, I'mma take this to Mr. Alvarez," said Safia as walked off toward the diner's end to see a man in a suit playing chess with an older man in the back booth. "Here ya go, Mr. Alvarez," she said as she approached the booth.

"Oh, gracias, Safia," said the older man. Safia noticed his casual attire as he had on jeans and a jean jacket with a thick, grey beard.

"I see you're still dressing like you're from a denim commercial. Why don't you ever wear suits, you own your business, but we have never seen you in a suit."

Mr. Alvarez chuckled, "You know the suits, they make me feel all stuffy. Plus, I'm old now and stuck in my ways." He gestured to his companion ahead of him. "I shall leave the prim and proper suit wearing to the young ones such as my friend here."

"I appreciate the thought," said the younger man in the suit. "But it's not as if I enjoy it much either. But the school prefers that I look professional when recruiting."

Never seen him before, thought Safia as she gave the man a quick look over. He was attractive enough, and the suit did look good on him. *School? I wonder if he's a teacher. I guess if they want him to wear a suit, then it must be for some type of fancy private school or something.*

"Today was the last day of school for you, wasn't it, Safia? I should have gotten you something."

"Oh, don't worry. You're alright, Mr. Alvarez," said Safia as she placed the plate of empanadas down before him, looking over the chessboard. "Are you winning again?"

"Ha, hardly," said Alvarez. "It seems I may have met my match today."

Safia took a closer look over the board and smiled, "Maybe you have." She then noticed that underneath one of the discarded chess pieces was the stained picture of a man in a blue coat. The base of the piece was covering up his face so it made her curious. "Who's that, Mr. Alvarez? Your son?"

The man in the suit moved one of his pieces as Mr. Alvarez picked up the picture, looking it over as Safia caught a glimpse of the boy. He seemed fairly attractive also. He had a nice face and a nice muscular build with dark hair that stopped at his cheeks.

"Hardly. It's my grandson. I'm bringing him here," said Mr. Alvarez as he stared down at the board for a moment while rubbing at his beard before finally moving his bishop across the board. "Hey, you still dating that Presden boy? If not, maybe you'd want to give Freddo a chance. He's a good kid, just needs someone to show him around when he gets here."

"Hmm, I don't know," said Safia as she pressed her lips together, giving Mr. Alvarez a look of suspicion. "If he's as sneaky as his grandpa. I might need to stay away from him. I can't have two of you around me here. I think just one of you sneaky types is enough for me." Safia watched as the man in the suit moved another chess piece. It was a play that made Safia shake her head in disapproval.

Mr. Alvarez smiled. "He's not as smart as me. He gets into trouble, but he's a good kid. You never know, if you meet him, you two may hit it off." He leaned out of the booth, giving a quick glance around the diner before once again looking back up to Safia. "Where's Yago? I haven't seen him all day."

Safia wagged her finger at Mr. Alvarez, scoldingly, "You both have been spending a lot of time together lately. Now, don't you go trying to corrupt my brother with your sneaky old man ways. He's already more than enough of a pain in my ass without you teaching him your bad habits."

"Safia," said Mr. Alvarez, placing his hand over his chest in mock offence. "You wound me. I am merely imparting the years of my wisdom on the boy. It will surely benefit him as he grows into manhood."

"Mmhmm," moaned Safia, with narrowed eyes not believing Mr. Alvarez's words, but then sighing in acceptance. "He's probably upstairs; I'll go check." She then turned to the man in the suit. "Oh, by the way, mister, I think you've lost."

"Huh," said the man, looking down at the board. "What do you mean?"

"You opened up your king, and it can't move straight because of the queen there and the bishop right there," said Safia as she placed her hand over Mr. Alvarez's queen piece, rocking it back and forth on the tip of her finger. "And all Mr. Alvarez has to do is move his rook forward and block him. Then you won't be able to take it with your king because then you'd be in the way of his bishop."

The man frowned at Safia before looking down at the board again. "Ah, fuck. You tricky old bastard," said the man with a chuckle.

"Smart girl," said Mr. Alvarez. "You saw that faster than usual."

"Don't worry, mister. He's beaten everybody here at least once. He used to make me and my brother play with him every day after school. And you can cancel that date with your grandson, Mr. Alvarez. I really don't think I can handle two of you coming in here every day."

Safia then patted Mr. Alvarez on the shoulder and walked off back to the counter, grabbing more empty plates from vacant booths on her. She gladly took the tips that were left for her on the counter tops, tucking them into her pocket.

Over an hour passed in the diner as Safia served the customers of Famosa's before she was able to take off her apron. Sweat dripped down the side of her arms as the smell of meats, vegetables, and bread were soaked into her clothing. She balled up the apron, pressing it up against her forehead to dry her face.

"Alright, Papa, I'mma head upstairs and wash off."

"Alright, honey. Tell Yago to come down here for a moment. I need him to change the shipment of fish to Wednesday."

"Okay," said Safia as she hopped up the stairs to the back of the diner. Above was a door to the second story of the building. Opening it, she found her brother sitting in front of a TV with a notepad before his eyes, along with paperwork scattered throughout the table. Their housing wasn't anything special. A mixture of hand-me-down mixed colored furniture, some of which was older than her. She'd often hear her father referring to it as 'vintage.'

"Yago, Papa says to come downstairs; he wants you to change a shipment or something."

"Alright, I'll go down in a second. Hey, you seen this drug bust in Florida?"

"Yeah, Maria told me about it," answered Safia as she took off her shoes. "What's so important about it? Doesn't drug stuff happen all the time down there?"

"Yeah, but a lot of the people aboard were illegals. A lot of Cubans are going to be sent back."

"I didn't know you were such a hero of our people."

"I'm just keeping up on the news."

"Although, judging from that hair," Safia leaned over the couch and started tussling Yago's hair. "I think you got mama's African more than you got papa's Cuban."

Yago knocked her hand away. "And I got pop's Spanish, while your Spanish is terrible."

"I can speak Spanish well enough. Besides, it's not like

all Spanish is the same."

"You're right. There's good Spanish and then there's whatever the hell you try to speak, also known as Saffy Spanish," said Yago with a smile on his face as he picked up some of the papers on the coffee table.

"Oh, shut up. And what are you looking at, anyway?"

"Invoices. Pops is trying to keep costs low. So that's probably why he was trying to move the shipment back for the stuff that's not selling much."

"Shouldn't he be doing this?"

"I'm better at it than him. I pay more attention to the details, which you need to start doing, since you always forget stuff so easily."

"I do not forget stuff easily. I just don't remember the unimportant stuff," said Safia, proudly.

"Uh-huh. Then tell me, who won the game today?"

"It was a tie," said Safia, looking away.

"You're a terrible liar," as he extended his hand out to her. "You owe me five dollars. Pay up."

"How did you even know that they would lose, anyway?" asked Safia as reached into her pocket, pulling out some of the one-dollar bills from the tips she had received, placing them in Yago's hand.

"You didn't see Kelly out on the red team, did you?" asked Yago, taking the money. "That's because her father was caught fucking Ms. Angela, the algebra teacher, yesterday. And since she's the star of the team, I figured she didn't not want to be bothered with people making fun of her on the last day of school."

"What? Really? I didn't hear anything about that," said Safia, looking shocked.

"That's because you never pay attention to stuff like that. But I promise you all the girls on the team knew. That's why I figured she probably wasn't gonna show up today."

"You think too much. And I thought guys weren't supposed to care about gossip like this.. Why do you even know this stuff?"

"Why don't you? Aren't you a girl?"

"Not everyone's mind works like yours does. You ever thought of going outside or getting a girlfriend like normal people do?"

"You mean like you and David? You still never told me what happened between you two."

"Why? So you can use it against me, like Kelly. No way. And you better not ask David either, or I'll make you regret it. You keep me out of whatever man-crush on my ex-boyfriend?"

Yago shrugged. "Am I not allowed to look after my little sister?"

"I'm older than you."

"Only physically, but you're still years behind me in thinking."

"Oh, ha-ha, Mr. 'Scholarship waiting on me after I graduate.' At least, you've got it nice and easy, so you don't have to worry about what you're going to do after you graduate."

Yago smiled back and stood up. "Don't worry, I'll give you a job when I'm all rich and powerful. But I'm going to need you to start thinking and remembering stuff more if you're going to be my Vice President."

"Great, so you and David both plan to be my hero's," said Safia, rolling her eyes. "I'm flattered, but both of you seem to have trouble just taking care of yourselves. I don't need you dragging me down with you."

"Oh that's right, I needed to call David and ask him something," said Yago as he stood up, stretching out his arms. "Want me to invite him over. It's about time you two made up before he goes off to college."

"Just shut up and mind your own business," said Safia with a frown. "And why do you need to talk to him, anyway? I don't remember you two being that close."

"I need his help with some work and I figured he wouldn't mind, especially if he gets to come over and visit you again."

"Hey!" blurted out Safia. "Don't just use me to get him over here."

"Don't worry. I'm not using you to help myself," said Yago with a smirk as he walked towards the door. "I'm using him to help you. You just don't know it."

"Help me? How?"

"Well, you've been all mopey since you two broke up. I'm just trying to help save my foolish sister who's too stubborn to make up with her boyfriend."

"Who do you think you are? Some type of relationship guru?"

"Well, if one of us has to be. I think it should be me. I'm the most qualified. You'd just mess it up."

"Oh, ha-ha fake guru. You think you know better than me about my own life. That sounds like something a villain would say."

"Of course, I do. I mean, isn't that why I'm always—" A flying pillow from the sofa flew perfectly through the air striking Yago in the face before he was able to finish the sentence.

"Just go downstairs and see what Papa wants, you idiot. And Mr. Alvarez was asking about you again. He probably wants another game. So go and flaunt that ego of yours down there with him."

"Alright, alright, I'm going," said Yago with laughter as he shielded his face from two more flying pillows. He quickly opened the door to the downstairs diner and hurried out before Safia could launch another volley.

Annoyed by her little brother, Safia headed over, entering her room. *Stupid Yago and stupid David. They don't understand what I'm going through. They both get to run away and I'm going to be the one stuck here.*

Her room was the standard inner city affair. Brick walls that were painted white and green to add some flair to the otherwise reddish orange that they had been before. In her window was perched an old oscillating fan. Maybe not the prettiest thing, but it did its job, sending in a cool breeze that partly made its way across the room. On the floor sat two mattresses, one on top of the other. And across her bed lay an assortment of stuffed animals from her now ex-boyfriend David. Closing the door, she pulled off her school clothes and put on her favorite oversized shirt, laid in bed, grabbing one of the stuffed animals, a soft oversized alligator, pulling it close to her.

Maybe it was my fault. I shouldn't have asked David to do that. It probably was my fault. I thought he would like it. Shows what I know, guess I'm just weird, thought Safia as the cool wind from the fan blew over her skin, providing her with a calming feeling as her anxious mind dwelled over past events.

But just as her mind began to calm down, the sound of her phone vibrating took her out of her own thoughts as she rolled over on top of the stuffed creature, reaching forward grabbing her phone off of a basket. She placed her thumb on the home screen and began scrolling over the feed of media sites and alerts. Her friends were posting pictures of parties, graduation gifts, and random inspirational quotes from famous people. But the souring thing to her mood was the pictures of the acceptance letters on display from the people she'd known most of her life.

A flash feed appeared across the top of her phone. 'Photos from NEWS TEN. Pictures of the exciting drug bust in the south of Florida.'

Why not? Everyone else seems so interested.

She tapped on the image and swiped. Pictures of an orange cargo ship, a bunch of money, and people being loaded onto trucks scrolled by as she moved her finger across the screen. She paused for a moment, freezing on a man in a blue shirt. He seemed familiar to her; his eyes, his face; it was as if he was clear in her mind, but still somewhat distant.

He kinda looks like the picture Mr. Alvarez had of his grandson, she thought before shaking her head and tossing away the conclusion. *And so does a million other dark-haired boys around here.* She flicked her finger more through the pictures of the drug bust. Her brother's words echoing in the back of her mind. *'Think more?' And exactly what am I supposed to think about, huh? About how much my life sucks?*

"Ahh, no, this is ridiculous," said Safia, smushing the pillow against the stuffed alligator in frustration, trying not to dwell on her life.

After not being able to relax, Safia would soon find herself back into her pants as she crept downstairs, towards the diner's entrance as she peaked over around the corner to where Mr. Alvarez was before. The man in the suit was gone, and Yago was sitting down in the booth across from Mr. Alvarez.

What have they been talking about these last few days? I know they play their game from time to time, but lately they've been together almost every day. Maybe Mr. Alvarez is teaching—

"Safia, what're you doing peeking around the corner at your brother. You looking for a job too?"

"A job? What job?" asked Safia, coming back from her thoughts and looking to her father, confused.

"Mr. Alvarez said he has a job opening down at the shipping yard in one of his warehouses. Gonna give Yago a job there for the summer. With him helping out there and you helping out here, that'll help us catch up on some bills, and when we're clear, everything's gonna be smooth from now on."

"Yago's getting a job? Wait, he said you're letting him handle the books now?"

"Yeah, I am," said her father as he scratched the back of his head, looking unsure. "At first, I didn't want to, but he insisted, saying that he wanted to get a business degree when he went off to college. That he needed to learn the money, you know. So I sat him down and taught him everything I could. He's done a good job too. I swear you both make me so proud."

Safia continued to watch as Yago and Mr. Alvarez conversed. "Papa, how long have you known Mr. Alvarez?"

"Over twenty years now? He was there the day I married your mother. Even gave us his blessing, and some money. Why? Something wrong with Mr. Alvarez?"

"No, he's always been nice to us."

"Okay, well, your mother will be home soon. You can ask her more about him if you like."

"Alright then." She turned back one last time to see Yago and Mr. Alvarez beginning to set up the chess pieces on the board before she headed back upstairs to lay in her bed. *It's not like I don't think enough. Thinking too much makes you paranoid, anyway. He's the one who's always playing games like that. Of course he thinks too much. Spending time with Mr. Alvarez, playing those games would make anyone think like that.*

Continuing to flip through her phone as she rolled over in bed, her mind wandered off until a dark-skinned woman with a scarf walked through the door an hour or so later. She wore jeans and her hair was tied behind her head in an afro puff, similar to Yago's.

"Safia, is everything alright?" asked the woman as she stepped into her room.

"Hey Ma, yeah, everything's fine. Why?"

"Your father, he said you wanted to see me. Asking about Mr. Alvarez or something."

"Oh yeah, it's nothing. Just me thinking too much."

"Oh, okay then. I'm about to go and get dinner ready then," said her mother before stopping in the doorway and turning back to her. "Safia."

"Yes, Ma."

"You sure you're okay with not going to college? I mean, we can't afford no big college, but maybe a community college, so classes from time to time. You might want—"

"No, it's okay, I might go next year or something, but I wanna help you guys out around here for now."

Her mother patted her hands against the door frame, staring down at her daughter with a half-hearted smile as she struggled to keep her eyes focused on Safia. She then took a deep breath. "Okay... okay, baby. You want anything special for dinner, since you're all graduated and everything?"

"Nah, it's okay, Ma. Whatever's fine. I'm tired. I'm just gonna rest for a while."

Her mother nodded her head, her eyes beginning to water as she turned away and went back into their home. The sound on the TV played in the background as Safia laid back down on her bed, turning on her side, watching the spinning blades of the fan as continue move but never actually go anywhere.

CHAPTER 2

The next morning, Safia awoke to a cold room, having fallen asleep with the window open. The chill of the now cold air nipping at her exposed toes as she quickly bundled herself back inside the blanket. *Ah! I forgot to take the fan out of the window.* Exposing one leg out of her warm blanket, she kicked the fan out of the window, causing it to slide down, closing itself shut. Bringing her leg back inside, she shivered, and clenched at the fabric above her.

She would lay in bed for a while as the heat from the rest of the house slowly seeped into her room providing a bit of warmth to her environment. During which time, she began to smell the delicious aroma of baked bread, which seemed to be tempting her out of her warm safe haven. This scent was soon followed by the sound of her family's muffled voices from outside of her door, accompanied with the drumming of their footsteps as they made their way around the home.

And joining that drumming came the grumble of her stomach. *Fine, I'm getting up,* thought Safia as her hunger and curiosity won out. She rolled out of bed and stood up with the blanket still draped over her shoulders as if it were a cloak. But her exposed legs still felt the sting of her now semi-cold room, as all she was wearing was the shirt she slept in.

Pressing forward as the cold nipped at the skin beneath her cotton shelter, she opened the door to her room. The heat from outside blasting its way past her, flowing over her bare legs and face as if the room were breathing over her. Dropping the blanket to her feet, she kicked it back inside of her room before quickly closing the door, locking in the cold of her bedroom. The smell of freshly baked bread filled her nose completely, pulling her out of her drowsiness as she looked ahead to see Yago. He was sitting down in front of the TV once again, looking over the shop's finances.

"Why are you up so early?"

"And good morning to you, Saffy" said Yago, raising a hand without turning around to look at his sister. "We had to take care of a few things this morning. Did you sleep with the window open again?"

"Yeah, and now my room's a freezer."

"You're gonna catch a cold if you keep doing that."

Safia leaned over the couch and poked her brother on the side of the head. "Yes Ma, are you going to fix me breakfast too?"

"That's already being taken care of," said Yago, turning around to his sister as he knocked her hand away with a frown. "You're really going to stay dressed like that?"

"Like what? I'm always dressed like—"

"Oh, wow," said David, coming out from the kitchen holding a tray of cinnamon rolls. "You really know how to welcome a guy."

"What? David, what are you doing here?" asked Safia, holding down her shirt, covering her thighs as she began creeping back to her doorknob.

"Wait," said David, holding up the tray.

"What?" asked Safia with one hand on her door.

"Let me just say; I was wrong?"

"Wrong? About what?"

"Marlena Palona," said David, with a nod to her legs. "With your pink panties, T-shirt, and that wild hair; you are way better looking."

"*Oh, shut up, you big dummy,*" said Safia in Spanish, as she dashed back into her room.

"Oh, she spoke Spanish to me. I rarely hear the language of love from her," said David as he turned to Yago. "That was Spanish, right?"

"That was Saffy Spanish; it's hard to actually claim that it's real Spanish. But for you, I guess it's good enough."

"I love you too, Safia," shouted David so loud that she could hear him clearly through the walls.

"Shut up, go home," shouted Safia back at him, with her back pressed against the door.

"I can't. I'm helping Yago out today. We're gonna be moving packages for Mr. Alvarez. So you should get dressed and come out and eat some cinnamon rolls. They're still fresh."

Minutes later, Safia came out fully dressed, her hair in a ponytail, with a little bit of makeup and eyeliner on.

"Ah, I was hoping for a cuter outfit."

"Just shut up and gimme a roll," said Safia as she reached over, grabbing one from the tray and turning back towards her brother. "Now Yago, why is this intruder in our home?"

"Intruder? We've known each other since we were kids

doing those silly magic tricks, pulling fake rabbits out of hats, trying to pick the right card. We even dated for two years. At least give me some respect."

"Fine. The illegal immigrant in our home."

"Now that's just being petty."

Yago flashed some invoices between the two. "He's helping me move supplies from the meat plant to the fish market downtown. And he's driving the truck."

"Shouldn't you be planning for college instead of goofing off around here?" asked Safia, placing her hands on her hips.

"Classes don't start till fall. I'm trying to earn some money before I head off."

"And why are you even working for Mr. Alvarez, anyway?" asked Safia, turning to her brother. "You could just work here and make money."

"Mr. Alvarez and I made a deal, so I'm working for him. Plus, I don't like cooking or waiting tables."

Safia frowned. "It's not like I enjoy it either. Wait, what kind of deal?"

"The kind that gets us money. Why? You looking for some work too?"

"No, I'm good, thanks," said Safia as she turned towards David. "And doesn't your family have money? Why are you working with Yago?"

"Hey, don't treat me like I'm some spoiled rich kid. I've been working on and off since I started high school. I'll have you know I paid for our dates with my own money."

"Is that why we never went anywhere?"

"You know, some low blows are just uncalled for."

"Fine, I'm sorry. That was mean," said Safia in a soft voice, as she placed her hands together with a smile. "I did enjoy our dates. Even though they were cheap."

"Thank you. I accept your half-assed apology."

Safia shook her head, still with a smirk on her face, as she turned back to her brother. "Hey, Yago. Since you brought up Mr. Alvarez. Did you... did you see that picture Mr. Alvarez had with him yesterday while you were with him?"

"Nope, we just talked. What was in the picture?"

"He said it was his grandson and I think... you know what, never mind. It's not important." *I'm thinking too much. Keep this up Safia and you're going to end up just as paranoid as Yago is.*

"Nope, why? You're looking for a new boyfriend?"

"What, really?" asked David with a silly face. "At least wait till I'm at college before you run into the arms of another man."

"You're both idiots. Just forget I asked."

"That's fine, since it's time for us to go. We have to head down to Maskel's to pick up the meat truck," said Yago as he stood up and walked towards the door with David following behind him.

"Bye, my pink panty princess," said David as he reached the door. "Triple P."

"Just get out," said Safia as she picked up another pillow from the sofa, tossing it and whacking David on the back of his head as he left the room.

"Ahh." said David as the pillow struck him. "Your sister's abusive Yago."

"Yeah," said Yago, his voice trailing off as he and David made their way downstairs. "Her aim with those pillows is more accurate than you'd think it'd be."

Safia sighed, feeling tired after having to deal with the two boys, decided to head back into her room, and once again embrace her still slightly cold bed. As her face hit the plushy alligator on the way down, she found herself hard-pressed, trying to fight the urge to scream into the softness of the green animal replica.

Hours later, after the heat of the rest of the house permeated her room thoroughly, she lifted herself up from the bed once again. Getting dressed, Safia headed downstairs, where the diner was filled with the early morning crowd. TV's blasted the morning news as honks from nearby cars sounded into and throughout the area. Hitting her nostrils was the smell of waffles and coffee, the usual smell of a morning at Famosa's, and this morning was no different.

"Hey, honey," said her mother as she hit the bottom step. "Did you see David? He and Yago just left. He was hoping to see you."

"Yes, mother," said Safia with pursed lips. "He did see me. Too much of me."

"Good. David really is a nice boy. He's even helping Yago with his summer job. I didn't expect to see him this morning, though. Have you two already made up?" asked her mother with a slight smile across her lips.

"No," said Safia in protest. "And stop asking about that. What about Yago, he said they were transferring meat for Mr. Alvarez. Does he own a meat company?"

"Mr Alvarez? No, but he handles some of the shipping stuff for the city, I think. Yago said they were just taking one of his trucks downtown and dropping it off down there. So maybe it's just meat this time. It's good that he's getting himself a job. After getting that scholarship, I was afraid he'd get lazy. But your father's got him handling the business side of the diner, so I guess I was wrong. Anyway, your father's out. Can you take out a few plates for me?"

"Sure, Mama," said Safia as she walked past her mother, grabbing an apron, and tossing it over her head.

"The calzones are for table four and the ham and eggs go to six."

"Alright, got it," said Safia as she began making her rounds through the diner. "Here you go Mr. Jacobs." She placed down the calzones.

"Hey, you hear about that big drug bust?" said the man

at the table.

"That's what everyone seems to be talking about, apparently."

"It says that some of the drugs were coming here."

"Well, it was a big bust, so I suppose it could have been."

"Well, I say, it's good they got caught. We've got enough drugs on the streets as it is without them adding to it."

"Yeah, I guess so. Well, enjoy your breakfast, Mr. Jacobs," said Safia as she walked a few tables down, dropping off the ham sandwich in front of an older woman with grey hair down to her shoulders. "Here you go, Miss Williams."

"Thanks, honey. Everything's been going alright with you?"

"Yes Ma`am, just working and helping out. You want anything else?"

"No, I'm fine," said Miss Williams as she patted Safia on the arm. "But it's good, you helping your family and all is important. They're the ones who have to look out for you."

"Hey, Safia. Got a few more orders for you," said Martin from behind the counter.

"Okay, coming!" replied Safia as she came back to the kitchen countertop. Taking more plates, she served customers for the rest of the day.

While waiting tables, she noticed the suited man that Mr. Alvarez was sitting with the day before had returned.

Oh, I didn't see him come in.

He was dressed in the same style of suit and tie as before and was sitting in the same booth near the window at the end of the diner, except this time he had a briefcase on the table in front of him instead of the chessboard. Safia watched him as he chatted on his phone, before noticing he had caught her attention and waved for her to come over.

"Yeah, I'll make the offer and report back to you soon," said the man as he ended the call.

"Welcome back, Mr. ahh... I just realized I never got your name," said Safia after walking over to him.

"Adams, I'm James Adams."

"Well, Mr. Adams, you here waiting on Mr. Alvarez again?" asked Safia as she looked around the diner. "I haven't seen him come in today, so you might have to come back another time. He's usually here on Fridays."

"No, today I'm just going to be handling some business of my own," said Mr. Adams, also looking around the bar, taking stock of the people inside. "Has today been an especially busy day for you?"

"Not anymore than usual. But usually I'd be at school right now," Safia sighed, thinking about her situation as she looked back at her father jovially laughing with one of the customers as he prepared their food. "But I guess this is just where I am now."

"Sounds like you're not too happy with your situation at the moment. Did you not have any other plans after graduation? College or perhaps picking up a trade? You're still young so the possibility is certainly there."

"Maybe next year or something after we've caught up with things here. But that is nothing for you to worry about. I'm sorry for bothering you with my problems."

"Oh, don't worry about it. I have listened to many complaints from potential students through the years. You'd be surprised at how many of them have stories similar to yours."

That's right, he did say something about working for a school. I forgot about that, thought Safia as she pulled out her pen and pad, trying to change the topic of discussion. "Did you want anything to eat?"

Just a lemonade and salad with ranch dressing, please if you don't mind."

"Right, just give it a minute and I'll have to ask them to get it ready."

Safia continued to serve the customers serving tables. Throughout the day she saw two men come to Mr. Adams' table at different times. Each one of the men seemed to be normal working-class men, although a bit large. They wore jeans and boots, not staying to eat. They just walked over to Mr. Adams and for each one, he would lift open his brief-case and hand the men a small envelope before they would walk out of the diner.

Wonder what that was about. They didn't look like students.

A few times during the day, Safia's mother came and went. But after returning home the final time, she changed her clothing and also began helping out in the diner. Both women made quick work servicing the customers, and Mr. Famosa continued his cooking in the kitchen.

"Safia, can you start cleaning the tables? I'll start restocking back here."

"Alright, mama."

The sun went down as they continued to work until only a few customers were left in the diner, including the man in the suit, Mr. Adams. He had just sat there most of the day, occasionally asking for a refill on his lemonade, but nothing else for the most part. Finally, as Safia's father was turning off the lights to close for the night, he opened the door and said bye to the last of the customers as they left. Well, everyone but Mr. Adams, who was still sitting at the end of the bar with his briefcase on the counter in front of him.

"Hey, buddy, we're gonna close," said Safia's father as he began flicking off the lights.

"I'm sorry, but I was waiting to speak with you, Mr. and Mrs. Famosa," said Mr. Adams, the nearby lights from passing cars casting an ominous feeling throughout the diner as he stepped from out of the booth and made his way towards them.

Her father turned to look at Safia and her mother, before then looking back to Mr. Adams, "Oh, yeah; and who are you? Do I know you from somewhere?"

"No, sir," said Mr. Adams as he stepped forward, his face passing in and out of the light shining in through the diner windows. "Mr. Alvarez asked me to come and deliver this to you and your family." Mr. Adams placed his briefcase on the counter, flicking his fingers on the latches that held it down as a loud clicking sound popped and filled the silence around them.

"Deliver something? And what's that? He gave my son a job and all, so I don't think he's got to give us anything. Wait, did something happen to Yago?"

"No, sir," said Adams as he lifted the lid on the briefcase, reaching his hand inside and pulling out a large brown envelope, handing it to Safia's father.

"What's that?" asked Mr. Famosa, narrowing his eyes in the dim light, hesitant to grab hold of the brown folder.

"I was informed that you had your son managing the finances of your diner here."

"Yeah, he wanted to learn the business. But what's that got to do with anything?"

"Well, Mr. Alvarez caught wind of that and decided to let Yago handle some of his logistics. Turns out your boy is very gifted and found a way to save Mr. Alvarez a lot of money. So much, in fact, that Mr. Alvarez said he would give the boy anything he wanted. And inside that envelope is what Yago asked Mr. Alvarez for."

Safia's father looked skeptically between the brown envelope and Mr. Adams. "So, you gonna tell me what's in that or what?"

"Yago wanted it to be a surprise. I'm merely following his wishes."

"Open it, honey, and see what it is," said Mrs. Famosa, still keeping her distance from the ominous man. "If this is the reason Yago's been working so hard, it's probably something worth looking at?"

Mr. Famosa looked at Safia and shrugged before taking the envelope from Mr. Adams, opening it and sliding out the paper and started reading. He squirted for a moment before turning back to his wife. "Hey, hit the lights, it's too dark in here for reading this thing."

"I got it, Papa," said Safia as she stepped over, turning back on the lights of the diner, which made them all squint for a moment as they readjusted to the lights.

"Thank you for your application," said Mr Famosa as he began to read aloud from the paper. "We here at Duke University would like to humbly accept Safia Famosa to next semester's class with full bene... what... but... what is this?" Her father asked, surprised, almost losing his grip on the papers.

"Turns out the dean of admissions is also from Cuba and apparently is married to Mr. Alvarez's daughter," said Mr. Adams with a smile on his face.

Safia ran out of the counter and to her father, grabbing the paper and looking it over. And to her surprise, it read exactly as he had spoken it. Safia's hands began to shake as she tried coming to terms with what she was holding. In shock, she just stared at the acceptance letter from Duke University, the school's logo feeling like an object of fiction in her eyes. "But... how?"

"Yago was very persistent on this," said Mr. Adams with a smile.

"So... I get to go to college?" asked Safia, trying to hold back the hope in her voice.

"Yes, as long as your family allows you to."

Safia turned to her father. "Can I go now, Papa?"

"What? Of course. I mean, if it's real. I'm not stopping my baby from going to school. Where's Yago? He should be here," said Mr. Famosa, looking back at Mr. Adams. "And why'd you wait till now to tell us? You were here all day. You could have told us anytime. Instead of sitting back there like some statue."

"I didn't want to interrupt your work-flow. I had intended to tell you on your break, but sadly, neither of you seem to take a break. So rather than interrupt your workday, I opted to wait for a time when you could receive this news in private."

"Well, of course. This is a hard-working family, you know. Especially my boy, but where is he? He should be here to celebrate with us."

"I just got off the phone with him, actually. Mr. Alvarez had him stay a little late to finish up. But he should be home within the next hour or so, I would guess."

"Well then, I'll just call him to make sure. I mean this is just a little hard to believe."

"Ah, please use my phone then; it connects straight to Mr. Alvarez's office," said Mr. Adams, after tapping a few buttons on his phone and handing it to her father.

Mr. Famosa started smiling as he heard his son's voice on the phone.

"Congratulations, Safia," said Mr. Adams with a smile. "Yago has been working on this for quite some time. He and that David boy he brought along are very hard workers."

"David too?" asked Safia, the paper shaking in her hand, as she could barely hold in her excitement.

"Yes, although he asked for you to get into Hamilton with him, as well as Yago. But Mr. Alvarez doesn't have connections in New York, unfortunately. But I hope you enjoy Duke."

Hamilton? Is that where he decided to go? Thought Safia, before focusing back on her own situation. "Of course I will! I mean, thank you." Safia smiled, allowing herself to take a breath and believe this was real.

"Yago said he would be home soon," said Mr. Famosa as he gave Mr. Adams back his phone. "He's getting David to drop him off."

"Well, I'm sure you all have a lot of things to discuss. Because of the speed at which this is being handled. She will need to start her enrollment a week from now if that is okay with you."

"A week," said Mrs. Famosa. "That's hardly anytime at all."

"But what about the shop?" asked Safia. "Who's going to help you two out?"

Mr. Famosa looked at his wife. "Martin might appreciate a few more hours, I guess. But if we need, we could just hire a part-timer. I mean, money's already a little tight, but I'm sure we can make it work out."

"Oh, Yago's already saw to that. In exchange for him to keep organizing the books at the warehouse, Mr. Alvarez will be increasing his pay. The extra money should cover the cost of hiring a part-timer. All we ask is that we continue to use the services of your son."

"Seriously?" asked Mr. Famosa as he began scratching his head. "The hell you got my boy doing down there, shoveling gold?" he asked skeptically.

"Hardly. You should feel quite proud of your son. He managed to save the company a lot of money just by changing where we spend it. Come down and visit the office one day when he's not out running errands and see for yourself."

"I mean, I knew the boy was smart and all because he saved us a bunch of money by cutting back on the stuff we ordered. But wow, I'll be damned if I knew he had that much of a head for this business stuff."

"Well, he did get a full scholarship already," said Mrs. Famosa.

"You two have done a great job raising him," said Mr. Adams. "He fit in at the office almost immediately. Even I must admit that I was surprised when Mr. Alvarez called me to inform me of the situation he had. If he's this smart at his age, he's going to be a millionaire before turning thirty. But that's enough from me; I still have a few more stops to make. You all enjoy yourselves."

"You two, sir, and thank you," said Mr. Famosa, opening the door to the diner for Mr. Adams before locking it behind him and jumping around, shaking his hands. "My boys a fucking genius. I can't believe it!" He hugged his wife and Safia, kissing them both. "He said he's gonna be a millionaire. I might even have my own chain of Famosas' Diner's by then."

"Come on, let's go celebrate and get things ready for when he gets home," said Safia's mother.

After turning off the lights and locking up, the three of them headed upstairs and waited for Yago to return.

A little over an hour later, Yago and David opened the door to the upstairs home. Mr. Famosa, Mrs. Famosa, and Safia all greeted them at the door, only to have the boys come into the light looking more disheveled than Safia had ever seen them before. Both boys looked exhausted. Their shoulders were slumped, their eyes were heavy, their eyes and hair was a mess, and their faces and clothes had some type of red dirt covering large portions of their bodies.

"Boys, what happened to you? You both look half dead."

"Good," said David. "Then I look exactly how I feel."

"It's my fault. I wanted to hurry and finish up the last truckload at the warehouse. But the last truck must have had a rough trip. Because the moment we opened the back we were hit by a mountain of red dirt."

"Dirt?" replied Mr. Famosa, not understanding.

"Yeah, apparently they use some type of special dirt to season the meat in while they transport it. I wanted to have a look at it, but I didn't expect it to fly out of the truck and hit me," said Yago as his father patted him down while covering his own face as a small dust cloud appeared around him.

"I didn't even know you could season food with dirt," said David, as he stayed close to the door. "But Mr. Alvarez said he brought it all the way up from Mississippi. Mr. Famosa, you mind if I use your bathroom to clean up?"

"Sure, David. Go on. You know where it is. Bring a wet towel back for Yago."

"Yes, Sir," said David as he carefully stepped his way towards their restroom, trying not to get dirt on anything.

Safia noticed the tiredness in his eyes as he passed by.

"I'll go get that wet towel for Yago," said Safia after a

moment of watching her father continue to dust off her brother.

Following behind David, she made her way to the bathroom, the sound of running water in her ears as she got closer. There, David stood with the door open, his shirt off on the floor beside him as he pressed a wet towel against his face. Safia couldn't help but notice that his body was still toned from his years playing baseball. He had a few scars on his body that she remembered fondly caressing her fingers over when they'd laid next to each other. But also, there were a few newer scars that she didn't recognize. Watching the water from the rag drip down his body as he sighed with the warm cloth over his face, her hand began to raise itself, to reach out for him.

"Hey, alligator," said David, as he removed the warm cloth. "I hope you've been enjoying this day more than I have."

"How could I not, after getting that news?" She said, pulling her hand back before he noticed. "Hey, I see you still have that scar on your stomach from our first date. You really did fall down really hard back then."

"You mean how you pushed me down, fell on top of me, and rammed your skates into my ribs. Yeah, that was a wonderful first date."

"It wasn't that bad," said Safia, still smiling at him. "Hey, they sent me to get a rag for Yago."

"Oh, okay," he said, removing the rag from his face as the now reddish dirt dripped from the towel to the sides of the sink, falling down to the bathroom tiles below. He had done a terrible job of getting the reddish dirt from his face, leaving a decent amount above his eyes and a bit around his ears and neck.

"Gimme that," she said, stepping forward and taking the rag from his hand.

"So forceful. I see that part of you hasn't changed."

"Shut up. You said you liked my forcefulness."

"It has its places, but I wish you'd learn to turn it off during our private moments."

"You know I tried," said Safia as she began wiping off the dirt around his face. Slowly, around the eyes, she took her time. Dipping the towel back down into the running water. "But some things are hard to turn off."

"I know. Maybe it's my fault in a way as well. I probably should have said something earlier."

Feeling the warmth of the rag against the skin of her fingers, she squeezed it tightly, letting the water drain back into the sink. Bringing it back up to David's face, she dabbed it at the corner of his nose, the steam from the rag raising up, washing over his almond eyes.

"I take it everything went okay?" asked David as he breathed in deeply the warmth of the cloth around her fingers.

"What do you mean?"

"The college that Yago got you into. When he came to me for help. I had no idea how he would manage it."

"Wait," said Safia, pausing her attempt to cleanse his face as she stared up at him. "So you knew about it too? How long have you been at this?"

"Of course I knew. I wouldn't be standing here covered in dirt otherwise."

"I thought you were doing it for money before you head off to college?"

"That helps too, but the main goal was for you to go to school. I figured your folks would have no reason not to let you go if they didn't have to pay."

"So you've been doing all this for me?" asked Safia, unbelieving.

"Of course I have. You're a smart girl. You should go to college."

"Even if it's not the college you're going to? And that reminds me," she said as she gave David a whack on the shoulder. "I didn't know you were going to Hamilton. You could have at least told me, you jerk.”

“Ouch, hey. I didn't decide on where to go until just recently,” said David as he rubbed his shoulder. “And trust me, I tried to get you into Hamilton, but Mr. Alvarez said that he didn't have connections there. So we take what we can and make the best out of what we have. That's what my father always says.”

“I'm not a child. I'm sure I would have found a way to go to school,” said Safia, looking David up and down. “Why do all this when I'm not even your girlfriend anymore?”

“Can't I just help out a friend?”

Safia frowned at David with narrowed eyes. “Really, that's your excuse?”

“Okay, so Yago asked me, and I owed him a favor. But I would have done it anyway. You may not be my girlfriend anymore, but you're still my baby.”

You corny idiot, thought Safia as she brought the cloth back up to his face, dabbing it around his ears with a smile on her face. “And does Sara know I'm your baby?”

“Let's just keep that part a secret. She goes off to California soon to live with her aunt anyway, and I'll head off soon to. So, at the very least, I'd like to try and enjoy the last few days with my high school girlfriend,” said David as he peeked out the door, seeing an old magic kit on the counter. “Hey, do you still do those magic tricks like when we were younger?”

“What? No, I haven't touched that stuff in years.”

“That's a shame. I was hoping you could show me one of your secret magic tricks,” said David, giving her a smirk.

“Well, I do think you deserve some type of appreciation, but I guess since you have a girlfriend, that can't happen.” She said with a chuckle as she dipped the cloth once again. “Too bad for you, no more magic tricks.”

“Well, if that's the case; I can think of two ways you can repay me that are less sexy magic and more just feel good magic.”

"And those are?"

"First would be a kiss."

"And a kiss isn't sexual?" asked Safia with a raised brow.

"My Grandma is French. They kiss all the time there?"

"And are you French?"

"I am now, dammit."

Safia laughed despite herself, but leaned forward and tilted her head upward. Lifting herself up, she pressed her lips against his. They were still warm from the heat of the rag, but the feeling of her skin pressed against his... *Oh, I missed this so much.* She savored the feeling of him finally touching her again after their breakup. A feeling that she knew all too well that she couldn't forget. The way he softly stroked his hand against her cheek as she heard the sound of his breath exhaling was really only a taste of what she truly desired. But their desire would only meet for only a moment before she pulled her lips away from his, taking a step away.

"I had forgotten how good of a kisser you were," said David after he took a moment to stare at her.

"And you've gotten a little better at it."

"Only a little?"

"Okay, so maybe a little more than a little, but that's one, what's the other one?"

"Well." David bit his lip with a smirk as he looked her over. "While I was out working very... very hard for you. The only thing that kept me working was a single thought. That maybe, just maybe, I'd get to see you strut around in that t-shirt and panties again. You know, before we head off to school and all."

"Oh, for the love of God," said Safia, smiling and shaking her head as she turned around, walking back towards her family. She saw that her parents had sat Yago down in a chair as their mother kept knocking the dust from his hair.

"I hope you were wearing a mask around all that dirt. I heard it can cause breathing problems if you breathe in too much."

"We weren't there long," said Yago.

"Here you are, Yago," said Safia, holding out the wet rag for him.

"Thanks," he replied, quickly grabbing it and started wiping his face. "They will come and pick you up Monday and take you to the airport."

"Who will?"

"Mr. Adams."

"Oh, the creepy guy who gave us the envelope," said Safia's dad, shaking his head. "You know I was about to whip his ass when he walked up to us tonight."

"Hector, stop that."

"What? I thought he might try to rob us. You know he was kinda creepy; that's why you and Safia hid behind the counter."

"We did not hide. Stop being silly."

"I'm telling you, you were about to watch your husband whoop some ass," said Hector, and he balled up his fist, raising it to his face.

"Yeah, Mr. Adams just gives off that kinda vibe," said Yago, shaking his head. "But he's harmless. At work, he just sits down and eats his peanut butter sandwiches."

"I still can't believe both my babies are going to college," said their mother excitedly.

"Safia's going. I'm not in college yet."

"Oh, it's just another year, and Mr. Frolani said as long as you keep up your grades, then you'll get the scholarship."

"That's what he says, but anything can change."

"I swear, my son's always been the type to look on the negative side. I wonder where you get that from, certainly not your father or me. Maybe Hector's father, he was always a negative person."

"Hey, my father was a man of wisdom. Everyone used to go to him for advice."

"Come on. Cheer up for once, Yago. You've earned it."

"Just being realistic. Few things work out the way you want, and the things that do, chances are someone made it happen."

"Alright," said David, walking back into the room. "Thanks for letting me use your bathroom, Mr. Famosa. I'll be heading home now."

"No problem, David. Thanks for helping Yago out. I swear if you learn Spanish, boy, I wouldn't mind you marrying Safia."

"Papa!"

"It doesn't matter," said Yago, standing up from the chair, heading towards the washroom. "Saffy can barely speak Spanish, anyway."

"Yago!"

"Now, now, come on. Stop teasing your sister, and let's get you cleaned up," said their mother while their father escorted Yago to the back, leaving David and Safia alone.

"Okay," said David, opening the door. "I'll see you again before you head off to college."

"Bye, David, see you next time."

David opened the door and placed one foot on the steps. "You know, you never did say if you'd grant me the second wish."

"No, I didn't," said Safia with a smile as she stepped behind him, placing her hand on the door. "But you might want to start showing up in the morning again. Yago might need a little bit more help. And, who knows, you might see something you like." And with those words, she fully closed the door behind him; her last sight of David was of him with a stupidly big grin on his face.

Safia turned around, placing her back against the door, and shook her head thinking about David. *He really is just a big dummy.* Taking a deep breath to clear her mind of that stupid smile he had on his face, she headed back through their home. The sound of the shower catching her ear as she walked into her room. Grabbing her phone, she laid in bed beside her stuffed animals and began glancing over at all the things people had shared throughout the day. More parties, more well wishes, and info posts about the drug bust in Florida; they even had a video of the mayor talking about it. More pictures of the money they seized and a video of ICE escorting immigrants into vans. *People are still talking about this.*

Deciding to click the video, she watched as hundreds of people stood at a port with the huge tanker behind them. So many that she could see from the helicopter view that the police had to section the area off from the increasing public that was gathering. *I don't understand why people go to these places after they hear about it on the news. If the police are there, doesn't that mean it's dangerous? Maybe that's just how Florida people are.*

Safia blinked at a part of the video where she thought she recognized a man's face in the crowd as the video scrolled by. Clicking on the video to scroll it back, she paused it in a freeze frame and squinted her eyes staring at the screen. I feel like I've seen him before. Safia's eyes went wide with recollection. *No way. That kinda looks like Mr. Alvarez's grandson. But wasn't he...*

Giving the situation more thought, she could have sworn that he was also one of the men that were handcuffed the day before as they were escorted off the ship. But now, he was in the crowd, watching as the rest of the detainees were put into a van.

No... No, I'm probably just thinking too much. This isn't some crazy movie. People don't just do things like that. I'm just being paranoid. I need to stop thinking about this and start thinking about what I'm going to do when I get to college.

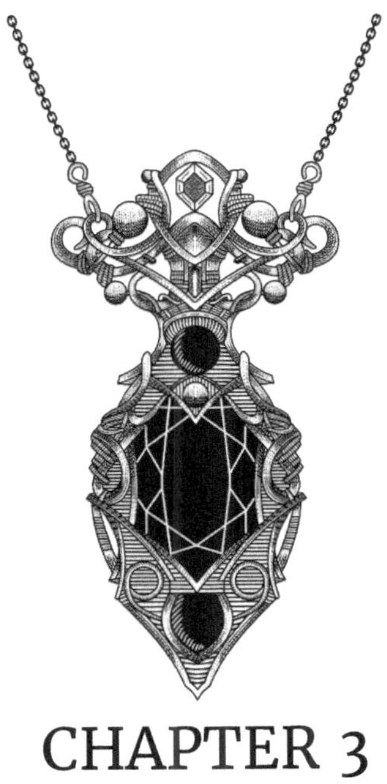

CHAPTER 3

The days went by quickly as Safia worked at the diner serving food to customers, and running errands for her parents. She had to admit that the days serving in the diner were a lot more pleasant for her now that she knew she was leaving.

In the mornings David would pick up Yago for work, but was pleasantly surprised to see Safia answering the door in panties and a shirt that barely reached her hips if he got there before Yago woke up. A few kisses and mild touching would ensue between the two before Yago would awake, and both boys would go off to work and come back at night.

But from then on, they both would stay clean for the most part.

The day before Safia was to head off for college, they all took off from work to celebrate. Their father even closed the diner early to take them out to dinner, with David tagging along with them to a nice restaurant.

The restaurant was more upscale than they would usually go to. Servers wore freshly creased black slacks, along with matching vest and dress shirt underneath. Safia couldn't help but make comparisons between herself when she was a waitress in normal street clothes and their uniformed attire. Whereas she would just have her hair in whatever style she felt like that day, the servers here had well-manicured hair; from the men and their short cuts to the women, and their stylish buns with braids that hung around the side.

I wonder how much they make working here? Way more than I ever did. What I would make in a week, they probably make off one tip. And with that thought, she couldn't help but look around the restaurant, taking a glance at the other patrons. Most had on business attire and seemed more upscale than the people who came to their little diner. Even the building itself seemed expensive; with its cool climate control atmosphere and fancy dimmed soft orange lighting fixtures that accented off the large black wooden beams that they used to highlight the style of the establishment. *How much is all this going to cost?*

"Congratulations to my Safia, who will be the first in the family to go to college," said Mr. Famosa as he sat at the head of the table. "And to my brilliant Yago who got her there. This is how it should be. Family helping each other to do better." He smiled at his wife. "You see, Samantha, this is why I say we should have had three children. We make good babies together."

"And who was going to have the third? Not me. Two is enough. Just because you came from a big family of six

44

kids doesn't mean you're getting that from me," said their mother, shaking her finger at her husband.

"You see, Yago, this is what women do to you. They trap you and take your dreams away," said Mr. Famosa, slapping his son on the arm playfully. "So be careful when you get a girlfriend. I once had a dream of becoming a famous magician. I was going to do those card tricks that I used to show you and Safia there for a living, along with pulling the rabbit out of the hat and all those things. But your mother made me give up on my dream, my one true passion."

"Your magic tricks were always too dangerous," said their Mother, pointing her fork at her husband. "Remember the time you almost burned down our home with that flaming handkerchief trick?"

"Oh, I remember that," said Safia, pointing her finger at her father. "He made me help him in the kitchen with that. I had to get a whole new dress after that."

"Hey, what is this?" asked their father, frowning at his wife and daughter. "Why the ladies gotta team up on me, huh?" He tapped Yago on the shoulder again. "Be careful Yago, you might think girls are all soft and sweet, but when they get their claws into you it's over. The next thing you know, you have two kids and you've given up on your card tricks."

"You weren't going to support a family by playing card games with your friends on street corners," said their mother in protest to their fathers foolishness.

"See? She never understood. It's too late for me boy, but don't let a pretty girly take your dreams away, like your mother did to me. You're my last hope, you see."

"That'll never happen," said Safia, giving Yago a superiorly smug look, "Yago is always in his books or paperwork for the shop. Too busy to get a girlfriend. I don't think I've ever seen you talk to a girl for more than five minutes."

"Wait, what?" asked David, looking around the table, confused. "But doesn't Yago have a girlfriend? I mean, she's been bringing him lunch every day, at work."

Suddenly, the table grew quiet as everyone turned to Yago as he pulled the fork from his mouth.

"What?" asked Yago, looking around the table innocently.

"What do you mean, what? You had a girlfriend and didn't even tell your father?"

"You never asked."

"I shouldn't have to ask. I should just know these things. We're supposed to have that talk, you know, father and son. I mean, I'd expect you to bring her over, introduce her to us or something. I've never even seen you on the phone for more than five minutes. Who is she? Do we know her? What about her family? Does she go to your school?"

"Yeah, you know her, it's Liliana."

"Lilli... Liliana? Wait, you mean Mr. Hernandez's Liliana; the prissy one with the big hips and the blonde hair?"

"Hector!" said their mother in a harsh tone.

"What? The girl has big hips. You have big hips. It means, like father, like son. That's something to be proud of."

"Yeah, that's her."

"But isn't she in college? Wait, how old is she?"

"Nineteen?"

"But you're sixteen. What does she even see in you?" asked Safia, genuinely flabbergasted by the current discovery.

"That's what I thought too," said David, as he shrugged his shoulders. "But they eat lunch everyday together."

"That's my boy, getting himself an older woman. You know that's because he's mature for his age. Wait, isn't there some type of law against that?" asked Mr. Famosa in a low tone. "I mean a sixteen and a nineteen-year-old; I can't have my boy going to jail."

"That... that's actually a good question. I never thought about that," said David as he stuffed his face with a piece of fish.

"It's okay. We like each other."

"Hey, hey, I'm sure you do," said their father with a chuckle as he wrapped his arm around the shoulders on his son. "But it's not about what you feel. It's about the police and how they feel. Your mother here is African-American. Your father is Cuban. They already don't like either side of our family. We don't need to give them any excuses. I mean, if it was like white boy David over here, then sure, maybe he'd get away with it."

"Hector!"

"Papa!"

"What? It's not like I'm telling a lie. Look at everyone at this table and tell me who's going to be pulled over first. It damn sure won't be David, I'll tell you that."

"I'm sorry, David, my husband is being inconsiderate."

"It's alright. I found out recently that he's probably right. That might be why Mr. Alvarez asks me to drive his trucks so much."

"There, you see, Samantha? Even the boy knows it," said their father as he gave a sideways glance to his son before leaning in. "Hey, you and her, ah, you know. You got her in the back of a truck and had yourself a little—"

"Hector!" said Safia's mother in a stern tone as she wacked her husband on the shoulder. "Stop that."

"What, I'm doing what a father should. The boy might need some advice."

The sound of a jingle came as Yago's phone rang. "Hello," he answered as he shook his head disapprovingly at his father. "Oh, hey. Yeah, I'm out with my family for dinner. Can you swing by Molando's if you're nearby? Okay, I'll see you when you get here then."

"Who was that?" asked their father. "Was that that Liliana girl? Are you going to introduce her to us properly now?"

"No, it was someone from work. I left my watch there, and he was just bringing it by since he was in the area making deliveries."

"Hey now, that's a good friend."

"Safia, honey," said her mother, "Have you decided what your major is going to be?"

"Probably psychology. I want to try and help people."

"You mean like the people who come and sit on the couches and tell you their problems?" asked her father as he rubbed the side of his chin. "Aren't they the people who deal with the crazies?"

"No, they help people," said Safia, annoyed by her father's blanket description. "A lot of the time people just need someone to talk to and not feel like they aren't going to be judged for it."

"But outside of the people who need to talk, there will be some crazies, right?"

"Hector!"

"What? She's my daughter. I'm not allowed to worry about my daughter now? You seen them movies. The therapist is always getting kidnapped or being brought out when they do something crazy. Then the police gotta bring them in to talk."

"Don't worry about your father; he's just being stupid."

"You say that now, but I remember when Safia was making you pull your hair out down at that school after arguing and fighting with them boys down there. You know she's prone to getting into trouble, just like you were. Oh, your mother was a demon when she was younger, let me tell you."

"Hector enough, no one wants to hear about your made up stories."

"Fine, fine, I get it; everyone ignores the father until my baby girl winds up trying to talk down some crazy person up on a roof, or at gunpoint."

"How are you going to be a therapist when you barely pay attention to anything?" asked Yago, sliding his phone back into his pocket. "Not to mention you already have a bad memory."

"I do not have a bad memory. You just always remember the boring stuff."

"Oh, yeah. Then tell me why you lost the volleyball bet with me. What happened to Kelly?"

"Ahh." Safia tried to think back about what happened. She could remember something about it having to do with the girl's family, but she couldn't remember exactly what it was.

"Kelly?" questioned Safia's mother, catching on to their conversation. "Oh, I heard about how her father was caught with one of your teachers at the school. That poor girl must be so embarrassed."

"Yeah," said Safia, chiming in. "Her father got caught having sex with Mrs. Angela. See, I can remember stuff."

Yago raised a brow at his sister.

"Who did what now?" asked their father. "A teacher and a student? You see Yago, this is why we should have that talk. You got some crazy things happening down at that school."

"Not a teacher and a student. It was a teacher and the parent of a student."

"Oh. Then that's not so bad then. That's someone who really wants their kid to get an A plus."

"Hector, stop that."

David couldn't help himself but laugh at the antics of Safia and her family. "My family is nothing like yours, Safia. You all really do have a lot of fun together."

"You think this is fun? How would you feel if your father acted like mine? Embarrassing you all the time."

"Well, my home would certainly be a lot more lively, that's for sure," said David as he turned to Safia's father and mother. "What will you both do a year from now when Yago is out of the house? Then, both your children will be gone. My sister's only five, so my parents will have their hands full with her while I'm gone."

"That is why I say we should have another child. Samantha needs another baby to take care of."

"You can keep dreaming as much as you like. But unless you want a divorce, then I don't think any more kids are in your future."

"I guess, I will have to settle for grandkids one day."

Yago's phone rang again as he swiped across its screen, then placed it to his ear. "Oh, he's outside. I'll be right back." He then stood up from the table and made his way outside into the night air.

Safia watched him from the window as his friend approached from the parking lot's shadows into the dim light near the restaurant's window. She instantly recognized his face; it was the man from the picture Alvarez had. And from the news feed on her phone.

No way. Okay... okay, there's no way I'm just paranoid. That's him, that has to be him.

"Safia? Safia, everything okay, honey?" asked her mother, noticing the look of worry that had unconsciously crept across her daughter's face.

"Huh?"

"Your father asked if you have all your clothes packed for tomorrow."

"Oh, sorry, Papa. Yes, I do. I'm ready."

"That's good; Mr. Adams said we could ride with him to the airport to see you off. We don't want you to miss your flight."

Yago soon walked back in, holding a watch in his hand, sitting back down at the table.

"Hey, that's a nice watch. Looks kinda thick, though," said Mr. Famosa.

"Yeah, I got it because I figured it wouldn't break easily. We're always moving things at work and slamming our wrists against stuff all the time."

"Yeah, that's good thinking."

Safia couldn't help but stare at Yago the whole night, wondering what he had been up to. But one thing very much stood out to her through the rest of the night. Whereas Yago left the diner with one phone, he now had two clipped onto his side.

Where'd that one come from? He must have gotten it from that man. But why? What the hell are you up to, Yago.

But after eating their meal, they all left the restaurant and headed home. David and Safia drove back together, parking Mr. Alvarez's delivery truck around the back of the diner as their parents walked around the building.

"We're gonna stay out a little longer. I just want to say goodbye," said Safia.

"Okay, you two lovebirds, say your goodbyes, but don't stay out too late. We gotta get you to the airport tomorrow," said Mr. Famosa, as he and his wife headed up the back stairs into their home; her mother giving her a smirk on her way up.

"Okay, what's going on, both of you?" asked Safia when their parents had gone inside. "Fess up!"

"What do you mean?" asked David, looking confused at the random question.

"The guy who came to give Yago that watch. That's the guy who was on the news, and Mr. Alvarez had a picture of him. None of this is making sense anymore. Papa and Ma may just accept it, but something about all of this seems wrong."

There was a moment of silence between the three as David and Yago stared at each other and then back at Safia.

"Well, I guess it was just too good to be true, that she wouldn't ask questions, Yago."

"She always starts thinking when she gets mad, but out of all the times for you to think too much, I can't believe now is the time you decide to use that brain of yours," said Yago with a sigh.

"What do you mean?" asked Safia, looking between the two boys.

"I mean, you're right. That man you saw me with is Palito, one of Mr. Alvarez's sons."

"You mean grandson."

"No, I mean his son. He brought him here from Cuba to oversee his business."

"Business," said Safia as her mind went back to the cargo freighter that had all the drugs and money that the police confiscated. "Wait, Mr. Alvarez can't be involved with drugs, he's been sitting at the diner since we were babies. He's not a drug dealer."

"He's not, but he knows them. He knows a lot of people. Sometimes, he allows them to move the drugs in his trucks."

"Wait, then how... Mr. Adams?"

"Yep."

"You mean a drug dealer is picking our family up tomorrow?" asked Safia as she felt a chill go down her spin." Are you crazy? Am I even going to college? How do you know I won't be sold into some crazy sex dungeon or something?"

"Because we've already paid for you to go. Mr. Alvarez made sure of that."

"What do you mean, paid? We don't have money like that... Wait... We... You knew about this too, David?"

"Uh oh, she's mad at me again."

"Of course, I'm mad," said Safia as she began slapping David on the chest before turning her fury on her brother as they both raised their hands, blocking her slaps. "What did you two do?" she asked, looking between the two of them angrily.

"We took some packages to Chicago, that's all."

"Chicago? But that's like six hours away!" Safia's eyes opened wide as her mind started piecing together all the nights before. "That's why you've been getting here early every morning and returning late." She pushed David and Yago. "You idiots, what if you'd been caught? What would Ma say?"

"She really does figure stuff out fast when she's mad," said David, shrugging his shoulders.

"Shut up," said Safia, placing her hands on her hips.

"Answer me, Yago. What if you had gotten caught? That would have killed Mama."

"We were careful, Saffy," said Yago as he pointed at David. "But Pa was right; the police really didn't check David. We were able to pass right through one of the police checkpoints."

"Oh! God help me," said Safia, shaking her head as she turned towards the meat truck. "Wait, then what about when you came in with all that dirt on you?"

"They had everything in the back of the truck covered in some type of red dirt, or sand, or whatever it was," said David. "That damn stuff was sticky and got everywhere."

"Oh Lord, help me, you're both idiots. My idiot brother and my idiot boyfriend."

"Ex-boyfriend."

"Shut up, I know what you are."

"Yes, ma'am."

Safia threw her hands over her face. "I can't believe you two. How long are you going to keep this up?"

"Oh, we're done," said David, waving his hands around. "The deal was for three deliveries to resupply what they lost in that Florida bust. Apparently, they've already brought in another load from New York. Now we just work in the warehouse and I take the meat downtown."

"Well, that's good," said Safia as she nodded her head. "At least, now I won't have to worry anymore."

"You'd worry about me. That's sweet."

"Shut up."

"Yes, Ma`am."

"Ahhh, you're both so frustrating," said Safia as she began to pace back and forth biting on her bottom lip. The sound of her steps echoing in the silence of the back alley of the diner as she continued to think about what she should do."

"So, do you still plan to go to college?" asked Yago, looking at his sister nervously. "It's not a scheme or anything. You really are going to college."

"What? Of course I'm going. I can't just not go. Ma and Papa are so happy that I have to go now. It's just… It's just it's all so messed up now."

"Then, it was worth it," said Yago, with a sigh. "I didn't want everything we did to go to waste. And then I'd have to explain it to Mr. Alvarez. That wouldn't be fun."

"Why even do all this. It wasn't worth what could have happened to the both of you."

"You know what things are like around here, Saffy. If you don't go now, chances are, you'd never go."

"It was fine. I was fine with not going. Especially if it meant you both would become drug dealers."

"Technically, it's drug transporters," said David, wagging his finger. "We never actually—"

"Didn't I tell you to shut up?"

"Yes, ma'am."

"But you're both sure you're done, no more drug stuff?"

"Yep," said Yago. "David will be in New York soon, and I'll be at the warehouse and helping around the diner. Mr. Alvarez was clear about that part. He wasn't exactly happy about us doing it, either."

"Okay… okay then," said Safia as she attempted to gather her thoughts.

"Don't worry about it anymore. You can't change what's been done. Instead, just when you get there, you better work your ass off. We didn't almost go to jail so that you can just live a regular college life."

"I know that. Of course I'm going to work hard," Safia answered back heatedly.

"Good, then I'll leave you out here with David, so you both can enjoy a lovey-dovey moment. I still need to work on the finances of the diner," said Yago as he headed back up the steps and into their home; the wooden boards of the steps creaking beneath his feet.

Safia and David stood in the darkness outside her home,

not speaking, the silence only being interrupted by some type of animal knocking over a glass bottle somewhere.

"Aren't you going to say something or—"

"I'm still mad at you."

"I know. What we did was stupid."

"Very stupid."

"But," said David, raising his hands, "Yago called me and asked me for my help. At first I thought he was crazy, but the more he talked about it, it didn't seem so crazy. You should have seen it, Safia. He knew where the police would be, what roads to take, how long it would take. He knew everything."

"He always acts like he knows everything."

"No, I mean it, he knew everything. Even the people at the drop-off place knew him. We were only there like three minutes before we were back on the road again. I don't know what Yago is into, but I'm sure he's done things like that before."

Safia glanced up at the steps. "He never really tells us anything. We just thought he was the quiet type." She turned back to face David. "Fine. What do you get out of this? He's my brother, so I have to accept whatever stupid thing he does. But why'd you—"

"To see you dance around in your panties every morning was fun. Especially the ones with the cute dolphin on the back. I love those."

"Stop that. I'm being serious."

David sighed. "Is it so hard to believe that I want you to be happy?"

"Yes, I mean, no. But that's not enough reason to do all of this."

He turned around, walking over, taking a seat on the steps, before gazing up in the dark sky above him. While there were no stars to be seen in the city, there were the lights coming out of nearby buildings that blocked the view of most of the sky that wasn't directly above them. "I love you,"

"I know that, but--"

"I don't think you know how much I love you, but I'm not stupid. I have a free ride to college, and I'm going. I told you before with Sara, I don't think long-distance relationships work. That goes for us as well."

"So, why do all this?"

"Because I want you to be happy. And as much as I know you love your folks, you've always seen this place as if it was some cage."

"I never said that."

"You didn't have to. I've been watching you since we were eight, and you forced me to do those silly magic tricks with you and your father. You think I didn't notice how you'd slump your shoulders when you'd put on your apron, or how you'd sigh every time I'd walk you back home because you needed to help out at the diner."

"It's not like I did it every time," said Safia, feeling embarrassed by the conversation, while at the same time feeling flattered that he'd paid that much attention to her during their time together.

"I can't stay for you, Safia. But that doesn't mean I can't help you leave. And, now, we both are about to head off to college and live our lives. Probably drink too much, have our hearts broken, and both walk out four years later with a future that's more than just working in our parents' kitchens."

Safia walked over to David as he slid to the side, giving her room to sit. Instead, she placed her hands on his shoulders, sitting down on his lap. "So what now? We just walk away and never see each other again?"

"Probably," he said as he wrapped his arms around her waist, taking in a deep breath of her smell. "Feel free to send me pictures every time you try on new panties, though."

"What is it with you and me in panties?" said Safia with a giggle. "I thought all boys' just like naked girls."

"How dare you lump me in with such filth as other boys my age? I shall have you know my taste in women's attire is refined. The panty line around cute hips is the highest form of erotic art. Why, I dare say that it's up there with the Mona Lisa and the Sistine Chapel."

"Really, you think so?" she said, shaking her head.

"Trust me, I have an eye for these things."

Safia looked around the darkness, her eyes stopping on Mr. Alvarez's meat truck. "What's in that thing, anyway?"

"What, the truck? Nothing now. I delivered everything this morning. He just allows me to drive it when I need to."

Safia bit at her bottom lip in contemplation. "You think two people could fit in the back?"

"Of course, it's… Safia, your parents are upstairs."

"It's your choice, Mr. Panty man, and for your information, I went out and got some new ones. I'm wearing them now."

"Oh, that's not fair; you're teasing me."

"Yes, I am."

"Your father would kill me."

"I think Ma's keeping him busy."

David slid Safia off his lap and stood up, walking over to the back of the truck, with Safia following behind him.

CHAPTER 4

The next morning, they were all at the airport, saying their goodbyes. The terminal was louder than she thought it would be. The sounds of chatter from the many people around them as their luggage squeaked on its wheels, next to the sound of their footsteps. Every few minutes over the intercom, a voice would announce the loading of a certain flight at a particular gate with its sounds flowing through all the open space above their heads. Safia looked ahead with her family and stared out of the gigantic widows that showed the dozens of large aircraft down on the runway below.

"Have you never flown before?" asked Mr. Adams as he stepped up to Safia's side.

"No, we never really went anywhere before unless to visit family that was nearby and then we'd take a car."

"Don't worry, it will be a smooth experience after we get up in the air."

"Hello Sir," said a young blonde-haired stewardess as she approached Mr Adams. "Your flight is available, when you're ready just head down to door thirteen and I will be waiting for you."

"Thank you," said Mr. Adams as he turned back to Safia and her family. "Go on and say your goodbyes. We've got a decent flight ahead of us."

Mrs. Famosa, reached out, hugging her daughter. "Don't get into any trouble down there and call us if you need anything."

"I will."

"And don't get involved with any bad people," said her father as he also stepped in for a hug, kissing Safia at the crown of her head. "I've heard about what happens at college. Don't drink anything you didn't pour yourself."

"Hector, stop that. She's a smart girl, she knows not to do that," said her mother, giving an eye roll.

"What? She's a young girl; she has to be careful."

"Don't worry about me; I'll be fine."

"Study hard, Saffy. You're going to have a chance to do well," said Yago, giving his sister a quick hug.

"I know, I won't waste it," said Safia as she turned to face David. "Aren't you going to say anything?"

"I'm going to miss you," said David as he reached out, grabbing her hands in his, leaned down, and gave her a kiss.

"Yeah, that's right. You think of David while you're away. At least I know him, and I can beat up his father if he does you wrong."

"Hector, stop making a fool of yourself."

David pulled his lips away, resting his forehead against

hers. "Try to send me pictures, preferably ones with dolphins."

"Shut up, you," said Safia with a smile on her face.

"Are you ready, Miss Safia?" asked Mr. Adams.

"Yes, I'm sorry. Let's go," she said as she walked away from her waving family, following Mr. Adams through the airport. They stopped at gate thirteen's entrance where the previous woman who had informed of his flight waited for him.

"Are you ready, sir?" asked the woman with a smile.

Safia noticed that the blonde-haired lady seemed close to her own age and was actually really pretty. With a golden pin in place to keep her cap firmly seated to her hair; she wore a brown skirted uniform with blue accents. But what really caught Safia's attention was that across her neck hung a beautiful pendant that shimmered in the sunlight.

"Ah yes, we can go now," said Mr. Adams, giving the young woman a smile. "Did everything go well this time?"

"Yes, sir. The plane has been refueled, and all of the assignments were handled around a day ago. Your flight now awaits you downstairs."

"Good, thank you." said Mr. Adams as he allowed the stewardess to lead both him and Safia through the doors into the loading tunnel.

Safia looked out of the window to the large pane ahead. *Downstairs?* Ahead of them she could see the opening of one of the larger places, but instead they turned at an opening in the tunnel and headed down a flight of metal stairs into the open air and sunlight. "Ahh, weren't we catching that plane?" She said as she cautiously followed behind him.

"The jetliner? Oh no, our plane is over there," said Mr. Adams as a small white private jet with a brown stripe across the sides sat over in the distance ahead of them.

"We get our own jet?" asked Safia, staring across the concrete as the sound of planes soaring above filled her ears.

"Of course, the campus has its own airport. So, there's no need to fly commercial," said Mr. Adams before turning around. "Unless you would prefer that. I'm sorry, I just assumed, but if you'd prefer to, we could buy tickets for the next flight."

"No, no. This is fine. It's just that I've never been on a plane before and now I'm getting on something like this." *I didn't even realize Duke had its own airport.*

"Oh, that's... you did say that. Well then, you're in for a treat. Steven is a wonderful pilot," said Mr. Adams as they all walked over to the plane. The door of the jet detached from itself, folding down, revealing a set of stairs for them to use to enter.

"You both can have a seat and I'll go and tell the pilot that we're ready," said the stewardess as she made her way towards the cockpit.

Stepping aboard, Safia and Mr. Adams took a seat. The inside was beautiful, with leather cream seats, trimmed in gold with the maker's name sewn into the headrests. It read 'Apex.' as Safia noticed the same logo on the carpet.

"We will soon be on our way," said Mr. Adams with a smile as he glanced out the window before turning back to Safia. "Are you excited to be starting your new life; filled with textbooks and not enough sleep?"

"I would be," said Safia as she continued to look around the cabin of the jet. "But that sounds a lot like my current life."

"I must admit I am curious about you, Miss Safia."

"Me, why?"

"Well, it's just the school has never really changed their plans before and how they rushed me to have your paperwork finalized. Just how did you manage that?"

What? They changed their plans? Then what were there plans before? Wait... doesn't he know about what Yago did. I don't think I did anything special. My brother was the one who did all the work. In truth. I'm just as surprised as you are."

"I see. Well, that brother of yours is quite the motivated one. Mr. Alvarez really did take a liking to him."

How much does he know? I can't just tell him that my brother transported whatever types of drugs to Chicago to pay my way through college. "Mr. Adams, how long have you known Mr. Alvarez?"

"Not that long, really," said Mr. Adams as he scratched his head. "I mean sometimes the school sends me to him to drop off some private letters or ask him to make arrangements for some of their alumni. But they send me everywhere, so I guess I know him just an acquaintance. Why, is there something I should know?"

"No, I was just curious. I mean, we've known him all our lives," said Safia as she felt the jet shake as it began to move forward. "So I was just curious if you had met his wife or kids."

"What's that?" asked Mr. Adam with a smirk across his face. "Are you having second thoughts on dating his grandson now? I remember you not being so keen on the idea back at the diner."

"What? No... I was just curious, is all."

Mr. Adams laughed as he leaned back in his seat. "Don't worry, I'm just teasing you. I'm not blind. I saw you kiss that fellow back there. You seem pretty content for the moment. Is he your boyfriend?"

"Yes, I mean no," Safia sighed. "We broke up a while ago and we decided it's probably not the best thing to try and have a relationship when we're so far away."

"I'm sure that decision couldn't have been easy," said Mr. Adams with a sigh. "But long-distance relationships are hard. After all this is over and you're both living your lives. There's a good chance of rekindling your time together. I do believe there's a term for that scenario called second-chance romance."

"Yeah, That's what he said. So I guess we will find out

someday."

Patting the soft leather armrest, Mr. Adams rested his head backwards. "Would you mind if I closed my eyes for a moment before take-off? It has been exhausting getting everything ready, and this would be my first chance to rest."

"Oh. No, go ahead. I'll probably do the same after a little while."

"Thank you, Miss Safia," said Mr. Adams as he closed his eyes, leaving Safia to stare out the window, still thinking about her time with David.

A few minutes later, the stewardess reemerged from out of the cockpit while putting on lip gloss.

"Okay, everything's ready," said a stewardess as she walked up to Safia, "Would you like anything while we wait for takeoff?"

"Just water, please," said Safia, finally taking notice of the stewardess's name tag. "Ah, Addison?"

"Oh already? Sure no problem. What's your name?"

"Safia."

"Safia's a pretty name," said Addison as she leaned forward, dropping her lip gloss, then reaching down to pick it up. Safia caught the faint smell of lemons as she did. "Well, Miss Safia, let me go and get you that water then." She then walked forward into a small cabinet in the plane. Leaning in, she grabbed a bottle of water and came back, handing it to Safia. "Is this your first time flying?"

"Yes ma'am," said Safia as she took the water, untwisting the top. She couldn't help but stare at the shimmering pendant that hung from the woman's neck. "We don't really get to travel much."

"Well, don't worry, sweetheart. It's not that scary when you're up in the air. But you'll probably miss it if we stay on the ground much longer."

Safia took a swallow of water while looking at the woman, who really didn't seem to be much older than her, "Have you been working here long?"

"Who, me? Oh no, I'm just doing this because I need the points."

"Points? Are you still training?"

"I guess that's one way of looking at it. I'm about to start my second year, and I need to have a certain number of points to graduate. I kinda messed up on a gamble, but the school is always offering ways to make up the extra points for those who want it. I was only off by a few and they offered me this job to make them up."

"So... like an internship, then. How many more flights before you graduate?"

"Hopefully, this will be the last one, but I still have another year. Then I'm off to start a wonderful life." She patted Safia on the shoulder. "But if you're going there. A bit of advice, try not to make as many mistakes as I did. I've seen that place drive a lot of people crazy."

"What... you... I don't... understand," said Safia as her head bobbed around. Her eyes started feeling heavy, and staying awake was becoming increasingly problematic.

"Ah shit, it seems to be working already. That's a shame. The trip's gonna be boring as fuck without someone to talk to. Oops, I shouldn't curse yet; I'm on the clock, but don't worry, I'll take good care of you."

And with the humming of the jet's engines in her ears, Safia's world went dark as sleep consumed her mind.

CHAPTER 5

Safia heard the sounds of singing as she woke from her slumber. The world was blurry and sideways to her as reached up, rubbing at her eyes. Blinking a few times she realized that she was laying down on a bed; her head resting upon a brown and gray pillow. Rolling over into the morning sun that shone in through a nearby window down onto her face, she squinted as her eyes adjusted to the light. With her vision clearing she noticed a woman across from her, sitting up on a bed.

"Oh, you're finally awake," said the woman as she finished humming her tune. "I was wondering how long you'd sleep."

"Huh? What happened?" asked Safia as she lifted herself up onto her elbows, her eyes finally adjusting to the light. But her body for some reason was hard to move, as if groggy and still half asleep. Looking down, she realized that she was on a bed and with a quick glance around her environment she realized that she was in what looked to be a dorm room. There were two beds on each side of the room, along with two work desks at the foothill of each. It even had a TV in the center of the room.

"What happened, indeed? You've been out for a good while."

What? How? How did I get here? Where am I? Safia turned back to the girl in front of her as if expecting an explanation. The girl had dark almond hair and wore a brown skirt with a short-sleeved button-up shirt tucked at her waist.

"I guess those drugs knocked you hard."

Drugs? What drugs?

The girl reached to her side and grabbed some type of glass tablet and began flicking her finger across its screen.

"Now let's see here," said the woman to herself as she scrolled across the tablet. "You're Sofia, right? Oh, that's an A. So, I guess it's Safia then."

Safia shook and she tried to stabilize her arms and rid herself of the drowsiness that still had a hold of her mind. "Who... who are you?"

"I'm Harmony," said the woman nonchalantly, as if it would explain everything.

"Where am I?"

"Now there's a good first question, but outside of a few staff, I don't think anyone here knows where exactly we are."

"What?"

"You must be a Trojan. There's always about half a dozen each year amongst the freshmen."

"A what?"

"It's going to be hard to explain until you fully wake up. You're probably hungry. You want something to eat?"

Safia waved her hand dismissively, "I'm fine, just... just... just give me a moment." She took her hands, rubbing them over her face as she sat up, allowing her feet to dangle in the air off her bed. The ping of sleepy muscles giving her mind something to latch onto as she orientated herself with the world around her once more. The feeling of cool air danced on the back of her neck, coming through a vent above her. She allowed the sun to coat over her body as she began taking deep breaths before opening her eyes again and focusing on Harmony in front of her.

"You feel better now?" asked Harmony as she placed the tablet down next to her.

"Yes, sorry. Am I at Duke now? I don't remember much after the plane," said Safia as she stared into Harmony's face. Something about her seemed familiar, as if she'd seen her somewhere before.

"Duke? Is that what they told you?" asked Harmony with a laugh. "Girl, this ain't no Duke. I can promise you that, but I guess it's better to show you than just tell you. Do you think you can walk without falling down?"

"Yes, I think so," said Safia as she slowly lowered herself from the bed. "Where are we going?" She said, suspicious of the girl's motives. *Wait, so I'm not at Duke? Then where am I? It is a school, right? I mean, this looks like a dorm room.*

"Just a trip around the campus. I'm getting points to be your tour guide and explain to you how things work here. So, I need to do my job."

Safia stood up, making sure her feet were solid under her. There were a few pings of sleep still in her legs, but she felt solid enough to stand. *Points? I think I remember the stewardess saying something about points.* She followed Harmony and continued to notice more details about her outfit. She wore a bow tie along with the button-up shirt. Inside the brown color of her clothing were blue accents that were sewn through the fabric, including the bow-tie itself. Below, she had on white stockings that went down into square-fronted latched shoes. *She's dressed like the people in old movies.*

"Well, it's a pleasure to meet you, Safia," said Harmony, extending out her hand.

Safia glanced down, reaching for her hand, but noticed the nicks and cuts that went along her wrists. *What happened there?* thought Safia as she shook Harmony's hand.

"Okay, let's go." said Harmony as she walked over, opening the door. Exiting out into the corridor, Safia followed as the girl led her through the area and down a flight of stairs.

"This is Marlone House. They always sort the freshmen amongst the houses. There's Marlone, Stoutfire, Yennefer, Grimdale, Cambridge, Marigold, and Duphfrey house. You'll learn them all by heart eventually, and who's the biggest threat."

"Threat? What do you mean, threat?" asked Safia, confused with the way Harmony was speaking. Following behind her escort after reaching the bottom of the steps, Safia passed the doors, stepping outside into an area as vast as she could see; the enormity of the campus now making Harmony's earlier words meaningful. Over a dozen buildings of odd design littered the campus as she watched numerous people make their way around.

All of them were dressed as Harmony was. Bow ties or neck ties of similar length; white shirts tucked into their trousers or skirts, along with the square front, brown or black shoes. The buildings all looked like something out of a fantasy novel. Concrete and brick walls, arches everywhere with pointy tops. The buildings on the campus looked like small castles or cathedrals. Places where the Pope might be seen coming out of rather than a bunch of well-dressed students.

"Welcome to the Apex Academy, where the future

leaders, singers, business people, and tech experts all go to learn," said Harmony as she stepped to the side, allowing Safia to walk forward and gaze over the campus. The walkway ahead was a spiraled labyrinth of confusion that twisted and turned in on itself in a way that seemed to be designed to be as annoying as possible. Just looking at it made her feel dizzy.

"What is this?" she said, stopping and pointing towards the walkways.

"Yeah, I wish I had an answer for you on that one. No one has ever been able to figure out why they created the walkways like this. Most of us here just accept that this school's architect was one of those crazy artistic types. That, or strung out on so many drugs that only his mind could make sense of it. But over time, you'll get used to it; or you'll just start sprinting through campus with reckless abandon. Either way, you'll figure yourself out here, like all of us did."

"Where are we?" asked Safia as she looked out over a field of green grass amongst the buildings scattered throughout the distance towards trees and mountains. There didn't seem to be anything that forced the students to stay. Just a line of trees that were far off. And down a hill from her, she saw a small lake next to an old looking shed that seemed to be in disrepair.

"Ireland, Scotland, somewhere in China; who really knows," said Harmony, also looking around the area. "We could be somewhere in the US for all anyone knows. All of us just woke up here, just like you."

"Everyone here was kidnapped?"

"What? No," said Harmony with a chuckle, "We all hoped to get here on day. We just didn't know how we would get here. Most of us at this school are trying to gain something or escape something."

Escape something?

"So one way or another, after learning about this place, we found a way to get here. Most of us probably have a mother, father, or uncle who went here, and that was our ticket. And if we were accepted, then we'd find ourselves waking up in a bed like you did a few days later." She then stopped and turned around to Safia, raising a finger. "And this is what brings me to my role in your journey here. I am to explain to you your current situation and answer any questions that you might have.

"But I didn't apply here. I was supposed to go to Duke."

"Yeah, that's why I called you a Trojan."

"A what?"

"Most of the people here come from wealthy families of influence of some type or another, but the people in charge here for some reason, invite people from unknown places to attend. Someone you know probably nominated you as a Trojan and the school came and picked you up. We all assume they do this just to mix it up and see if they will survive or be sent back."

"Survive?"

"Just a figure of speech, I promise," said Harmony, raising her hand in assurance. "After some time here, they will come and ask if you want to go back home. If you say yes, you'll be put back to sleep and probably find yourself back at home or wherever you came from. I've heard stories of people from poorer cities in America, Korea, China, and Brazil brought here, but I'm sure there are more. What about you? Where are you from?"

"Minneapolis, what about you?"

"I was born in Alabama, but grew up in California. If you're American, then you've probably seen my face before," said Harmony as she led Safia across the campus.

"You do seem familiar, but I can't remember?" said Safia truthfully, as the shape of Harmony's face did seem somewhat familiar, as if she had seen her before.

"Oh good, then it'll be more fun for you to try and figure it out."

Safia couldn't help but stare around at the similarly

dressed people as they went through the campus.

Marble statues of men and women were spread out through the green grounds as students sat beneath trees, reading and chatting with one another. Some had books, some had the same glass tablet as Harmony, and through-out the winding walkways were lampposts, where at the top of each one housed little black orbs that seemed as if they were looking at her as she passed them.

"So, this is a school then? What do they teach here?"

"Everything. They teach medicine, art, science. Probably not how to be an astronaut, though. I haven't seen any rockets going up around campus."

Is this even right? This is kidnapping, right? I mean, I thought I was going somewhere else. She took another look at Harmony as she continued her explanation of the environ-ment. *But there's no telling what might happen if I don't play along. I just need to pretend for a while. Then I'll see what's really happening.* "Everything just seems so weird. I thought I was supposed to be at Duke."

"Yeah, it's common to feel that way when you first get here," laughed Harmony. "I was in a taxi when they got me. I mean, you apply here, but you never know you're accepted till they come for you. I heard that one of the Trojans before kept having panic attacks every day, so much so that they had to sedate him and send him back home. I understand this place isn't for everyone, but the graduates from this school usually end up becoming very famous or powerful people. Presidents to Dictators, many are said to have come from here."

"Presidents? That can't be true."

"You'll probably see for yourself soon enough; the proof is walking around this campus somewhere. But like I said, if you don't want to be here, they will send you back. It's your choice at the end of the day," said Harmony as they came across a dozen people sitting down on the grass in a circle, where in the center of them sat a girl and a guy on a blanket. The girl held three playing cards in her hands that she was displaying out for the guy in front of her to inspect.

"What are they doing, playing a game of card shuffle?"

"Yeah, but it's a bit different in terms of rewards. Come on, this will be a good chance for you to learn," said Harmony as she stepped down onto the grass and strolled over to the group with Safia trailing behind her.

"Learn… learn what? I know how to play a game of card shuffle."

"Hey, Harmony," said a dark-haired boy sitting on the grass. "What you up to? Looking for your boyfriend?"

"Nah, just showing a new arrival around. Apparently, she's a Trojan."

"Oh, really," said the boy as he looked Safia up and down. "I see she hasn't started wearing the casual uniform of this place yet. She's cute though."

Thank you, I guess, thought Safia twisting her lips in response to the boy's remarks.

"It's her first day. I figure it's best to just show her around before we get her into the pleated skirts."

"Makes sense," said the boy as he slid over, making room for them. "Well, take a seat; the show's about to start." He reached out his hand to Safia. "I'm Gregory, by the way. Most people around here just call me Greggy."

"I'm Safia," she said as she shook his hand and lowered herself down to the ground, sliding between him and Harmony. "So what's so special about a game of card shuffle?"

"Nothing really," said Greggy. "Especially this game. They aren't really waging any high bets. So it's nothing too dramatic. Just messing around mostly."

"Yeah, but it's a good way for her to gain the concept of how this school works if she just watches it."

Safia watched as the boy ahead inspected the three cards before handing them back to the girl.

"Okay, I accept that the cards are real," said the boy.

"So you approve of the game then?"

"Yep, let's go."

The girl placed her hand on a pendant across her shirt's breast pocket, tapping on it, making it click, as the outer white rim of the pendant turned red. "I, Catarina Mondana, challenge Drylan Fillian to a game for ten points a game. And we shall play until one of us has lost a total of fifty points."

The boy on the blanket placed his hand on the pendant across his blazer, also tapping it, making the outer rim of the pendant again turn white. "I, Drylan Fillian, accept the challenge."

Both their pendants turned back white. "Challenge has been accepted," said a dual voice from both of their pendants.

Safia glanced around, looking at the people around her, and noticed that each of them had a pendant on their person. One girl had hers clipped onto a large braid in her hair; another boy had his clipped onto his pocket. Then she remembered the stewardess. *That's kinda like the pendant that she had around her neck on the plane. Is that what she meant by 'She was just doing it for the points'?*

Safia rubbed her shoulder, feeling nervous as she watched Katerina lay the cards down in front of her, she then revealed the Queen card to everyone before beginning to shuffle the three cards in front of her. Katerina's hand movements were very quick. One card on top of the other. One hand movement from left to right. Then from right to left. The cards flew in the air from hand to hand with such skill that it seemed as if she was doing it effortlessly. Safia observed the girl's movements in quiet awe as the cards shuffled back and forth. *She's really good at this,* thought Safia as she sat mesmerized by the girl's hand movements.

"Okay, now take your pick," said Katerina, as she placed the three cards down in front of Drylan.

"Well, I'm thoroughly fucked on this one, aren't I," said

Drylan as he tapped his fingers against the blanket.

"You can always just guess and hope for the best," said another boy behind him.

"Seems I don't have a choice. I can't back out now, can I?" asked Drylan as he reached for the left card. "I'm going with this one."

That's the wrong one. It's the card on the right.

He gripped the card and flipped it over, revealing a joker. "Ah, shit."

Instantly his badge turned red, while Catarina's badge flashed blue.

"And just so you know, I didn't cheat you," said Catarina as she flipped over the rightmost card revealing the Queen.

"So, I have a thirty-three percent chance of winning if I can't follow those shifty hand movements of yours."

"If you want to concede now and just give me another forty points, I'll accept that too."

"And go back to the boredom of waiting for orientation to be over? Not a chance. Let's go again."

Safia watched the two continue their game, their badges flashing red as they both won and lost the card game for several rounds, but eventually, Catarina emerged victorious to the sound of the applause of those around them.

"Catarina is the winner of the bet and is awarded a total of fifty points," spoke the tiny pendants attached to the two.

"Well, it was fun while it lasted," said Drylan, throwing up his hands.

"I can always challenge you again if you want."

"No, thanks, you've taken enough of my points today. Now, I gotta try to ace the next test to make up for it."

"Or you could just hand over all your points to me and become my discarded. I'll be sure to treat you well."

"No thanks, I like my freedom," said Drylan as he picked up a card and playfully tossed it at Catarina. "Next time, we will play a game that I will decide on."

"Well, that's that, I guess," said Harmony as she stood

up, dusting blades of grass off of her skirt before reaching her hand down to Safia. "Come on then, I'll finish showing you around the school."

"Alright," said Safia as she reached out, grabbing Harmony's hand, lifting herself to her feet. She couldn't help but take another look at the cut marks on Harmony's wrist. A large amount of them seemed to graze across her skin and some seemed fresh, as if she'd been clawing at them. They weren't that deep. They seemed just surface level really. But they drew her attention nonetheless.

"I'll catch you two later," said Greggy as he laid down on the grass, closing his eyes. "I think I'll try to take a nap here."

"Always the lazy type," said Harmony, shaking her head, smiling.

"Are all the bets like that?" asked Safia as they continued on their way through the campus.

"What? You mean with the cards? Goodness, no. They were just wasting time, is all.

"Wasting time? How?"

"Well, since the new crop of students are coming in. No one is really making any big bets until you guys get settled. So for the most part, since classes are on hold. Mostly everyone is just at a standstill until everything kicks back off. You're required to bet at least once a month here or you will get penalized. So you will see that once or twice."

"Penalized?"

"Yeah, but it's nothing major unless you go two months in a row, so don't worry. You'll understand."

"If you say so." *I knew this place was weird. Dammit, Yago. Do you even know what you've gotten me into? Is this school some type of gambling cult?* thought Safia as they headed toward a large building with arches and sharp edges on its roof. She couldn't help but gaze up at the structure. "Why do all the buildings here look like this?"

"Yeah, that's a question I'm not sure of," said Harmony

as she walked up to the building and placed her hands on its concrete walls. "Perhaps the people in charge here really just like old roman architecture. Arches, domes, vaults, you're going to find these themes all throughout the campus. And pillars, a whole bunch of pillars. It's actually quite pretty, if not a little pretentious."

"What's this building for?"

"Come on in, I'll show you," said Harmony as she walked forward, grabbing the circular metal handle of the large wooden door to the building and pulling it open. A cool air struck them both in the face as the door opened.

"Wow," said Safia as she gazed inside at a mountain of books that spread across dozens of shelves.

"Welcome to the library," said Harmony as they walked forward. "Well, one of them, there's another one just like it across campus. It doesn't cost anything to enter here. Oh, but the cafeteria is free until orientation, then it's three hundred points a month."

Safia had never seen so many books in one place. Shelves upon shelves of books littered the building in sectioned off aisles. The only thing to separate them were the pillars that held the roof of the building. Even amongst the walls were shelves filled with books that went two stories high. The only free space on the walls were for the windows that allowed the sunlight to shine in through an assortment of mosaic windows that housed art work of people that she didn't recognize.

As she stared up at the images on the windows, the sounds of some rolling came as she saw a student gliding on a moving ladder as he came across to grab a book from one of the higher shelves.

"So many books," said Safia in awe.

"And the other one's just as big. If you are a bookworm, then this is probably the place you will spend most of your time," said Harmony with a chuckle as they walked past several aisles of books. "The reading area is back here."

Ahead of them in a small open area at the back of the library were a set of six tables spaced out amongst themselves with a few students who were studying; two boys and a singular girl. The girl was wearing the same uniform as the rest of the students here, except for a few minor changes. She wore long sleeves that came down to her wrists instead of the short sleeved dress shirts and vest that the others had on, and she wore a scarf around her head and neck so that only her face was revealed.

"Well, this is lucky," said Harmony. "It seems we've found ourselves another Trojan. Maybe you two can become friends. That'll be more points for me." She waved at the girl in the scarf as she walked over. "Hey, Hammy, I brought you a friend to play with."

"It's pronounced Hashmi," said the girl, looking annoyed. "Why must you intentionally mispronounce my name?"

"Because Hammy and Harmony sound better together."

"I did not realize we were 'together' since I have not seen you in two weeks."

"Don't worry about her," said Harmony to Safia, "She looks grumpy, but she's just a cute baby inside. I'm the one who showed her around the campus when she got here a little over a month ago."

"Yes, and then you dumped me when your boyfriend appeared."

"That's not fair. We had a good opportunity to win some points."

"And I was assaulted by the other students; each of them trying to challenge me to their dumb games. Even though I'm not even allowed to bet by the rules of the school. I ended up having to tell them that gambling was prohibited in my religion just to get them to leave me alone."

"Okay, I'm sorry I left you," said Harmony as she pointed to Safia, "But look, I brought you a new friend as a peace offering."

"You mean you're trying to get more points?"

"Why can't it be both?"

Hashmi sighed but extended her hand over to Safia, "Hello, don't believe anything she tells you. If we become friends, then she gets more points. That's why she's doing this."

Well, she seems normal, at least. "Why is everyone here so obsessed with points," asked Safia as she reached over the wooden table to shake Hashmi's hand. "Do grades matter that much?"

"You haven't explained it to her yet?" asked Hashmi, narrowing her eyes at Harmony.

"Hey, don't look at me like that," said Harmony as she threw up her hands in innocence. "She's barely been awake for an hour. I was getting around to it."

"Explain what?"

"The point system here," said Hashmi, placing a marker in her book before closing it. "This school runs off of it. Anything you want, you can buy if you have enough points and if the person agrees to sell it. If you want something that's not here, all you have to do is request it, and the school will figure out a point total for you to have it, and if you have enough, then, it's yours."

"Anything?"

"So far, yes," said Harmony, "I haven't heard of anything being denied. Only people not having enough points for some ridiculous items, such as tractors or something else foolish. But, as new students, we aren't allowed to make any wagers with our points until after orientation and we've agreed to the school's terms."

Terms? So they make you sign a contract? Wait, is it like some type of extortion thing? "The point system here seems really confusing."

"The school will explain it better than us," said Harmony. "Just try not to fall too deep into the points game here. I've seen people do crazy things trying not to get expelled."

"Ah, okay." *I'm afraid to ask what she means by crazy things.*

"Come on. I'll show you the rest of the school."

"Okay," said Safia as she waved bye to Hashmi. "It was nice meeting you."

"It was nice meeting you, as well. Try not to let Harmony be too much of a bad influence on you."

"Oh, ha-ha, you just put your head back into your book. I've got points to make," said Harmony as she led Safia out of the library and through the concrete walkways of the campus. "That's the cafeteria, the gymnasium, the theater, and most of the dorms." She pointed out different things as they made their way back around the campus. Most of the buildings had the same design as the library, but off into the distance, after passing a corner, she saw the top of another structure over a side wall.

"What's that one over there?"

"That's the school," said Harmony as they rounded the wall, allowing the school to come into view.

"Oh, wow," said Safia as she saw the full scale of the school. It was a massive three-story arched monstrosity of a building. The design across the spires looped over each other, all connecting to a bell tower at the center of it all.

"Yeah, that's how most people react the first time they see it. But it becomes less intimidating the longer you stay here. Most classes will be held there unless we are having exams, but since you're a first-year, your class will be on the first floor, so at least, you won't have to deal with those steps."

"Oh come now, you can do better than that," said a male voice from ahead of them.

Safia rounded the side of the building to see a group of people sprawled out amongst the grass in front of a fountain as they watched and laughed, as a boy and a girl with their sleeves rolled up, both splashed around in water as if searching for something. There at the edge of the fountain, Safia saw what was surely there belonging; two sets of shoes alongside a set of socks and stockings.

"We just had to run into them," said Harmony with a sigh as she spotted the group of students.

"Oh, looks like we have some visitors," said one of the boys, laying down on the grass, holding a smiling girl in his arms.

"Oh, is that so? Do you think we should be charging an admission fee? I'd hate to think of others getting free entertainment from our private sports," said a girl with her head relaxing on a man's lap as he waved a fan over her face.

"Now, don't be like that, Amanda. It's our responsibility to be accommodating hosts," said the boy as he waved over at them. "You two, come over here for a moment."

"It's best not to piss them off," said Harmony in a low tone as she shook her head. "Come, follow me, and stay close."

"Okay." *I guess bullies exist in college, too. That must be one of those universal truths Mr. Wilcock kept talking about in science class,* thought Safia as she and Harmony walked over to the group with the two in the fountain continuing to splash around in the water.

"Well, if it isn't Miss Harmony," said the dark-haired boy with the girl in his arms. "And who's that you have with you there?"

"Hello, Dario. She's a new student. I'm just showing her around."

"You're still doing those charity cases for points?" asked Dario, shaking his head sympathetically. "That's a shame. If you want points to restart your career, all you had to do was ask. With that body of yours, I'm sure we could work something out."

"No, thanks. I'd prefer not to be your pet. And I don't think my boyfriend would like that very much," said Harmony with disgust in her tone.

"That's the problem with you, men," said the woman with her head in the man's lap. "You're always looking to break down and control women. While I, on the other hand, make my toys better than before I claimed them."

"Ha, I found it," yelled the boy in the fountain as he raised his hand out of the water with a coin that was silver on one side and solid pink on the other.

"And thus, my point is proven," said the woman as she sat up from the boy's lap and reached out her hand to the other boy in the water. "Now, come here and bring me the coin, Ricardo."

The boy in the water did as he was told, stepping out of the water; his soaking wet button-up shirt revealing his body beneath as it stuck to his skin. He made his way over, bringing the coin to the girl, and suddenly, the badge between her collar turned blue, along with Dario's badge on his shoulder strap turning red.

"Amanda Chastain has won and has been awarded five thousand points," said both their badges.

"Screw you, Amanda. I swear you're cheating somehow," said Dario as he began to get frustrated and turned to the girl in the water. "Get out of there. You're going to go again."

"Yes, sir," said the girl as she stepped out of the water, walking over to Dario, her face and clothing also soaking wet, revealing the bra she had on beneath.

"God, you're useless," said Dario as he grabbed her by the arm, pulling her forward towards him. "How are you ever going to pay off your debt to me if you keep losing?" He looked down at her revealed bra showing through her clothing. "Take off your shirt. If you're going to cost me points, I can at least enjoy the sight of your tits bouncing around while you do it."

The girl looked around at the other boys, "But... but there are people around."

"What, you wanna be expelled, is that it?"

"No, I'm sorry, please don't send me back."

What? How can he just treat her like that? Thought Safia as she felt a quiet rage fill up inside of her that was about to peak.

"Oh my," said Amanda, laughing at Dario. "Talk about over-compensating. I swear that penis of yours must be smaller than my pinky finger."

"What?" responded Dario as he let go of the girl, snapping his attention towards Amanda. "You've got some nerve. If we were out in the real world, I'd have your tongue cut out for that."

"Poor Dario. That temper of yours will always be your downfall. You simply don't know how to play with your toys," said Amanda as she turned towards the soaking wet boy who had brought her the coin. "Ricardo, take off your shirt and show Dario here what a real man is supposed to look like."

"Yes, ma'am," said the boy in wet clothing as he began to unbutton his shirt, pulling it from his wet body, exposing himself. He had a large chest, well-defined abs, as well as strong muscular arms and shoulders. He looked like a model out of a magazine more than a student. Even Safia caught herself staring at him as the leftover water from his shirt dripped down his body, soaking into his pleated pants.

"You see, Dario, even the girls in your little fan club admire my man here," said Amanda, as she slowly slid her hand over Ricardo's chest, kissing him on his shoulder. "You need to learn to take better care of your pets." She pressed up against him from behind and grabbed his ass while taking the time to run her other hand across his chest. "While discarded they may be, you can still get plenty of fun out of them."

That's a thing to say, thought Safia before she had a moment of self-reflection about her own previous relationship. *But I guess I'm not really one to talk.*

Amanda reached her hand around, rubbing her fingers across Ricardo's crotch; The wet fabric of his trousers dark in the morning sun. "Well, at least I can have fun with mine. I doubt you have enough down there to satisfy any woman, let alone that child you have there."

"You bitch, if you think I'm just going to—"

"How about we make another bet, Dario?" asked Amanda as she reached for her pendant. Safia noticed that it was shaped like a star. As she tapped her pendant with one hand and reached down, unbuckling Ricardo's belt from his trousers. "I, Amanda Wilson, challenge Dario Rossilini to a contest to see who has the bigger cock. Either my discarded Ricardo Reigns or Dario Rossilini himself for the sum of five hundred thousand points in exchange that he transfers over the discarded rights of Mallory Polana."

What is happening? Are all the people in this school like this? Is no one going to say anything? Wondered Safia as the surrounding crowd gasped at the number of points being wagered.

"You, bitch. You dare make fun of me," said Dario, his face starting to flush as his lips twisted, revealing his teeth.

"Bitch, this. Bitch, that. I swear men like you have such a limited vocabulary. It's simple, Dario, dear. If you're such a big strong man as to pick on a little girl like that, then surely you must be hiding a wondrous cock down there. And I do believe Miss Mallory still has the ability to be transferred If I'm correct." Amanda unbuttoned another button on Ricardo's trousers, allowing her finger to circle around the third. "Come on, Dario, it's half a million points, and they're all yours. All you have to do is show us how much of a man you are."

Dario's pendant flashed red, its colors going through its spiraled design. "Dario Rossilini," said the voice from his pendent, "do you accept or decline the challenge? You must answer, or you will forfeit the right to wager for a month and lose two hundred and fifty thousand points as a penalty."

"Come on, Dario. The cock - oops. I mean, the clock is ticking," said Amanda with a sly smirk as she patted Ricardo's crotch. "And please understand, I'm very anxious to show you all what I get to play with at night."

Dario's teeth ground in his mouth, and Safia swore she could see the hate behind his eyes. But there in the morning sun, Dario then stood up straight and tapped the pendant on his shoulder.

"I, Dario Rossilini, decline the challenge."

"Ah... really? And here I thought we were finally going to see the moment when Dario Rossilini finally acted like a man. But I guess you are coming up short again, Dario. As I'm sure many women in the future are destined to find out. And thus be just disappointed as I'm sure we all are now."

"Be careful, you sharp-tongued bitch. I'll make you choke on those words."

"And I'm sure the odds of that are just the same as me choking on your so-called cock," said Amanda with a mischievous smile as she narrowed her eyes at Dario. "Because as I've just proven. It doesn't exist."

Dario's eyes went wide as he stormed off, followed by his entourage and the girl he was just accosting.

"I guess that settles that," said Amanda with a sigh as she patted Ricardo on the back. "Put your shirt back on, Ricardo. Oh, but please do try to keep that cock hard. I may have use of it later on tonight."

"Yes, ma'am," said Ricardo as he wrung out his shirt, sending a stream of water to the ground.

Amanda sighed. "Such a shame. I had hoped that goading him like that would have forced him to wager that poor girl and I could free her. But I guess I should have chosen a wager where he may have thought he could win. I mean, how was I supposed to know he had a small cock." Amanda then turned her attention towards Harmony and Safia. "Oh, but where are my manners? Hello, girls, and what brings you out here? Oh, that's right, you said you were escorting this lovely new student around." She stepped forward, looking Safia up and down. "Well, aren't you cute? And your hair's all curly."

What... who is this. What even just happened? Thought

Safia as she looked down into the woman's face; Her gray eyes looking poised and filled with the mischief of a child waiting for the next item to throw their attention at.

"Hold on, Amanda," said Harmony as she stepped in front of Safia, trying to protect her from Amanda's curiosity. "At least let her get settled in before you before you wrap her into your games."

"Harmony, you know that I only have the purest intentions," said Amanda with a smirk as she raised her hand up Harmony's face and caressed her cheek. "And, besides, you didn't seem to mind my attention that much for the time we shared together."

"A time that gladly has passed," said Harmony, slowly removing Amanda's hand from her face.

"So, it seems it has," said Amanda in a sour tone. "Oh, well, far be it from me to hold up your tour of the campus. I wish you both well."

And with a quick turn, Amanda turned and walked back over to the two men waiting for her. The shirtless man had decided to stay that way, as he had gathered his items and was holding them in his arms as he waited for her. Then together the three of them walked off, leaving Safia alone with Harmony to contemplate the absurdity of the previous few minutes.

"What was that?" asked Safia, unable to wrap her mind around it. "Are they allowed to treat people like that here? Why doesn't anyone stop them?"

Harmony sighed as she started making her way towards the school ahead of them, with Safia following behind her again.

"I know it doesn't seem that way, but the girl who Dario was abusing. She's letting him do that to her in order to stay in the school?"

"What? Why?"

"Everyone's got their own reasons, I'm sure. But the short version is that if you lose all your points, you'll be expelled. The only way to stay after you have no points is to essentially become someone's property."

"Property? Like a slave?"

"Kinda, I mean. Ahh! What a pain it is to explain this," said Harmony, scratching her head. "That girl and Dario made some type of deal. I don't know exactly what that deal is. But he essentially takes care of her. He buys her food, her textbooks, and whatever else she needs that costs points."

"I don't care what he buys me. I wouldn't let anyone treat me like that."

"You'd be surprised what people will do when they're desperate enough. And I know it looks bad, but Dario has a risk involved with her also. If she's penalized any points, then it comes out of his account. So, the person who takes you in has to have a large number of points to take care of you. Otherwise, they might risk being expelled just by having you."

"I just... I don't get it."

"You will. You'll understand the point system here soon enough if you decide to stay."

They reached the building where Safia saw a few more students cleaning the halls and nearby classrooms. The floors were shiny and seemed as if they were made of marble. One of the boys up ahead caught Safia's eyes and seemed familiar.

"Wait," said Safia as she recalled the boy's name. "Isn't that Randall Justin, the Vice-President's son?"

"Oh, you recognize him, then. Yeah, that's him."

"But... but why's he here cleaning the floors?"

"Helping others get points, I'd guess. He organizes a lot of events for students with low points. Such as cleaning the grounds and study sessions for hard exams. He is one of the few people here that's mostly liked by everyone. Well, him and Jericho."

"When will classes start?"

"In a week or two. The teachers haven't arrived yet. Only

the administration is here; they're the ones that handle the class schedules and get everything ready." She stepped forward. "But that will be in the main building. Come on, I'll show you the store. You're going to need to know how to buy things."

"Okay," said Safia as she followed Harmony through the massive building and up a flight of stairs to the second floor.

"And here's the store."

Safia looked around at everything on the second floor. Whereas the first floor seemed like your standard school, with its long corridors and classrooms, the second floor looked more like a shopping market. There were shelves with books and accessories, and racks with clothing, short and long pleated skirts for girls and pleated slacks for boys. Against the wall, she could see an assortment of electronic devices. Each of which having large red tags next to them with numbers on the side.

"Now, let's see," said Harmony as she walked up and began flipping through a rack of white short sleeve shirts, before picking one and coming back to Safia, holding it out in front of her chest. "Well, at least you'll look cute in it."

"Why do the pants and the skirts have different colors?"

"Each color represents a different house. It doesn't really matter so much except during team exams. But that's second-year stuff."

Safia nodded her head, but noticed the red price tag hanging off the shirt. "It's fifty dollars?"

"No, It's fifty points," said Harmony with a smile as she waved her hand around the room. "Money doesn't mean anything at this school. You buy everything with points here. From the food you eat to the clothes you wear."

"Wait, so I can't eat if I don't have points?"

"Nope. Eating here costs three hundred points a month. And if your points get below that and you can't afford the food budget, then they'll just expel you and send you back home. Don't worry, you won't starve on campus or anything," said

Harmony with a giggle and a dismissive flick of her wrist as she wandered around the store examining different items. "If this school were that masochistic, I doubt any parent would allow their child to go here. There are multiple rules put in place to keep the students safe from other students, or from themselves."

Safia, shook her head, watching Harmony's head bobble back and forth behind the book rack. "Why do people even come to this school? Why not just go to a normal school?"

"Now, that, I think, will be better if the administration explains to you. They have a whole presentation on it, but, trust me, you'll understand soon enough why so many people are here, and even more so, just who these people are."

"If you say so... but no one's going to stop me if I try to go back? I won't be shipped off to some foreign country or something?"

"No, I call some of the graduates from here from time to time, as well as a few who left the school voluntarily, because they didn't think it was worth it. Not to mention those like Miss Abigail, who came back to teach at the school."

"I think I'm starting to understand, but all of this still just seems so weird." *Okay, I'm at some secret school or something like out of those TV shows. Oh, Yago and David are so dead when I get out of here. Just who are these people?*

"Oh, I'm sure," said Harmony with a laugh as she walked over, finished with her exploring of the store. "But come on, let's head on back. I think I've been as much of an informative guide as I can be for today."

"Okay," said Safia as she and Harmony headed back down-stairs and out of the building, once again back to the winding concrete walkways. Safia noticed that if she focused on the ridiculousness of the spiraling walkway, she would soon find herself feeling a bit light-headed as she went through the twists and turns of its confusing paths.

"So, Miss Trojan student, I've told you everything I can

think of, but do you have any questions for me?"

Of course I have questions. Not that I'd get a real answer. Who made this place? Are you sure you're not being held hostage? Is this really a rich people cult? "Not really, I mean… I mean, it's weird here. Like the people cleaning up, who decides how many points they get for doing that. Is there like a sign posted up somewhere that says you will get points for such-and-such?"

"That would be helpful," chuckled Harmony. "But sadly, no. We just do things that we think would benefit the school and wake up the next morning or in the next few days with more points. Sometimes, the school asks us personally to do things, but even then, they never say how many points we'll get."

"Wait, you said you were getting points for showing me the school. Does that mean you don't know how many points you'll get?"

"Exactly, I haven't a clue. I'll wake up one day, and it'll be in my journal."

"Journal? Will I get one?" asked Safia as she took another look at the students of the campus, who just seemed to be going about their leisurely way. "I mean this is a school right. But I haven't seen anyone with backpacks or anything."

"Oh, that's right, you haven't gotten one yet. Remember that tablet-looking thing I had in my hand when we first met? That's my journal. You might want to get one of those when you have enough points. They're super useful."

"Ah, okay. I'll try to remember that," said Safia as she followed Harmony through the campus till they reached the dorm where Safia had awoken. Making their way back up the steps, Harmony opened the door and plopped down on the bed.

"Ah, it feels so good to be back. Being an escort is hard work. Not to mention that we ran into Dario and Amanda the moment we left," said Harmony as she smushed her face into the fabric of the pillow before turning to Safia. "Are you like one of those people that's bad luck to be around or something?"

"What? No," said Safia with a frown as she walked over, sitting on the bed opposite Harmony's. She grabbed a remote from the windowsill and turned on the TV. Feeling a bit dirty from her journey throughout the campus, she looked around the room for her luggage and noticed that it wasn't anywhere to be found. Thinking about it, she wasn't sure it had ever arrived. "Hey, do you know where my things are? I want to call my family. I told them I'd call when I got here."

"That may be a problem," said Harmony as she grimaced at Safia. "Seeing as no one on the campus is allowed a phone."

"What?" shouted Safia in shock.

"Yeah, that's one of the bad things about going to school here."

"But why not? They can't just keep us here, and what about the rest of my stuff?"

"You'll find a change of clothes in your closet along with any medication you might be on. And it's not to keep you here, I don't think. But remember when I said that this school has some of the children of rich and famous people here?"

"Yeah."

"Remember the Vice-President's son, well he's not the only important person here. This school has had the children of a lot of rich and powerful families here. Can you imagine the type of problems it would cause if suddenly half the people here were kidnapped and held for ransom? Children of dictators, drug lords, presidents, ambassadors all attend this school."

"Then... then... are we safe here?" asked Safia, looking around nervously as she thought about what Harmony was saying.

"As far as I know, sure. I mean, I've never heard of

anything bad ever happening here. Well, outside of being expelled, I guess. But don't worry, you'll get to call your family when they come to get you, they just monitor the calls, is all. I guess it's to make sure you don't tell them where you are. But it does feel kinda creepy with them watching over you."

"But I don't know where I am."

"Good," said Harmony as she placed her hands behind her head, stretching out on the bed. "Then, that means you have nothing to worry about."

CHAPTER 6

That night Safia washed herself in the dormitory bath and slipped into the pajamas. It was another brown a white set that the school had assigned to her. All clothing sets, she realized, matched the standard uniforms of the campus. Feeling mentally exhausted she lay in the bed assigned to her. The day's happenings flowed through her mind as she tried to process everything that she had seen.

To her, everything that happened seemed as if it was a dream. This mysterious campus where everything seemed to run on points. But try as she might, she couldn't deny the truth that there was a campus filled with others; who themselves had chosen to come and participate in this madness. A concept that she was forced to accept as the truth of which lay asleep in front of her.

These thoughts plagued her mind until she awoke the next morning to the sound of knocking on her door.

"I'm coming," said Safia, as she tried to force herself awake, rolling out of bed and fumbling her way to the door while scratching her head. She pulled the latch, opening it to find a tall man in a suit before her. His size towered over her as he wore a look of sternness across his face that was covered by the jet black hair that hung down just at the tip of his eyes. His appearance startled her, causing her to take a step back into the room.

"Ah... may I help you?"

"You are Safia Famosa, correct?" said the man with a deep voice.

"Ah, yes, that's correct?"

"It's time for your entrance exam. Please, follow me," said the man as he turned and walked off down the hallway.

"Ah, wait," she said as she hesitated at the door in her pajamas. Turning back towards Harmony's bed for some type of assurance, Safia realized that she was gone. Her bed had been made and the few items she did have on the table before the bed were also gone. *Okay... okay. This isn't bad. I just need to follow along. They're plenty of other students here. Nothing bad is going to happen to me,* thought Safia, in order to accept the situation. While cautious of him, she closed the door, following behind the man and quickly caught up to him. "You could have given me some time to get dressed at least."

"There will be plenty of time for that when we arrive, and you will be given proper clothing there. I was asked to speed up the process because you wish to have a conversation with your family."

"Yes, I did. Can I talk to them now?" *Is that where Harmony went? Did she tell them I wanted to call home?*

They left out of the backside of the building, moving into the open area of the campus. The sun had only barely come over the horizon, and the grass was still wet from the dew of night as they quickly made their way across campus.

The winding way walk still made Safia feel a bit dizzy as she traveled along its route. *Argh, I hate this. Why couldn't they just make it straight like normal people? It feels like I'm walking in circles.* Soon Safia saw where they were headed. It was another colossal two-story building down from the actual school where at the steps stood a heavy looking wooden door. But there were no latches on the door; instead, there was a small electronic device on the side of the wall.

"This is it," said the man as he reached inside of his breast pocket, pulling out a small key card, and swiping it over the electronic device. Safia heard a loud clicking noise as the wooden door split, sliding on its sides, and opening the way forward for them.

Safia blinked and grabbed at her shoulders as an enormous rush of cold air from inside rushed out to meet them.

"Come. We have a phone inside."

The building had tiled floors, integrated into black and white sections like a chessboard. This design was mimicked across the roof as well and on the lower sections of the wall. Instantly Safia felt the patterns begin to mess with her eyes the moment she gazed in. Blinking, and waiting for her eyes to adjust, they both stepped in.

Throughout the hall were large windows where she could see inside each of the rooms. They all were empty, but thankfully didn't share the same checked pattern as the hall. Instead, one room was completely white and the next would be completely black. Inside each were desks and chairs along with some exercise equipment; one room looked to have some type of large computer terminal. Between the chilled sterile air and the lights inside the squared ceiling, it gave Safia the feeling of going through a hospital.

I'm okay. I'm okay. Keep calm. I've come this far, just a little more, and I'll be able to talk to my family. She glanced back at the hallway and back up at the man in the suit. *I hope.*

"This way, just a little further," said the man as he stepped inside with Safia trailing behind him. After passing a few more of the odd rooms, they stopped in front of one. Through the glass, Safia saw a black room that had sectioned off stalls mounted onto the walls. And inside of each stall looked to be phones with stools below them.

"Here you can speak with your family," said the well-dressed man as he led Safia inside of the room. She instantly noticed a white door in the back. The contrast with the rest of the room was so glaring that she couldn't help herself but to stare at it for a moment.

"So, can I just pick one and—"

"Here she comes now," said the well-dressed man.

She? Who's she?

The white door in the back of the room opened and in walked a dark-haired woman in a brown full body skirt and a lab coat holding a tablet similar to the one she'd seen Harmony use.

"Hello there," said the woman. "I'm Abigail, and I take it you must be Miss Safia Famosa."

"Ah, yes, Ma'am." said Safia, surprised by the woman's appearance, but somehow felt comforted by the sight of another woman.

"Oh, just call me Abigail. No need for the Ma`am. Now, please follow me, and we can get started on your tests," she said as she turned around and began to head back through the door.

"Tests?" blurted out Safia as she took a step back, instantly on alarm. "What tests?" *Now what do I do?*

"This one would like to speak with her family before she accepts the terms of the school," said the well-dressed man. "I have brought her here for that reason, and if she agrees, then you can perform her physical."

"Oh," said Abagail with a smile. "I'm sorry. I just assumed you were here to get your physical over with. "But yes, please, take a seat at any one of these booths and we will have you connected to your family in no time."

Safia looked between the man and woman cautiously for a moment before she stepped in the nearest booth. Opting to keep standing and facing the two, she reached forward grabbing the phone. It was then she noticed that it was an old type of phone with a long rubbery cord and a rotary dial.

Is this a pay phone? Do I need to use points? She stared at it. *I've never actually used one of these before.* She then placed the headpiece to her ear, but didn't hear anything. She reached for the rotary dial. *In the movies, I think they…*

"Wait a moment, please," said Abigail as she began to play on her tablet. "I haven't activated it yet. And unfortunately, one of us will need to listen in on your call. We usually do things by sex here. So Derrick will assist the men and I will listen to your call. It makes things a little less embarrassing if something were blurted out that you'd not want others to know. You know, girl secrets and all that."

Safia turned back to the large well-dressed man. *Derrick? His name's Derrick.* Thought Safia as she remembered that she had never actually gotten the man's name.

"Ah, okay," said Safia, just wanting to speak to her family. "Can I call them now?" *This place is beyond weird. And I thought nothing could be worse than working in the diner. This place is… well, I don't know what this place is. I just know that I want out.*

"Sure," said Abigail as she began flicking her finger across the tablet's screen. "Let me just activate booth number two and you should hear a dial tone soon."

And sure enough, after a few disturbing sounding clicks from the phone, then came the sound of the dial tone.

"Okay, I hear it now."

"Who would you like to call first?"

"Ah, my father, Hector Famosa."

"Okay, now do you know the number, or would you like me to look it up?"

"I know it."

Abigail walked up to Safia pulling out a stool from a nearby booth and took a seat. "Okay, have a seat Miss Famosa."

Safia cautiously did as instructed, noticing that Derrick was now further away from before, standing with his shoulder leaning on the corner of the room. Turning back to Abigail, she noticed that now that she was closer to her; Abigail couldn't be much older than herself. *I wonder how old she is. Maybe early twenties?*

"Is something wrong Miss Famosa?"

"Huh, oh sorry. No." She turned back toward the phone and immediately sighed. "How do I... I mean, I've never used a phone like this before."

"Oh, of course. I'm sorry. Just tell me the number and I'll dial it out for you."

"It's seven, five, seven, four, three, five, seven." After telling Abigail the number, Safia placed the phone back to her ear and watched as Abigail slid her index finger in the loops ahead of each number.

"Now remember. Your family thinks you're at Duke and we'd prefer it if you ensured that they think this way. Remember, everything here is a secret."

"Oh, ah, okay," said Safia, as she nervously watched the rotating dial spin. *I just gotta be careful what I say. But Yago will know something, then I'll be able to go home.*

The phone's earpiece made another clicking noise as it rotated back into position after each turn. But soon after the clicking of the telephone came the sound of a ring, and then another. The phone rang several more times, which to Safia felt like forever. And then after nine or ten rings, finally, she heard another clicking sound.

"This is Famosa's'. How can we help you?" came her father's voice from the other end.

"Papa? Hey papa."

"Oh! Safia baby, I'm so happy to hear from you. We were starting to get worried, you know. You never called. What happened?" There was a clicking sound on the other end.

"I'm sorry, Papa, the ahh... the phone doesn't work out here. Might be too many mountains," said Safia as she looked over at Abigail, who smiled back at her and nodded.

"Hey? Whose phone is this, anyway? I'd hear this strange ringing in the home and I had to look all over before I found it. Why'd you not call the house phone?"

"Oh, that's Yago's phone. Mr. Alvarez gave it to him for work?"

"Dang boy, should tell his father these things. I find out he's been hiding a girlfriend and now he's hiding phones. I tell you Safia, this is how it starts. Next thing you know, my boy is out selling drugs or something. I can't wait till he's in college like you are, then I won't have to worry so much."

Her father's words brought a small amount of regret into her heart because of what she was now mustering up the courage to tell him.

"Yeah, sorry. I knew. I guess I should have told you."

"Bahh, don't worry. It's not your job to rat your brother out. But forget about him for now. Did you make it okay? Do you need anything?"

"No, I'm fine. I just ahh... wanted to tell you that I'm ahh... I'm okay." Safia shook her head, struggling to confess to her father that she wanted to come back home. "Is everything going well there?"

"Oh, yeah, everything's fine. I'm just relaxing today, watching the TV. Oh, that Mr. Alvarez is downstairs, sitting in the back as usual. I've been thanking him every day for what he did for you. You're the first one in the family to go to college. That's something to be proud of, ya know?"

"I... I know, papa," said Safia as her eyes began to water.

"Here," whispered Abigail as she reached in her pocket and pulled out a handkerchief, handing it to Safia.

"Is everyone doing okay?" asked Safia, dabbing at her eyes with the soft cloth.

"Oh, we're all fine here. Hey, there's your brother. Hey, Yago, your sister's on this phone you got that you didn't tell me about. How many secrets are you keeping from the family, huh? You some type of secret agent or something. Now, come over here and say hello to your sister before you head off to work."

"It's not a secret phone, you just never asked," said Yago's voice in a muffled distance away from the phone before Safia heard a shuffling sound, and then came her brother's voice.

"Hello? Saffy? What's wrong?"

"Yago, hey. Nothing, I just ahh. I just wanted to let you know I made it safe, and everything's okay here."

"That's good to hear. Try your best there. You're a lot smarter than you think you are."

Safia laughed. "You think so?"

"Of course. But don't worry about the school, okay. I wouldn't have let you go there if I thought you couldn't handle it. Just try not to lose all your points, okay."

Safia's eyes opened wide when he mentioned the points as she turned to Abigail, who was also staring back at her, confused. She clutched the phone to her ear.

"You... you know about this school?" asked Safia, hearing another clicking sound from the other end of the call.

"Not really, but I've heard about it. I got invited to go myself, but after I got my scholarship. I decided you should take my place. Be safe up there, little sister. I know you can do it."

"I'm the big sister," she corrected him, "and I will," said Safia as she heard a horn blow in the background of Yago's call.

"That must be my ride. I gotta go. And sis?"

"Yes."

"Remember, it's okay if you just want to come home. If anything, David sure misses you, although he'll be gone in another week."

"Thanks, Yago."

"See ya soon, Saffy."

After talking with her brother, Safia spent a few more minutes on the phone with her father and found out her mother was out handling orders for the shop before she then hung up the phone.

"And this Yago is your brother?" asked Abigail.

"Yes," said Safia, already knowing that there was no need to lie about that to the school. They more than likely knew everything about her family.

"Any idea how he found out about the point system of this school?"

"I don't know. I only found out about it after I got here."

"Well, that's fine. They will look into it, I'm sure," said Abigail, tapping her finger on her knee. "Sorry for all the questions, but it's part of the procedure."

"It's okay. Harmony explained everything to me."

"Okay then, I'll move along," said Abigail as she stood up from her seat and, in a formal tone, spoke. "Miss Safia Famosa, with everything you know now, I have to ask the question. Do you wish to attend Apex Academy? If so, you will be enrolled into the current semester and provided room and board for two or three years unless you are expelled. But you may also refuse enrollment, in which case you will be sedated and returned to your family."

Safia looked up at Abigail. "I have to decide now?"

"Yep, the moment you entered this room, you wouldn't be allowed to leave without an answer to this question. That's one of the reasons Derrick's here. This is the moment where you decide the type of life you want for yourself."

"What if I say yes, but decide I want to go home in a month?"

"Then, the same will apply. You will be sedated and escorted home. However, we encourage anyone from here to not disclose any information about the school to anyone other than former staff or students, which is why I'm curious as to why your brother had the information on our point system if he's never attended before. And according to our recording we have never officially offered an invitation to Yago. Unless it's a very recent action that hasn't been updated in our systems."

"I... I don't know. Yago's always been like that, always knowing weird stuff." Safia then looked around the room one last time. The blackness of the room made her feel as if she was going to be swallowed whole any moment. *I wonder if I should have told papa I wanted to come home. But he seemed so proud and they said I can go whenever I want.* She then glanced back over at Derrick, who was still leaning with his shoulder against the wall. *I guess I've made up my mind then. I hope I'm not making the wrong decision,* she thought to herself as she turned back to Abigail. "If I can, I'd like to try and attend this school?"

"Good, we're happy to have you. There are a large number of benefits to graduating from Apex. The main one, I imagine, that people come here for is the influence. Graduating from here with a high number of points will almost guarantee you a life of influence in the world. You're from America, so the idea of you being a governor or a senator isn't out of the question. Well, as long as you can handle the campaign trail. There are some things we can't fix, like if a presidential candidate decides he wants to strip down naked and run through the streets of Washington on election night."

"Wait, that was Senator O'Connell. Was he from this school?"

"Yes, and apparently, they had such high hopes for him until that incident," said Abigail, shaking her head disappointingly. "I don't believe even this school could control the news spinning enough to salvage anything out of that situation, the complete disaster that that was."

"I remember that night. He was all over TV the next day. They even made memes of him in country music videos."

"Oh, we are aware of the memes that sprouted out from that travesty. But as long as you don't go and pull an O'Connell on us and graduate like a regular student, then getting you in some type of high office shouldn't be out of the question."

"Can you really do all that?"

"Me? No? I'm just a teacher here. But the people in charge, they can. Some of the people I went to school with here have become everything from astronauts to world-class chefs."

"Harmony said you can't turn people into astronauts."

"We don't exactly send people off into space from campus. But we can get them in the programs that might. Apex gives them the opportunity. The school simply opens the door for people to succeed. As we have just spoken about the tragic circumstances of Senator O`Connell, there are some things that are even beyond this school's control."

"Oh. I guess that makes sense." *Am I doing the right thing by staying here? Of course I'm not. I'm an idiot,* thought Safia as she nodded her head, closing her eyes for a moment. *What else is there for me? Serving plates for the rest of my life. No. If this is real, then I want this. Yago and David did this for me. I can't just go back home after what they did to get me here. Plus, Yago knows now, and it looks like I can at least call home if I want.*

"Now, since you decided to stay, will you please follow me," said Abigail as she lifted herself from the stool and turned, heading for the door.

"Okay," said Safia as she began to follow, but noticed Derrick watching her as he stayed behind. "Is he not coming with us?" asked Safia, feeling a bit self-conscious as she followed Abigail towards the next room.

"Who, Derrick? Not unless you'd like for him to see you naked."

"Naked?" Safia blurted out loudly.

"Only partly; it's part of the exam. It's why they asked me to do it since I'm female, and they'd assume you'd be more comfortable with me there." Abigail waved her finger with a smile on her face. "Unless having him watch you getting undressed makes you feel more comfortable. I'm sure Derrick wouldn't mind."

"No, he can stay there then."

"Yes, I guessed as much," giggled Abigail. "Don't worry about him; he'll be fine. Just follow me."

The next room was just as black as the previous. But inside there was a work desk with a rolling chair on one side and another old rotary phone against the wall on the other side of the room. But what caught Safia's attention the most was what looked to be a dentist's chair in the center of the room, with a light above it. It was long, white, and reclined back for people to lay on.

After Safia had entered the room, Abigail closed the door behind her.

"Okay, take off your top and lay yourself down in that seat over there, and we can get started?"

Safia looked around the room self-consciously before grabbing the side of her pajama top and lifting it over her head, revealing her bra. She then reached behind her for the clip on the back.

"Oh, not the bra. We only need to see your shoulders."

Handing the pajama top to Abigail. Safia then walked over and laid herself in the dentist looking chair. "What happens now?"

"Well, first," said Abigail as she reached down and opened a drawer beneath the seat, pulling out a breathing mask with a little bottle on the end. "We're going to have you breathe into this."

"What's that?" Safia asked, leaning her head away

slightly.

"Just something to knock you out for an hour or so, so that we can implant the tracking chip."

"Tracking chip!" blurted Safia with surprise before the mask was placed over her mouth and nose.

"Oh, it seems Harmony didn't tell you everything, after all. That's going to cost her some points," said Abigail as she squeezed the little bottle at the end of the mask.

Caught up in the moment, Safia took in a quick breath and felt her mind begin to spin as the world turned blurry. *Tracking… you didn't say… tracking…* A cloud of white smoke filled inside of it over her nose, and as Safia felt her eyes getting heavy, the rest of the world drifted away, fading into a blackness that matched the color of the room.

Safia awoke sometime later in the dentist's chair. It was still dark except for the light above her. She squinted and turned her head away as the world slowly started to become less blurry and her mind came back to her. Once focused, she noticed a woman sitting next to her. She tried to look at her, but the light was in the way of her face.

"Wha… hmm…" mumbled Safia as her senses returned.

"Oh, she's coming back to us. That's good," said the woman as she stood up. "Welcome back, everything went okay, and you're good to go."

"Wha…" said Safia, still drowsy from the sedative.

"Just give her a minute, and she'll be fine," said the woman as she headed for the door. "I have to go and enter her into the system or she'll show up as an unknown."

"Okay," said Abigail, who was sitting in the rolling chair in front of the desk in the room. She then rolled her way around as Safia began blinking her eyes, trying to adjust to the light. "Just give it a minute, and you're going to be fine. It takes a bit for it to wear off."

Safia tried to catch a glimpse of the doctor's face as she left the room, but all she saw was her backside, noticing that she had blonde hair that was wrapped into a bun.

After a few moments of Abigail rubbing Safia's shoulder, she slowly felt herself come back to consciousness. Her shoulder and neck itched as she wiggled her fingers, trying to reach up to scratch her back. That's when she felt the pad at the top of her shoulder blade.

"Stop that," said Abigail in a friendly tone as she reached over and pulled Safia's hand down to her side. "No scratching at the device. It's just a small cut that should heal a week or so if left alone. So, try not to irritate the area."

Safia took a few breaths and tried to get out of the chair as Abigail turned off the light above her.

"Okay, let's try and get you up, shall we," said Abigail as she grabbed Safia by the hands and guided her back to her feet.

Safia's legs felt heavy as she struggled to maintain her balance for the first few minutes on the tiled floor, but Abigail was patient and led her around the room, holding her hands until her feet felt solid under her once again.

"There we go," said Abigail as Safia regained her ability to stand on her own once again. "I swear, every time I do this, it feels like I'm teaching a child to walk all over again."

"Do you… do this a lot?" asked Safia as she continued to walk around one side of the room with her hand supporting her against the wall.

"Not as much as you might think. The school only has around a hundred and fifty students, and about half are boys. I only chip the girls, usually," said Abigail as she walked back over to her desk and picked up her glass tablet and began tapping on it. "This is just my second year doing it, so maybe I've done around three to four dozen so far."

"Why do I need tracking? Do people try to run away or something?" *Isn't this what they do… to… animals? Is that what I am now?*

"Huh, oh no. This is merely a safety precaution. We keep track of every student on campus. If something were to happen to you, we would need to know where you are as fast as we can if you need any assistance. Say you're in the library alone one night, a shelf falls on you. A circumstance like that has happened before. The tracking chip alerts us when you are under high amounts of stress. Then we look into the matter and try to contact you. If you don't respond, we send someone to the location of the chip."

"Oh... okay. That makes sense."

"Don't worry, a lot of students are curious about that. But when you consider this school's high profile students, it does begin to make a bit of sense. I don't imagine any parent wants to hear that their children that they have entrusted us with have gone missing. Don't worry, you can opt to have the chip removed upon graduation."

Safia could see her picture through the tablet as well as some writing and check mark boxes. She continued pacing, looking around the black room. After a few more laps around the dentist's chair, she noticed one of the small black orbs that she had seen around the campus was in the top corner of each side of the room. They so closely mirrored the shade of the walls and floor of the room that she hadn't noticed them before.

"You think you're ready to go to the next stop?" asked Abigail, snapping Safia out of her gaze.

"Ah." She tapped her foot against the floor. "I think so."

"Good," said Abigail as she reached over, grabbing a keycard from the desktop, along with Safia's pajama top, and stepped forward, handing it to her.

"Thank you," said Safia, taking her pajama top and sliding it back on. "What do I do now?"

"Now, we take you shopping," said Abigail with a smile as she walked over to the door. "Let's go and get you dressed up."

Safia followed Abigail out of the room, where Derrick

had taken a seat at one of the booths as he waited for their return.

"Oh, you've come out together. I guess that means you've got it from here," said Derrick, as he stood to his feet.

"Yes, everything has been taken care of, and there were no complications. Miss Famosa here is chipped and registered as a student of Apex."

"Then, I guess my job here is done," said Derrick as he stood from the stool, adjusting his blazer. "Welcome to Apex Academy, Miss Famosa. If, from now on you have anything that needs to be taken care of, please do contact me."

He's acting a lot nicer than before. "Yes, thank you. I will. But how do I contact anyone? Do I just come back here?"

"Oh, that will be through the school's pendant after you receive it. Just tap it for any type of assistance, and I or anyone of my associates will receive the call."

"Yes, sir. I will do that then."

"Good," said Derrick with a smile. "I'll be on my way then."

"See you next time then," said Abigail as she and Safia watched Derrick leave the room before they left.

"Aren't we going to the other building with the clothes?" asked Safia as Abigail went back into the checker patterned hallway outside, seeing Derrick go towards the other door heading out into the campus grounds.

"Oh, you mean the store?" asked Abigail as she led Safia down the hallway past all the windowed rooms. "No, that'll be for you after your full enrollment into the point system. For now, we just want to get you dressed so that you don't stand out as much."

"What are all these other rooms for?" asked Safia as she walked through the windowed hallway.

"Training rooms mostly, I think. I've never seen them used before, actually," said Abigail as they approached the end of the corridor. She swiped the keycard, causing the doors to slide apart, and they walked into another room.

This room had a cream carpet, unlike the others, and atop the carpet sat racks of clothing for both men and women. There was even a huge mirror that covered the entirety of a wall, like the ones you would see at a ballet studio.

"Go on then, I'm sure you don't expect me to dress you," said Abigail with a giggle as she took a seat in one of the chairs near the door. "I'll wait here. Just pick out what you like."

Looking around the room, Safia glanced over the assortment of brown and white pleated skirts and slacks that hung down from their circular racks.

"You can wear slacks if you desire," said Abigail. "There's no rule that says you must wear skirts. A few of the girls here have done that. Just pick what makes you feel comfortable."

Safia walked forward, grabbing different pieces of clothing into her hands. "Is there a dressing room?"

"You're standing in it. Don't worry; no one else is going to come in while we're here. But, if you prefer, I can turn around for you if that makes you feel comfortable."

Safia looked around the room cautiously, but didn't see anyone except for the small black orbs at the corners of each side of the room. She shrugged. *Well, I did decide to stay after all, and that probably isn't one of those two-way mirror things.* Safia hesitantly dropped her pajama bottoms and stepped into one of the long-hem pleated skirts. She tried walking in it but found that it was a little long for her size and dragged across the floor. *I mean, I'm kinda tall, but I wonder how tall is the girl that this would fit..*

"Oh, dear, perhaps I should have asked for a tailor after all," said Abigail, as Safia stepped out from behind the clothing rack.

"It's fine. I can wear a shorter skirt; one that stops at the knees," replied Safia as she slipped back out of the long hemmed skirt, stepping over and grabbing a shorter skirt, sliding into it. This one did stop just below the knees. She then walked around, taking off her pajama top and grabbing a white button-up shirt.

"I heard from Harmony that she took you around the campus to see everything. Did you meet anyone that you'd like to be roomed with?"

"Huh… is Harmony not my roommate?"

"Unfortunately, no. She's a second-year, and she was only meant to be your guide. Starting tomorrow as a student here, you will be moved to a first-year dorm. I was curious if you'd met any other first-years whom you would prefer to room with."

"No, not really. Well… there was one girl I met in the library, but I'm not sure what her name was. H something, maybe. She seemed nice. Oh wait, Harmony called her Hammy, if that helps."

"Hammy? That's certainly an odd name. I'll try and see if I can find her." said Abigail as she held up the glass tablet once again. "And you said that you met her in the library? Do you know when it was?"

"No. I mean it was yesterday, but I'm sot sure what time it was."

"Okay then, I'll try to have a look."

Safia finished buttoning up her shirt, tucking it into the hem of her skirt. She then peaked her head over the rack to see Abigail's tablet showing footage of the library. The video was moving fast as it skimmed through the past days' events.

"Ah! There you are," said Abigail as she slowed the footage down. "Now, let's see. Is she the girl in Hijab?"

"Yes, that's her."

"Margaretto Hashmi from the UK."

"Her first name's Margaretto?"

"Yes, it says here that it is… oh, well, looky there. It seems that she has also requested to be roommates with you."

"She has?" asked Safia with genuine surprise. "She didn't

already have a roommate?"

"It doesn't seem as if she did. You're a late admission and arrived as new students are picking who they want to partner up with. You must have made a good impression."

"I guess so. She's just the only other first-year that I can think of," said Safia as she reached out, grabbing hold of a bow tie and a regular tie, holding them up for Abigail to see. "Wanna help me decide?"

"Well, your hair's brown, so why not go with the long brown one," said Abigail, checking another box on the tablet.

Safia picked out some white stockings, sliding them up to her legs, along with some square-toed heeled loafers, and went over to the large mirror to inspect herself. *I can do this. If this really is a school that can make my life better, then I have to try my best here.* She thought to herself, trying to make herself feel a little less on edge.

"Well, don't you look snazzy?"

"Is that everything?" asked Safia as she walked back over to Abigail.

"That's it. Orientation will begin soon enough in the school's auditorium. There, you will be assigned to your dorm. As I said, I am one of the first-year teachers here, so I'm sure that we will be seeing more of each other. So, you can follow me out, and you are free to go wherever you like."

"Okay, is there any place I should go?"

"No, not especially. I understand if you feel lost here at the moment. But as soon as classes start, you will find your way into a rhythm like everyone else. Most new students I see just spend their first few days here learning the campus and where everything is. So I encourage you to do the same. I'm sure you've noticed that the walkways here are made in a bit of an eccentric fashion. All those twists and turns make me dizzy just looking at them."

"Yeah, they make me dizzy whenever I walk them for

too long. Why couldn't they just make sidewalks like normal people?"

Amanda giggled at Safia worlds. "I have often wondered the same thing myself. But even when I was a student here, they've always been that way."

"I will try to get used to them," said Safia with a sigh, but found that she enjoyed talking with Abigail. The woman seemed kind and understanding and not at all rude, overbearing, manipulative, or an overall crazy person. Which she couldn't say for some of the people she'd met around the campus so far.

"Yes? What is it? You're looking at me as if there's something you're curious about."

"What? No… I mean, yes if you don't mind."

"Ask way,"

"It's just, don't you think that all of this is weird. I mean this school out in wherever we are? And the betting that people do. My first day here, there were these people betting on their cock sizes."

"Oh my," said Abigail, taking aback by Safia's forwardness. "I guess you have been through a lot of your first day haven't you." She then turned to the door as it opened the way to the checkered corridor once again.

"Is that normal here?" asked Safia as they made their way to the front of the building.

"Humm, it's not uncommon to have wagers that some would find questionable. Especially if people are desperate for points. I'm still not ready to say that comparing cock sizes is normal here. But I'm also not in charge of the boys here. Perhaps they have superior penis rituals that us girls are simply not aware of."

Safia shook her head. "I can't believe I decided to stay here."

"I know it can seem a bit overwhelming here at times. But I do hope you find a way to make the best of your time here with us. And you can always come and talk to me anytime you wish to express what's on your mind.

"Thank you, I'll remember that."

"Oh, and be sure to wear that outfit during orientation."

"Yes, ma'am. I mean Miss Abigail," said Safia as they neared the end of the corridor, "Hey. what about those little pendants that I see everyone wearing?"

"You will get one of those after you've been awarded your first round of points, after orientation." The door to the outside opened as they both stepped back out into the fresh morning air. "But don't be in such a rush to acquire that just yet, Miss Famosa. While this school has a wealth of possibilities for your future," Abigail looked out over the campus with a sigh. "There have been many who, I'm sure, regret ever coming here."

"I think I know of at least one, already," said Safia as she thought back to the girl in the fountain whom Dario was mistreating. She then turned back to Abigail, who had stopped on the inside of the door. "You said that everyone comes here of their own free will, but in my case, I didn't even know I was coming here. But that makes me wonder if everyone is staying here of their own free will."

Abigail looked down at the start of the concrete walkway, nodding her head before stepping back with a sort of sadness in her eyes. "Well, I can't deny that there is probably a bit of truth in that. But If you're smart enough to realize that now, just after a single day. Then I think you'll be fine here, Ms. Famosa, and I wish you good luck with your studies," she said as the doors closed in front of her.

Safia heard the door click and lock as she watched the card reader icon turn from green to red. She then closed her eyes and stood there for a moment, accepting everything that had just happened and the choices that she just had made. The morning sunshine descended upon her in her new pleated brown and white outfit as she took a deep breath, embracing a slight breeze that blew in, flowing through her hair.

Right, I've decided to stay. For better or worse, I'm here now. And if what they said is true, then I'll be able to make something of myself here. And not just working for mama and papa. She smirked. *Maybe I'll be even more successful than David. But knowing that idiot, he'd probably proclaim himself as a house-husband and happily send me off to work every morning. Wait, what am I thinking about? That idiot and his silly proposal actually have me thinking about marriage. I wonder if he even knows I'm here and not at Duke.*

She turned around, her new skirt flowing above her knees, and started making her way back across the campus.

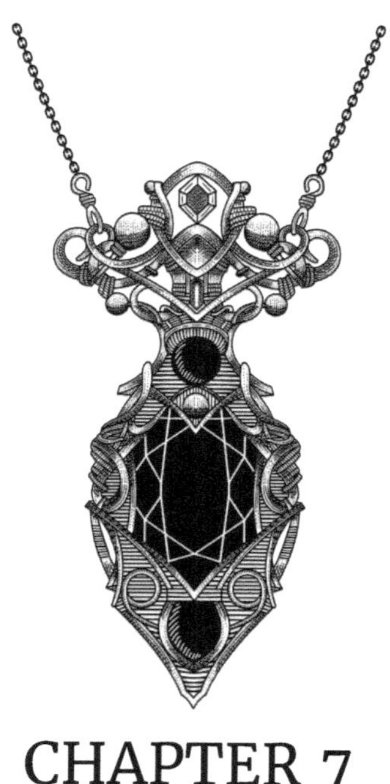

CHAPTER 7

Safia spent the next few days walking around the campus, getting accustomed to the buildings that she was allowed to enter, and trying her best to understand the spiraling walkway system that they had. But the more she walked around it, the more confusing it became to her. It seemed as if it was purposely made to extend the time of even the simplest journey a needless amount.

Eventually she learned where the major facilities were, including the cafeteria. She found that there was a large assortment of food to choose from. And if you were willing to pay extra points, you could order special foods or be allowed to use the kitchen for personal use. But between the confusing walkways and the journey to learn the campus, Safia had a large amount of time to think over her situation. In which time she thought about her parents, her brother, and David. Wondering if they were all really doing okay.

After those few days of aimlessly wandering the campus, just as Abigail had said, Safia awoke to find Derrick knocking at her door. Still as intimidating as the first time they met, his tall suited stature stood before her as she opened the door.

"There will be an orientation at eight am in the auditorium beside the main school building," he said in his deep voice.

Safia turned back to look at the old clock hanging on the wall. "Is there anything I should do beforehand?"

"No, just the attire that you were given when I took you to the communication room will be fine," said Derrick as he turned, making his way down the hall, and knocking on another door.

I guess he's a busy person. Thought Safia, turning back into her room and changing into her new uniform. Soon she was dressed and headed out of the door. Leaving the building, she immediately noticed a few dozen other students all headed towards the school.

So, I guess I should just follow the ground then.

They all navigated the confusing walkway in the brown and white pleated outfits, twisting and turning the confusing route along the way. Many of their faces wore the smiles of their excitement; ready and willing to commit themselves to the lives that this school had surely promised them. But to Safia, all she felt was nervousness as all the brown outfits intermingled in the midday sun, spiraling into a smaller concrete building to the side of the school like a funnel, slowly drinking down anything that happened to fall inside its circular trapping.

Once inside, she found the students sitting amongst

rows of foldout chairs. The inside walls of the building were still as ancient looking as the outside. The concrete arched roof contrasted with the wooden flooring beneath it and along the walls were giant screens that were angled down towards them. A mixture of old architecture and new technology that did nothing to appeal to the eyes.

Safia and the rest of the students all took their seats before a stage at the back of the building, where atop it stood a singular podium with a microphone attached. Around the room, Safia didn't notice any guards or authority figures, but she did see Abigail up ahead near a door, along with two other men standing beside her.

I wonder what happens now. Will they hand out class assignments? thought Safia as she sat amongst the rest with nervous anticipation. She had to admit to herself that even though she had chosen to stay, the eerie feeling of being here amongst these people still felt as if it was unreal. It was a sense of apprehension she soon realized many of the other students shared. She picked up on the chatter of a few nearby classmates as they nervously conversed amongst each other.

"This is weird. I wasn't told anything about these outfits. I feel like I'm in a cult," said one of the boys ahead of her.

"Yeah," said another girl. "My grandmother told me about the time when she went here. She says it can get crazy during the game nights."

Okay, see. I knew I couldn't have been the only one, but she said that her grandmother went here. I wonder how old this place is, thought Safia, feeling reassured in her way of thinking, now that someone else expressed hesitancy after seeing the ongoing events around the campus.

"Well, there certainly are a lot this year," said a loud female voice from behind the students as they all turned around to see a small woman wearing a brown pleated overall skirt and a long brown trench coat. She held a microphone in her hand and Safia saw the two black speakers behind her by the doors, which were amplifying her voice. "Good morning, everyone. I'm happy to see that so many of you have decided to join us this year." She said, making her way towards the front of the room, followed by two large male guards.

Whispers of "Who is that?" flowed throughout the students as the small woman made her way up the steps towards the podium.

"My name is Champ Champ, the headmaster of this school, and this will be my third year overseeing the activities here," she spoke as her voice changed locations after she reached the podium, now coming in from all around the room.

Champ Champ? Is that a joke?

"Yes," she said, smiling out at the crowd, "That is my real name. The word Champ, said twice. Trust me, if I could change it, I would. But here on this campus, that is how you are to refer to me."

Well, that answers that question. What the hell kinda name is Champ Champ?

"Now, some of you might be wondering, what is Apex Academy? Well, allow me to answer. We are the leaders of the world. If it's foreign policy or dictators needing to squash a rebellion that upset a third world country, more than likely we have our hands in it."

Champ Champ left the podium and walked forward, sitting down on the edge of the stage, her feet kicking in the air. "We influence everything from what music is popular in what country to what the next tech innovation will be. What I'm saying is that graduation from our school will immediately put you in a position to be at the forefront of almost whatever you desire. Now, obviously we can't save you from yourself if you do something as stupid as go on a cocaine binge and go streaking through a city naked during the night of a critical election."

Oh, that seems to be a sore spot here.

"But, outside of a catastrophic amount of stupidity, all of you that graduate from this school will be given the opportunity to thrive in this world. I'm sure a lot of you know how the news always talks about the one percent? How the one percent control over half the world's wealth. Well, I can tell you that ninety-two percent of that one percent are graduates from Apex. And, here, we only have one goal. Survival of the highest level."

Survival?

Champ Champ hopped down from the stage, the sound of loafers hitting the wooden floor sounding through the small room. Then with a smirk across her lips, she began to pace in front of the stage. "I'm sure, by now, you've heard of our wonderful point system. You gain points by simply being good students here; helping out around the campus and such. And while finding cute little projects around the school and doing well on tests can certainly get you through our system here, leading you to a comfortable life. For those of you that are hungry enough, there is the betting system, where you can challenge other students directly for their points in almost any type of game imaginable. And you can wager anything in exchange for points. We don't discriminate here with the methods you use. Now, obviously, physical harm is not allowed unless agreed upon by both parties, but, other than that, if it exists, you can bet on it."

She stopped in front of the new students. "And for those who don't realize how seriously we take our games here, allow me to display an example which is very personal to me." She pointed upward and a picture of a brown-haired, blue-eyed man appeared on the wall to the left of them. He looked like an ordinary man except that his face had two scars that ran across the left side.

He's a student here?

"You see that wonderful man on the wall? He's in his third year here. You might see him around, so feel free to stop and say hello to him. Don't let the scars on his face fool
118

you, he really is just the loveliest man."

Wow, that looks like it hurt, thought Safia as she gazed up at the image on the screen. The man's picture showed clearly, and the flesh on his face was scarred deep. The facial fissure twisted in two lines from his jawbone to his cheek and from the top of his lip, stretching to just before the top of his ear. *I wonder how that happened to him.*

Champ Champ raised her hand and displayed a ring on her finger. "That man is my husband. In my first year as headmaster here, I was a little arrogant and perhaps foolish, which allowed me to accept a wager that he tricked me into. I won't go into the details, but I eventually lost that bet and as a result, I had to marry him."

You married someone because you lost a bet? Is that like one of those Las Vegas things where people get drunk and end up together?

The crowd began to mumble amongst themselves at the revelation.

"So not even I am immune to this school's rules," said Champ Champ as she gazed up at the wall with a smile before walking back over to her guards. Turning back around, she then faced the new students with her arms wide. "You will all be awarded two thousand points for entering this school. The rest you are to earn on your own. Try not to spend it all at one time, or like many former students, you'll soon regret it." She then threw up her hands in a flamboyant motion above her head, clapping them together as colorful ribbons exploded from the sides of the room, flying over the students' heads. The material floated down, draping itself over Safia and the rest of the students before landing on the floor. Looking down at the ribbon that lay stretched out across her, she saw that words were embroidered in the fabric. It read, "Welcome to Apex Academy."

I don't even know what to think about this anymore, thought Safia as she lifted her head just in time to see Champ Champ turn and leave the room, followed by her two guards. *And now she's gone. Almost everyone on this campus must be insane.*

"Wow, that was something," said a boy in front of Safia.

"You think she really got married because she lost a bet?" asked a girl next to him.

"Considering where we are, I wouldn't doubt it. But damn."

"Ahem," said another woman on the microphone as she stepped up on the podium. "That was our headmaster, Champ Champ. Next, we will start assigning houses to the students here. So please stand up when your name is called and head towards the door. Now first is..." She flicked her finger across a tablet. "Trevor Tallin, please head for the door."

A boy in one of the front rows stood up and walked toward the door. The class turned around to see that three people had set up a small station near the exit. They asked the boy a few questions, gave him his school pendant, and allowed him to leave the building. Another two or three dozen people were called before Safia heard herself be summoned.

She stood up and walked towards the exit, where a brown-haired man sitting down in a chair greeted her. She couldn't help but feel excited and a bit nervous as she came and stood before the man.

"Hello. Are you Safia Famosa?"

"Yes, sir."

"Okay, you're going to be stationed in Yennefer House. We will have your new clothing sent to your dormitory."

"Will it be any different from what I'm wearing now?"

"Oh no, it will pretty much be the same, but instead of the pure brown and white pleated set, you will be given a more ah... I think the Yennefer dorm has the purplish pleated set to represent the colors of their house."

He reached to his side and grabbed one of the pendants on the table. It was a simple design, unlike the previous ones she had seen around the campus days before. Instead, this one was a circular pendant with a jewel at its center with a ring of glass around it.

"Now, which shoulder did they implant the chip in?" asked the man as she held up a metal paddle looking device.

"Ah... this one, here," said Safia as she reached up, tapping herself in the spot where the chip was placed.

"Okay, turn around and hold still for a moment. This won't take long," said the man. Safia did as instructed, as the man pressed down on the jewel inside the pendant, causing it to make a clicking sound. He then waved the paddle over her back, and it beeped. "Okay that will do it." The glass around the jewel began flashing colors before it went back to normal.

"All done. Here you are," said the man as he handed Safia the pendant. "You now have two thousand points. But you will not be able to wager any of them until classes start, which will be soon. Nevertheless you will be able to purchase food, clothing, and other items from the campus stores. Do you understand?"

"Yes, sir,"

"Good. Do you have any questions?"

Safia looked down in the basket where he grabbed her pendant from and saw that it was filled with similar pendants. "I saw some students with different types of these. Do they change each year?"

"Oh, no. After being here for six months, you are given the option to design your own pendant. Of course it will cost a few points, but many students here change their design throughout the course of their time here."

"Okay, thank you. I was just curious."

"No problem. Anything else?

All I have are questions. But which ones could I possibly ask. "No. sir."

"Then you are free to leave."

Safia left the building beside the school, back out into the sunlight. Next to her towering as if it was an impregnable fortress was the main school building that cast a shadow over her and the building she was just inside. Shaking her head as she gazed over the green lawn and black lamp posts ahead of her, she began making her way back through the confusing spiraling concrete walkways, looking for Yennefer house. It still made her head feel weird as she traversed it, even after days of doing so. So much so that she began to get confused as to which was the right way to any of the dorms. Looking over the campus, she stared out at the many buildings in the distance. They all looked the same from far away.

Agrh. How am I supposed to even find where I'm supposed to go? Everything either looks the same or just looks weird.

Giving up searching alone, she ended up asking other students for directions as she hadn't seen Yennefer house before. And eventually, over time and after one or two more inquiries as to the house's location, she found it.

The house stood atop a small hill on the campus grounds. A two-story building with an elliptical arch above the entrance with the word *Yennefer* etched into the stone. Below it were purplish flowers that laced the soil around the walkway leading to the entrance. Safia walked up the steps, and at the top were even more flowers around the pillars of the archway. She peeked her head inside, looking around. There was a wooden floored lounge area where two students sat quietly reading on couches and a spiraling ladder that was directly to the left of her. And to her right was a desk with a book atop it.

"Ahh, hello? Is anyone here?" said Safia in a high tone in hopes to be heard.

"Oh, is someone down there?" asked a male voice from above the flight of stairs. Soon the sound of stomping feet came through the foyer as a dark-skinned boy made his way downstairs, his dye-tipped dreadlocks bouncing over his face with each hard step. He noticed Safia and smiled. "Hello there, you must be another newbie. What's your name?"

"Safia... Safia Famosa."

"Well then, let's have a look-see," said the boy as he walked over to the book that sat atop a wooden desk near the front door. He flipped through a couple of pages before scrolling down it with his finger. "Ah, there you are, Room B-Seven. Follow me then, Miss Safia." He turned around and began going back up the steps, with Safia following behind them. "So, tell me, what part of the world are you from?"

"Ah, the US. I'm from Minnesota."

"Nice, I'm from Texas myself. My Pops wants me to take over the business, so he sent me here to try and hob-nob with the other rich bastards here. What about you?"

"Not sure. I was told I'm a Trojan, if that helps."

"Ha, a Trojan? So, they sent another one over. I'd heard they might stick one or two of your types in each of the dorms to spice things up a bit from time to time. But putting you together, I guess that happens too. So, where'd they pick you up from? Were you homeless or about to go to prison or something?"

"What? No, I was just working in a diner with my family." *They pick up criminals and bring them here?*

"Really? That's a little less exciting than the stories I've heard, but maybe we just got the two boring ones. But don't worry. How much money you got doesn't mean shit here. Only how many points you have." They stopped at the door to a room. "Speaking of which, do you know how to check your points?"

"No, they never said how."

"Figured as much. I've had to show a few others. You got that pendant they gave you?"

"Yeah, I have it," said Safia as she reached into her pocket, pulling out the pendant.

"Okay, tap it till it clicks and ask it how many points you have."

Safia looked at the pendant and did as the boy had

instructed, pressing down on the jewel in the center as she had seen the man earlier do. It clicked. "How many points do I have?" It was silent, not responding to her. She looked back up at the boy, confused.

"Oh, sorry. You have to say it in the right way. Say, I and your name, then ask for the points."

Safia clicked the pendant again. "I, Safia Famosa, would like to know how many points I have." There was another long moment of silence.

"Safia Famosa has a total of two thousand points," spoke the pendant.

"It will start responding faster the more you talk to it. I guess it's learning your voice or something. Like, if I clicked your pendant and tried to ask it a question, it wouldn't respond to me. So, it seems each pendant is locked to your voice and that chip they put in you." He reached over and opened the door for her. "Well, this is your new room."

"Thank you."

"No problem, but be careful sharing how many points you have from now on. It's okay for now since you're new and everyone can guess how many points you have. But when school starts, you might want to keep it to yourself."

"Okay, I'll try to remember that," said Safia as she peeked inside and saw a room much like before, just a little bigger. There was a bed on each side of the room, both covered with brown comforters and pillows, along with two closets, and a desk at the foot end of each bed. The main noticeable change now was that the floor was made of a dark black-purplish wood, and the beds were bigger.

"Go on and have a look around; they will be delivering your clothing in a day or two. I just gotta put in that you've been assigned to your room. By the way, my name's Austin; I'll be downstairs if you need me."

Safia turned back to him with her eyes squinted. "Your name's Austin and you're from Texas?"

"Hey, don't ask me. My parents aren't exactly the most

original people," said Austin as he stood in the door.

Safia caught him staring at her a little longer than needed. "What? What's wrong?"

"Nothing. It's just... well, you're actually the first black person they stuck in our dorm. So, I'm just curious, is all."

"Oh, about what?" asked Safia with a smile. "You want to share hair care secrets?" She pointed to his dreadlocks. "I'm not sure my shampoo would work well with what you have there."

Austin chuckled. "Does that mean you don't know how to twist locks? I could really use some help with these things." He pulled at a dreadlock on his head. "They take forever."

"Sorry. I can do braids. But I've never tried locks before."

"That's a shame. Alright then, another question since we're sharing. Your skin's lighter than mine, what race are your parents. Both mine are African American."

"My father's Cuban and my mother is African American."

"Cool, can you speak Spanish?"

"Not as well as my father. But I can get by. Why? Do you want me to teach you?"

"That might not be such a bad idea, it'll..."

"Hey Austin," came a voice from down the hall. "You got someone down here?"

"And there we go. I guess I'll see you around. Things will get pretty busy when classes start. But say hello from time to time when you see me." Austin patted his hand against the door frame and headed down the corridor, back towards the stairs.

Safia closed the door as she stepped inside, looking around the room. But it was mostly empty. *There's no TV here and no phone. Things really are going to be boring here, but I guess that means I'll have plenty of time to study.* Even the closet was empty except for a sealed toothbrush and other sanitary items. She then walked over, sitting on one of the beds, before lying down and closing her eyes, trying to take a rest. Once again the thoughts of the day's events flowed through her mind.

What kind of name is Champ Champ? That's like naming myself winner winner or house house. Everyone is a crazy person. Well, Austin seemed pretty normal. And then there's Abigail, she didn't seem like she enjoyed the things that go on here.

Around an hour later, Safia awoke to a knock on her door.

"Everything okay, are you dressed?" asked what she recognized to be Austin's voice as the door slowly creaked open.

"Ah, yes, you can come in," said Safia as she lifted herself from the bed.

"Good. Okay, you can follow me in," said Austin as the door opened and walked in followed by the girl Safia had met in the library when Harmony had shown her around.

"Hello again," said Hashmi to Safia as she walked inside the room, glancing around. She was wearing an outfit, similar to the one she had seen her in days before. A long hemmed plaid dress with a sleeveless vest. Underneath was a long-sleeved dress shirt that covered her arms. And around her head, she wore another scarf. A purplish one this time that matched the mascara that she had on her eyes.

"Hey," said Safia.

"I have brought your prison companion," said Austin jokingly. "I hope you two can manage to get along."

"I think we'll be okay," said Safia as she left the bed, rolling her eyes at Austin.

"I'll leave you girls to chat amongst yourselves, then. Just holler for me if ya need anything," said Austin as he closed the door behind him, leaving the room.

"I was told that you asked for me to be your roommate," said Safia to Hashmi as she walked over to the other bed.

"Well, I had to pick someone, and you were the only girl I figured didn't have a roommate since you arrived late. And you didn't seem like such an odd person to me. So that was a plus."

"It's nice to know I'm not the only one here who thinks this place is weird."

"No, you're not. I've experienced a fair amount of weirdness since I've arrived also. I saw you walk by during orientation. Are you adjusting to the school okay?"

"Well enough, but it's not like I have a choice anymore. I decided to stay here for better or worse."

"That's a choice we all made. Many of us have our own reasons for being here. Although judging from my experiences so far, most are not as savory as they would have you believe."

"Yeah, I can imagine," said Safia as she extended her hand to Hashmi. "Well, thank you for choosing me as your roommate. I hope we can get along and not piss each other off all the time."

Hashmi smiled back at Safia and reached forward, shaking her hand. "Likewise, I think we'll get along well and even if I could have roomed with Harmony; I'm sure she would've just spent most of her time with her boyfriend, anyway."

"Yeah, she never came back to the room after showing me around. I guess that's where she went," said Safia, looking Hashmi over. "Is this the part where we get to know each other and become best friends forever, then?"

"If we were to go by what the telly tells us, then yes, this'd be it."

"Okay, I guess I'll go first. Where are you from? I was told you're from the UK. Which part?"

"Yes and no, I was born in Germany but grew up in Indonesia. My mother is an English teacher, so we traveled a lot for her work, going back and forth from Germany and Jakarta. We live in Liverpool now, though."

"Jakarta, where's that?"

"It's in Indonesia. What about you? Where do you hail

from?"

"Minneapolis, Minnesota, I've been there all my life for the most part. So not as fancy as you."

"I doubt it will be as fancy as you think it is if you ever visit."

"Maybe not," laughed Safia as she walked over to her closet and began fumbling through the toiletries. "I was told everyone comes here for different reasons. I mean, I thought most people go to college to get an education so that they can get a good job. But according to what that Champ Champ lady said, this seems like a place where everyone takes things way too seriously."

"You think a woman who calls herself Champ Champ is taking herself too seriously?" asked Hashmi with a smile. "Then, I'm fairly curious to see what your definition of ludicrous is."

"Okay, that's a good point. So, maybe I am thinking a little too much about it. But it's hard for me just to accept that everything I've seen here is just another normal day at any other university."

"Do you not want to become a ruler of the world, like the rest of them?" asked Hashmi as she fiddled with the sheets on her bed.

"Ha, please," laughed Safia, "I'm not even a ruler of my own life. I really don't think I could handle managing the world. If what that lady said is true, then my plan is to stay away from the crazy betting people and just go to class and graduate."

"I shall try to avoid the betting also," said Hashmi as she laid down on the bed. "That's not exactly permitted in my beliefs."

"So here we are," said Safia, turning around, holding the sealed toothbrush in her hand, pointing it at Hashmi. "Both of us at a crazy gambling school, and us the No-Betting-Girls are roomed up together."

"Perhaps it is fate," said Hashmi, sitting up, looking

around the room. "Do you think we should go to the store and buy the things we need before it closes?"

"I was told that we could spend our points when I got my pendant. But do you think we should, I mean, this school seems pretty concerned about points."

"That's what some of the other students said they had planned after they left orientation. But I don't plan to spend much. Just a few things should work."

"Okay then," said Safia, looking around the room, "So what do you think we need?"

"I don't know, really. A telly for sure and maybe just some basic things, more toiletries for certain though." Hashmi pointed at Safia's hand. "That toothbrush looks horrible. If possible, I'd like to get an electric one."

"Let's go then," said Safia as the two girls got up and headed out the door, out of the dorm, and through the campus. The moment Safia saw the spiraling concrete path ahead of her, she reached for her head, covering her eyes. "Oh god I hate this part. Just looking at it makes me feel dizzy."

Hashmi laughed, "I see you still haven't gotten used to the walkways yet."

"No, how can I? It's like it was made just to torment me."

"It used to bother me to no end as well. But there's a trick to it. Want me to show you?"

"Please, anything that will make it go away," said Safia, still covering her eyes.

"Here, give me your hand."

Safia did as instructed, allowing Hashmi to hold her hand. "Okay, now what?"

"Now we walk forward," said Hashmi as she began to guide Safia along the path. "The trick is not to focus on the walkway. Instead, focus on the distance ahead. Like those buildings over there, or better yet, just focus on each of those black lamp posts as we pass them. They will give your mind something to focus on."

Safia did as instructed, and as she made her way through the spiraling walkway, she didn't focus on the path. Instead she focused on each of the lamp posts one after another as she passed them. And to her surprise it was actually working. No longer did she feel an ever-growing migraine as she looked over the campus.

"It's working."

"There, you see. Nothing to worry about."

"Thank you. But why would they make such a confusing walkway? It all seems so pointless."

"They do seem a bit over-engineered for such a simple purpose. But I'm sure that we can add that mystery to the numerous others that we might have about this campus and its ongoing activities."

No longer feeling distraught by having to navigate the campus. Safia and Hashmi quickly made their way to their destination, upon which they found themselves in a crowd of people going in and out of the building.

It really is a lot, thought Safia as they made their way inside the structure. Following the crowd, the two girls made their way upstairs to the store. There they saw an assortment of items to purchase: televisions, handbags, alternate clothing, and so much more. Spotting what she had mentioned earlier, Hashmi let go of Safia's hand and made her way over to one of the medium-sized televisions.

"Will this one do?" asked Hashmi, patting the top of the television while holding up one of the red tickets that displayed its price.

"I guess so. It's not like we need some super big TV." She looked around and saw a boy up at the front desk. "I hope they don't expect us to lug that up there for him to scan," said Safia, while trying to judge the weight of the object and the distance to the front desk.

"No, you needn't do that," said a male voice from behind Safia. "You just need to grab one of the red tickets there and take it up to the counter. He'll handle the rest."

"Ah, thank you," said Hashmi, turning around to greet the man, her eyes going wide as she saw the man's face. It had two scars across the right side, from his chin to his cheek, and from the top of his lip to near his ear.

"Yes, thank you, ah..." said Safia, also startled by the man's looks and sudden appearance.

"Don't worry about it. I take it you girls are first-years?"

"Yes, that's right. We just finished our enrollment."

"That's good," said the man, walking away, gliding between the different sections of clothing. "Try to enjoy yourselves and don't spend all your points up here, or you'll regret it. This campus has a way of bringing out the worst in people."

The girls just watched him walk away into the back of the store before Safia turned back to Hashmi.

"Was that him?" Safia whispered.

"Who?"

"You know, the husband? The one that little headmaster was talking about. She had his picture blown up on the wall."

"Oh, I think you're right!" said Hashmi, as her eyes went wide with recollection. "I doubt anyone else on campus has scars like that. She did say that he was a third-year here. Do you really think he's her husband?"

"You could always go over and ask him if you like."

"Ah, no," said Hashmi, looking back at the man before waving the red ticket around. "I think I'll just go and try to buy this."

"But it's four hundred points. That's a bit much." said Safia in protest.

"How bout we split it, then?"

"Can we do that?"

"I don't see why not. They said that practically every-thing is allowed in this school. Let's go find out then," said Hashmi as they both went up to the counter. Sure enough, they were able to split the difference between them, each only spending two hundred points.

Safia noticed two glass tablet things behind the man. The small one was for eight hundred points, and the large one was for fourteen hundred points.

"Hey," said Safia, "what are those?"

"Huh…" said the boy at the counter, turning around. "Oh, those? They're essentially just information devices. They keep records of everything you do in school here. You can also have your textbooks put on them if you like."

"I see," said Safia, remembering Harmony's words about them. She thought about her points and took a deep breath. "Can I get the small one, please?"

"Sure, let me grab it," said the boy, turning around and reaching upward towards them.

"Are you sure?" asked Hashmi, with a tinge of worry on her face. "It's eight hundred points. You're already halfway through with what they gave you."

"Honestly, no," said Safia, "But I'm about to find out if it's worth it." *I probably shouldn't do this, but I've seen so many people walking around with those things. It has to be useful or else they wouldn't have it. Even Miss Abigail had one.*

"Here ya go," said the man behind the counter, handing Safia a white box. "Just plug it into the charger when you get back. I've already assigned the TV to your room, and it should be delivered there before the day is over."

"Thank you," said Safia as she took the box and both she and Hashmi left the store, headed back down the stairs, exiting the building. "Hashmi, want to go get something to eat?"

"Sure, I haven't eaten since yesterday."

Both girls then headed back through the campus, with Safia taking extra care to make sure she was focusing on the lampposts as they found their way over to the cafeteria, where there was a rowdy crowd of people outside.

"What's happening here?" asked Safia as they neared the cafeteria, where she saw a boy at the front of the line arguing with the people at the base of the steps into the building.

"You can't get in unless you have a food pass," said another boy wearing a chef's outfit, complete with the mushroom hat.

"The fuck! What do you mean a food pass?" asked the angry boy, as he began waving his hands around.

"As I told you, sir. You can buy a food pass for three hundred points a month."

"And I told you, I ain't got no three hundred points," said the boy irately. "I spent most of 'em in that store trying to get everything I needed."

"Then, we can't help you, sir. Perhaps if you won a bet and earned more points—"

"You, idiot. I'm a freshman. I can't bet yet. They said I have to wait until classes start."

"Then, perhaps someone will give you their leftovers, or you could eat out of a garbage bin. But could you please move? You're holding up the line."

"The fuck you say to me," said the boy as he grabbed the other boy in the chef's attire by the collar, shaking his chef's hat from his head as he drew back his fist. "You think you can treat me like this. You know who I am?"

"Help!" screamed the boy in the cooking attire as he pressed his pendant, making it turn red. "I'm being assaulted by a student. He's physically assaulting me."

"I ain't done shit yet, but I swear if you don't—" suddenly the boy started spasming on his feet before falling to the ground, his body twitching at the bottom steps to the cafeteria. He screamed out in pain as his body shook uncontrollably, rolling from the concrete walkway, down onto the grass. The other students stepped back in horror at the sight.

Soon, two men came from across the campus, grabbing the boy by the shoulders, and dragging him across the grass, out of sight.

What... what's happening to him? Where are they taking him?

"Now," said the boy in chef's clothing as he reached down, grabbing his mushroom hat, patting the dust off of it, and placing it back on his head. He then looked over at the remaining students as they stood there in shock and yelled. "If you don't have three hundred points, then I suggest you leave and find a way to get those points, or you're not going to eat." He said with a devilish grin on his face. "Either that or you can try your luck like the last one and experience what he got."

Immediately, over a dozen students left the line and began walking away from the cafeteria. They're mumbles of horror, disgust, and panic fueling the horror of the situation to Safia.

"Okay then," said the boy in the chef's hat. "Who's next?"

Safia then turned to Hashmi, who was looking just as shocked as she was. "Ah... Hashmi, after we get that food pass. I think... I think I'm going to stop spending my points from now on."

"I imagine that might be a good idea considering the circumstances," said Hashmi as they both walked to the end of the line; their minds having to come to grips with what they just witnessed and what it could mean for them if they're points became low enough.

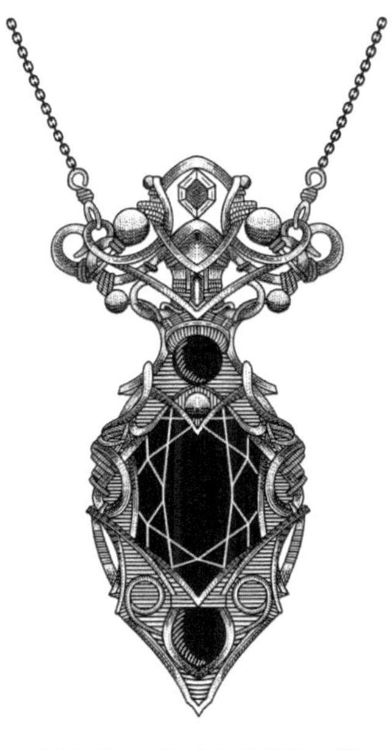

CHAPTER 8

Throughout the next week, Safia and Hashmi organized their room to their liking, making several more trips to the store to pick up a few small items that they found they needed. They made sure to be frugal with their points, only picking out cheap items. Delivered to them on the fourth day were their class schedules, and they found that they had the exact same classes. It seemed that all freshmen had the exact same classes, just shuffled around into different times. Some classes she shared with Hashmi and some she didn't, and they would only be sorted into their preferred majors in their second year at the academy.

Eventually, the first day of classes arrived, and the students made their way out in the morning sun. As Safia left her own dorm, she quickly noticed that the colored accents sewn into the clothing of the students that she passed. Across their blazers and trousers were shades of reds, pinks, yellows, and a wide variety of other colors were on display amongst the green grass as she made her way throughout the campus. The winding path was no longer giving her the dizzying spells from before. She made sure to not focus on the ludicrousness of its design.

Safia herself opted for a purple accented vest with a dress shirt beneath that tucked neatly in her skirt. While the design was what she considered to be old-fashioned, she did admit that she felt more refined every time she looked in the mirror. She opted to continue to allow her hair to flow normally as it hung loose from her head and rested on her shoulders.

Hashmi stood beside her adorned in the same; her long hemmed dress, covering her legs, and long-sleeved dress shirt that went down to her wrist. Even Hashmi's scarf that she always seemed to wear over her head and wrapped around her neck was a perfect purple shade to match her outfit.

I mean it is morning, but doesn't it get hot wearing that? thought Safia as she looked over at Hashmi, but opted to stay silent, as didn't know if asking such a question would be offensive. The weather wasn't hot, but it definitely wasn't cold either. It was a mild day and the breeze that flowed against Safia's leg felt pleasing as the girls continued on their way.

"So many people," said Hashmi as she gazed ahead of them. "I thought they said that this school only had around a hundred or so people."

"If that's the case, then I guess they're all here now then," said Safia as she pulled out the small glass tablet from her handbag. Pressing her thumb on top, it began to light up, showing her different options. "It says that our first class is world economics."

"That thing looks handy. Can I see it?"

Safia handed the glassed pad to Hashmi, and instantly the lights and information went away.

"Oh, all the words are gone."

"I guess it only works when I'm holding it," said Safia, taking it back. Instantly, the words on the screen appeared again, showing her the schedule for her day.

"It seems you're right," said Hashmi as she leaned over, looking at the screen. "I guess it's some type of security issue in case someone tries to steal it."

At the top of the screen, it read Apex Systems version six hundred fifty-seven.

"I hope I don't have to pay much for my books," said Safia as she swiped across the tablet, trying to get used to how to properly navigate it. She had spent the first few days on the device, but this morning it had updated again and now everything was different. "I really hate how it looks now. All the icons are shuffled around, and I don't know where anything is anymore."

"Has it been useful so far?"

"Not yet, but I hope that the textbooks are cheap on this thing, I really don't want to lose any more points."

"Well, they did say that you could put your books on it, but it seems kinda small to be reading off of," said Hashmi as they approached the school, making their way up the steps. The thick wooden doors were already opened as students made their way in and out of the building.

Inside, everything seemed even more spotless than the last time she entered. The marbled floor and concrete walls gave off the appearance of a concert hall. Safia looked up towards the roof of the first floor, watching the illuminated crystal of the chandeliers above her twinkle as she walked forward. There were no windows in the hall for her to look inside, but beside each door was a rectangular piece of glass that flashed and showed the class's name, along with the number assigned to it.

"Class one-o-three, that's us," said Safia, as she and Hashmi entered the room. While there were no windows inside the wall to look inside each classroom, there were, in fact, huge windows that reached up into the second floor of the building on the outer walls of the school. Scattered through the room itself were several sets of chairs and desks, all organized into rows for the students, a few of which had already arrived and taken their seats. Safia and Harmony made their way over to a set of seats next to one another, with Safia taking the one that was directly beside one of the windows.

The atmosphere was very much like a classroom, as the few other students chatted amongst each other about random topics of interest. Everything felt as if it was the standard classroom affair, if not a little old-fashioned. Dark wooden chairs, sitting under square wooden desks; light cascading into the room onto them through the multiple windows that allowed for a beautiful view into the clear campus grounds.

Outside they could see other students amongst the grass, lounging with each other in the morning sun. They were sitting underneath the shade of a tree listening to who Safia was surprised to see; Austin, his blonde tipped dreadlocks hanging down behind his back as he appeared to be reading from a book aloud to the lounging students as he paced along the grass.

"Welcome all to your first day of class. I hope you've been enjoying your time here," said a familiar woman's voice as she entered the room.

Taken away from her window gazing, Safia turned to see Abigail, who she had met when she decided to stay at the school. Instinctively Safia reached towards where the chip had been implanted in her, begging to rub at the cloth above her skin, remembering that awkward conversation with her family.

I guess she really is a teacher here.

Abigail walked forward. In her hand she held a large book and a glass tablet that was clutched under her arm. No longer in her doctor's clothing, she instead wore a simple a white button-up blouse along with a tight black skirt. Her hair was pulled back into a bun and her shoes were black with a white line down the center that matched her blouse. She plopped down the book on the desk as she turned and faced her students.

"It's nice to see we have so many new students," said Abigail as she gazed over the crowd. "Now, does anyone know what this World Structure one-o-one class is about?"

"It's about how to control the world," said one boy with dark hair and glasses as the other boys around him chuckled.

"Although you said it as a joke, you're not wrong. I'm sure most of your parents have informed you about the importance of this school. I, myself, was a student here two years ago, and I—"

"Yeah, but then you failed out," said the previous dark-haired boy. "My brother told me about you. You got kicked out because you lost all your points. And you've become a teacher to pay off the debt you owe."

She did? Safia asked herself while finding herself taking a sort of protective dislike towards the boy because of the tone of his words towards Abigail.

"That's not exactly wrong," said Abigail with a raised brow, but still remaining unfazed by the remark as she nonchalantly leaned back, taking a seat on the teacher's desk behind her. "You're right; I did lose all my points. But it wasn't because of a bet. Remember what the headmaster Champ Champ said during admissions." Abigail raised her finger, whirling it around whimsically. "Anything can be bought with the points here. And my sister had gotten sick. So, I went to the headmaster here and proposed a trade. I didn't have enough points to buy what I needed, so I traded my services working here for points. I gave them all the points I had and traded in ten years of working here in service for my sister to get all the proper care she needed. And because of that, my sister is alive, and I have around seven more years here to repay that debt."

That... that's good. If she saved her sister, and the school is just letting her work off her debt, Safia thought about her family. *I would probably do something like that too.*

Abigail then placed her hand under her chin with a frown on her face, "But I guess that Mr. Fontain here is the type to forsake all family for his own good," she said as she picked up a glass tablet from on top of the book and began flicking it downward. "Humm, it says in your records that you have a little sister. I sure do hope she stays healthy, since her brother is the type of man to just leave her to die."

The class grew silent as Mr. Fontain narrowed his eyes hatefully at Abigail.

"Oh, nothing else to say?" asked Abigail in a smug tone at Mr. Fontain, then she looked over the rest of the class. "Well then, does anyone else know what this class is about?"

"Is it about world relations and such? Like how we trade for oil in them Saudi countries?" asked another male voice near the back of the classroom.

"Good, that's exactly right. This class teaches you how our leaders and business owners manipulate the world to further their own needs. This school is a miniature ecosystem for trade. I know that some of you may think that betting is the only way to acquire points, but there are many other ways to achieve success here in this school outside of betting."

"And how's that?" asked a girl on the other side of Safia. "That headmaster lady sure did seem excited about us betting."

"Well, you can clean the school for one," said Abigail as she pointed her finger towards the windows of the building.

"I know you all have seen how well-groomed our campus is. But we don't really hire out any contractors to keep it clean. All this is done by the students, including cleaning the school and the dorms. You can even buy services from other students, like a tutor to train you in your studies, or swimming."

"So, this school operates on the barter system?" asked a dark-haired girl.

"Yes and no, it may have started on the barter system a century or so ago. But I assure you, that's not the case now. The betting system has taken over whatever this school used to be."

"But in certain situations, when betting is not optimal, some have reverted to the barter system and have been successful in completing their studies here."

"More like the begging system, if you ask me," said a brown-haired boy in a white shirt. His sleeves were rolled up to his elbows; tattoos ran down his arms in some sort of tribal design. "Most of us know why we're here. This school wants us to crush as many of our fellow students as possible in order to achieve success in this world. And I'm willing to play along. I just gotta wait a little longer before they'll let me bet."

"And that's the reason why the barter system was replaced, Mr. Tristan," said Abigail, sighing. "The people that this school recruits always seem all too eager to try and prove their superiority over their fellow man."

"Of course, we do," said Tristan, shaking his head. "It's human nature to try and prove you're better than everyone else. Why should I be expected to play nice when almost everyone else here will be playing the game?"

"One might think that if they were going to change this school, then it has to start somewhere and with someone," said Abigail as she looked over the class. "This world changes all the time. Politicians change alignments, the countries change allegiances to who has the highest chance of winning. Who's to say that this school won't be able to change to a different system, rather than trying to bankrupt one another and perhaps cause a forced expulsion."

"And those that try to change it either wind up as the discarded or whatever the hell you are," said Tristan, flipping his hand in the air. "No, thanks. If this school wants me to play their game, then I'm damn sure gonna play."

What are they even talking about? thought Safia as she tried to follow along with the conversation. But she was having a hard time understanding everything and only really understood that Abigail wanted to change how the school worked. Which, given what she'd seen so far, she felt compelled to agree with.

"Then, let's get started," said Abigail, shaking her head. She then began walking around the class, handing out papers. "You'll find pencils and erasers under your desks."

"A test on the first day?" asked a girl at the back of the class.

"These tests are another way for you all to gain points," said Abigail as she walked through the aisles, continuing to pass out papers. "There will be many in all of your classes. But not all tests have incorrect answers. Many of them are just situational questions as to how you would handle a situation."

Safia received her test and began skimming over the questions. They all seemed normal to her, if not a little complicated.

Iraq has closed down trade negotiations with the US, Russia, and China. This is during a time of economic downturn and the oil market has run dry. What are the necessary steps to retrieve the oil from the country?

A foreign third-world country has developed nuclear weapons and decided to launch them on a world-ending terror- ist barrage. How would you handle the situation?

"Mr. Jericho, I know you might find my class boring, but would you please try to stay awake," said Abigail, accosting
142

one of her students.

Safia turned around to see a brown-haired boy with his arms folded across the desk, with his head down.

"I'm awake. I'm just resting my eyes, is all. Trust me. I'm listening to every word you say. I just don't need my eyes to listen."

"Well, you need your eyes to read the questions on this test. So I would appreciate a little cooperation from you."

"Unfortunately, I can't argue with that," said Jericho as he lifted his head and began rubbing his eyes. "Okay, let's get this over with. Hand me the test?"

"Oh, wow, have none of you been taught how you should speak to a teacher? Especially when said teacher is the one who will be grading you and does in fact have some influence over just how many points you receive."

"What do you mean?" said Jericho, as she stretched out his arms. "I'm one of the most loving students you could ask for. I'll even bring you an apple from the cafeteria."

"Well, aren't I happy to see you're being so co-operative, and thoughtful," said Abigail with a non-believing look on her face.

"Well, I want to try and make the teacher happy," said Jericho with a grin.

"Then, do well on all your tests and try to stay awake. That'll make me happy."

"I can do the first part, so one out of two ain't bad."

"Just take the paper, smartass," said Abigail with a smirk on her face as she playfully wacked Jericho oh the held with the test sheet.

"Yes, Ma`am," he said with a mock salute.

"Always one, every year," said Abigail, shaking her head, but still keeping her smile.

Safia shook her head as she watched the two go back and forth, but frowned when she turned back to her test, re-reading the questions again. *What type of questions are these to answer?* She then looked around to see all the other students and even Hashmi writing on their papers with their heads down. *I guess I'm just the weird one then.* She grabbed her pen and began to write her name on the paper and saw that it was already there. *Is everyone's test different? I guess that makes sure you can't cheat.* Giving up on procrastinating any longer, she shrugged her shoulders and began trying to answer the questions as best she could, not fully understanding what a lot of them meant.

Sometime into the test, she began to close her eyes, trying not to strain them by looking at the paper so intensely. As she opened and closed her eyes, rubbing at the bridge of her nose, something caught her gaze out the window as her focus returned. Gone were Austin and his reading group, and instead there was now something white on the grass. Her eyes still blurry, she squinted to see what it could be. The white figure floated on the green lawn providing such a stark contrast that it seemed to demand her attention. As her eyes came into focus, Safia realized it was a girl in a large white dress. She seemed so out of place that she had trouble recognizing her as an actual person.

Safia looked around the room for reassurance that she wasn't hallucinating, but all the other students all had their heads faced down on their tests; the quiet atmosphere occasionally being interrupted by the sound of erasers rubbing or papers being flipped over. Turning back to look out the window once again, she watched as the white-dressed girl danced her way around the tree, disappearing behind its trunk.

What in the world? She turned back to the class to once again see everyone still with their heads down, focusing on their tests. *How am I the only one who saw that? Does this place have ghosts?* Safia then shook her head, trying to get the image of the girl out of her head. *No... No... I'm not doing this right now. This school is already weird enough without me thinking that it has ghosts. That wasn't real, I'm just tired or something.* Forcing her attention back on the test and it's confusing questions, she began marking her answers and trying to finish up as best she could. *Focus, Safia.*

"Okay, that'll be the end of the class," said Abigail after another half hour or so. "You can leave your tests on the desk, and I will pick them up. If you have any questions, you can stay after class and I will answer them as best I can."

The students then stood up to leave, as Hashmi leaned over towards Safia.

"You want to get something to eat?" asked Hashmi.

"Huh," said Safia, losing her battle with curiosity as she stared out of the window at the tree where the girl in white had been. She then turned back to Hashmi and smiled. "Ah, sure, let's go."

Uplifting themselves from their seats, the two girls grabbed their things and made their way towards the exit. But as they reached the door, Safia noticed a tall man just standing by the door looking at Abigail. His hair looked a bit disheveled, and his eyes looked tired, as if he hadn't slept in weeks. He smiled at all the students as they walked past him on their way out of the classroom.

Who's that?

"Does no one want to stay and ask any questions?" asked Abigail with a smile on her face, but her eyes were glancing over to the man, as if she seemed a bit nervous about him being there.

"Safia? What's wrong?" asked Hashmi.

"It's nothing," said Safia, but as they made their way closer to the door, Safia specifically chose to go through the aisle of chairs that lead up to Abigail's desk. She plopped down her bag on her desk and reached inside grabbing a few blank pieces of paper. She then leaned over to Abigail and whispered to her as to make sure no one else overheard her. "Is everything alright? You seem a little nervous." She nodded to the man in the corner. "Is it because of him?" She had seen girls and boys getting bullied in school and Abigail was giving her the same vibes as they did back then.

"Me? Ah… no, it's not that," said Abigail after sighing. "I'm just avoiding my responsibilities, that's all. You girls go on ahead. I should probably take my test as well."

Test? What test? Is he your teacher or a principal here or something? "Okay, then," said Safia, confused by Abigail's statement, but not really convinced. "Well, I guess we'll see you next class, then."

Allowing herself to let the topic go, she and Hashmi walked out into the marbled hallway of the school with the other students and headed for the door. After making their way down the steps and on to the beginning of the walkway, Safia couldn't help but gaze out at the tree that she saw the girl disappear behind as she rounded the corner of the school. She was surprised to see that at the base of the tree she saw something white sticking out.

So I wasn't seeing things. I wonder who that— "Oof," said Safia as she bumped into a boy heading in the opposite direction. Losing her balance, she began to fall backwards, only to have the boy slide his feet between her legs and wrap his arm around her waist.

"Hey, you okay?" asked the boy that she bumped into.

Safia blinked, shaking off the impact. "Oh, sorry, I wasn't paying attention," She allowed the boy to pull her back up. "Thanks for catching me." She said, looking up at the boy. He had dark skin, dark eyes, and wavy hair, along with the stubble of a small beard that was starting to come in.

"Hashmi, who is your clumsy friend?"

"This is Safia, she's my roommate," said Hashmi, shaking her head with a giggle at Safia, before turning back to the boy. "Safia, this is Nasir. He is also a first-year here, just six months ahead of us."

"Hello Nasir," said Safia with a smile. "I didn't know Hashmi knew anyone else. Are you from the UK also?"

"Algeria, actually, but I spent a lot of my time in Russia and the US for schooling."

Safia stepped back, looking the boy over. His slacks had

a yellow shade in their pleated design, along with a scarf around his neck that shared the design and color scheme. She could see that he was quite well built as his broad chest filled out the button-up shirt.

"Well, if you're okay, then all is well," said Nasir as he smiled at them. "I must be heading off. I have to attend a gathering that I'm pretty sure I'm already late for."

"Oh, sorry for making you late then," said Safia.

"Don't worry yourself over it," said Nasir as he walked forward, turning back to the girls. "Hashmi, bring your clumsy friend the next time we have lunch," and he took off up the steps and into the school.

Safia glanced at Hashmi with a smile, "I didn't know you had a guy friend."

"Who, Nasir? I met him on my first day. He's just friendly, is all."

"You, sure? He seemed to take an interest in you."

"Oh quiet, he said to bring you along. So maybe he likes you instead. And besides, he apparently already has a girlfriend. He told me that they came to this school together. Anyway, let's go and get something to eat."

Safia glanced back at the tree where the white was still showing over the base of the tree trunk. "Actually, Hashmi, you can head on without me. There's something I want to check out."

"Are you sure? I can come with you, if you want."

"Nah, it's okay. I'm just making sure that I'm not going crazy. You go on ahead?"

"Okay, if you say so." responded Hashmi looking confused. "I guess I will see you back at the dorm then."

"Yeah, I'll see you then," said Safia, smiling back while stepping down from the walkway onto the grass. After passing the school halls, Safia was struck by a gust of wind that flew through her hair and the branches of the tree, sending the leaves spinning downward toward the ground as she approached the tree. Feeling cautious, she slowed her pace as she made her way closer, stepping lightly as she rounded the base of the trunk. Peaking around it, she was surprised to see someone was sitting behind it wearing a white dress with a hat to match. Nature had adorned her with an assortment of leaves that had fallen down, now scattered through her white clothing.

"Ah, hello? Is everything okay?" asked Safia as she cautiously stepped in front of her. She squatted in front of her and was surprised to see it was a young girl asleep with her back against the trunk of the tree. She looked like a small doll in her outfit, with pieces of the sun piercing through the leaves above shining down upon her.

The dress looked like it was made for some type of costume party. It was big and puffy and had frills all over it, even down the arms, where across her lap lay a white rolled up sun umbrella. But something was off. There was a feeling of familiarity that nagged at the back of Safia's mind as she exclaimed the girl's face. Then, with eyes wide, the memory came back to her.

This is her. This is the headmistress of the campus. The one from orientation who had the weird name, Champ Champ. Confused as to why the headmistress of the entire school would be out alone like this. Safia quickly began looking around for anyone nearby. But the two of them were alone. Only people nearby were the students that were walking the spiraling walkway off in the distance. *Why is she out here?*

Perhaps feeling a disturbance around here, Champ Champ began to open her eyes and noticed Safia squatting down, staring at her. She then blinked and yawned while stretching out her arms. The small head mistress leaned for a bit, her arms still outstretched and suddenly jumped at Safia, wrapping her arms around her as they both fell over on the ground with Champ Champ landing on top of her.

"Hey, what's wrong?" asked Safia in a state of confusion, as the grass beneath her tickled the back of her neck and arms. "Is everything alright?"

"Yes, hello," said Champ Champ as she continued to lay on top of Safia with her arms around her neck. "You smell like a new student. Are you enjoying our school?"

Smell like? What does that even mean? thought Safia as she laid in the grass; the sun above shining down on them both. "Ah, what? Wait, aren't you the headmaster?"

"Oh, yes, that's me," said Champ Champ as she pushed herself back up, rising to her knees and blinking her eyes curiously. "Why? Do you want to make a bet with me? I'm afraid I can't marry you. My husband has already won that bet."

"What? No," answered Safia as she also lifted herself to her knees. "I mean, what are you doing out here?"

"I was bored and wanted to get some sun," said Champ Champ as she stood up, wiping pieces of grass off of her person. "Organizing all these events for the start of classes has been hard on me, so I felt I needed a break. What about you, Safia? Are you enjoying yourself here? I hope you're not bored."

"You know my name?" asked Safia as she stood up, again noticing how small the girl was compared to her. She barely even came up to her chest.

"Of course. However, it took a minute to recall your face. But I was taking a nap, so I guess that's to be expected. But when I'm awake, I know everyone's name. I try to remember everything about my students," said Champ Champ as she pointed her finger at Safia. "You are Safia Famosa, age seventeen. Your brother is Yago Famosa, Father, Hector Famosa, Mother, Samantha Famosa, and your boyfriend, David Reynolds. You also like to have sex in the back of meat trucks."

"What!" yelped Safia before looking around to make sure no one else heard. "How do you know that?" she whispered.

"We looked into you when we found out you were selected to attend this school instead of Christopher Alvarez," said Champ Champ, reaching down and picking up a white sun umbrella.

"Wait, I thought I was taking my brother's place?"

"Oh, that's just what we told him. Things were already complicated enough without adding that extra bit. Hey, how was it?" asked Champ Champ as she took a step closer to Safia.

"How was what?" asked Safia, trying her best to keep up with the information the little girl was spewing out.

"The sex. I've never had sex in the back of a meat truck. Was it fun? But I do imagine that it smelled like meat, though. Is that a fetish you have? A meat fetish?"

"Oh no," said Safia, placing her hands to her face in embarrassment. "Don't tell anyone about that, okay?"

"I won't. That would spoil the game, but we needed to make sure that it was safe to acquire you, and so we had to check up on you. You have a violent school history, fights between both boys and girls in your youth."

"That... that was years ago. I'm not like that now," said Safia in protest.

"I certainly hope so," said Champ Champ, folding her arms in front of her. "We take the safety of our students very seriously. There are to be no fights here, useless it is agreed upon by both parties."

Safia looked down at Champ Champ, narrowing her eyes at the girl. "What do you mean, both parties? And why are you even interested in me and David? Wait, how old are you?"

"Twenty three," said Champ Champ, looking up at Safia curiously. "Why?"

"But you're so small, and why are you dressed like that?"

"I know, right," said Champ Champ, looking over her dress and shaking her head in disapproval. "My husband forces me to wear these things. He makes me so mad when he shows up with these stupid outfits."

"He forces you? Why?"

Champ Champ sighed and spoke in a monotone voice.

"Because he said that if I'm going to look like a child and act like a child, then I may as well dress like a child." She shook her head in disgust at her own words. "And I have to say that every time someone asks about my clothing."

"What? Why is that? Is this a part of the bet you were talking about during orientation? The one where you said you became someone's wife?"

"Yes," said Champ Champ, continuing to use a bored monotone voice. "Because I lost a bet to my darling husband, now I have to play the role of the good wife and good little wives listen to their husbands." Champ Champ huffed, blowing out a breath of air. "And yes, I also have to respond like that when people ask me why I listen to him." She then placed her hands on her hips. "Can we not talk about my marriage? He's a good man, he just likes to annoy me."

"Okay, but can I just ask, why are you listening to him if you don't like it?"

"Oh, that's because that was our wager," said Champ Champ with a cheerful smile on her face. "You never expect to lose, but that sure was a fun day."

"But just because you lost, that doesn't mean you have to do what..." Safia stopped when she noticed Champ Champ's demeanor change; her whimsical nature vanishing as her face took on a serious expression.

"To not honor a wager will result in immediate expulsion from this school, and we will ensure that all wagers are paid in full," said Champ Champ as she took another step closer to Safia. "You are free to resign from this school at any time, Miss Famosa. But if you wish to leave because you lost a bet and refuse to pay, then we will ensure that any agreements you made while on this campus will be upheld, even after you have left this campus. Do you understand this, Miss Safia Famosa?"

"Ah, yes ma'am," said Safia, quickly, as she felt a cold chill go down her spine at the sudden change in tone of the small girl before her. Her quick response surprised even her. She found herself a little afraid of this apparent grown woman in front of her. *Am I afraid of her?*

"Good," said Champ Champ, who had switched back to her whimsical nature. "It's important that we all take responsibility for our actions," she said, turning around, picking up her umbrella that had fallen from her lap and pointing it back towards the window of the school. "Look, even Miss Abigail understands how important it is to honor her bets."

Safia followed where Champ Champ pointed her umbrella and saw Abigail through the window of the school. Through the glass, she could see the man she saw waiting at the door beforehand. He was caressing the side of Abigail's face with his palm until she turned her away from him. They were saying something, but Safia couldn't tell what. She only knew that whatever it was, Abigail didn't seem too excited about it. "What's happening? Is he trying to bet her or something?"

"What? Oh goodness, no. Abigail's wagering days are long past her. She found herself in a bad situation here a while ago when I was still a student. Needless to say, she wound up working for us to pay off her debt."

"Wait, she was saying she did it because of her sister."

"Oh, she already spilled the beans. Good, then that makes it easier to talk about."

"Talk about what?"

"She owed this school ten years of her life in return for saving her sister's life. It was a deal she and my grandfather worked out. I think it was a bit excessive given the number of points he asked from her, but she accepted it. So, who am I to judge?"

"They why... I mean, does she owe him anything, then?"

"What? Killian?"

His name is Killian then? wondered Safia as she looked back through the window.

"No, of course not, he was just a freshman then," said Champ Champ, shaking her head. "No, the school owns the debt. My grandfather set it up so that she would graduate and still get to go home to her family in exchange for ten years of her life in service to the school. And with a large amount of money, since we pay our teacher a hefty amount for their services. Plus, her father invests his money in businesses that work through our companies. And she didn't want her debt to affect their family's lifestyle. She really is a good daughter. I hope I'll have one like her one day."

Safia frowned down at Champ Champ. "Then, why is she tolerating him? Why not just leave? Isn't he harassing her?"

"Oh! That's because he's trying to buy her debt from the school. Amazingly, he's spent the last two years of his life collecting points so that he can buy the next seven years of hers. It's actually ironic in a selfish love type of way. Perhaps when he's done, he should write a book about it, leaving out the name of the school and our involvement in it of course. I would love to know how he views things from his perspective. I imagine he fancies himself quite the hero; saving his love from the oppression of the school and what not."

"Wait, what? What do you mean, buy the years left of her debt? So he wants to pay it off?"

"Not exactly. What Abigail owes this school is her servitude. He wants to buy that."

"What? Can he do that? I mean, are you going to sell her?" *This must be a joke. That's... that's like slavery, you can't just sell a person off like that.*

"If he can come up with the points required, then, of course the school will sell; it's already been decided. I was told to inform him of this two years ago, and the school won't go back on its word. Although, at the time, I convinced them to set a number I thought he would never reach. After all, I do so enjoy having Miss Abigail here, but that boy Killian has been absolutely singular-minded in getting points these last two years. If he keeps going at his current pace, then I'm afraid he will end up buying her debt before he graduates. He's a very persistent man."

"How many more points does he need?" asked Safia, still looking through the window at Abigail and Killian and what appeared to be a very uncomfortable interaction.

"Now that's between us three. You may ask him about it if you like, but you will not get that information from my end. Everything I've told you so far is a bit less than common knowledge amongst the third years, which granted there's only about two dozen or so of them left here, and it seems Miss Abigail has already told you a bit about her entanglement. But the actual points, that's between us three. But feel free to confront those two about it. Perhaps they will be willing to share if confronted directly."

Safia stared down at the small woman and then turned back to the window, unbelieving of the situation that she had heard.

"Oh, don't worry about it," said Champ Champ. "There are always a good number of students who graduate from this school, that never placed a single bet during their entire time here, and go on to live very fruitful lives. The wagering system doesn't apply to everyone. It's just for the select amongst us who wish to take risks because they desire something greater in life."

"You act as if there's no other way to succeed, besides this school."

"Is that so? Well, that's certainly not the impression I want to give. You don't need this school to be successful. Graduating from here just opens up more doors and gets you connected with the right people. Our graduates have more access to certain benefits that others simply do not. It's not just career opportunities."

"What else is there?"

"You name it, and we have access to it, from the best to

developing countries, the best health care, auto manufacturers, or perhaps political adjustments that can sway the thinking of an entire country. Apex doesn't just claim to make the world's next leaders. For the last three hundred years, this school has handcrafted this world economy, from wars in third world countries to crashes on the stock market."

"But I've never heard of this... Apex Academy," said Safia, looking around her. "In fact, none of this seems right? It just seems like a place for terrible people to be terrible?"

"And who's to say that terrible people don't run the world, Miss Safia," said Champ Champ as she waved her hand over at the students that were making their way throughout the campus. "Look at them all. Each one of them is a marvelous bundle of potential that will one day leave here and push their influence out into the world. Whether it be for good or bad, who knows?" She then brought her hand around, stopping it in front of Safia. "Some may be terrible, some may not. But each one according to our tests, has the potential to be a leader. And that brings us to you. Our tests have shown that you have the same drive as they do. And let's not forget that you chose to stay here in this place. So that must mean you want something, something that you think this school can give you. Or else you simply would have gone back home and lived a modest life in the parents' establishment."

Safia wanted to disagree with the head mistress, but found that she could not find the worlds. She could only stand there with a solemn look on her face.

"Don't look so glum, Miss Safia. While that truth may be hard to swallow. It just means you're as human and flawed as anyone else. And the proof of that is you're standing here before me."

Safia stayed silent as she gazed back out over the campus. *Am I really the same as everyone here? That can't be true, the things I've seen. There's no way I'm as bad as them. I wouldn't treat people that way.*

"Cheer up Miss Safia. This is a rare opportunity for you. You should embrace all it has to offer," said Champ Champ as she puffed out her parasol and began to twirl it around. "This place only used to invite the wealthy and elite, but my grandfather was a betting man, and he always thought that the only difference between the predator and prey was that the predator had more opportunity to kill."

Champ Champ spun around whimsically, allowing her parasol to twirl in her hand as her extended foot slid along to top of the grass. "But on those rare occasions throughout history, where you might look close enough, you would see the tables turn when the hunted would become the hunter. And it was in those moments that you would truly get to see something magical." She stopped her twirling and raised her parasol above her head. "I do hope that you decide to give us a good show during your time here, Miss Famosa. I would relish another chance to witness my grandfather's miracle."

"Miracle? What miracle? I don't understand. What does any of this mean?"

"Of course you do. You just haven't realized it yet. In fact, I do believe you've met our miracle, although your encounter was brief. You were certainly able to witness firsthand the result of it."

Is she talking about a person? Who did I meet? Though Safia has her mind flipped between the assortment of people that she had met on campus since her arrival. But no one that she could think of fit with what the headmistress was saying.

"Oh, it seems my break is over. I must get back before they come for me. Take care Miss. Safia," said the tiny woman as she turned on her heels and strolled off out from under the tree and through the campus's well-manicured lawn, once again twirling her parasol in her hand as it rotated above her head.

Shaking her head in total confusion as she watched Champ Champ stroll off, Safia then turned around and began to head back, but stopped after noticing some deep markings in the tree. Leaning down, inspecting the bark, she noticed that the markings spelled out two words. *I Win* was etched deep into the bark of the tree.

She then turned back to where Champ Champ was, but the girl was gone. Feeling anxious about what was just revealed to her, Safia shook her head, walking back towards the campus with thoughts of Champ Champ and what she had said in her mind as she made her way through the winding concrete path.

She eventually made her way across the whole campus and found herself at the door to the test facility, where she had the chip implanted into her. Outside of the building, she saw a shirtless male student with a shovel in his hand. Alongside him, were several small trees that had the base of their trunks wrapped in black bags that were tied by small pieces of rope.

I know that face. I think he was in my class. thought Safia as she walked up to the building. Looking at the key reader beside the door, she realized that she didn't know how to actually enter the building or contact the people inside. Looking around for a moment, she noticed one of those black orbs above her on the wall; its black lens reflecting off the sun up above as it seemed to gaze down at her.

"Ah, hello," said Safia, looking upward at the black orb. "I would like to use your phone, please." She then waited for some type of sign that they heard her, but no response came.

"You're doing that the wrong way," said the shirtless boy as he drove his shovel down into the ground, stomping on it with his foot to drive it deeper before scooping up a large mound of dirt. "You're not going to get their attention like that."

"Oh, yeah, then how am I supposed to talk to them,"

said Safia in a much harsher tone than she meant to. "I'm sorry, I shouldn't have snapped at you like that." She looked over at him and tried to collect herself.

The boy drove the shovel down into the dirt again, this time sticking it into the ground. "You got your pendant on you?"

"It's in here," said Safia, raising her handbag.

"I'll show you how to use it then," he said before walking over to his discarded shirt that was laying atop the grass. He reached in, pulling out his own pendant. It was the same type as hers, indicating that he was a first-year student. Safia noticed that his clothing had a red accent to it.

Red? I wonder which house he belongs to.

He then held out his pendant for Safia to see. "You have to do it like this," he said before clicking the pendant. "I, Jericho Andrews, would like to talk to my family."

"Please wait outside the Communication building, and someone will soon come to meet you," spoke the pendant.

"There you go," said Jericho, tossing his pendant back down onto his clothing and walking back over to one of the small trees. "Don't worry if it takes them a little longer to answer. I think it takes the system a little while to get used to your voice." He undid the wrapping at the base of the tree, pulling on the string of small rope and exposing the rich soil inside the bag that held the roots of the small tree. Then, reaching his hands around and gripping the soil at the bottom of the tree, he lifted it, carrying it over to the hole he had just dug before dropping it inside.

Feeling more calm, Safia couldn't help but notice the boy's muscles as he went about his work. The sweat and dirt spread throughout his body and up to his arms, painting him in a more primal tone than she expected. He was an attractive boy, perhaps not a model, but he was not hard to look at by any means to her.

"Thank you," said Safia, stepping onto the grass towards the boy until she remembered the name he'd used. *Jericho?*

Moving her eyes from his body back to his face, her mind went back to the sleeping smartass in her class. "Wait, I remember now. You were just in my class."

"I was? Are you sure?"

"Yes," said Safia, giving the boy another look over. "You were the one sleeping and got into trouble with Abigail."

"Everyone just assumes I'm sleeping," said Jericho as he clapped his hands together, trying to shake free the loose dirt on his fingers. "Is a man not allowed to rest his eyes from the harsh realities of the world without judgment?"

"Harsh realities? Don't you think you're being a bit overly dramatic?"

"Depends on your sense of dramatization, really. Considering what some people have seen so far here, they might think I'm totally justified in my response to this school."

Well, I can't say he's wrong, considering everything that's happened so far, thought Safia as she looked back at the communication building. *And I guess that's kinda the reason I'm here.* Safia shook her head, trying to wipe the thoughts from her mind. "Well, thank you for showing me how to get in, I guess."

"Don't worry about it. People come here from time to time wearing that face of yours."

"What face?" asked Safia, narrowing her eyes at him.

"That face like someone just killed their favorite pet," said Jericho as he walked back over to his shovel. "I'm guessing you're thinking about going home."

"What? No, I'm not."

"Oh, was I wrong? Damn, and I'm usually so good at reading people. All right, then," said Jericho, placing his hand on the hilt of the shovel, waddling it in the ground until it was loose enough to free from the soil. He then picked up and began digging another hole.

Safia watched him scoop up another two shovels of dirt before deciding to be more honest with him. "Okay, so maybe I am, but don't you think this place is weird? This whole betting thing. The discarded. This place is fucked up."

"Yeah," said Jericho as he scooped up another pile of dirt. "Can't argue with you there, but that's just the people here. Places can't be fucked up. Places are just places. If you deal with fucked up people, you're bound to become just as messed up as they are." He then turned back to Safia, smears of dirt on his face mixing in with the sweat running down his cheek. "But everyone's got their reasons for being here. And I don't think they care much whether you or I agree with them."

"Okay, fine then. Why are you here?" asked Safia as she waved her hand around at the campus. "Or is that a secret like everything else in this place?"

"My sister asked me to come. She wanted me to make all these rich people my friends."

"What?"

"Exactly what I said; we're all here for different reasons. I'm here for selfish family reasons. To make friends with the elite so that I can make use of them later. So, tell me, what's your reason for being here?"

"I... ah... my brother. He and—" said Safia before the door beside her opened, and a man in a lab coat came out of the double doors to greet them.

The man looked around before spotting Jericho with the shovel in his hand. "Get dressed, and you can call—"

"Actually, it's not me. She's the one who wants to call," said Jericho as he pointed his thumb at Safia before driving the shovel back into the ground, bringing up more dirt.

"I see," said the man before turning towards Safia, "What's your name?"

"Safia... Ah, Safia Famosa."

The man pulled out a small glass tablet from his pocket and began scrolling through a list of names until Safia's name appeared. He touched on it, and her face showed up on his screen along with an assortment of other data.

"Okay, follow me, and I'll take you to have your call," said the man as he turned around, walking back inside.

"Good luck," said Jericho, "I hope you get what you want."

Safia glanced back at Jericho one more time; the sun gleaming off the sweat on his back and arms before she turned and followed the man inside. The building still gave off the vibes of a doctor's office, with its sterile smelling air and checkered tiled floors, walls, and roofing. *Why do they make everything so weird here?*

They passed the first set of rooms just like before and walked down the corridor. The large windowed offices that she could see in were much the same as before. But in one of them she saw a brown-haired boy sitting reading a book. He looked no older than ten. They stopped at the same door as before as the man led her into the room and gestured to the walls, where the rotary phones were mounted in their identical stalls. Each one next to the other.

"Okay, please use booth number five and have a seat."

Safia walked forward, looking around the room until she saw a large number five sign above one of the stalls that housed the phones. After she sat down on the stool, the man walked up behind her, and after having inserted an earpiece, he sat down next to her.

"Please, start your call. But remember to keep any specific details about the campus out of your conversation."

"Okay," said Safia as she looked at the rotary phone, trying to remember how Abigail used it. *Its hard trying to remember the numbers by heart. I usually just assign a name to a number and forget the number in my phone. Let's see, it was two, seven, six, eight, four, three, seven.* She placed her finger in the hook of the number dial and began spinning it. Her finger slipped on the numbers once or twice. *Dang it, did I do it right? I think that was a three instead of a two.* She thought to herself, but soon after a few rings, a familiar voice answered the phone.

"Hello," said Yago's voice.

"Hey, Yago, it's me," she said as she felt a wave of relief wash over her upon hearing her brother's voice.

"Hey, Saffy! How's school going? Are you getting accustomed to campus life?"

"I... I'm not so sure anymore." She glanced over at the man beside her as he fiddled with his glass tablet. "It's hard getting used to classes and stuff, but I think... I think I'm gonna be okay. Ah, how's Pa and Ma? Is... is everything going okay there?"

"Yeah, Pa's still downstairs in the diner, and Ma's here," said Yago before Safia heard an echo of her brother on the phone, "Hey, Ma, Saffy's on the phone." Then came the sound of the phone being handed off.

"Hello? Safia, is that you?" came her mother's voice into her ear.

"Hey, Ma," said Safia, dropping her head as she clenched the phone in her hands. She pressed the side of the phone against her ear as if the gesture would shorten the distance between her and her family. "I... miss you."

"Ahhh. I miss you too, baby. We were all just talking about you today, and everything's been so busy, too. David and your father have both gone out to get a new oven for the restaurant."

"A new oven?" asked Safia, comforted by the sound of her mother's voice. She found pleasure in hearing about things at the diner, about a life she never realized she could miss so much.

"Oh, yeah, Mr. Alvarez gave your father that money he promised, and your father said that he wanted to use it to fix up things around here. So, David's been helping him move stuff around before he heads off to college."

Safia laughed, thinking about David, as she heard a clicking sound on the other end of the phone, then her mother's voice began to fade away.

"Ma… Ma… Hello?"

"Safia? Baby, you're breaking up. Is everything okay?"

"Can you hear me, Ma?"

"Okay, that's better," said Safia's mother, as her voice came back into the phone. "Are your studies going okay, honey? Do you need anything?"

"No, I'm fine," said Safia as she cherished the sound of her mother's voice. She then noticed that all the aggravation and confusion that she felt earlier had mostly subsided. "I… I just wanted to hear your voice. That's all and make sure everything is going okay."

"Tell me, have you found a new boyfriend yet?"

"What? No. And I'm not looking for anyone. Why are you asking that?" asked Safia to the sound of her mother giggling over the phone.

"I'm just teasing, but everything is going fine here, so don't worry about us. Just focus on your studies. We're all so proud of you, and I tell all the girls that my baby is off at college making something of herself."

"Yes, Ma, I will," said Safia, and after a little more conversation, she finished up the conversation with her family and hung up the phone. She then lowered her head as she looked down at her skirt and her brown square-toed shoes with a smirk on her face. *I'm such a child. Look at me, having to call home and talk to my parents every time I feel upset? Maybe I am the little sister, after all.* Wiping at a few hints of moisture at the edges of her eyes, Safia lifted herself up from her seat and turned to the man that had escorted her in.

"Are you finished?" asked the man.

"Yes, that's it. Thank you."

The man then stood, removing his earpiece, and led Safia back out of the building. She realized she hadn't been inside long, as the sun was still high in the sky when she walked back outside. And to her right, Jericho was still there planting his trees, sweating in the midday sun, although now there were two more small trees in the ground along with an extra shovel that she wasn't sure was there before. The doors closed behind her, and she took a deep breath before walking over to him.

"Ah, excuse me. It was Jericho, wasn't it?"

"Hello again," said Jericho after stomping his foot around the soil of one of the trees he planted. "Yeah, I'm Jericho Andrews. And your face looks different from before. Do you feel better now after talking to your family?"

"What? How can you…" Safia stopped herself, raised a finger, and spoke again. "Yes, I feel better now. How could you tell I wasn't feeling well?"

"I'm good at reading people's facial expressions and body language," said Jericho, waving his hand at her. "You looked pretty stiff when you spoke to me, and you were shortening your words as if you were in a hurry."

"I guess that'll help you fit right in at this school with its betting system then."

"Maybe, but I'm not interested in betting. I'm only interested in controlling my own little world," said Jericho as he knelt, picking back up his shovel. "I'll make a friendly bet once a month, but after that, I stick to just helping out around campus to get points. Plus, I do tutoring on the side, so I'm sure I'll be fine."

"How does that work? Do you request to be a tutor, or do they offer these jobs? Is there somewhere I can apply for them?"

"Oh, no. If you see something that you think needs to be done on campus, just tap your pendant, say your name, and say what you want to do. You'll receive an answer in a day or so. Speaking of which, where's your pendant?"

"It's still in my bag. Why?"

"Oh, that won't do," said Jericho, walking up to Safia with his hand out. "May I?"

Safia gave him a suspicious look but decided it was okay and knelt, reaching into her handbag, pulling out her pendant.

Taking it, he then turned around, walked back to one of the wrapped plants, plucking off one of the strings tied to the base before returning to her. He then knelt beside her bag and looped the string in a hole in the back of the pendant and tied it to the side of her carryall. "There, now you're all set, and you won't have to go fiddling in your bag the next time you want to use it."

Safia looked down at Jericho, who had dirt all over his hands and now on her pendant that was dangling from her bag. "I guess after I clean it, it will look nice."

Jericho looked at his dirt covered hands, "Oops, well sorry about that, ah... actually, I don't think I ever got your name."

"Oh, did I never introduce myself?" asked Safia with a smile. "My name is Safia Famosa. And why do you have two shovels? What's that one for?"

"Well, Miss Famosa, that one belongs to someone who's been helping me, but he hasn't come back yet. He kinda has this habit of being a passionate gambler and ran off to make a bet. He's very dedicated to gaining points here. So perhaps I'll see him again soon, but probably not today."

"Sounds like your friend's addicted to betting like everyone else here. Are you sure you're not a gambling fiend? You know what they say, like-minded people tend to stick together."

"Sorry, but that guy's in a league of his own when it comes to betting. I think I'll stick to my little chores around campus to get by. That seems a lot less stressful than the obsession over points that most here seem to have."

"Can you make a lot of points by doing stuff like that?" asked Safia as she pointed to the shovels.

"No, not really, but it all adds up, I think. And as for my friend, well, he has his uses. But it's good to meet you, and I look forward to seeing you around. Who knows, maybe we will end up being friends."

"You sure?" asked Safia with a giggle. "My family isn't rich."

"That's fine. Not everyone can be a sugar momma."

"Seriously? Is that what you're here for?" asked Safia, not letting go of the smile on her face.

"Hey, we're all here for a reason. Some reasons are just more selfish than others."

"Okay, bye, Jericho. Hopefully, I will see you around, instead of just sleeping in the back of the class," said Safia as she walked back through the campus, headed off towards Yennefer house.

Halfway through her trip back, she felt a slight vibration on her hip and reached inside her pocket, pulling out the glass tablet to see she had a message that appeared on the screen in the form of a little icon of an envelope. Tapping on the envelope, the message icon opened.

'Apex System awards you seventy points' was written across the tablet.

Safia squinted her eyes at the message. *Seventy? Why did I get these points? Was it because of the test I took today?* She pondered the questions as she made her way back to Yennefer house where at its flower-filled steps she looked up to see that a few other students were going in and out of the building. And up on the steps watering the flowers was Austin, who had shown her to her room.

"Ah, excuse me," said Safia, walking up the steps towards him and showing him the message on her device. "It says I got seventy points. I'm guessing that's for the test I took earlier. Is that good?"

"Hey, hey," said Austin, reaching forward and pushing Safia's hand down. "Don't show me that. Always keep your points a secret. Other people might get an advantage over you."

"Oh, ah, okay. I didn't think about that." *Advantage? How? I mean, how can someone use my points against me?*

"It's fine. Just be careful, okay," said Austin with a sigh.

"But, yeah, that is typically normal for a test here. We get tested multiple times a month here. So, seventy points is pretty good. I guess they must have liked your answers."

"What was up with those questions?" asked Safia, placing the device back into her pocket. "None of them made any sense."

"No idea. I don't know what questions you had," said Austin, shrugging his shoulders. "As far as I know, everyone's tests are different. That's why, when you get your paper, it already has your name on it. There's a lot of things about this school that most here don't understand. I myself just roll with it. As long as I graduate, it'll be fine."

"Oh, I guess that makes sense. Thank you."

"Are you enjoying this place so far? You're new, so I bet its kind of a shock."

"I'm not sure enjoying is the right word."

Austin laughed. "Yeah, I was like that too when I first arrived. But you'll get used to it. If you need anything else just ask."

"I will, thanks," said Safia as she turned to leave.

"Hey," said Austin, stopping Safia before she could go.

"Yes?"

"Soon, they are going to release the restrictions on freshmen not being able to bet. Be careful after that. This place changes when that happens. You don't want to get too caught up in what's about to happen."

What's about to happen? That doesn't sound good. "Ah, okay... But don't worry. I don't plan on really betting here," said Safia before making her way into the dorm house and up the steps towards her room.

She opened the door to see Hashmi in her pajamas, on her knees, with her head pressed against an ornately designed rug.

"Oh, I'm sorry. Should I come back later?"

Hashmi raised her head, looking at Safia with a smile. "No, I've finished, unless you would like to join me?"

"I'm not very religious," said Safia, coming into their room and closing the door behind her. "I never thought to ask your religion, but I'm guessing you're Muslim?"

"Yes, and since you're from the States, I'm guessing you're Christian."

"I guess. My parents never really practiced it, though. I can't even remember the last time I went to church."

"Ha, my mother is the same," said Hashmi as she sat up, placing her hands on her lap. "She's not a very religious person. So I've only been a practicing Muslim and wearing Hijab for about two years now."

"What's Hijab?"

"In simple terms, it's the scarf around my head and neck," said Hashmi as she stood, rolling her prayer mat into her hands.

"Oh? Wait, two years ago? So, you weren't Muslim before that time?"

"No, I suppose, I really wasn't."

"Do you mind if I ask why you started? I mean, if that's not too personal?"

"No, not at all. Originally, it was to develop a better relationship with my father. He asked me to try it one day while we were out shopping. It felt right, so I've been doing it ever since. Although, I often forget to do my prayers at the right time. So, I'm probably not the best example of someone who practices the Muslim faith."

"And I know I'm definitely not the best example of the Christian faith," said Safia, shaking her head with a laugh. "So, I think we both might have a long way to go." She then pointed to the mat on the floor. "Do you always pray on that?"

"Yes, It's a prayer mat. My father actually made it for me in celebration of me coming here," said Hashmi as she held up the mat for Safia to see. The carpet had a golden border and a sky-blue interior. Inside were five golden symbols at the top that she didn't know how to read, and at the base was the picture of an odd-looking building with three cone-shaped tops.

"It's very pretty. Are you and your father close?"

"Now we are. But for the longest time, we weren't. It's gotten better over this past year, and we're trying to grow a better relationship. What about you and your family?" asked Hashmi as she rolled up her prayer mat again and set it beside her bed. "Are you close with them?"

"As much as it can be expected. We argue and fight, but we mostly get along. Well, except for my know-it-all brother. My mother is African, and my father is Cuban, so when they fight, it gets loud. But they've mostly calmed down now."

"I guess that's most families, then," said Hashmi, shaking her head. "My father is from Israel, and my mother is from Liverpool. They met in college and had me, but father had to go back home, where he married another woman. So, I spent a long time hating him for that."

"But you said you're trying to make a better relationship with him. Has it worked?"

"For the most part, yes, but we still have our arguments from time to time since he wants me to be more like his idea of what a Muslim should be, the type in Israel, and I wish to find my own meaning of why I wear Hijab."

"And what about dating?" asked Safia with a raised brow and a knowing smile across her face.

"I've only had one boyfriend, and father didn't exactly like him, but I guess all fathers are like that? Was yours the same?"

"Not my father. I dated this boy named David, and my father loves him. He even started calling him his son while we were together," said Safia, shaking her head. "He'd always say," Safia tried her best to put on her father's accent, "You dating that white boy. He from that rich family, that's good. You marry him, and you won't have to work. And your mother and I won't have to worry about you."

"And was he from a rich family?"

"Well, yeah, I guess. His father owns some type of lawyer's office."

"So what's wrong? Did you not like him?"

"No, we got along well, I guess. Except that he was a pervert most of the time."

"I think that's all men," laughed Hashmi as she gestured her hand over her clothing. "In fact, my religion asks that I dress this way precisely because of that issue."

Safia smirked and pointed her finger at Hashmi. "I thought you said it was to make your father happy."

"Oh, it is," Hashmi smirked, "But that doesn't make it any less true."

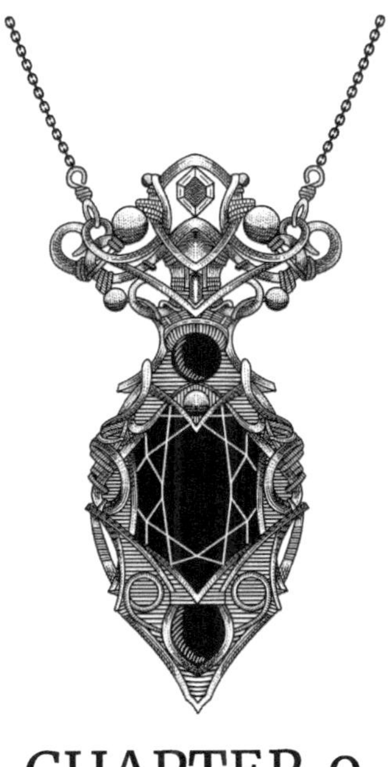

CHAPTER 9

The following week, Safia stood in her room getting dressed for her classes. After finishing the final button on her blouse she heard a noise outside the window. Stepping forward and looking through the glass, she saw the boys of her dorm running back and forth on the lawn. Around them were a crowd of onlookers shouting their cheers. One of those onlookers was Austin. He stood beside a set of runners with his hand raised as they got into position. And as he swung his arm down the runners took off across the grass.

What are they doing?

It was only when another set of boys lined up, and Safia watched as multiple group members tapped on their pendants, did she realize what was happening.

They must be betting. But there's so many people.

Safia turned around as the door to her room opened and Hashmi walked in, fully clothed and holding her bathing materials.

"What's wrong, Safia?" asked Hashmi, noticing the odd look on her face as she turned back to her.

"Look," said Safia, pointing out the window.

Hashmi walked over and sighed. "Harmony said it would be like this. I guess that explains the noise from downstairs."

"What noise?"

"If you go out in the hall, you'll hear it. It's loud. I guess they're playing some type of game downstairs."

After getting dressed, Safia and Hashmi headed outside of their room on the way to their morning classes, and upon stepping out into the hallway, she did indeed notice the sounds coming from below them. The two girls both headed downstairs and saw the students of Yennefer House and a few other students from other houses betting in the common area of the dorm. Some had dice; some had cards, while others played games that Safia had never seen before.

What is happening? Is this what everyone has been waiting on? Just for when the school allowed them to bet? Safia watched as the students tapped on their pendants.

"Hey, Hashmi. You wanna make a bet to see who winds up with the highest number?" asked one of a few boys coming in behind them.

"You ain't gonna win any points off that one, mate," said another boy, tapping him on the shoulder. "That's one of them Muslims. Don't ya see that thing on her head. The school gives em some sort of special rule that they ain't gotta play the game,"

Hashmi frowned, shaking her head at the man.

"What about you, then?" asked the first boy, looking at Safia. "You wanna make a bet on who wins?" he said, pointing towards some boys rolling dice on a table.

"No thanks, I'm not interested."

"Come on, it's just a friendly bet. What? You one of them Muslims, too?"

Safia took a good look in the boy's face, "To you, I might as well be," and grabbed Hashmi by the hand, walking out of the door with her.

"You didn't have to do that," said Hashmi as she allowed Safia to lead her out of the door and down the steps.

"What a horrible way to start the day, meeting a dumbass in the morning."

Hashmi laughed, "Are you okay? You seem more upset about it than I am."

"I am upset," said Safia, turning around looking at the smile on Hashmi's face, "What? Did I say something wrong?"

"No. It's sweet that you care. But really, I'm used to it."

"Why? Aren't you upset? What he said was rude."

"Because I'm used to it. I told you before that I only started Hijab about two years ago. So, imagine what it was like in school for everyone to go from seeing my face every day to suddenly seeing me in Hijab. What he said was no worse than anything else I've heard, and I promise I've heard a lot worse."

"Oh, well... that still doesn't make it right."

"After everything we've seen here so far, I don't think the people here care about what's right or wrong," said Hashmi with a smile. "Come on, let's go to class."

"Ah, okay," said Safia as she felt Hashmi squeeze her hand and lead her off through the winding concrete paths towards the school.

On the way, they saw that the campus was lively with a lot more activity than usual. Conversations were happening between crowds of people along the path, and Safia caught more than one or two people staring at them as they made their way into the school and towards their class. But on the winding path to school, she caught a glimpse of a girl with her arms spread out on a bench. She wore a brown skirt with yellow accents, along with a loosely buttoned-up shirt that exposed more cleavage than necessary, Safia thought. But as they neared the girl, Safia couldn't help but stare at her face.

Why does she seem so familiar? I don't think I know her.

"Safia, are you okay?"

"Huh?"

"I'm not sure," said Safia in a whisper as she passed the girl.

"You're going to walk by and not speak? I figured you had better manners than that," said the girl.

"Do I know you?"

"Ah, you forgot me already. Now that's fucked up. I had to play stewardess and babysit your ass for half that flight. I at least expect a damned thank you."

"You… you're that stewardess who drugged me."

"Oh, now you remember me. I swear, tying your ass down so you wouldn't fall over was a pain. You know they made me take that damn sleeping stuff again when we got in the air. I was half tempted to roll your ass on the floor so I could just sleep on top of you."

"Who are you?"

"Doesn't even remember my name. You're no better than a man after a one-night stand. Well, fine," she said, placing her hands on her knees and standing up. "I'm Addison, ex-stewardess and second-year student. And you are Safia. Who's the Muslim chick you're hanging out with?"

"Excuse me, but the Muslim chick has a name," said Hashmi, looking annoyed.

"Yeah, and I just asked for it, or didn't you hear me with your religious earmuffs on?"

"Is there a reason you speak like that, or were you just raised to be abrasive?"

174

"Pretty much been a bitch all my life. No point in hiding it like you hide that face of yours and everything else under all that getup you're wearing."

"I do this because of my beliefs in being modest, something I could certainly teach you a thing or two about," said Hashmi, pointing to Addison's exposed bra through her partially buttoned-up shirt.

"Oh, is that so?" asked Addison, as she began to undo another button on her shirt. "Well, come on and strip Miss Uppity, you put on my clothes, and I'll wear all that carpet you have on."

"What?"

"Don't back out now. If you want me to cover up, then I expect you to undress and put on my clothes. Or does that God of yours not believe in fair exchange? Because if I'm putting on, then you're taking off."

"I will do no such thing."

"Stop," said Safia, grabbing at Addison's hands as she reached the final button of her shirt. "What's your problem?"

"My problem? I'm just putting the princess's words here to the test. Or are you just all talk?"

"I never said I would swap clothes with you. You're just making things up."

"No, you said you could teach me modesty. Well, in exchange, I can teach you how to forget that modesty and stop giving a fuck what people think."

"I'm not going to play your game. Forsaking my beliefs for your ridiculous thinking is unacceptable."

"So, it's okay for you to place your modest beliefs on me, but when I ask the same, suddenly you turn tail. What a hypocrite."

Safia could see the annoyance building in Hashmi as her face began to twist. "Stop, both of you. This whole thing started because of nothing, so just leave it alone."

"Fine," said Hashmi, as she closed her eyes and regained her composure.

"Are you okay now? Will you please button up your shirt?"

"Yeah, fine. Let her have her little pity party."

Wow, what the hell just happened? "Now you said they put you to sleep also, so does that mean that even you don't know where we are?" asked Safia, trying to change the subject.

"Yeah, they put me to sleep after you, and I woke up at the airport. The only reason I knew where I was is because they let me walk around the airport until you arrived. When I woke up, we were already here, and that guy you were with was gone. They probably dropped him off somewhere else."

"Can I ask why you were on the plane? I mean, you said you're a student. But you had on a stewardess outfit, and... oh." Safia nodded her head in understanding. "It was because of the points."

"Exactly, that's what they wanted. When I woke up, they already had the outfit for me. And they wanted me to speak all proper for you. I hate talking like that," said Addison, making a disgusted look on her face. "Reminds me of my shitty ass father." She buttoned up one of her buttons. "So, why'd they pick you up? Your folks send you here too?"

"Ah, no. I was told I was something called a Trojan."

"Ah, that's cool. We had a few of them last year. That bitch Amanda even picked one up. You better watch out, or you'll wind up discarded or expelled like a couple of those fools did at the lunch line."

"I saw that. One of the boys looked like he was having a seizure."

"What, seriously? Ha, the poor fucker must have put his hands on somebody. Dumbass, should have known, you put your hands on someone here, and they report it. Wham," she slapped her hands together. "Instant expulsion."

"Really?"

"Oh yeah, I've seen some dumbasses get expelled like that before. But that's only if they report it. Sometimes, they turn it around on 'em and threaten to expel them if they don't give 'em something." Suddenly, a buzzing sound was heard, and Addison reached into her pocket and pulled out a tablet, taking a look at the screen. "Fuck, my boyfriend is calling. I forgot to meet up with him."

"Oh, okay, then. I guess you have to go."

"Yeah, he gets all pissy when I'm late," said Addison, placing the tablet back in her skirt pocket. "Alright, catch you later, Trojan girl, and you too stuck-up Muslim chick. How about you learn some manners next time I see you?"

"Oh, piss off," said Hashmi with annoyance in her voice as they both watched Addison run away with a smile on her face.

"Wow, she really got to you. I thought you said you were used to that."

"I am. But that one; such an insufferable woman. I hope to never see her again."

"Come on, then. Let's go get you cooled down. We still have to get to class," said Safia with a smirk as she rubbed Hashmi's shoulders and pushed her off down the winding path.

They soon entered class, where a man was sitting behind the desk.

"Alright, come in, all of you, so that we can get started," said the man as the students all made their way in.

Safia walked over and sat beside a window. Looking around the room, she noticed that Jericho was also in this class, although he already had his head down and eyes closed. *I guess I shouldn't be surprised,* thought Safia as she smiled, noticing that he was also in the same position as the last time, at the back of the class. She then reached down for her bag, and her finger nudged the pendant that he had tied there for her. *I guess you can just sleep through all your classes. No one ever said you needed to do well on tests. You just need to have a certain number of points at the end of the first and second years. I wonder how many points he has.*

"Okay, class, welcome to World Finance," said the older

man in a brown blazer with large, rimmed glasses.

So that's what WF one-o-one stood for.

"I am your teacher for this class, Mr. Highlander, please take your seats," said the man as he fiddled with a few pieces of paper, his unkempt swaying over his face.

Mr. Highlander? Safia took another look at the man, and her eyes went wide in shock? *That's the guy who I see on television talking about money. Isn't he supposed to be some big-time money broker?*

"Okay, now that we're all seated," said Mr. Highlander. "Who here can tell me the most financially viable countries in the world?" He looked around the class as no hands were raised. "Anyone?"

"The US, Russia, and Canada?" asked a girl ahead of Safia.

"That's a good guess, but no," said Mr. Highlander, looking over the room. "Those would be the top three if we were talking about their military. But we're talking about finance. And that mostly depends on a country's resources." He then raised his hand, extending a finger into the air. "Resources are what drives a nation these days, not the military. What they have to trade is far greater than any weapon."

So, we're going to learn how to trade goods now?

"Whereas a weapon can kill; if you kill trade to a country that depends on you, then you can cripple and exploit that country. It's the reason China is such an economic world power, or the reason the US has gone to war so much in oil-rich countries." He made a fist, bobbing it up and down. "That's where real control lies. If you go into a country with war, then you can expect rebellions and upheaval. All terrible things to have to deal with. However, if you can cripple a country and then go in as its saviors, then you can control them. Not through war, but through influence. And influential control is a more gradual but also a more stable form of control."

"Why's that? Don't most small countries just go to war, anyway?" asked one of the boys next to Jericho, who still looked dead to the world.

"A good question. And yes, that's true. But those are small countries. Places like that have little influence on the world as most other countries see them as having little value. This is why most first world countries just allow their wars. Because, to them, it would cost more resources to try and fix those areas than it'd be worth. So, we happily sit back and treat their atrocities as if they are invisible."

"So, we should only help those that provide us with some type of resource?"

"You all are already doing that. You just haven't realized it yet," said the man as he began to pace in front of his desk with his hands behind his back. "This whole world is built up on its resources, whether intangible or not." He raised a finger. "Your parents, for example, raised you, provided you with clothing, food, a roof over your head. They gave you their resources, and you, in turn, will carry their genetics or their ideals into the future."

"But they're our parents. They love us. That's what they're supposed to do," said a girl at the front of the class.

"Really? How old are you, Miss?"

"Eighteen. Why?"

"And have you ever had a boyfriend before?"

"Yes. What does that have to do with anything?"

"Well, I'm sure your boyfriend bought you nice things, took you to nice places. Am I right?"

"You mean dates. Of course he did. We were a couple."

"Well, let me ask you, even though he loved you, do you think he'd still do that if you were also dating or flirting with every other boy in your school?"

"Probably not, but—"

"Exactly. Love is not unconditional. That man was willing to spend his resources on you as long as he received love from you. Love is also a valuable resource. And whom you choose to share it with can affect your entire life." The old man chuckled. "Some of you might become third world countries of love, where no one cares about you or is willing to give you anything. And that is because the rest of the world will assume that you have nothing to offer them."

"Well, that's a messed-up way to think about dating," said another girl in class.

"Really? If you think about it, that's all this school is. I came to this school forty years ago, and every year that I come back to teach, one thing remains the same. Nothing is ever truly free. Each and everything here you will pay for, one way or another."

"Forty years? Why do you even come back? Aren't you rich?"

"Depends on what you think rich is," laughed the old man. "A couple dozen million is enough for me. I mean, most entertainers and football players have more money than I do. Granted, statistically speaking, ninety percent of them will be broke less than five years out of their career. But rich in resources and rich in stupidity are not two things that mix well when one wants to consider financial success."

A little over half the class chuckled at the joke.

"But as to answer your question as to why I come back here each year. Well, think of it as a bit of philanthropy in my old age. I come here and try to impart a bit of my wisdom upon the younger generations, and I get to watch and see if anything that I am teaching takes root." He leaned back, taking a seat on his desk. "Being a teacher is a lot like being a gardener. You try your best to plant these ideals in people's heads. Sometimes, it works, sometimes it doesn't. But it's always interesting to watch the garden grow and see which seeds will take root."

"Well, that's better than my last teacher, who tried beating the lessons into us with test after test until you wanted to die. Our graduation turned into a celebration just to be rid of him."

"I have a question," said another girl.

"Yes?"

"You mentioned before about small countries not having resources. Well, what about smaller countries that do? How do we control them?"

"Ahhh, yes," said Mr. Highlander, lifting himself back off the desk and onto his feet. "And there, we have a seed taking root. Influence, my child. Influence is how it's done. We provide the countries with things they need and threaten to take it away if they don't acquiesce to our demands."

"So, we just bully them then?" asked a familiar voice.

Safia turned around to see Jericho with his face up. *Now is when he wakes up? To ask questions about this weird topic?*

"It's not necessarily bullying, but it is a form of global manipulation."

"And what if the country doesn't adhere to your demands?"

"Well, that simply means that you failed in establishing a total dependence on your resources. The goal is to make them totally dependent on you to the point where refusing you would result in their total destruction. Therefore, it's still their decision to make. But in reality, they had no choice at all. It's all a form of global manipulation, you see."

"So, it comes down to resource management in the end."

"Yes, but it's a lot harder than it would seem to make them totally dependent on you. That's where the true power of finance lies. Because when you boil it down, the purpose of money is for trade. And the need for trade is to try and acquire the things you either need or desire. And desire is the heart of finance."

The class continued as more and more students rattled off questions to Mr. Highlander. But the conversation between Jericho and the professor was the highlight of the class as they argued back and forth on the proper way to handle the world's economy until the bell sounded, signaling the end of the class.

"Okay, now class. I want you to write a five-page paper on how you feel finance has influenced the world. Based on your own personal analysis."

Safia stood to leave and saw a group of people over by Jericho's desk. He was now smiling with a few girls and guys who were around him.

Well, I guess arguing with the teacher for an hour is how you make friends. But I guess it proves that he wasn't lying earlier. He really wasn't asleep, thought Safia as she headed toward the door. As she approached Mr. Highlander, she stopped to speak with him.

"Excuse me," said Safia.

"Yes."

"I'm just surprised to see you teaching here. My brother and I saw you on TV about a month ago."

"Oh, that's not such a mystery, my dear. Most of the faculty here are Alumni of this school in some form or fashion. As I said during class, this place is like a garden for me, and a man needs to have a purpose. After raising my children, this old man just wishes to try and be of use a little while longer before he goes off into the sunset."

"You're not that old. You were pacing around that desk pretty fast."

"Ha. That's good to hear you think so. But perhaps you're right. I can probably squeeze another decade or two out of these old bones of mine. What about you, my dear? Are you enjoying your time here?"

"Yes, Sir... I mean, I think I am. I honestly don't know yet."

"That's fine to feel that way. When I attended, I felt much the same. Tell me, what's your name."

"My name's Safia and this is Hashmi."

"Hello, Sir," said Hashmi.

"It's nice to see two young ladies taking an interest in this class. There are many life lessons to be learned in finance, ladies. Lessons that will prove invaluable in life. So please ask as many questions as you like and say hello if you see me on the campus from time to time. I'm always in need of a bit of company," said Mr. Highlander as he headed out of the class.

"Yes, Sir," said both girls.

"Hey, what's your name?" asked a boy behind Safia as she watched Mr. Highlander leave. She then turned around to see a boy with blonde hair and a smile on his face.

"Safia."

"Well, Miss Safia, you wanna make a bet on who gets the highest grade on the report we gotta do?"

"Huh?" asked Safia, not understanding why she would do such a thing.

"Ahh, don't worry, it's just a friendly bet between class-mates," said the boy as he turned around, waving his hand back at the rest of the group that was surrounding Jericho's desk. She looked back at Jericho as he waved back at her. "We're getting everyone to bet one hundred points each. So far, the pot is up to twelve hundred points."

"One hundred?" asked Safia, thinking of her points. "I'm sorry, I don't have enough points left. I need to save them."

"Ahh, that's a shame. Oh well, suit yourself," said the boy as he ran back over to the group.

Safia watched as Jericho laughed with them as they made their betting plans and smiled. *I thought you weren't the betting type, but I guess that everyone here has their own plans.* Safia shook her head in disappointment and left the classroom.

"Oh, I forgot my book. I'll meet you outside," said Hashmi as she turned back, heading to her desk.

Safia walked out of class. In the hallway, she pulled out her tablet device and began flicking through the screen icons. *I wonder how many points I have. I shouldn't have spent too much since I bought the food pass for the month.* She continued to flick through the buttons. *Now which one was the one that showed you your points?*

As she continued to flick her finger through the icon, she heard her name being called throughout the hallway. She turned, thinking it was Hashmi finally leaving class, but instead, she saw another girl who had startling pink hair holding the same type of glass tablet as her.

"Ah, are you, Miss Safia..." She looked down at her tablet. "Famosa?" asked the pink-haired girl, walking up to her, looking a bit out of breath.

"Yes, that's me. Is something wrong?"

"You're wanted in the transport room. Apparently it's urgent."

"What, me?" asked Safia as she began to get nervous. "Is something wrong? What's the transport room?"

"Oh, yeah, sorry... that's the communication building, the one with the phones. They sent me to find you. They said that it was important. Will you please follow me?"

"Okay," said Safia, looking down the hallway. "But my friend Hashmi is waiting for me."

"Well, as long as you know where the building is, I can go and inform Miss Hashmi to meet you there."

"Thank you, I'll go there now then," said Safia as she quickened her steps and headed out of the school towards the building with the phones. It didn't take long for her to reach it. She knocked on the door, but no one answered. Looking around, she noticed the plants that Jericho had placed into the ground and remembered how to get their attention.

Safia then lifted her bag, grabbing for her pendant, clicking it. "I, Safia Famosa, require access to the ah... communication room." She then held up her bag towards the black orb against the wall so they could see the pendant.

"Someone will be out to see you soon," spoke a voice from the pendant.

She paced back and forth. *Is everything okay? I mean, I don't think I've done anything wrong.* Soon, the door opened,
184

and out walked the man in the suit from when she first arrived.

"Thank you for coming, Miss Safia. Please come inside," said Derrick, as he led her in and down the corridor.

"What's happened? Did I do something wrong?"

"Oh no. You've done nothing wrong," said Derrick, as they entered the rooms with the phones. "I'm afraid I have some bad news."

"What... what is it?" asked Safia, her heart starting to feel tight in her chest.

"Your father, I'm afraid he's been shot."

"What? How? I mean..." Safia fumbled her words as her shoulders began to tremble and her knees started to feel weak.

"We don't know much ourselves yet. We just found out because we try to keep track of the happenings of our students' lives outside the school. And when we got the police report with your father's name, we immediately decided to call you. We have opened up phone line number four for you. Please, call your parents and talk as long as you need to. I shall leave you alone for this call out of respect, but please remember not to speak of any details of this school."

Safia stumbled her way over to the phone in booth number four, taking a seat. Her hand shakily reached out for the phone, pulling it off the hook and placing it against her ear. The sounds of her own breathing aiding in her anxiety as she swallowed, trying to control herself. Slowly, her fingers entered the loop and pulled down the number. The clicking sound made her feel as if it were a countdown to the worst news she could hear about her father. After a final click, there was a bit of silence, only to then be followed by a ring. *Please be okay.* Another ring. *Oh God, please, Papa, please.* Another ring and then a click that was followed by the sounds of her mother's whimpering voice coming back through the phone.

"He... hello..."

"Ma... it's me Safia, is everything okay?"

"Oh, Safia baby. It's your father. He's in the hospital. He's in the hospital," said her mother, her voice trembling through the phone. "Someone came into the restaurant with a gun wanting the money, and you know how your father is. He jumped at the man grabbing the gun, and they started fighting and your father, he... he... oh Safia, it's bad. They got him hooked up to this machine with lots of tubes. He hasn't woken up at all."

"It's okay, Ma... don't worry. Pa... Pa's strong, he's gonna be okay," said Safia, realizing that even with tears in her eyes, she would be the one to have to comfort her mother. "Where's Yago, Ma? Is he there with you?"

"No... He's downstairs talking to the police about what happened. They've been asking us all kinds of questions, and we don't... Oh, your brother, he's back." Safia heard a clicking noise along with muffling on the other end of the phones.

"Hello? Saffy, is that you?" asked Yago's voice through the phone.

"Hey, Yago, is Pa okay?"

"Yeah, he's gonna be okay, don't worry. Hey ma, you go and sit with Pa for a while. I'll talk to Saffy and tell her what happened," said Yago, and then the phone went silent as Safia heard the sound of a door closing.

"Saffy, you there?"

"Yeah, I'm here. What's going on, Yago? Is Pa really going to be okay?"

"We... we don't know. Pa... he got shot in the chest, and the bullet is stuck in between some hard-to-reach place or something like that."

"What... where is it? They get it out?"

"I don't understand it all yet, but I will. I just need more time to talk to the doctors. I'm not going to lie to you Safia, Pa might not make it. They got him on this breathing machine, and he's been like this all day. We've been here for like sixteen hours. They took him to emergency surgery, but they don't know what to do yet. They're talking about letting the bullet stay in and all kinds of crazy stuff!"

To Safia, the world started spinning, as she couldn't envision a world without her father being in it.

"The only reason pops made it was because Mr. Delanie was in the diner for breakfast. He had his ambulance parked outside when it all happened and they..."

Yago's voice trailed off as Safia's mind went dazed off inside of it itself. *This can't be happening. This isn't real. It must be some type of dream...*

"Saffy... Saffy," said Yago into the phone over and over, until finally, snapping her out of her haze.

"I'm sorry... I... I just... I'm coming home, Yago," she responded, shaking her head, feeling the water at the edge of her eyes. "I'll get them to send me home, okay."

"Okay... I'll tell Mom you're coming back. I gotta go now... the police... they still got questions for me. So... I'll see you soon, Saffy."

"Okay, Yago... I.... I'll be home soon," said Safia as she listened to the phone click. Even after the call ended, she held the receiver close to her ear, with tears flowing from her eyes. Even as the dial tone filled her ears, she sat there in the booth, just listening to the nothingness.

It took a while, but eventually, she composed herself enough to stand back up from her seat and walked towards the exit. Opening the door, she saw Derrick sitting down in a chair against the wall, waiting.

"Is everything okay?" he asked, standing when he saw her.

"No, I want to go home."

"Are you sure? Once you leave, you will not be allowed to return."

Safia nodded, "I... I'm sure. I have to go home."

"Okay, then. We will call for one of our jets to come and

get you. It may take about twelve hours to route one here. But give us a few hours to get everything sorted, and we will call you and have you sedated and sent back home."

"Thank you," said Safia as she was led out of the building.

"Go and get some rest, Ms. Famosa. We will call you as soon as we have secured your way back home."

Safia nodded and turned, walking away. Everything seemed so foreign to her now. As the doors closed, she just stared at the trees that Jericho had planted beside the building. The leaves on them were greener than before, all except for one. Half the tree had its leaves turned brown. Safia stared at it. *They'll probably just get another one to replace it.*

She blinked away the last traces of her tears and started walking towards Yennefer house. Throughout the campus, she could see people laughing and joking while playing their little games. They were tapping on their pendants and making bets. Whereas before it was something she found too risky, now it all just seemed like a waste of time to her. *Is any of this even important?*

Eventually, she made her way to her dorm's steps and walked inside to see people were downstairs making more bets in the dorm's common area. Ahead of her, she saw some boys standing around a new machine that was there. It was an old arcade machine, and the boys were waiting for their turn at it.

"Welcome back, Safia," said Austin, who was standing by the door looking at his book. "Hashmi came back looking for you."

"Huh? Oh. Right, I need to go see her," said Safia as if in a daze. "Where did that machine come from? The arcade game the boys are playing around."

"Oh, they just brought that in today. Greggory bought it with his points from racing the other day. He's now charging the people five points to play it. It's actually kinda smart. Now that bastard can sit around and make points without ever having to bet. He said he's trying to put one up in each of the dorms when he gets enough points."

Safia just stood watching the boys play the game, and the memories from days before started to play into her mind. That day in the auditorium, her time with Harmony, her conversations with Jericho all came rushing back into her mind. And then, in a snap, she blinked as her reality came back to her. She began looking around the dorm as if lost.

"Safia, are you okay?"

"Huh?" asked Safia, turning around, "I ah… I need to go." She then turned and ran out of the door and down the stairs. Running through the campus in the midday sun, her eyes frantically looking around in search of something, she soon made her way back to the school and hopped off the concrete walkway, sprinting across the grass over to the tree that was outside of her first class's window. Making it to the tree, she began to look around more, but didn't see anything. Panic and frustration pierced her mind as she rested her hand on its bark and started looking around the campus grounds. Nothing and no one was there, just the words *I Win,* that were still etched into the tree.

Where… Where is she? If I can find her then, maybe… Safia's eyes opened wide as thoughts of being with Harmony on her first day entered her mind. *Find her, I just need to find her.* She then dropped her bag on the ground and knelt beside it, reaching out and grabbing her pendant in both hands, tapping the crest in the center, and hearing it click. "This is Safia Famosa. I would like the location of Champ Champ, the school's headmistress. I would like to speak with her."

Safia breathed heavily as sweat slid across her fingers onto the pendant as she waited. She sat there in silence for a long moment until the pendant finally spoke.

"Permission granted. Directions will be sent to your Apex device."

She then opened her bag and began fumbling through it

until she found the small glass tablet. Placing her finger on the button, the screen lit up, and across the top was a short message that said, Champ Champ. She tapped on the name and, instantly, a three-dimensional map of the school, along with two dots, appeared on the screen. One was blue, and the other was red. The map was very detailed and even had an image of the tree she was under next to a blue dot that represented her location.

Okay, so that one's me, then where is...

The red dot was nearby, and it showed that it was in the school. She moved the map with her finger, trying to get a better view of it, and noticed that the red dot wasn't in the school. It was above the school. Safia peeked out from under the tree, looking up at the walls of the building. It seemed even more intimidating now, with its sharp spikes that arched over its top like some type of castle from a horror movie she'd watch late at night.

Fine, I just need to go up there.

She got up and headed towards the school. As she began to move, the device showed her a trail to follow in the form of a set of yellow dots. Following them, she found herself inside the school, walking down its long hallway.

It was empty now, since classes had ended for the day. The solitude gave off an eerie feeling to hear her footsteps sounding off the walls and echoing back at her. But she continued to step forward until she reached another wooden door. While placing her hand on it, she could instantly tell it wasn't wooden at all. The cold chill of metal pierced her fingers the moment she touched the supposedly wooden surface.

Looking around, she didn't notice a way to open the door. There was no doorknob, no latch, no handle, or even a nearby card reader. The dots on her device clearly showed that she needed to go forward, except that there was no way forward. She continued to feel the crevices of the door, desperately trying to find how to get through it.

She pushed, but it wouldn't move. She knocked, but got no answer. Only after a long moment of despair did she hear a clicking sound and felt the door give.

She stepped back after hearing the loud click, anxious about what might be behind the door. Slowly, she stepped forward and placed her hands back on the cold door. Pushing it forward, she was hit in the face with a large gust of air that ruffled her clothes and lifted her hair. She raised her hand to shield her eyes, turning away from the gust of air until it finally subsided. Through the open door, she could hear the constant bussing of machinery. Gone were the quiet halls of the school, replaced by what lay behind the facade. Stepping inside, she let go of the door only to have it seal shut behind her, and a cold chill quickly took control of the room as the vent above her began to shoot out chilled air. Conduits for cable work littered the concrete walls here. Instead of marble floors, she saw metal grates and a hand railing for steps that led up above her.

There was another door next to the stairwell with a large yellow sticker in the front, labeled 'Security Tapes.' This door also didn't have a latch or a handle. Safia slowly walked forward and peered upward into the stairwell. It seemed to go on forever. But with determination, she took a deep breath and placed a foot on the bottom step, making her way upward.

Each step she took seemed to mimic the beat of her own heart as it thumped inside her chest. The eerie humming of the machinery below her filled the stairwell and provided just enough white noise to drown out her thoughts, but not enough to wash away the dreading fear that slowly crept into her mind the higher up the circular steps she climbed. The cold of the climate-controlled area nipping at her ankles beneath her skirt as she continued to make her way upward until, finally, she reached another door. This one did have a handle, an old-fashioned golden plated circular door knob on another wooden door. She reached out, touching the knob of the door and found that it was, in fact, a wooden door, not just a painted facsimile.

Once again, taking a deep breath, she twisted the golden knob and felt the door give way, opening her way back into the world outside. The air inside ruffling her skirt and hair once again as it escaped out into the warm climate. Stepping forward and allowing the door to close behind her, she found herself looking over the entire campus, with the top of each building off in the near distance. Behind them were three mountains that she'd never really noticed before now, but what must have surely been there all along.

Ahead of her, on the roof of the building, sat a small girl in a yellow dress along with a yellow sun hat. She was on her knees, and as Safia walked forward, she could see that there was someone in front of her, with their head in her lap.

"Hello, Miss Safia. I do hope that it was important for you to come up here and interrupt our alone time."

"You… you don't know why I'm here?"

"No, but it is certainly a rare thing for me to receive a message saying that one of my precious students was looking for me personally. And to be so forceful as to use her pendant to call upon me. There must be something of importance you wish to discuss. So, don't be shy. Come over here and tell me what you desire."

"Then, how do you know I want something?"

Champ Champ laughed. "My dear, look where we are. Or should I say look at where you are? I'd say that it's fairly obvious you want something, and it must be something big to compel you to travel all the way up here. So come on, don't be shy."

Safia did as she was bid and stepped closer. Ahead, she could see that the person with their head in her lap was a man, and after walking up beside them, she remembered him. Or was it easier to say that it was hard to forget him? To ignore those two large scars on the side of his face that

Champ Champ was then so gently rubbing with her thumb as she rested her hand on the side of his face.

"Oh, don't worry about him," said Champ Champ as she smiled down at her husband. "I had him take a few pills to sleep. He's been working so hard lately, and I just couldn't let him go on without some decent rest." She turned her head to look at Safia. "Now, come on, tell me what you want."

"My father... he's... he's in the hospital."

"Oh, dear, I'm sorry to hear that. Are you trying to go back home? If so, we will be happy to send you back. Family is, of course, very important."

"They said my father has a bullet inside that they can't get out. Does this school know people who can get it out?"

There was a moment of silence between them as a gust of wind came by that lifted Champ Champ's hat off of her head and sent it soaring into the air and over the side of the school.

"Miss Famosa, I admire your need to help your family. But do you realize what you're asking? Nothing in this school is free."

"Then what?" asked Safia, getting frustrated. "What do you want me to do, bet? I'll bet whatever you want if it will keep my Papa alive."

"You? Bet Me?" asked Champ Champ with a laugh. "Hardly, you couldn't begin to imagine the games I play. No, if you're serious about this, then how about we propose a trade."

"Okay, what do you want? I'll give you whatever you want."

"Goodness, you act like that and expect to survive here," said Champ Champ with a sigh. "And you even tried to bet me." She shook her head. "No, Miss Famosa, I'd prefer not taking advantage of your desperation here. Instead, you will be given a fair trade like everyone else." Champ Champ closed her eyes, thinking for a moment. "Okay, this is the trade I offer. I will look into your father and offer the best services I can."

But I know there has to be a cost. The school seems to be all about that.

"And If we can save him, then you are to relinquish to me one thousand points a month for your first six months. Then for every six months after that, the points will be subsequently doubled until you graduate or you become the property of this school. This will have an exception for two months out of the year due to the enrollment process. So that equates to eight thousand points this semester since a month is about to pass."

"And if I can't afford to pay, will you just let my father die?"

"Oh, goodness no. I believe that we had a discussion on how Miss Abigail spilled the beans as to her current relationship with this school. No? I imagine you'll serve out a decade here doing much the same. Only if you do not honor your end of the bargain, will we be forced to take drastic measures. But if you fail to pay your debt, then the next ten years of your life will belong to the school. It will control where you go to work, live, and even appoint you with a spouse of its choosing if need suits it. But if we can't—"

"I accept."

"Wait, let me finish," said Champ Champ, raising her hand. "But if our efforts to save your father prove unsuccessful, then the trade is null and void, and you will not be required to fulfill your obligation, and any points you have given towards this debt will instantly be refunded. Do these terms sound acceptable to you?"

"Do I really have a choice?" asked Safia with her head down and her hands in front of her, rubbing at her wrists.

"We always have a choice, Miss Famosa. But it's in being able to make the hard choice that's where you will find out the type of person you are. And you seem like a person who loves her family very much. I'm sure there are many amongst the current crop here who would have just let their father die, rather than take up the trade you've just made."

"Then, why not just help me? Why do we have to do this?"

Champ Champ stroked the side of her husband's face, letting her finger trail over his scars, "You see the scars on my husband's face?"

Safia glanced down at the man.

"I did this to him. I put a blade to his face and cut at his flesh."

"Why?" asked Safia as her face contorted at the thought of the pain it would have taken to make those scars.

"Oh, there were a few reasons, but none of them are important now," said Champ Champ, placing a finger to her lips in a thinking fashion. "Now, as to your question as to why do all this. Well, the answer is simple; that's because everything has a cost. I think I mentioned earlier that this man here, and I played a game, and the outcome for me was that I would become his wife. Well, to that same fact, the outcome for him was this face that he wears everywhere he goes. That was his price to pay."

Champ Champ then turned her face up with what seemed to be tears in her eyes. "And if I were just to give you the gift that this man was willing to risk his life for. Then as a good wife, I wouldn't be honoring him at all, now would I?" She blinked, shaking her head as a single tear fell down to her cheek. "No, Miss Famosa. If you wish to save your father's life, then I'm going to expect you to risk the life you had planned to do so."

Safia stared down at the small woman before dropping her head, closing her eyes, and clenching her teeth. Another slight breeze came by that nipped at her arms, making her grab at her shoulder as her hair blew over her face.

"Okay, so what do I do now?"

Champ Champ took a deep breath and gazed over the horizon. "You simply go back to your dorm, lay down in your bed, and try to get some rest. And starting tomorrow, you join us in our madness here. And if you believe in God, then I suggest that you pray, and you pray hard that by the end of next month, you have those thousand points."

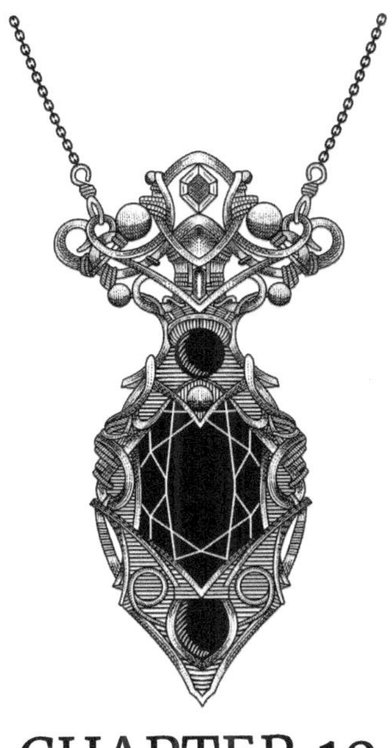

CHAPTER 10

The morning came, and a light shone into the dorm window where Safia lay in bed with her eyes open. In her hand was her tablet, where she looked at a number on the screen. One thousand and four. Her eyes were heavy, and her mind was tired. Throughout the night, she just replayed the previous day's events in her mind.

Two days... two days ago, everything was fine. Then everything changed. She rolled over on her side, looking into Hashmi's sleeping face. *She mumbles in her sleep, apparently.* Safia wasn't sure if those were prayers or just the rambling of her subconscious mind.

Soon, their alarm rang, signaling the start of another day of class. Hashmi awoke to see Safia in bed with a tablet in her hand.

"Oh, you've made it back. I was worried you'd run away since I didn't see you yesterday. What time did you get in?"

"Sorry about that. You were asleep when I got back, and I didn't want to wake you. I probably got in a little after midnight. I just needed some time to think is all, so I went for a walk."

"Why? Is everything okay? You've seemed distant this last day or two."

Safia turned back, looking into Hashmi's worried face. *Why not? What harm could it do to tell her?* "It's my father. He's... he's been shot."

"What? Really? How?" asked Hashmi, fumbling her words. "Oh, I'm so sorry. Is he okay?"

"I don't know. I mean, I hope so. But I'm not sure anymore."

"Will you be going back to see him?"

"I can't? I have to..."

"What do you mean you can't?" asked Hashmi, looking shocked as she sat up in her bed.

"It's not... It's not that simple."

"Safia, your father was shot. You should be there," said Hashmi, with a noticeable amount of judgment creeping into her voice.

"I can't. Okay," said Safia, anger seeping into her own voice, "Why are you getting angry? He's my father."

"Because you're the one who said your father was a good man. If it were my father, I would be on a plane out of here at this moment. And you're just lying there looking at your tablet like you don't even care."

"How can you say that? Of course, I care," shouted Safia back at Hashmi before she started to see water form up in Hashmi's eyes from beneath her hair. Safia felt a tiny bit of guilt come over her, looking at Hashmi and calming her voice. "Hashmi, look, I don't want to fight. Not over this, it's hard enough as it is. Can I... Can I just ask you to trust me when I say I can't go home? There's a reason why I must stay here."

Looking back at the seriously solemn Safia, Hashmi also quieted her voice and took a deep breath, wiping at her eyes. "I'm sorry too. I... I shouldn't have started yelling. I just started thinking about my own father, and I lost my temper. I apologize."

"So, we're okay now?"

"Yes, we're okay, but promise me you're not just acting selfishly by not going back."

"No, I promise I'm not acting selfishly."

Hashmi stood up and walked over to her closet. "Fine. Then, you can join me this morning."

"Join you? What do you mean? Join you in what?"

Hashmi pulled out two rolled-up prayer rugs from her closet. "We are going to pray."

"What? But I'm not even religious, and I'm Christian."

"Then pray to whomever you like, and I will pray to Allah," said Hashmi as she walked back over, spreading the prayer mats on the floor beside each other. "You asked that I trust you; that there is a reason for you to stay here. Then, in return, I ask that you pray with me."

Safia stared down at Hashmi, who was on her knees on the floor, on her mat, looking up at her. "Okay, I guess it couldn't hurt." She said as she strolled out of bed in her pajamas and knelt down beside Hashmi on the prayer mat. "Okay, so how am I supposed to do this? Is there like a chant or something I should say during prayer?"

Hashmi stood up to her feet, laughing. "Well, we should wash our hands first, and I should be in Hijab. But I think Allah will forgive us for being a little off in our prayers this time." She then reached out her hands towards Safia. "First, we stand."

Safia took Hashmi's hand allowing herself to be pulled

up.

"We stand this way, facing Qibla."

"The Qi-what?"

"The cute little building there on the mat. The arrow above it there points us towards the Kaaba," said Hashmi, pointing towards the top of the mat.

"Okay," said Safia, placing her feet away and standing beside Hashmi, trying to keep an open mind.

"And just follow my hand movements," said Hashmi as she placed her hands up towards the side of her face with her palms out forward.

Safia mimicked her motions by placing her hand down by her belly button, but frowned when Hashmi began speaking in a language that she didn't understand.

"Ah, I don't think I can say that?"

"It's okay," said Hashmi with a giggle. "I'm saying it for both of us," and she repeated the words with a smirk at the edge of her lips.

Safia watched and followed along to the best of her ability, repeating the process. She bowed, then dropped to her knees, placing her head against the prayer mat.

Whoever may be listening, please protect my Papa. He's a good man who only tries to look after his family. He works hard and tries his best for us... and.... and... Safia's fists clenched against the fabric of the prayer mat as she placed her forehead against it. Her teeth clenched. She began to breathe deeply, trying to control the flood of emotions that were finally breaking in. Harder, she gripped the mat as tears glimmered on the edge of her eyes.

But then she felt Hashmi's arms over her shoulder and across her back, pulling her into her arms. Hashmi slowly eased Safia's face into her lap, trying to comfort her, and with that physical contact, Safia's resolve finally broke. There, on the floor, her head across Hashmi's legs, she began to cry. All the frustration, confusion, and pain that had boiled up since her arrival at the school finally being laid bare on two crumpled-up prayer mats and in the arms of a woman from half a world away.

Safia stayed there, her face buried in Hashmi's lap until she felt comfortable with rising back up to her knees, where she knelt in front of Hashmi, too embarrassed to look her in her eyes.

"Do you feel better now?" asked Hashmi.

"I... I do," said Safia, still keeping her head down until Hashmi reached forward, gently placing her fingers underneath her chin and allowing her thumbs to graze across her cheeks. Safia took a breath and embraced the compassion she was being shown as the last few tears left her eyes, dropping down the side of her face, only to be rubbed away by Hashmi's fingers.

"It's okay now. Allah has heard you, just as I am sure your God has as well," said Hashmi as she leaned forward, pulling her face closer and placing her lips at the crown of Safia's head.

Safia breathed deep. The sweet scent of rose oil drifted past her nose as Hashmi's hair hung over her face, grazing against her skin. She felt the pressing of Hashmi's lips atop her forehead, and it began to seem as if a heavy weight had been lifted from her shoulders. She then reached forward, grabbing Hashmi's hand as they both stood up.

"I'm sorry, I've cried on your pajamas."

"That's fine. They needed to be washed anyway," said Hashmi with a smile. "Come on, let's get ready and go get us some breakfast. We've gotta put these points to good use."

Safia gave a chuckle and nodded her head as the girls separated from each other and began to get ready for their morning.

An hour later, they were dressed in their matching brown and purple accented attire and headed out towards the campus cafeteria. On the way, Safia saw over in the distance, a boy sitting down on a bench with a sketchbook in his hand. Stopping, she stepped forward, staring at him before she realized who it was.

"Safia, what's wrong?" asked Hashmi, as the boy noticed them and waved with a smile on his face. "Do you know him?"

"I do," answered Safia, walking towards him with Hashmi beside her. "Hello Jericho, I'm surprised you're not sleeping. You do it in class so much."

"And here I thought a woman would appreciate a man getting his beauty sleep. Besides, I've said before how I don't need to have my eyes open to listen."

"And what are you doing out here, looking for a new place to rest your eyes?"

Jericho turned his book around and showed the girls a sketch of the campus he had been drawing. "It's not much, but it's a fun way to waste time."

"I didn't realize you had a talent for art," said Safia, leaning down to look at the sketch. "Wow, it's actually good."

"Hey, that hurts. You make it sound as if you didn't expect me to have any talent," said Jericho, wagging his finger at Safia as he balled up his lips.

"I didn't," said Safia honestly, laughing despite herself. "But it does make me wonder what other secret talents you're hiding."

"Oh, I have more secrets than you can imagine. Maybe, one day, you'll get to see some of them."

"Hashmi, this is Jericho. He is someone I met out planting some trees into the ground a while ago," said Safia as she gestured to her friend. "And Jericho, this is Hashmi. She is my friend."

"Hello, Miss Hashmi. I've seen you in class, but it's nice to formally be introduced. And I'm glad that Safia has a friend. The last time I saw her, she didn't look so well. But she seems to be in high spirits now."

"Yes, she was that way a little while ago, also. But she's better now. Tell me, are you trying to become her boyfriend? From how she reacts around you, I don't think she'd be amiss to the idea.

"Hashmi, stop that."

Hashmi giggled after her teasing of Safia.

"Me? I'm not sure I could handle her. She seems like quite the handful."

"I agree, but I think she'll be worth it."

"Okay, enough of you both teasing me," said Safia, waving her hands around at the two. "What are you working on now, anyway? Looking for more places to plant your trees."

"Not this time, but I will probably have to replace one of them that I planted before. I'm always looking for new ways to make the campus look better."

"What about down there?" asked Safia as she pointed downhill towards the lake behind Jericho. That shed looks pretty beat up. Why not just fix that? I'm sure it'll be with some points.

"Probably not that one. I've actually been looking for places to build a gazebo."

"A what?"

"A gazebo, it's a place outside where people can sit down, relax, and get all lovey-dovey with each other," Jericho said, while giving Safia an obvious stare and smile.

"Why are you looking at me like that?" asked Safia with an equally obvious smile on her face.

"Well then," said Hashmi, looking between the two. "Don't I just feel like I'm imposing. Do you two plan to share a kiss under your gazebo?"

"That sounds like a fun idea," said Jericho. "You know when they build ships they christen them with bottles of wine. Who's to say a kiss underneath a gazebo wouldn't be in order."

"Stop looking at me like that," said Safia, still smiling,

"You won't be getting any kisses from me underneath your little play-house."

"Does that mean, I will in some other places?"

"Smart ass."

"I am that. But who knows what the future holds?"

Safia looked around, trying to change the subject and saw many other students just sitting on benches or on the grass. "There seems to be lots of people who've already found a place to sit."

"True, but look over there by the school."

Safia and Hashmi turned to gaze over the distance at the large school structure with its arched peaks and concrete walls.

"I don't see anything odd about the school," said Hashmi, turning back to face Jericho with a look of confusion on her face.

"Exactly. There's nothing there. Just that big ugly concrete monstrosity that they call a school. Look at all that clear green grass that surrounds it. They don't even have trees there. It's like they're trying to force you to only see the ugliness of this school."

Hashmi chuckled, "Your friend has an interesting way of viewing things, Safia."

"Oh, are you my friend?" asked Jericho with a raised brow. "I didn't realize that. When did that happen? Should we do something to celebrate?"

"Well, seeing as you said you are here to make friends with the rich and the powerful, I doubt that we will ever be friends, since I am neither."

"Oh, well," said Jericho as he closed his sketchbook and leaned forward on top of it. "Acquaintances it is then." He then pointed over to the school. "I plan to build a gazebo over there for the students to sit during their breaks between classes. That'll be a good way for me to earn a fair number of points."

"Oh, that reminds me of why I came over here. You said

before that you would get points for planting those trees. Can I ask how many points you got?"

Jericho raised a brow at the question.

"Safia," said Hashmi, "It's frowned upon to ask another about their points here. Information like that could be used against you, if people knew how many points you had left."

"Oh, sorry, I forgot about that," said Safia to Hashmi before turning back to Jericho, "Okay, then can I trade you for the information."

"Trade me?" asked Jericho, twisting his head sideways, still looking at Safia.

"I understand. Nothing in this school is for free. I get that now. Maybe I can help you with homework or something as a trade for the information."

Jericho looked between Safia and the expression of worry on Hashmi's face. "Sixty-seven points, that's how much I received for planting the small trees."

"What? But I didn't—"

"It's fine. I assume there's a reason behind you asking me this. So, what else would you like to know? I'll answer anything you want outside of directly telling you the total amount of points I have."

"Why would you do that?" asked Safia, looking confused. "I'm grateful, and all, but aren't you supposed to charge me points or something? That's what everyone else at this school does."

"I just feel like being charitable, is all," said Jericho as he shrugged his shoulders nonchalantly. "So, go ahead, ask away. This is an opportunity that you should take advantage of."

"Okay then, let's say that I wanted to earn over a thousand points a month. Could I do it by just doing what you do and helping out around the school?"

Jericho stared back up at Safia for a long moment, but then sighed, "No, given the amount of work you would need to do, at most, you'd get about half that in a month. And if you ace the three tests a month here, which keep in mind no one ever actually does, then at best, you're looking at around eight hundred points a month. If it's over a thousand points you're looking for, then you're going to have to bet. No question on that."

"I figured as much," said Safia, rubbing at her wrists. "I don't suppose you know of any easy bets."

"Safia, what's wrong," asked Hashmi. "Are you actually going to try and start betting here?"

"I... I'm just going to try it out, is all."

"Be careful," said Jericho, "I've seen what getting too deep into the games here can do to the people."

Safia thought back to the girl and the boy, splashing about in the fountain for coins on the day Harmony showed her around. "Yeah, I know. I've seen it too." She then grabbed Hashmi's hand and turned to walk away before turning back to Jericho. "Thanks for telling me this. I appreciate it."

"No problem," said Jericho, waving her off. "I guess it's good to be nice once in a while. But, if you'll excuse me, I think it's time for my mid-morning, thinking nap." Kicking up his legs, he then stretched out on the bench, opening up the sketchbook and placing it over his face. "Remember, if you're going to bet, bet the odds. You're not cut out to start betting people directly yet."

Safia smirked at the sight of him with the book over his face. "I'll remember that," she said before heading back off into the campus.

"Safia, are you going to tell me what's going on?"

"It's fine, Hashmi," said Safia, gazing around at the people. "Everything is fine now." *Bet the odds, not the people. So that means I should look for games with more than one person then? Or maybe board games based on chance?* Safia turned to see Hashmi's worried face staring at her as they walked along. "Don't worry. I'm not going to go crazy with betting like everyone else here. I'm just going to try it out."

"Okay, if you say so," said Hashmi, not looking convinced.

"Come on, let's go and get something to eat."

Together, they walked towards the cafeteria, with Safia still gazing around at the people who were out and about playing their games. *How can I win more points? I have a little over a thousand now. She said I have a month. But if I spend it and don't bet, then I won't have anything to bet with next month. And then there's the food budget, that's three hundred. So, including that, I need to make thirteen hundred points each month. Plus my monthly supplies, so many fourteen hundred in total.*

Safia shook her head, trying to consider more ways to gain points, but she couldn't figure out how to earn more. She continued to think about this as she and Hashmi entered the cafeteria and walked over to the counter to order her food.

"Well, if it isn't my two best Trojan friends," said a familiar voice.

Safia turned around to see Harmony walking up to her with a big smile on her face.

"Hey, Harmony," Safia smiled back at her. "I haven't seen you in a while. Where have you been?"

"She probably ran away to her boyfriend again," said Hashmi.

"You're never going to let that go, are you? I said I was sorry."

"I'm not angry anymore. I'm just giving an opinion, is all."

"Well, either way, I've been busy with classes. We, second-years, have a harder work-load than you, firsties," said Harmony, grabbing a tray and standing behind them. "So, what have you two girls been up to? Been making any good bets lately?"

"No," said Hashmi with a frown across her face, "although you seem to be eager enough. Let me guess, you want to make a bet and take advantage of us."

Harmony placed one hand over her chest. "Hammy,

that hurt. You know I only have your best interests at heart. And besides, there is nothing wrong with a friendly little bet, is there?"

"Spoken like a true addict," said Hashmi.

"Now that's just sour grapes. What about you, Safia? How about a friendly bet?"

Safia looked into Harmony's smiling face and sighed, "Fine, if it's a friendly bet, then sure."

"Safia, don't," said Hashmi, disapproving.

"Don't worry. I have to make one bet a month anyway, remember. I don't get the religious exception that you have, so I might as well get it over with."

"Oh, I forgot about that."

"Oh, really?" asked Harmony. "Well, let's just play for something simple. How about a coin toss? Something simple and easy to understand."

"Fine, how much?"

"Well, let's say fifty points, just to make it interesting."

"Fifty?" asked Hashmi. "Don't you think that's too much?"

"Fine," said Safia. *I guess it has to start sometime. Why not now?* "How are you going to catch it? In the palm or on the floor?"

"Oh," said Harmony, looking surprised. "Ah, I guess I'll catch it, flipping it over on my wrist."

"In that case, I'll call it after it's on your wrist."

"Ah… Okay," said Harmony with a frown, "I guess that's fair."

Hashmi watched the interaction between Harmony and Safia with a disapproving look on her face.

"Okay, I guess we can get started," said Harmony, pulling a coin from out of her pocket and taping the pendant. "I, Harmony Davis, challenge Safia Famosa to a coin toss, for a total of fifty points."

Safia looked down at her pendant beside her handbag and soon saw it flash red. She then left her tray on the counter. Raising her bag up, she tapped the pendant with her other hand. "I, Safia Famosa, accept the bet."

"So, I will flip, and you will call it when it lands, okay?"

"Okay," said Safia as her chest began to tighten from the nervousness of the situation.

Harmony smiled back and placed the coin against her thumb, heads up. "On the count of three. One, Two. Three," she said before flipping the coin.

Safia watched the coin float into the air, the spinning rotation seeming to slow down in her mind. *Head or Tails, Head or Tails, which one will it be?* She watched the coin come back down, and Harmony quickly snatched it out of the air before slapping it down on the back of her wrist, her hands covering the top of it.

"Okay, now guess which side it landed on," said Harmony with a grin on her face.

Safia stood there, looking down at Harmony's wrist. Her palm slapped against the back of her hand, where the coin lay underneath and back up to Harmony's smiling face. "Heads," she said and watched the smile of Harmony just briefly change as she moved her hand and revealed the coin that was set on heads.

"Oh, it's heads," said Hashmi as she sighed with relief, staring down at the coin.

"Oh, it looks like I lost," said Harmony with a smile. "That's a shame. I don't suppose you'd want to give me a chance to win my points back in another toss?"

I guess everyone here is like this. I probably shouldn't be surprised. "If you want to. I guess that would only be fair. I don't want to run away since you helped me out so much when I got here."

Harmony smiled, "Okay, let's try again." Harmony placed the coin on the tip of her thumb, flipping the coin into the air once again. Safia glanced down at Harmony's hand and then back up into the air as she flipped the coin before watching Harmony once again snatch the silver piece out of the air, flipping it over on the back of her fist once more.

"Okay, now which side is it on this time?"

"Heads," said Safia, looking into Harmony's eyes as if looking through her.

Harmony frowned, revealing the coin, which was once again heads. "Wow, you're really good at this," said Harmony. "I guess I can't win against you." She then placed the coin back into her pocket. "I guess, maybe I'll try a harder game next time."

"Harmony," said Safia with sadness in her voice. "You said before that everyone is here for a reason. Why are you here?"

"What? Isn't that kinda personal? Information like that might cost you in this school. You should be more—"

"I'll trade you back your hundred points if you answer me honestly."

"What? Why? Why do you even care?" asked Harmony, getting a little irritated.

"Because," said Safia with the same sad voice, looking directly into her eyes. "I want to know if what you just did was worth it. And I think if you tell me the real reason you're here, then I'll understand."

"Ah, well," said Harmony, fidgeting and looking around, her smile slowly leaving her face. She then tapped her pendant again, and Safia's pendant spoke.

"Safia Famosa has been awarded one hundred points," said the pendant on Safia's bag.

"Look, Safia, try not to take anything personal around here, okay? This is just how things are. We all might need the points for one thing or another." She then turned to leave them and waved. "I'll see you girls around, okay?"

Safia sighed, watching Harmony head back over to a table where it seemed as if a boy was waiting for her. She plopped down in his lap and began rubbing his face.

"What was that about?" asked Hashmi, looking at Safia

with curious eyes.

"I'll tell you later," said Safia, turning back to the lunch counter and grabbing her tray. "Suddenly, I don't really feel like eating anymore. Can we get out of here? I just want to go on a walk."

"Ah, sure," said Hashmi as she picked back up her tray. "But are you sure you're okay? You look kind of angry."

"Hashmi, can you promise me something?" asked Safia, still looking over at Harmony, who was laughing and joking with the others.

"What is it?"

"Can you promise me that you'll never try to bet me? I really do think that's the only way we'll ever be able to stay friends here."

Hashmi followed Safia, gazing over at Harmony, then turned back to her. "Sure, I bet you that I will never try to bet you," she said with a smile.

Safia turned back to her friend, seeing the smile on her face, and smiled back. "I think I'll take you up on that. Come on, let's go." And they headed back out towards the school.

"Will you tell me what happened with Harmony?" asked Hashmi, walking beside Safia. "How did you know it would be heads both times?"

"I didn't on the first flip, but the way she wanted to flip the coin was odd. She wanted to flip it over on her wrist. Which I thought was fine at first. I've seen people do it before. But after the coin flip, she kept both her hands closed. Usually, both hands are open, the palm at the top and the palm open at the bottom. So why keep her hands closed?"

"Was she hiding something?"

"Yeah, it was another coin."

"What? How did you know?"

"Did you see what she was wearing today?"

"What?" asked Hashmi as she tried to think back. "Ahh, pretty much the same as everyone else."

"She had on long sleeves today, even with the weather

being as sunny as it is. You have on long sleeves, also. But you wear this because of your religion. I don't think Harmony is a Muslim."

Hashmi took a gander around at all the students, still wearing their spring clothes. Short skirts and blouses that exposed their forearms were everywhere.

"Plus, when I first met Harmony, she had on short sleeves. On her wrists are a bunch of scratch marks. I thought they might have been from some type of self-harm. But now I'm thinking they came from the coin up her sleeve, always grazing up against her skin."

"Are you secretly, like a smart person?"

Safia laughed. "You're probably the only one who would think so. I only know all this because my Papa has always liked learning magic tricks as a hobby. As kids, he'd teach my brother and me all kinds of tricks. I guess I just remembered one at the right time, is all."

"Wait, then how did you know the coin was heads?"

"Oh, that's the easy part. That's because she used the same hand. Right over left. Each hand had a double-sided coin."

"It what?"

"Right hand was heads, and the left hand was tails. She would swap between the two when she passed one hand over the other. It's still a gamble for her, depending on how the coin toss is called. She couldn't let it fall on the floor because that would expose the trick. And if I were to call it in the air, then she could switch the coins whenever she liked, so she'd win one hundred percent of the time. But if I called on her flipped wrist, then it's back to a fifty-fifty chance unless I know the trick. Then, it's a hundred percent chance I win. It's just too bad for her that I've seen that trick before."

"Wait, then why didn't you confront her about it."

"I didn't think it was worth it. She showed me around school and introduced me to you. And she didn't seem like
212

a bad person then. So I just figured, I was winning anyway. So just let it be. But I would have liked to know why she tried cheating."

"Well, either way, you wanted points, and now you have an extra hundred. I hope it helps you."

"It's a start, I guess."

CHAPTER 11

A few days later, Safia was sitting at her desk near the window of her world economic class as Miss Abigail stood in front, teaching the students. She was trying to listen, but her mind continued to focus on her father and the points she needed. Her mind was in a daze as Miss Abigail continued her lecture on world politics and how the world truly worked.

Waking from her daydream, she felt her pocket begin to vibrate. Safia quickly reached in and pulled out her tablet and saw that she had a message from Champ Champ. Clicking on the pink envelope icon that appeared on the tablet, the icon unfolded in a display of colors on her screen.

Dear, sweety sweet Safia, I have news about your father. After classes today, please meet me by the pool inside the gymnasium. Also, I think I've put on some weight, do you think I have? I swear cakes put on a lot more pounds than you think they would. Sweet and fluffy demons are what they are.

Safia stood up in the middle of class.

"Safia, is something wrong?" asked Abigail, looking worried.

"I have to go." Safia reached down and grabbed her bag.

"Well, class is almost over, so I guess—"

"Thank you," said Safia as she quickly headed out of the class and down the hallway, out of the school, and sprinted down the spiral walkway towards the building beside the gymnasium. Barreling past people as fast as she could, she forced students to step off the sidewalk to avoid being hit, making her way towards the pool area. Eventually, she arrived at the building and dashed inside, passing a few girls and guys in their swimming attire. She made it to the pool and began looking over and around the water frantically.

"Oh, there you are, Miss Safia," said Champ Champ, sitting down on concrete bleachers beside a hand railing. She wore a brown one-piece swimsuit with her hair twisted in two tiny buns on her head. "I'm glad you came. And so quickly too, I thought for sure you'd be in class for another half hour or so."

Safia quickly walked over to Champ Champ, standing before her winded and breathing heavily as she looked at the sweat dripping down her own face as her hair hung over her eyes.

"My... My father... you said you had news."

"That I do," said Champ Champ, patting the concrete beside her, "But please do take a seat. You look as if you're about to pop a blood vessel."

"Please, just tell me that he's okay."

Champ Champ looked around at the other people in

swimsuits, looking at them and sighed, "Yes, your father is doing fine. Our surgeon was able to remove the bullet from near his heart, and he's expected to make a full recovery." She patted the concrete beside her once again. "Now, would you please take a seat? I don't think you'd be wanting others to find out about our little arrangement, now would you? Because people are starting to take notice."

Safia took a sigh of relief after hearing the news and sat beside Champ Champ with her hands over her face, trying not to cry.

"There, there," said Champ Champ, patting Safia on the back, trying to comfort her. "Goodness, what we must look like. But I guess there's no helping it. I did call you out here after all."

Safia raised her head, looking at Champ Champ, "Thank you so much."

"A thank you. That's unexpected. But don't thank me, I only offered you the deal. Your father's life is safe now. We even have ensured that he is being taken care of through some bogus insurance payout that he didn't know he had. So, you needn't worry about your little diner. Instead, you should worry about yourself. You only have another two weeks before your first payment is due."

"I hope you're prepared for what's about to come. If not, then your thanks may turn to curses really fast."

"If... if I can't pay the points and I lose, will you still allow me to visit my family?" asked Safia, wiping the tears from her eyes.

"What? Of course. We're not monsters," said Champ Champ as she placed her finger under her chin with a smile. "Well, okay, maybe we are. But we're not heartless. Even if you end up in servitude to the school, you will still be able to make periodic visits to your family if you wish. Even Abigail has visited her sister many times since her arrangement."

Safia wrapped her arms around Champ Champ's neck, hugging her. "Thank you so much. You don't know how much this means to me."

"Okay, I get it. I get it. You're grateful," said Champ Champ as she pried herself free from Safia's embrace and hopped down to the pool's floor. "Goodness, I look like a child, and you act like a child. Nothing about this makes sense. Well, I'm done with you. I just wanted to inform you of the details on your father. I think I'm going to go for a swim. You can head back now."

Champ Champ then turned toward the pool. "Hey, Katerina," she shouted.

"Yes, ma'am," said a woman near the pool in a two-piece swimsuit.

"Let's go swimming," said Champ Champ as she dashed towards the pool, tackling the girl.

"Ahh!" screamed Katerina as she lost her balance and went hurdling into the water with Champ Champ latched onto her.

Safia stood there in shock as the two splashed about in the pool.

"Ma'am, please stop," said Katerina as she stood up, splashing about in the pool with a smiling Champ Champ, still latched on to her.

"Play with me, Katerina."

Safia just stared at the girl's rough housing before she got up from her seat and left the pool area as everyone gathered around the pool, trying to see what all the commotion was about.

Exiting the pool house, she found herself wandering aimlessly through the campus.

"Well, hello there," said a voice from the side of a building as she passed.

Safia turned to see a woman with two men at her sides, "Ahh, hello?" she said, confused as to why the woman was speaking to her.

"Oh, have I been forgotten already? And here I thought I made quite the lasting impression on you last time."

Last time? Thought Safia as she looked at the woman when her memory came back to her. "Amanda?" she asked herself, questioning if her memory was correct.

"And there we go. Now I feel better." She walked up beside Safia, grabbing her by the arm. "And you would be Safia, if I remember correctly. Come, walk with me for a bit." She said as she strolled off down the walkway with Safia's arm wrapped around hers. "How are you today? Are you enjoying yourself here on the campus?"

"Ah, I honestly don't know anymore," said Safia, being honest.

"I thought so. You were looking like one of those animals that gets caught in the headlights. Which really is a shame if you're going to be spending the next two years here, you really should enjoy yourself," said Amanda as she turned around and waved her hand at the boys behind her. "These are my boys, and they'll very much ensure that I enjoy myself here."

Ricardo smirked, "I think you sometimes enjoy yourself a little too much."

"Perhaps. But that's only because you two spoil me so much," said Amanda as she rubbed her hand down Safia's arm. "Tell me, Safia, have you ever wanted to be a discarded? I could really use more girls beneath me."

"You said that term before, when we first met. What exactly is that, again? I remember how Dario treated that girl. It didn't exactly look pleasant."

"Yes, that was Mallory. The girl made a poor choice in picking Dario as her handler. I tried to buy her from him on multiple occasions, but he's a petty bastard who only seeks to control others."

"It seems like that's what everyone here wants, that or more points. Or they used points to try and control your life."

"Well, I can't argue with that. But for me, I only desire two things."

"And what's that?"

Amanda quickened her steps, walking in front of Safia, stopping her. She then raised a finger with a smile on her face and placed it against the temple of her own head.

"The first is to be remembered."

"That's an odd thing. Do you think people will forget you?"

"Of course, they will," said Amanda as she turned her back to Safia, gazing around the campus. "Memories are a fleeting thing. The moment something leaves your immediate vision, your mind is already trying to find ways to replace it. Why, did it not just happen moments ago? You seemed to struggle quite a bit to remember me."

"I guess that's true, but it has been some time since I saw you. Anyone would have forgotten."

"Really? Is that so?" asked Amanda with her back still turned to Safia, "Then, tell me, what color are my eyes?"

"What?"

"Come on; I was just standing next to you. Tell me, what color are my eyes? I'll bet you a thousand points right now, and all you need to do is tell me the color of my eyes."

"Well," said Safia, trying her best to remember her eye color, but soon slumped her shoulders, realizing she couldn't bring the thought back to her mind. "I... I don't know. I didn't pay much attention."

"See? Already replaced by another thought," said Amanda as she turned back around, revealing her gray eyes. "And that was only seconds ago. But don't worry about it. That's just human nature. We move so quickly onto the next thing that strikes our fancy. Who needs a telly when life flips channels far faster than any clicker ever could?"

"I... I suppose you're right then," said Safia, raising her head back up. "Can I ask you a question?"

"Of course, I'm always happy when someone takes an interest in me."

"How did you get so many points?"

"Oh, that," said Amanda, placing her hand under her chin. "I guess that would be a mystery to you then, wouldn't it?" Amanda stepped closer to Safia. "Now you should know that information isn't free. But for a small price, I can show you how I have earned the points that I have."

Safia shook her head, sighing, "I don't think I can afford to give away any points at the moment."

"Points?" asked Amanda, "Oh please. I have more than enough points to last years here. Instead, you promise me three favors, and I'll show you where and how I earn my points."

Safia glanced back at the men. "I won't become one of your discarded, if that's what you want."

"Miss Safia," said Ricardo. "You seem to be misunderstanding something. We willingly became discarded under Amanda."

"What? Why?"

"Honestly, I just got tired of the games that people played here. One day, I was considering quitting the school when Amanda just suggested that I become her discarded. Then I could just go about my studies and no one would bother me about the stupid games they play here. It's worked out well enough so far since discarded don't really have points. No one's pestering us for games. If I wanted to, I could just quit this school now and go home, but doing it this way still ensures that I will graduate this year and not have to deal with the hassle."

"That's the same for me as well," said the other man. "It's not like she ever mistreats us or anything. We'd just leave if she did. We have no reason to stay here beyond our education."

Amanda walked back to the men. She then reached forward and kissed Ricardo on the lips before turning to the other man and kissing him on the cheek. She then whirled around on her heels in a dramatic fashion, facing Safia. "There, you see? Not everything is so black and white here,

Miss Safia. You would do well to remember that. So, tell me, do you still refuse my offer?"

Safia thought for a moment, staring at the gray-eyed woman and her companions before sighing, "What are the favors?"

"Nothing big, I promise," said Amanda with a smile. "I simply require your time to fulfill three of my goals, is all. I promise they won't be putting you at risk of any harm to yourself or your points. Just be ready, and I will show you how I make my points." She then turned around and started to walk away with the two men. "I'll send Ricardo here to come and get you when everything is ready."

Safia stood there for a long moment as the gray-eyed woman and her two men wandered back into the campus. *I wonder what I just agreed to. Probably something stupid. But at least I'll get to know how to earn more points.* She ran her fingers across her face, taking a deep breath. *They said that they could leave this school whenever they wanted. But if that was the case, why did the girl with Dario allow herself to be treated like that?* Safia then looked over at the school once again. The sharp peaks and arches that decorated the structures of each and every building. They looked even more intimidating and disgusting the more days she spent looking at them. *What am I even thinking? It's not like I can just go home now either. I'm sure that girl has her own problems, just like I do. Maybe even worse, considering how this place works.*

She once again started aimlessly walking around the campus until she found herself at the doors of the left library of the school. Stepping inside through the heavy wooden doors, she was once again greeted by the sight of thousands of books sitting upon layers and layers of shelves. The smell of old papers and wood was as if a perfume of time was drifting through the air. As she made her way into the library, for some reason, she felt as if her body was gliding through the aisles.

Her fingers went up beside her, rubbing against the

bindings of the books as she passed them. The feeling of her fingers gliding against books soothed her mind. Step by step, her finger flicked from binder to binder, the ridges of each book's back cover easing her mind more and more.

At least I can relax here. She took another breath, breathing in the smell of worn paper all around her. *Why has this smell always felt so good to be around?* She stopped and pulled out an old-looking book from the shelf and took the tip of her finger, running it down the rough leather casing. *Secrets of the World by Amy Anderson,* it read. *I wonder if there's a book called 'Secrets of this school.' That would come in handy.* She smirked. *But Papa's okay now. That's all that matters. The rest I can deal with as long as he's okay.*

She opened the book to the first page.

"Just a little bit longer. You wouldn't believe how close I am," said a man's voice, piercing Safia's newly found comfort zone that she was slowly making in her mind as she began to flip through the pages.

She stopped, annoyed by the words of the man, and once again tried to find that place in her subconscious where she could escape back to, if only for a few more moments.

"Why don't you just give up already? Can't you find something better to do with your points? Chasing after me this long is ridiculous," said a familiar woman's voice that halted Safia in her mental tracks.

Was that Abigail?

"Look, I know you don't particularly like me," said the man's voice. "But I can't help how I feel about you. I think about you when I sleep, when I eat. I just... I can't control this. You even said so yourself, that you didn't dislike me."

Safia took a few steps back and began to look around, trying to find where the voice was coming from. *Where? Which way?* She turned around and tried peeking through the space between the bookshelves, and she made her way down the aisle. It didn't take long before she found them. There, with her back against one of the shelves, she saw

Miss Abigail standing with a book clutched to her chest. Beside her, with his hand against the books behind her, a man leaned over, looking down on her.

"Well, just because I don't dislike you, it doesn't mean that I'm fond of you either," said Miss Abigail, looking up into the man's eyes, frowning. "Don't you see how you're acting? You're like a child who won't accept being told no."

The man pulled back from Abigail and placed his back against the bookshelves, folding his arms in front of him and closing his eyes. "You think I don't know that? I've thought about what I've been doing for the last two years, Abigail," he said, rubbing his fingers over his elbow. "Thinking I must be crazy doing this for a person who doesn't even want to be with me." He opened his eyes and looked up at the rows of shelves above him. "And yet, here I am in my third year. Trying to buy my way into freedom from this incessant need."

"Your need? What about what I want? You're asking me to just sit back and give you seven years of my life."

"And if the school ordered you to be with me for those seven years for the sake of your sister, would you do it then?"

"That's not the same thing and you know it."

"No. What I know is that this school has the right to pick your mate for the next seven years, and I'll be damned if that's going to be anyone other than me. If I buy out this damned contract, then may... maybe I'll finally be free from this, and I'll get my life back."

"Excuse me, Miss Abigail," interrupted Safia, stepping into their view, halting their conversation. "Sorry, I left class early, but I was wondering if you still had time to tutor me." She raised the book in her hand for them to see.

Abigail stared at Safia for a moment before brushing a strand of hair out of her face and regaining her senses. "Ah, yes, of course, dear," she said as she walked past the man towards Safia. "We can grab a seat at one of the tables in the back. She then reached out, linking her arms with Safia, and headed towards the back of the library as the man went in the opposite direction, heading out of the door.

The two women walked over to an empty table away from the few students that were there and pulled out two chairs, sitting down next to one another.

"I'm sorry you had to see that, but I do thank you for getting me out of that situation."

"Is he always like that? He seems... kinda..."

"Killian isn't a bad person. He's just... obsessive," said Abigail with a sigh as she ran her hands over her face. "And that obsessiveness has had him trying to buy my debt ever since he's found out."

"Your debt? Is that what they were talking about in class that day?"

Abigail looked at Safia with wide eyes, then with realization, "Yes, I forgot you were in that class." She then took a deep breath. "I guess there's no harm in telling you now, is there? Especially now, since apparently, Killian is close to getting the points he needs."

"My... my sister... she had a bad heart growing up. Then, one day, while I was here, I received a call saying that she had collapsed on the floor while trying to cook breakfast. Needless to say, I was distraught. You may not know this, but this school has access to some of the most advanced things in the world. Clinical trials for cancers that won't be available for the next ten years, new technologies, and for me, I wanted a new heart for my sister.

This story started sounding all too familiar to Safia as it was for this reason that she herself went to the headmaster to propose a similar trade and knew that more than likely she got the idea because of Abigail's situation.

"Well, after finding out and asking to be sent home to be with my sister. The headmaster at the time, lady Champ Champ's grandfather, offered me a deal; he said that he would give my sister a new heart, in exchange for two million points."

Two million? Is it even possible to get that many?

"He said I would have until I graduated school to pay off the debt, which I knew was some type of joke. How in the world was I going to get that many points?"

"Did you try to?"

"Of course. What choice did I have?" asked Abigail, clenching her fist. "For those next two years, I worked my ass off. I gambled on bets that had the highest chance. I worked around the campus, tutored; anything I could think of outside of selling my body, I did. But at the end of it all, it wasn't enough. How could it ever be? The headmaster came to me and said that since I had gotten around half the required amount, he said they'd cut the debt in half, so instead of twenty years given to the school, I only needed to give ten. And that was three years ago."

"Then how is he... I mean. How can he just buy you?"

"That's what many people in this school don't realize. But during the orientation, I'm sure you heard Champ Champ say that 'you can buy anything here with points.' Well, that includes other people's debts. And if Killian buys my debt, then he essentially buys me. And if he cancels my debt, then not only my life but my sisters will be ruined. And I can't let that happen, not when she's been through so much."

"Wait..." said Safia, now remembering her conversation with the headmistress. "So if he's almost able to buy your debt, and you had half, and you've already been here three years. Does that mean he almost has seven hundred thousand points?" asked Safia, trying to figure out the math.

"Thank goodness it wasn't only just seven hundred thousand," said Abigail with a reluctant chuckle. "I may have lost the bet to Champ Champ's grandfather, but it was Champ Champ and not the previous headmaster who was in charge of the debt after she took over. She told Killian the debt to buy my remaining time was still two million, regardless of the time left. We both thought that would give me a bit of security, since it seemed like such an impossible goal. Even me working my ass off for three years could only achieve half that. Well, we were shortsighted in his dedication. Killian is, by all means, a genius and very single-minded."

"Within his first year here, he had already gained more than half of what he needed. He burned through almost all the seniors' points, bet after bet. The only reason he didn't finish in his second year is that the freshmen who heard about him the year before and were too scared to bet him the following year. So, it slowed him down. But his final school year has just begun, and apparently, he's really close now. So, I'm pretty much stuck at this point. It looks like he'll win."

"Is there nothing you can do?"

"Not unless someone has an extra two million points lying around. I don't think there's much anyone can do," said Abigail as she leaned back into her chair and stared up at the ceiling, her eyes showing just a slight hint of water at their corners.

"Does that happen to a lot of people here, where they end up working for the school?"

"I don't know anyone else in my situation. Most of the teachers here besides me are here of their own accord. But if any of them are, then I hope they keep it a secret or they might find themselves in the same situation as I'm in."

I guess that means. I need to keep this to myself, then.

"Miss Abigail, is that you?" asked a girl that passed by in front of them, holding two books against her chest.

"Oh, Mallory, how are you? Can I help you with something?"

"Oh, yes ma'am. I was just looking for textbooks on the history of Africa's trade with foreign countries for tomorrow's test."

Where do I know her from? I feel as if I've seen her before. The conversation with Amanda came back into Safia's mind.

Maybe I do need to pay more attention to the people around me.

"You're looking in the wrong section, Mallory. You should be looking for the exportation of precious gems from the country which would be in the other library. Not this..." Abigail's words caught in her mouth as she stared at the girl. "Mallory, come here for a moment."

"What, why," said the girl defensively, keeping her distance from the table and turning away. "Ah... I have to go now."

"Mallory Polana, you come here this instant, or do you want me to call the campus medical staff to have a look at you?"

"What? No, please don't do that."

"Then, bring yourself over here," repeated Abigail in a stern manner.

"Yes, ma'am," said Malory as she made her way over and around the table, still with her head facing down. She stopped just before Abigail and started looking around, trying not to look the teacher in her eyes.

"You've got a black eye," said Abigail as she reached out, touching the girl's face and smudging her makeup a bit.

And there it was. Safia could see it clearly beneath the smeared makeup, a significant black mark under her right eye.

"Did Dario do this to you?"

"No, I ah... fell down, that's all."

Abigail frowned. "Dammit, Mallory, why don't you just report him?"

"I can't. Then, they'd send me home too."

"Home can't be any worse than this," said Abigail, as she gently rubbed the side of Mallory's face.

Mallory narrowed her eyes and pulled her face back from Abigail's hands. "That's where you're wrong, Miss Abigail. I promise you; things can get a whole lot worse than just being here under Dario." She then turned around and quickly walked back into the center walkway of the library towards the door.

Abigail stared at Mallory as she left before sitting back down and began rubbing her hands against her head in frustration, "Well, one thing's for sure, I might not like the idea of Killian buying off my debt. But I can promise that whatever he has in store for me is a far sight better than whatever that poor girl's going through."

"But I thought you weren't allowed to hurt anyone at this school."

"That's only true if you report it. If you allow it to happen, then the school doesn't take part in any resistance. I'm sure if someone like Champ Champ sees it, she would do something about it, but who knows what anyone sees nowadays?"

"I see," said Safia in a somber tone.

"Thank you, Safia," said Abigail, placing her hands on the table and nodding her head. "It actually felt good to have someone to talk about this with. That mess with Killian, I mean. The only other person who knew was Champ Champ, and talking to her is rather confusing, even at the best of times."

"It's fine. Thank you for sharing this with me. But can I ask you one more question before you go?"

"Sure, I can't imagine it being more difficult than what I've already shared."

"That name, Champ Champ, how did she get it? I can't be the only one who thinks it's an odd name."

Abigail smiled back at Safia shaking her head, "Now, that, you're going to have to ask her yourself. I'm not sure I could ever do the story justice."

CHAPTER 12

Days later, Safia and Hashmi were in their pajamas, sitting together on the floor of their room. Flipping through the pages of a book Hashmi had picked up from the library, they discussed how their next assignment would go.

"Okay, so, is it true that World War Two started over a payment for some telegraph poles?" asked Safia as she ran her finger across the words of a page.

"That's what it says, but I don't know if that's what people consider the actual start of World War Two," said Hashmi, writing down her notes in a notebook. "I was always taught that it started when Japan attacked Pearl Harbor."

"Ah, this is so confusing," said Safia as she dropped the book from her lap and laid down with her head on the rug of the room. "Why is everything written so vaguely? Every book just tells stories about each side as if it was just a guess? Nothing ever points to what truly happened."

"I think that's the whole idea," said Hashmi, picking up the book and placing it in her lap. "They want us to give our interpretation as to what caused certain events in history."

"I wish Yago was here. He loves stuff like this. I'd just ask him to help me out."

"Yago, who's that?"

"That's my little brother. Have I never told you about him?"

"You said you had a brother, but you never said his name before."

"Oh, well, he's alright; just an ass most of the time. But unlike me, he's smart. He even got a full scholarship to college."

"I don't know. You seem pretty smart to me. You figured out that coin trick pretty fast."

"That was only because I've seen it before. Yago is the one who somehow got me into this school. I'm not even sure how he even found out about it. If it weren't for him, I'd still be in my father's diner, serving plates for the rest of my life."

"Well, at least you know your brother. I've never met mine before."

"I didn't know you had a brother."

"I told you before how my father and mother had me in college. Well after graduation, father went home and selected himself a proper Muslim family. Together, I have two half-sisters and one half-brother. But I've never met them before. I don't even know if they know that I even exist." Hashmi rubbed a page of the book between her fingers and she allowed herself to get lost in her thoughts. "He and mother argue about it sometimes, but there's really

230

not much to be done about it now."

Safia reached her hand over, rubbing Hashmi on the back, bringing her back to reality.

"But didn't you say that you were getting to know him? So that means he must come to visit. Has he never brought any of them with him?"

"No, he does visit. It's just that he never stays long. Only a week or so every couple of months. It's not like he treats me badly or anything. And he always gave mother money for my schooling and stuff when I was growing up. I just wish he'd... well, you know."

"It seems we both have family issues," said Safia, sitting up while still rubbing Hashmi's back with her hand. "But you did say that you and your father had a close relationship. Can't you just ask him?"

"Sometimes, I try to. It's just I don't know how to bring it up. And we've been talking more lately, so... I don't want him to get mad at me. But it would be nice just to meet them, if only once, you know," said Hashmi, reaching over and placing her hand around Safia's wrist for comfort. "If only just to say hello to them. But how would that even work? Hello Nazia, Laaya, and little Rashid, I'm your big sister Margaretto." Hashmi laughed, "It sounds so silly when I say it aloud."

"Is that why you prefer for everyone to call you Hashmi? You want them to use your Muslim name?" asked Safia as she shuffled behind Hashmi, wrapping her arms around her and placing her head on Hashmi's shoulders, to embrace her.

Hashmi was quiet but nodded her head, grazing her skin against the side of Safia's face, and in return Safia held her close to her until they both could feel the warmth of each other's bodies pressed against one another, trying to provide some comfort for her friend in this moment.

"I guess no life is ever really perfect. Everyone will suffer in their own way," said Safia, rocking back and forth with Hashmi still in her arms.

"Yes, no matter who you are, everyone has their battles they must fight," said Hashmi.

There was another moment of silence between the two girls.

"Hashmi, when we leave here, do you think we'll still be friends?"

"What? I hope so. After this, maybe you can show me the place where you come from. I've never been to the U.S. before."

Safia looked around the dorm room. "For all we know, we could be in the U.S. now."

"I guess that's true."

"Okay, come on," said Safia as she removed her arms from around Hashmi and stood up, reaching out her hand. "Enough moping around the room. We promised we'd help out today to get a few more points."

"Alright then," said Hashmi, grabbing Safia's hand and allowing herself to be pulled up by her friend.

Both girls walked over to their closets and began putting on their clothes. Safia with her standard purplish skirt and the button-up blouse and Hashmi with her long skirt, except this time instead of a white-collared shirt, she put on a darker tone brown and purplish shirt. Safia noticed that Hashmi put on a different type of Hijab than the usual one that covered her hair and wrapped around her neck. This one was longer and draped down over her shoulders and hung below her chest, stopping near her stomach.

"Oh, that's a different one. I've never seen you wear one like that before. It's longer," said Safia as she looked over the head garment while buttoning up her shirt.

"Well, I figured we might work a bit today, so it's best to be a little more modest," said Hashmi, as she took another look over Safia's attire.

"What?" asked Safia, noticing Hashmi staring at her.

"You should try one," said Hashmi, her eyes showing

the excitement of the idea in her mind.

"One what? Wait, you mean a Hijab. No, you're kidding," said Safia in protest, shaking her head. "I'm not even Muslim."

"Oh, come on, you should try it. And it's not like it's exclusively Muslim to wear one."

"I can't, it wouldn't..." said Safia, looking at her friend's face, seeing how happy she was at the idea and remembering the story of her wanting to meet her family. *I have Yago, but I guess it's different if you don't have any other siblings.* "Okay, but just this once," sighed Safia.

"Really? Oh, good. I have the perfect one.," said Hashmi, turning and reaching back into her closet, pulling out a brown and purple scarf along with a black head wrap, along with a little box. "Okay, just have a seat, and I'll put it on for you."

Well, at least she seems to be having fun, thought Safia as she walked over, pulling out a chair from her desk and sitting down in it with her hands on her knees.

"Okay, here you go, hold this," said Hashmi, as she gave Safia the scarf and the box to hold and she walked around her with a long comb in her hand. Then softly made a few strokes through Safia's hair to make sure it was straight before wrapping her hair up in a bun behind her head. She then took a black opened cap, rolling it up between her fingers, stretching it out, and bringing it down over Safia's head, around her neck. She then stretched it back out, pulling it back up over her eyes, and let it stay at the crown of her head, wrapping it around her hair and ears.

"Oh, it's a bit tight on my ears," said Safia, feeling the cap snuggle around her head as Hashmi placed it on.

"It feels like that at first, but it gets easier the longer you wear it," said Hashmi as she reached into Safia's lap and grabbed the scarf, wrapping it over the top part of her head, above the cap, leaving the top exposed. "This is the first time I've ever done this for someone else before," said

Hashmi with a giant grin on her face.

"Well, I'm happy to be your first, I guess."

Hashmi then took the rest of the scarf at the top of Safia's head and wrapped it under her chin and back over her head, folding the side back. "Okay, can you open that box for me?"

"Okay," said Safia, opening the box, revealing an assortment of different types of pins with ornaments on them. "Wow, these are so pretty."

"They're all my favorites. I had to ask specifically that they, along with my Hijabs, be allowed to come with me."

"I don't know which one to pick."

"Hmm," mumbled Hashmi before reaching her free hand down into the box. She then pulled out a crystalline jeweled dragonfly pin, its wings glimmering in beautiful sapphire and emerald crystals. Placing the pin into the side of the cloth, it locked the fabric in place at the side of Safia's face near her ear. Then, taking the other half of the material, she wrapped it loosely around Safia's neck, letting the rest hang freely behind her. Hashmi then reached over, grabbing a hand mirror from her bed and placed it in front of Safia.

"Ah… my face looks so tiny like this."

"It draws the attention towards the face since there is nothing else for them to focus on," said Hashmi, walking around to stand in front of Safia, still wearing a smile on her face. "Do you like it?"

"It's different," said Safia with a genuine smile back. "But I do like it. Are you sure it's okay for me to wear this?"

"Of course. There's no rule that says you aren't allowed to dress this way. Plus, it looks good on you."

"Okay, if you say so. But I'm not sure I could wear it every day, though. But just for today, I don't see why not." She then placed the mirror back down on Hashmi's bed along with the box of pins and grabbed Hashmi's hand. "Come on. Let's not keep the boys waiting."

"Wait, what about your pendant? You might need it."

"Oh, yeah. Well, I don't need my bag today, so..." Safia walked over to her bag and knelt, untying the rope around the pendant and holding it in her hand.

"Why not wear it like a necklace? You have it on that strong rope, anyway."

"Okay," said Safia, tying the rope back into a knot and placing it over her head, letting the pendant hand around her neck. "Okay, let's go."

The two girls left their room, went downstairs, and headed out of the dorm, making their way across the campus. It wasn't long before they arrived at the side of the school, where a dozen or so students were out near a bunch of lumber and bags, along with shovels. Safia and Hashmi stepped off the walkway to the grass and made their way over to the group.

"Sorry, we're a little late," said Safia as they approached.

"Don't worry about it, we were just about to sta..." said Jericho as he raised a brow, looking at Safia and Hashmi. "I didn't know you were the religious type. Has Hashmi converted you already?"

"Oh, ha-ha," said Safia, "I let her dress me up today, so I hope you aren't planning to work us half to death out here this morning."

"No, far from it. We're just going to have you help with the lumber and the foundation today. The lumber's come in but doing this will take a few days to get done with just us here."

"Salaam sister Hashmi," said Nasir as he approached. "And hello to you too, oh holy and most devoted and revered, sister Safia," said Nasir, with a sly smile on his face. "If I had known you were so interested in our culture, I would have brought you a Quran myself," he said with a chuckle.

"Oh, now everyone wants to be a smart ass. I think you've been hanging around Jericho too much," said Safia, frowning at Nasir.

"Now, stop picking on my friend, you two," said Hashmi, wrapping her arms around Safia with a big smile. "You must admit, she looks lovely wearing Hijab."

"Well, I can't argue with that, plus she still has that rope I gave her. It's a symbol of our forever friendship."

"Yes, and just like our friendship, it was dirty."

"Alright, smartass," said Jericho with a smirk as he turned back to the buckets on the ground. "You two, come along, and we'll get you started. Let's put our dirty friendship to good use."

As Safia followed behind Jericho, she noticed the unexpected face of Killian leaned over on some lumber, making the side of the wood with a marker.

"What's he doing here," asked Safia. "I thought he had a bunch of points."

"Oh, Killian," said Jericho, following Safia's gaze. "He always tries to help me out around campus. He helped me with the plants when we first met. That's who the other shovel belonged to, but he left early after dropping them off."

"Do you not like him or something?" asked Hashmi.

"No, it's just I heard he has a lot of points, is all. So, I was just curious why he's out here."

"Oh, now that part's most certainly true," said Jericho as he reached down, picking up two buckets filled with sticks. "I've heard stories about how most people on campus are too scared to even try to bet him. They say he's only ever lost a single bet since being here. No idea what he's planning to buy with all those points though," he then turned to Killian, "Hey, come over here for a second."

"Yeah. How can I help?" asked Killian, marking up another piece of wood before making his way over to them.

"Meet your new assistants. I and the rest need to finish digging up the foundation. So, you have the girls here to help you finish cutting the boards. We're not making magic here but try to have the measurements as close as you can, and don't vanish on me this time."

"You sound like you don't trust my abilities," said Killian with a smirk.

"Oh, I trust your abilities to know what you're doing. I just don't trust your ability to stick around till the project's done."

"Hey, that's not fair. Someone wanted to challenge me to a bet, and I needed the points."

"Yeah, yeah. You damn point freak. Well, I'm using those two to look after you this time," said Jericho with a smirk as he turned back to Hashmi and Safia. "You hear that, girls? If he tries to run, tackle 'em to the ground."

"Yeah yeah, alright. You win. I won't leave till the job is done," said Killian, looking up at the horizon, then turning to Hashmi and Safia. "The morning is still early, but I'm sure you girls don't want to be working out in the hot sun when it comes up. I'll help you two move the supplies to that tree over there, so we can continue to work in the shade."

"Ah... Okay," said Safia, looking at the tree that was downhill from them.

"Good, here, take these," said Killian as he reached over, grabbing two pairs of gloves off an upturned bucket, and handing them to the girls. "Put these on. You don't want to get splinters in your fingers."

"What are we supposed to be making here?" asked Hashmi, taking the gloves and sliding her fingers into them.

"Today, it's just the foundation to a gazebo that Jericho wants to build," said Killian, walking over to the wooden supports holding a plank between them. "But I imagine we'll also do a bit of the structure today as well. The roofing will need to be done another day." He then removed the wood on top of the supports and laid it on the ground. "Can you two grab that support piece there, and I'll grab the one on the right?"

"Sure," said Safia, walking to the wooden supports and picking it up with Hashmi. They both then lifted it and began walking in unison, trying to balance the support in their gloved hands as they made their way over to the tree.

"You girls are both first-years, right?" asked Killian, as he knelt beneath the support between the wood and lifted it up onto his shoulders. "You both liking the school so far?"

"Yes, Sir," said Hashmi, "But how long have you been here?"

"Me? I'm in my third and final year."

"Third? What made you stay past the two that they require?"

"There's something I want and I need this school's points to get," said Killian as they made their way over to the tree. He knelt, placing the wooden structure on his shoulders back down on the ground. "So, I'm still here." He then walked back to the girls and took the wooden structure from them before looking down into Safia's face.

"What?" asked Safia, looking back up at Killian. *Did he remember me?*

"Have we met before?" asked Killian. "I feel like we have."

"I don't think so," said Safia. "But I meet a lot of people around campus with Jericho, so maybe we have." *Oh, thank you, Hijab. I'm sure it would get awkward if he remembered.*

"Mr. Killian, are you perhaps enraptured by the beauty of my friend here?" asked Hashmi with a smirk.

"Ha," laughed Killian as he turned, placing the wooden structure down, its side facing the other. "While I admit you're both lovely ladies, as much as I hate to admit it, there's only one woman I'm interested in."

Yeah, and you trying to buy her, you bastard.

"Oh, is it a love story then?"

"A one-sided love story perhaps," said Killian, turning around. "Come on. Help me grab my tools." And they all went walking back. "What about you, girls? Anyone around campus that you fancy? Your name was Hashmi, right? Maybe you've fallen for Nasir?"

"Oh, goodness no," laughed Hashmi. "Just because he is Muslim does not automatically make us love interests. Besides, he already has a girlfriend."

"There... Can you girls grab my hammer and nails there and I'll grab a few of those two by fours?" asked Killian as he walked over, picking up the pieces of wood while the girls picked up his tools. "Whether he has a girl or not doesn't matter to some people. The heart very rarely responds to logic, if it did then it'd be a different matter altogether." Killian looked towards the horizon while the lumber bounced on his broad shoulders. "We want what we want. There's no use questioning it."

"It sounds like you are very much a love-struck man, Mr. Killian, or a hopeless romantic."

"Well, I doubt she sees anything romantic about it," said Killian with a laugh as they made their way back under the tree. He then placed the lumber down, setting it to the side as he grabbed one piece, bringing it over, and setting it atop the wooden supports. "Okay, you girls just apply some pressure to each end to make sure it doesn't move that much while I'm cutting it."

Both Safia and Hashmi leaned down on both ends, as Killian looked over the wooden board before reaching down, picking up the saw. Safia noticed his school pendant was chipped to the outside of his pants pocket. But she was surprised to see that his pendant was the same as hers and all of the first years.

Why does he still have one like ours? Aren't you allowed the design you own when you become a second year?

"Aren't you going to measure it first?" asked Hashmi.

"Nah, I would if I was going to have someone else cut it, but I already know the measurements of what Jericho has planned," said Killian, placing the saw against the board.

True to his word, Killian cut every piece of wood without measuring it. And, to Safia's surprise, when they were done and stacked on top of each other, the boards seemed to measure perfectly aside one another.

"Okay, now we just have to—"

"Well, it's nice to see the little worker bees having themselves a fun morning," said an annoying voice from behind them.

Safia turned to see Dario and his entourage behind him. It didn't take long for Safia to also notice that Mallory was also a part of the crew.

From the stalker to the asshole.

"I didn't even know we had Muslim women here. Are you two out here trying to get some points? I can think of a few ways for you to earn points way faster than this."

"I see you're still being an asshole, Dario," said Killian, squatting down with his back turned.

"Wait, is that the point freak? I didn't recognize you with your back turned. Why are you even out here helping these people?"

"Not everyone wants to bet like us, Dario. Some people actually come here to learn and, you know, enjoy themselves."

"Then, they should have gone somewhere else. This place is meant to break you down. Well, except for the two Muslims you got with you. With their little religious exceptions. Honestly, them being here is just a waste of a spot."

"Perhaps you should join Islam," said Hashmi, folding her arms in front of her, her tone growing harsher, "Then perhaps Allah will grant you some modesty and wisdom."

"Is that what your God teaches you? Tell me something; does that God of yours instill wisdom in you before or after you strap the bomb to your chest?"

"Dario, stop. We don't need you interrupting our work," said Killian, grabbing another piece of wood.

"I would love to comment more, but Allah would not appreciate the words I would call you. And I am beginning to think that even conversing with someone like you is too close to sin for my liking."

"Sin? You're in a school made for sinners. The heart of the beast is what's all around you. Don't think that little curtain on your heads is gonna protect you for long. Everyone falls in time."

"I think you're forgetting about the trade system," said Killian, trying to defuse the animosity in the air. "The school was founded on it."

"Nobody uses that shit anymore. I don't even think the people in charge know how it works."

"That just means we have something else to figure out. The school is filled with mysteries, after all. I'm sure there are some rules we don't even know exist." He then pointed at Mallory, "I heard for a long time that people didn't even realize that discarded even existed until one day someone made the offer out of desperation, and it was accepted. And now you and a few others get to run around like kings."

"That's because I am a king as far as she's concerned," said Dario with a chuckle, gesturing his thumb at Mallory. "But I'm surprised. I figured you'd be chasing another sucker who wants to bet you. Rather than building whatever the hell that is up there." He nodded to the rest of the group working up ahead of them.

"So, are you saying you're going to bet me?" asked Killian, standing back up and turning around to face Dario. "I'll happily take you on. It's been a while since I've taken your points."

"Like I'm stupid enough for that. I know you win all the damn time and I'll be damned if I fall for your shitty tricks again. No, I have a game planned for you where you can't cheat at dice or cards. One where we both are even."

"Oh, is that so? Well, I'm listening."

"Not now, point freak. Don't worry; you'll get what's coming to you. But only when I want it to happen, not because you say so."

"What a shame. And here I was hoping for some easy points," said Killian, turning to Hashmi and Safia. "Dario here once lost two-hundred thousand points to me in a single bet, on what he called a 'sure thing.' That sure was a good day. I've never gotten so many points so easily and so fast."

"Alright point freak, keep spouting off at the mouth, and I'll find a way to make sure you experience your second loss."

"Oh, I have no doubt you'll try, and I look forward to it."

"Let's get out of here and leave the point freak with his little Muslim harpies."

"I think I misspoke earlier," said Hashmi, her voice tightening around her lips. "I'm not sure even Allah could find forgiveness for a snake like you."

Dario spat on the ground, looked at Hashmi, and smiled, "Best compliment I've heard all day," and walked off.

Killian turned to Hashmi. "I didn't think you'd get so angry. Doesn't the Quran say something about not giving into anger?"

"Well, you don't expect me to lie down on the ground, now do you?"

"I'm not sure what that means?"

Hashmi turned around to face Killian. "It means we should take that wood you just cut to the others. I need to work off these feelings I am having." She then turned and walked off toward the pile of cut lumber.

"Your friend's got quite the spark to her."

"I see," said Safia as she watched Hashmi stomp her way back up the hill with some of the cut-off boards in her arm. *I didn't realize she had it in her.*

The three made a few trips back to where the rest of the group was, dropping off the wood they had cut. Killian grabbed a few more planks and took them back, while the girls grabbed a few cold bottled waters before returning.

I don't get it. Killian doesn't seem like the crazy stalker now, like he was with Abigail, thought Safia as she watched him place another piece of wood on the supports. She opened the bottled water, "How many more do we…" Suddenly, Safia tripped on a root of the tree and stumbled forward, squeezing the bottled water. "Ohh!"

Killian turned around and tried to catch her. The momentum from her swung them both around as he dropped the piece of wood from his other hand. He then knelt, sliding his foot over the grass before sweeping Safia off her feet and into his arms.

Safia, caught off guard by it all, closed her eyes, clutched the water bottle in her arms, and braced for the fall. But when she opened her eyes, she was greeted by the sight of Killian's soaking wet face gazing down at her. Looking around, she found herself hoisted into the air and cradled in his arms like a child.

"Oh, I'm sorry, I didn't mean…" *How did this happen? He picked me up so fast.*

"Well, this happened," said Killian, looking down at Safia in his arms. "You, okay?"

"Ahh. yes… I… I'm sorry."

"Oh, you're strong," said Hashmi with a smile. "You scooped her up so fast. I'm impressed."

"I'm not exactly sure how we got here," said Killian. "But Miss Safia, you may want to cover up."

"Huh, what do you mean?" asked Safia, still in Killian's arms. She then looked down at her shirt, which was now quite see-through and sticking to her skin, showing her bra. She quickly placed her arms over her chest. "Can you let me down now?"

"Sure," said Killian, with a smirk on his face. "I'm sure that will dry soon, but you can go change if you like. You're in Yennefer dorm, right? That's not too far off."

"No, it'll dry off fast. I'll just go sit over here for a moment," said Safia as Hashmi walked over, lowering the scarf of the Hijab down to cover her bra. They both walked over to the side of the tree together, while Killian went back over to the group to fetch more supplies.

"That was funny," said Hashmi with a smile on her face. "You got him good with the water, and he held you up like a princess."

"I'm happy you enjoyed it."

"Well, he did stop you from falling, but what's wrong? Do you not like Killian?"

"It's not that," said Safia, looking into Hashmi's eyes, trying to decide how much to tell her before finally looking around to make sure Killian wasn't around. She saw him heading over and turned back to Hashmi. "Look, I'll tell you about it later, but Killian isn't a good man. No matter how nice he seems now."

Hashmi looked at Safia curiously for a moment, but nodded her head.

"Is she properly covered up back there?" asked Killian jokingly as he walked back to the wooden beam, bending down and picking up his saw.

"Yes," said Hashmi, standing back up and walking over towards Killian, "She is drying up nicely now."

"Good. Well, can you grab that end for me? One person should be enough, really, and there's only a few more."

"Sure," said Hashmi as she came over, grabbing the end of the board. "Tell me, have you known Nasir and Jericho long? They seem friendly to you. And I don't see any other third-years over there."

"Well, there's not many third years in general, but there's at least one or two second years in there. And as for Nasir, I've seen him around and he seems like a nice enough guy. Jericho, though, I'm not sure I'd call us friends; he doesn't have friends as much as he has targets."

What does that mean? Thought Safia, listening to their conversation.

"I'm afraid I don't understand," said Hashmi, gripping the board.

"It's not really anything bad, per se. It's hard to explain," said Killian, turning around and looking up the hill. "He's a friendly fellow and all, but he has his faults."

Doesn't everyone?

Hashmi just stared at Killian for a moment. "I mean... I don't think anyone is perfect. We're all allowed to have our flaws"

"Yes, but Jericho is more of a specialized case. Hmm... It's hard to describe." He shrugged his shoulders. "Oh well, it's not like he's going to go on a killing spree or anything. He just doesn't seem to have the ability to empathize with anyone."

"What? Mr. I-just-want-to-makes-friends. He seems nice enough."

"Maybe he's just hiding his feelings from others," Hashmi joined in. "Many people can be introverted like that."

"You'll see what I mean if you start spending time around him. One thing's for sure; I'm happy I don't have to bet him, since he's just decided to try to be friends with everyone. It would be hell to try and read him."

That can't be true. Thought Safia, as she began thinking back to every time she had met up with Jericho. *That's definitely a lie.* She turned to the other side of the tree, looking up the hill. He was ahead with the others, sitting down with a bucket in front of him and stirring a large stick inside of it. *Get a hold of yourself Safia. You're taking the word of a stalker over someone who's helping you get points for Papa.* She peeked out, looking at Jericho again. *But it's not like he knows it's for my papa.* She shook her head, trying to free herself from the thoughts. *No, he's still helping me, and it's not like I'm some rich person like other people here. He has no reason to help me. He always seems friendly enough.*

Safia lifted herself and walked back around the tree, over to Hashmi.

"Hello again. Are you all dried off now?" asked Killian.

"Yes, thank you. Sorry about spla—"

"Ricardo Reigns would like to know your location,"

spoke Safia's pendant as it flashed different colors. "Do you accept or deny his request?"

"Huh," said Sofia, looking down at the pendant across her neck.

"Who is Ricardo?" asked Hashmi, turning to Safia.

Safia shrugged, "I don't know."

The pedant repeated the question aloud.

"Well, he's looking for you," said Killian. "You might as well accept. You're out here with us helping, anyway. So, I doubt it's for anything bad."

Safia then tapped on her pendant, making it click, "Ah… I accept his request."

"Well, you certainly seem popular, Miss Safia," said Killian, as he stretched his shoulder. "First Jericho, and now this Ricardo fellow, you seem quite the temptress for men whose name ends in the letter O."

Hashmi giggled. "I suppose I should be thankful that I am a woman. That seems to be the only reason I have survived your charms."

Safia frowned at the two. "Oh, ha-ha. I sure am glad you two are having fun at my expense."

"Well, now that you're all dry, would you mind coming over and grabbing the other end of this plank? They're probably ready up there for another batch."

Safia walked over, grabbing the other end of the plank, and Killian quickened his pace as they quickly went through the boards.

On the final cut, a boy walked up and waved at them. After seeing him, Safia instantly remembered him.

That's the one who was with Amanda, the one who was in the fountain. I must have forgotten his name again. Safia thought back to Amanda's words that night. *I guess she was right. If I don't regularly see it, then it escapes my mind.*

"Hello Miss Safia," said Ricardo, stepping up to them under the shade of the tree. "I hope I didn't catch you at a bad time."

"Hey, Ricardo. No, we were just about to take a break. Why were you looking for me?"

"Oh, that's because Miss Amanda wishes for you to join her for tonight's event."

"Event? What event? I haven't heard about anything happening."

"It's an event primarily for the second and third-year students that happens at the end of each month," said Ricardo.

"So, Amanda will be showing up tonight, then?" asked Killian, walking up beside Safia. "I wondered if she'd just decided to take it easy. She's been avoiding game night for a few months."

"No, Sir, she's just been busy. But she wishes for Safia to join her tonight."

"Game night," said Safia, looking at Killian. "You all get together one night and just bet?"

"In a sense, yes. But the bets are a lot larger and consist of more than just points. First-years usually can't go unless they are invited by a second or third year. So I guess you should feel honored. Amanda doesn't usually take guests, except for Ricardo there. But he's a discarded, so it doesn't really count."

"Are you willing to join Miss Amanda tonight?" asked Ricardo. "I need to relay your message back to her."

Safia looked between the two men. "Well, I did say that I would, so I guess so. There won't be anything weird at this game night, will there?"

"Define weird," said Killian, with a smirk on his face. "Because you're probably guaranteed to see something odd. If only for the type of bets that will be made. But if you mean dangerous, then no, game nights are completely safe, usually."

"That's not what I mean," frowned Safia, "But I guess that's the best answer I'm going to get. Okay, fine. Where will it be? Do I have to meet her somewhere on campus?"

"Oh, don't worry about that," said Ricardo with a smile as he turned and began walking off. "I'll come and pick you up when I bring your dress over." Ricardo then made his way back on the winding walkways and through the campus.

"You said game night happens once a month?" asked Safia, turning back to Killian.

"Yes, but the participants are random. Some people show up, some people skip. It's more of an event for those who have too many points to find new ways of losing them."

"He didn't say what time it was going to happen. Do you know, Killian?"

"It usually starts around nine."

"Okay, then, that's enough time to go back and change clothes."

"Safia, didn't you hear what he said?" asked Hashmi, tilting her head. "He said he's going to bring over a dress for you to wear."

"What? What kind of dress?"

"Oh, yeah," said Killian, scratching his head. "I guess I should have mentioned that sometimes the dress attire for game night can get a little odd."

"How odd?"

"Let's just say it might upset your Muslim sensibilities."

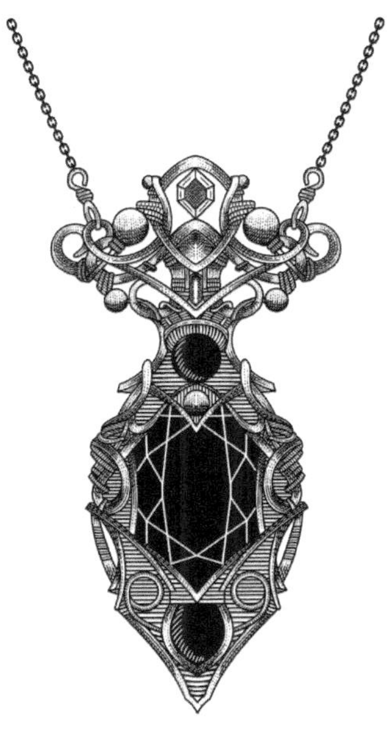

CHAPTER 13

Safia lay on her bed, staring up at the ceiling of her room. An uneasy feeling plagued her mind as the anticipation of the night kept her from getting any rest. Amongst the sheets of her bed, she lay in uncertainty of what was about to happen. *Game night, there's no way this will be something normal. Nothing here is normal.* She reached behind her head, grabbing at the pillow beneath, folding it over her ears and wormed around in bed. *Why do I keep getting myself involved in this stuff? Because I don't have a choice, that's why.* She closed her eyes, taking a deep breath. Between the ruffles of the soft fabric around her ears came the sound of crinkled paper as Hashmi, who sat on their windowsill, flipped another page of a book she had propped against her knee.

"If you're so apprehensive about going, then why did you agree?"

"I'm not..." said Safia as she let go of the pillow, looking over at Hashmi. "Okay, maybe I am. I'm just a little nervous, is all."

"Do you think he's really coming?" asked Hashmi as she flipped another page. Her skin glowing in the moonlight that shone down on her through the glass window. Recently out of the shower, her hair was wrapped in a towel as small droplets of water fell from loose hair strands down to the shoulders of her pajama top.

"Well, it's only around seven, so I suppose we still have time to find out."

"Are you sure you wish to go to the party?" asked Hashmi as she paused her reading, turning to look at Safia.

"Yeah, I said I would. Plus, Amanda said that she would tell me how she got so many points."

"Haven't you gotten enough points? You won some from Harmony, and we just did our test for the end of the month. That should be more than enough to live off of."

"No, not yet," said Safia as she began rubbing her fingers through her hair. "Don't worry, it's not like I'm going to become some type of gambling fiend or something. I just want to learn how the school works. And I'll probably learn a lot more at this game night thing they are having."

Hashmi bit her lip while looking at Safia, "If you say so, but I just don't want my friend to become one of those betting freaks."

Safia sighed. *It's not like I want that either. But I don't really have much of a choice in all this.* Safia rolled on her side, swinging her feet off the bed before sitting up. "Don't worry, that won't happen. Now come over here so I can comb through your hair. It's a mess, and should be dry enough now."

Hashmi removed the towel from her hair, rubbing it against her scalp as she walked over to a chair in front of their TV, while Safia got out of the bed grabbing a comb.

"Should I turn on the Tele?" asked Harshmi as she reached for the remote.

"No, let it stay off. I like that it's quiet. It helps me think."

"I guess you do have a lot to think about."

"Unfortunately," said Safia as she began to stroke Hashmi's hair. *I'm back at eighteen hundred, but the end of the month is tonight. So, starting tomorrow, I'll be back down to eight hundred, and then there's the three hundred for food. That doesn't really leave me with many options.*

"Safia? Safia?"

"Huh," blurted Safia as the sound of Hashmi saying her name brought her back to reality. "I'm sorry, I was daydreaming. What did you say?"

"I asked why did you say that Killian was a bad man today?" Hashmi turned around in the chair, looking back up into Safia's eyes. "He seemed nice enough to me."

Safia just shook her head and slumped her shoulders." He seemed that way, but he's a stalker; he harasses Abigail."

"Abigail, who's that? Wait. You mean Miss Abigail, the teacher?"

"Yeah, remember how she said she owes the school some years of her teaching or something like that? Well, it's more than just teaching. She gave away... I don't know how to say it. She pretty much allows the school to tell her what to do. Apparently, they can even pick her husband."

"So, it's like an arranged marriage then?"

"More like an arranged life for the next seven years, and then she's free. Killian is trying to buy those seven years now."

"Why would he do that, though?"

"I think to make her his wife or something. Whatever it was, she didn't seem too happy about it, and he didn't seem to care."

"And the school will allow this to happen?"

"They can't stop it. It's part of their system here; if you run out of points, you can sell yourself to someone who has a lot, and they will use their points to allow you to stay at this school."

"Yeah, that's the discarded system. I was told about that. But to me, that just sounds like slavery."

"Apparently they justify it because everyone here can go home when they feel like it. But if they quit school before graduation, they lose all chance of having this school's influence."

"Oh."

"Oh?" said Safia, confused by Hashmi's lack of shock at the ongoings of the campus." You sound as if that makes it okay."

"Not okay, but I can understand if that's the case," said Hashmi, dropping her head. "The people here, many of them come here with a lot of pressure from their parents. So, the guilt of not being able to live up to those ideals might make people tolerate a lot of abuse."

"I... I suppose you're right," said Safia as she thought about her own family situation. How her parents were so proud of her going to college. *I guess everyone has that. I mean, the only reason I'm still here is that I wanted to save papa. And Hashmi, she...* "Actually, Hashmi, why did you decide to come to this school? Did your family ask that you come here?"

"Oh, no. Mother doesn't—"

A knock came on the door.

"Who is it?" asked Safia, freezing the comb still in Hashmi's hair.

"It's Ricardo," said the voice from outside the door. "I've come to retrieve you, and I've brought the dress. Can I come in?" He said as the doorknob twisted, and both girls realized they had left the door unlocked.

Hashmi quickly jumped up and into her bed, pulling the blanket over her head as Ricardo stepped into the room.

"Wait," said Safia as Ricardo paused in the doorway, holding a green box in his hands as the door swung open.

Safia stood there with the comb in her hand as Hashmi hid under the covers.

"Let's go back out into the hallway."

"Ah... okay," said Ricardo, looking confused.

Safia put the comb down on Hashmi's bed, then walked towards Ricardo, escorting him back outside of the room, closing it behind her.

"I'm sorry, did I interrupt you two?" asked Ricardo.

"No, it's fine. You didn't know," *Even Yago wouldn't walk into my room like that.* "Do you have any sisters, Ricardo?"

"No, ma'am, I'm an only child," he said as he extended out the green box that he had towards Safia. "Here, this is for you."

That explains it, thought Safia as she took the decently sized box into her arms, holding it against her chest. "I hope that Amanda doesn't want to meet now. It's barely eight o'clock."

"No Mam, she would like to meet you around ten, but she preferred that I drop off the dress early and inform you that I'll be back to pick you up around that time," said Ricardo as he turned to go.

"Ah, Ricardo, wait."

"Yes, ma'am?"

"Amanda asked me for three favors. You wouldn't happen to know what those are, would you?"

"No Ma`am. But if you're worried, she might try to make a spectacle out of you or make you her discarded; then you needn't worry about that. Amanda is more of a free spirit type, but she tries to show respect for others. Just try to entertain her tonight, and everything will be fine."

"Why do you always call me ma'am? It makes me feel like an old lady. Although you have good manners for your age."

"Sorry about that, Miss Safia. My family is very military. So, I've just grown up saying it so much that it's become second nature."

"Okay, it's no big deal. Call me whatever you like. I was just curious. I'll guess I'll see you at..." Suddenly Safia realized where she was and who she was with. *Wait, I can ask him. He seems normal enough, I think.* "Ah... Ricardo, can I ask you about something?"

Ricardo tilted his head, looking back at Safia confused. "Sure, I suppose so, what's wrong?"

"It's just, you're Amanda's discarded. Don't you think this whole discarded system is messed up?"

"Oh, is that what has you so worried?" asked Ricardo as he leaned his shoulder against the way, folding his arms. "You believe you will fall victim to this fate?"

"No, I mean. I'm not trying to go so far as to be put in that situation. I'm asking what you, as a discarded, think about it."

"Hummm, I personally believe it has its uses. But I'm also not so blind and stupid that I don't see the abuse people here suffer under it. In my case, I'm more of a pseudo butler slash boyfriend. Which I accept because of my own personal feelings for Amanda."

Pseudo boyfriend? What does that even mean? Are you two dating?

For example? I believe I told you that I selected to be a discarded, but did you know that I had around four thousand points when it happened?

"What?" asked Safia in genuine surprise. "But I thought you had to run out of points, then you had to make a choice on if you wanted to become a discarded or not."

"That is certainly how it usually goes around here. But there is always more than one path to achieve a goal. This school has many rules that they don't tell you. You can't just assume that just because that's how it's done, that means that's the only way it's done."

"How? Did you know you could do that? I mean, has anyone else done it?"

"I can only speak for myself as I don't know the other discarded particular situations. But I think of this school as if it were a constant battle. Everyone here plays the game differently. I myself just found a roundabout way of not playing the game."

"And what if I don't want to play their game?" asked Safia, noticing how Ricardo's normally formal demeanor was now replaced with a more laid back side that she hadn't seen before.

He smirked. "Take a look where you are and what you're about to do. I think it's far too late to be saying that now, Safia."

"I... I guess you're right. I'm in this now. I'm going to have to see it through."

"I like you, Safia. You seem like an honest girl. So I'll reiterate the advice I gave you before. You needn't worry about Amanda. She just likes to have fun. I personally have never seen her act malicious towards anyone. To my understanding, she's for the most part just as carefree and simple as a child would be. You give her a new toy and off she goes to play with it. Among the second years, there are people way worse. I hope you never catch their attention."

"You make it seem like they are evil or something."

"No, perhaps not evil. But they are privileged and its best to—"

"Amanda Chastain would like to know your location," spoke the pendant on Ricardo's shirt collar as the glass around the crystal shifted colors from red to blue.

Ricardo raised a brow and reached up, clicking on the device. "Give her my location." He then smirked, looking at Safia. "It seems our conversation is over. She can be a bit needy when she's alone." Ricardo lifted himself from the wall, placing his hand behind his back, and assuming the usual stiff posture that Safia had come accustomed to seeing him in. "I wish you a good day, Miss Safia. I will return to pick you up at the proper time." He then turned around and headed off down the corridor as Safia watched him take the stairs back down.

Safia stood there for a long moment, processing everything she was just told, and surprised by the young man's quick swap between personalities. *"Who are you, Ricardo? Which one is the real version of you?" I don't want to think about that now. There... there's just too much to think about. Just focus on learning how to get more points. That's all that matters right now. Not other people's crazy secrets.*

Turning back around, Safia opened the door to see Hashmi back in Hijab. "Is everything alright?"

"Yes," said Hashmi, "I hadn't realized we left the door unlocked."

"Neither did I," said Safia with a smile as she fell back into conversation with Hashmi. "But I must admit, you jumped into that bed pretty fast."

"A woman must be nimble if she wishes to keep her modesty from the prying eyes of the people here and their wicked ways," said Hashmi with a smile as she jokingly did some stretches, as if warming up for exercises.

"I'm pretty sure Ricardo might be the least wicked person here." *Or at least the version of himself that he appears to be. But why did he reveal that side of himself to me? It's not like... No, no, don't think about that, Safia. Focus on tonight.* "Anyway, I'm about to go to a party with these wicked people. Do I not count in this group of heathens?" asked Safia as she walked over, plopping the dress box down on her bed.

"Well, you have promised me that you won't become a gambling fiend and you said that there's a reason you need the points. So, I trust in Allah that you are not deceiving me for selfish desires."

There was a moment of silence between the two girls.

"I am not deceiving you. If I could just go to class and

just make my once-a-month bet, then I would. But there really is a reason I have to do this."

"Then, I shall wait for the day when you feel that you can tell me," said Hashmi, walking over to Safia. "Now, let us see what type of dress you were brought. We must make you pretty for your date tonight."

"It's not a date," said Safia with a smirk as she opened the box, removing the soft paper inside. "I'm going for Amanda, not Ricardo." Inside, she could see crimson fabric. Reaching in and grabbing the ensemble, she lifted it, and her eyes went wide as she took a look at the dress.

"Oh my," said Hashmi as she took in the sight of the outfit and matching shoes. "I may have hidden under the sheets to hide my modesty, but if you wear that tonight, I'm not sure you're going to have any modesty left."

The crimson dress was long and had a deep V-cut in the front that looked as if it would come down to her navel. Across the middle were two pieces of fabric that connected the sides in an x pattern. The garment's back was also cut and had a circle at the center attached by two pieces of cloth that connected it to its sides.

Safia turned to Hashmi and held out the dress. "You want to try it on first?"

"I think I shall let you have the honor, sister."

"I don't..." said Safia, before she then turned back to Hashmi, smiling at being called sister. "Do you think you can help me try it on, then?"

Removing her pajamas and stepping into the dress, it took the girls some effort to properly fit the garment on Safia, as she tried to get all her parts in place.

"Ow, stop squeezing my breasts."

"Sorry, but they're bigger than I thought they'd be, and you're supposed to slip them inside, not have one hanging out."

"I know that. It's these damn straps," said Safia as she shimmied herself, while pulling at the shoulders of the dress. "They're in the way."

"Wow, your butt's way bigger than mine."

"Great, thanks for pointing that out. It's not like I can help it. I'm shaped like my mother. Ow, stop that. You're pinching me."

"Just stay still, almost there. Ahh, there we go. You're all in now."

"Well, at least she's allowing me to walk, I guess," said Safia as she tapped the back of her crimson wedged heels against the floor.

Hashmi then grabbed a black sash from the box and stepped behind Safia. "Okay hold still." Wrapping the Sash around Safia's waist, she then tied it into a large bow on her back.

"There, now you look like a butterfly. A very scantily clad butterfly."

Safia frowned back at Hashmi. "Hey, it's not like I'm used to wearing this either. And aren't you supposed to be supportive?"

"I am being supportive, or at least I'm giving you more support than that dress is. How are your breasts not falling out?"

"There was some sticky stuff inside. I slid it across the top of my breasts and that keeps the dress stuck to them. It came with instructions," said Safia as she showed Hashmi the note from under all the crinkled paper.

"Well, I guess that's something."

After fiddling around with the dress a little more, Safia allowed Hashmi to do her makeup before there was a knock on the door.

"Ah… It's me again," came Ricardo's voice. "Am I allowed to come in now?"

"Yes, you can come in now," said Safia. *I guess this is the version I'm going to be getting tonight.*

"I've come to get you," said Ricardo as he slowly opened the door, peeking his head inside. "Oh sorry, about last time,

Miss Hashmi. I didn't realize the religious implications."

"No, it's fine. I understand it wasn't on purpose."

"I brought you another package," said Ricardo as he held up a smaller box. "May I come in?"

"Yes, Ricardo. What's in it?"

"A small coat, I believe."

"Oh, good, more clothing. Every little bit helps at this point," giggled Hashmi as she made her way over.

Safia playfully rolled her eyes at Hashmi's comment, "Thank you, Ricardo."

He then knelt on the floor and opened the box, pulling out a short white coat, which he then held out and helped Safia put on. The sleeves fit perfectly and came down her arms to her wrists while the coat's base only came down to just below her chest. It did, however, allow her to cover more of her breasts. *As mother would say, 'Thank the Lord for small mercies.'*

"Ricardo," said Hashmi, "Don't you think that Safia's dress is a bit revealing?"

Ricardo stepped back and looked over Safia, which made her feel a little self-conscious as his eyes roamed over her body.

"Not especially, no. I'm sure there will be many others who have far more revealing outfits tonight. I think Miss Safia's outfit will be quite timid by comparison."

"Quite timid?" repeated Hashmi in surprise as she took another look at Safia. She then walked over to Safia and whispered in her ear. "You have to tell me everything when you get back."

"Oh, so now you're interested?" asked Safia, teasingly, "I'm sure I can ask Amanda to find a dress for you if you want to come."

"It's short notice, but I think Amanda might have something for you to wear if you wish to attend."

"Oh no, not in a million years," said Hashmi as she stepped back and hopped on her bed, letting her feet dangle in the air. "I think I'll just wait for you to give me the details when you get back."

"Mhmm," moaned Safia with pursed lips as she turned back to Ricardo. "Okay, I guess I'm ready to go."

And together they both left the room, heading downstairs, and out of the dorm, setting foot back on to the school's winding concrete walkways.

The campus was mostly silent now, except for the sound of her own heels as she stepped along the path and the insects talking to one another beneath the blades of grass all around them. Above her, Safia could see the full moon peeking over the school's sharpened arches ahead of them. The moonlight of the clear night illuminating the campus, giving the walkways a blueish-white tint as they made their way through them. Passing the school, they took a singular walkway along its side and ventured near the lake that was down the hill from it.

"Is the game night not at the school?" asked Safia, still feeling uneasy about where Ricardo might be taking her. The darkness and silent ambience of their surroundings doing nothing to add to her confidence.

"No, ma'am," said Ricardo as he pointed ahead of them. "It's there."

"You don't have to call me ma'am, Ricardo. I'm not your mother or anything."

"Sorry about that, Miss Safia. It's kinda ingrained in me at this point."

You say that. But I'm not too sure what's ingrained in you. Your mannerism now, is it just a character you play?

A little bit ahead, farther off from the lake, was the old abandoned-looking shed that she noticed when she first arrived at the school.

"In there? Are you sure?" asked Safia as she looked ahead, narrowing her eyes at the small house.

"Yes," laughed Ricardo. "I know how it looks. I was surprised too when I was first introduced to how it works."
260

How it works? I'm not suddenly in some type of horror movie, am I? Thought Safia as they left the walkway that was headed toward the lake. Stepping out onto the grass, they started making their way down to the old shed house.

Up ahead, Safia could see someone waiting on them in a suit. Their back against the wall, the person waved at them, and Safia realized that it was Amanda. She wore a button-down suit with slacks with white dress shoes. Her hair was tied in a ponytail behind her head with a black bow to match the bow Hashmi had fashioned on her back.

"Well, don't you look lovely, my dear," said Amanda, staring up at Safia. "I'm happy to see that the dress fits you."

"It fits me surprisingly well. How did you know my size?"

"Simple, I paid attention," said Amanda as she extended her hand for Safia to take. "It's one of my few admirable traits."

"I guess I need to follow your example then."

"Perhaps, but tonight, I simply ask for you to follow my lead."

"I don't think I've ever been invited out like this by a girl before," said Safia, reaching out and taking Amanda's hand. She looked up at the worn down shed house.

"Good, then hopefully you will remember me and this night." She then turned toward the shed door. "Now, shall we go inside?"

Ricardo opened the door for them and, instantly, Safia heard the sounds of people talking, along with the sound of a piano playing. Stepping inside the small wooden shack, she saw that it wasn't what it appeared. While the outside was coated in old wood, the inside was very modern and had metal walls along with two love seats on opposite sides. Ahead of her was a small stairwell that led downward into the floor. As she stepped forward and peered inside, she could see people walking around down below her.

"What is all this?" asked Safia as she turned back to see Amanda smiling at her. "A basement for parties?"

"It's a new world built for our enjoyment," answered Amanda as she stepped down, still holding Safia's hand. "So, let's enjoy it, shall we?"

Safia stepped down, following Amanda into the world of game night. The air was cool and the floor beneath was carpeted in a dark crimson tone that seemed to match her dress perfectly. The sound of a piano playing a soft melody floated through the air along with a pleasant aroma she couldn't place. And through the ceiling she could see the little black orbs in each corner.

"The cameras are even down here."

"Oh, I imagine they take everything here seriously, but to my knowledge, it's automated and no one ever watches them until they are asked." Amanda laughed, "Does this school really seem so lawless compared to where you are from?"

"What? No... well, maybe a little. I just don't understand how a place like this is possible. I mean not just here, but the whole school."

"Oh, I imagine there are a great many things possible that'd you'd never believe until you've seen it," said Amanda as she escorted Safia along the tunneled area.

The rest of the patrons were dressed in all varieties of clothing, or lack thereof. She could see booths with people sitting and smiling, holding drinks in their hands through-out the downstairs area. In front of them were reddish crescent-shaped tables with black rims. Some patrons were being served food and drinks, while others were simply enjoying conversing with one another.

"Wow, it is like a club down here."

"Come along, there is so much more to show you," said Amanda, guiding Safia by the hand through a set of black curtains covering a doorway. Inside was a lounge area where ahead on a stage was a gentleman at a piano, his fingers dancing on the keys, creating a classical melody. Beside him stood a woman with a microphone in her hand, singing a soothing tune for the enjoyment of the people who watched.

"Harmony," said Safia as she realized who was singing the melody. Beside her, Safia saw another familiar face playing the violin to accent the piano's tune. "Is that Addison?"

"Yes, so it would seem. It's well known that Harmony has a magnificent singing voice even since her days on television."

She was on television? Wait, I remember her asking if I recognized her. What show was she on?

But the truly remarkable thing is that the brutishly foulmouthed Addison has the talent and self-control to play such a delicate instrument. The world truly is filled with wonder."

Safia stared around the lounge as everyone listened to the unlikely trio on stage, serenading them with song. Suits and bow ties complemented by colorful evening dresses, much in the same fashion as Safia's littered the area. As the tune changed and the lights above them dimmed, she watched as a few patrons stood up and began to dance with their partners.

"I don't suppose you would like to dance?" asked Amanda with a grin, looking back up at Safia.

"Maybe when there's not so many people around. I'm not really such a good dancer."

"Next time then."

"Safia, is that you?" asked Jericho as he came walking up to them.

"Jericho? What are you doing here?"

Amanda smiled and placed a hand on Jericho's arm, "Jericho here is the one who convinced that songbird up there, and more impressively that surprisingly good violinist to play here tonight."

"Yeah, I'm tutoring her for her World Finance class, and one day, she just started singing. So, I figured she could come down here and sing for a few points," said Jericho as he quickly looked over Safia's outfit. "Well, don't you look lovely? A bold outfit, but definitely very beautiful."

Safia looked down at the floor, embarrassed, only to have Jericho place his hand under her chin, lifting it back up, looking into her eyes.

"Oh, no. Not tonight, Safia. Tonight, you have to walk with confidence. Show them all how beautiful you are, especially if you have the charming Miss Amanda as your escort. I'm sure she admires your beauty as much as I do."

"Why, Mr. Jericho, you really are a silver-tongued man, aren't you?" asked Amanda, as she turned her attention towards the singer on stage. "Picking out such a songstress from our current crop. You know how to spot other people's talents and put them to use. Even though you're a first year, I can already tell that you're going to go far on this campus."

Suddenly, the crowd started cheering and whistling as two people emerged from another room near the curtains. Safia turned to see a man and a woman who came into the lounge area, holding hands. But the shock was that the two were completely naked. They strolled forward through the crowd with smiles across their faces; the girl blowing kisses toward the male guests. And the female guests taking sideline glances at the man's member.

"Well, what do we have here," said Amanda as she bit her lip, looking at the couple as they came towards them, "Is this your doing, Jericho?"

"No, sadly not," said Jericho with a brow raised. "I do believe someone is trying to one-up me. And doing a fairly decent job at it if I must say so."

"Trisland and Harper," said Amanda as the two neared them. "What a pleasure to see that you're attending this game night. And it's even more of a pleasure that I get to see so much of you."

"Oh! Hello, Amanda," said the naked woman. "So, you've decided to come back down to game night this time?"

"Indeed, I have, Harper. And it seems I was fortunate enough to see you like this. I don't think the stories would have done your beauty justice." Amanda licked her lips as she took another look at Harper. "So, tell me, what spark brought on such a showing between you and your discarded here?"

Discarded? Is she making him do this? Wondered Safia as she tried her best not to stare at their naked bodies. An attempt that she was hugely failing at every few seconds or so.

"Well, I decided to try and bet our wonderful headmistress, and this is the result. A bit of exhibitionism for me and my little boy servant here."

"Are you sure? He doesn't look so little to me," said Amanda, looking down at the boy's cock.

"True," said Harper as she reached over, grabbing the boy's face and kissing him on the lips. "Trisland here has been a very nice partner to have. But I suspect we are the same. Do you not also have your own discarded to play with? I believe you have a very lovely one named Ricardo. Wasn't that his name?"

"That is true, although we haven't strolled through the campus in the buff yet. So, I imagine we aren't as far along as the two of you."

"I imagine not," said Harper with a giggle. "It wasn't exactly our plan either. But I lost the bet, so I must comply. The Headmistress here has quite the fetish for strange bets."

"I see," said Jericho with a smile on his face. "I must be sure to thank her for adding to tonight's entertainment."

"Be sure to do that," said Harper, "But if you'll excuse us. We promised to put on an exhibition of skin, and we must continue as per the rules of the bet. We're headed to the glass room to put on one final show for our little headmistress."

Amanda and Jericho stepped aside, allowing Harper and Trisland to pass by them as they walked through another curtain as more cheers and whistles were heard when they arrived.

"Well, I'm not sure I can top that tonight," said Jericho, turning back towards Amanda and Safia.

"Are you sure? I imagine quite a few people here on campus would love to see what you look like naked. I think Safia here might be one of them."

"What?" asked Safia, looking between the two.

"Well, as flattered as I am that you think so," said Jericho with a smirk at Safia, "I couldn't care less about promoting myself in that manner around the campus. It's the people who call me a friend that I hold on to after graduation that I care about. And as such, I wish to ensure that they know that I can provide them with entertainment. Perhaps even the birthday suit kind, if the reward turns out to be worth it."

"A brown-noser and an entrepreneur, and one who actually has a talent for the occupation. I think that you will do fine in this world."

"Happy to hear I have your approval," said Jericho, turning toward the stage as the trio was finishing their song. "They're almost done. I should go. Enjoy yourselves tonight, ladies." He then walked forward, stepping up on the stage, and grabbed the microphone when Harmony was done. "Ladies and gentlemen, how about a round of applause for our guests here for providing us this evening's entertainment?"

The crowd began clapping in appreciation.

"Is every game night like this?" asked Safia, watching the crowd's reaction.

"It varies. Some nights, there's not much happening as for entertainment. But I imagine if your friend Jericho there will be hosting a few more, then I suspect things are going to get far more interesting than before," said Amanda as she gazed up at Jericho, playing to the crowd. "He truly is a natural showman." She then grabbed Safia's arm. "Well, come along then. I did promise to show you how I earn my points, didn't I?"She then led Safia through the lounge area and through another set of curtains.

Inside the next room, Safia saw a vast open space filled with people huddled up toward games tables. At one table, they were rolling dice, and another they were playing cards. Through the entire room, games of chance and calculation were being played. And there, down on the far end of the room, was a bar. It looked to be made of complete glass as soft pink lights reflected over the area while a man inside went about his time serving drinks.

"Come along and let the games begin," said Amanda as she led Safia over to a dice table. But here, people weren't tapping their pendants; instead, the table had these slots on the side that the school pendants were lodged into. Before the man threw the dice, they would put their hands on the pendant and it would light up.

"How do you play?" asked Safia, looking over the table.

"Oh, it's a fairly simple game. You roll the dice on the table, and whatever number you land on, the people around the table bet on whether you can land on it again. But you lose instantly on the first roll by landing a two or a twelve, but people very rarely ever bet on a first roll. So, there's no real risk there. Now, the joys of winning are that you get the points of the people who bet against you. But the total will be split amongst the people who bet on your side. In fact," Amanda tapped on her pendant, "Inform Ricardo Reigns that I wish to see him."

Amanda grabbed Safia's hand. "Would it be too much to ask you to trust me?" She asked, looking up into Safia's eyes.

"Ahh, well..." Safia looked around the room. "Trust you how?"

"I want you to trust me with a few of your points?"

"Ah... I don't... I don't have that many. I can't really afford to make any more bets this month." *They're going to be taking another thousand away from me tomorrow. Then I'll only have eight hundred left. But maybe the points from helping with the gazebo will come in soon.* She wondered to herself.

"I understand. I won't ask for a lot. Seven hundred is the minimum bet here. Do you think you could trust me with seven hundred?"

Seven hundred? That's not a lot to you? Safia struggled to keep a smile as her eyes tightened at the number. *If I lose that, then I'll only have eleven hundred left. I can continue to pay the debt I owe. But what about food? That's three hundred. I won't have that if I lose. What am I going to do then?* Safia thought about the boy who was on the ground, twitching in front of the cafeteria. Then she looked back down into Amanda's gray eyes as they stared back up at her, waiting for an answer. *Oh, I can't believe I'm going to do this. Maybe Hashmi can sneak me out some food for a couple of days if I lose.* "So, only one bet, right?"

"Oh, good. Yes, only one bet," said Amanda with a smile on her face. "I promise just one."

They watched a few more rolls until Ricardo finally appeared through the curtains, and Amanda waved him over.

"Ricardo dear, would you do a roll for us?"

"If you want, I don't mind," said Ricardo, looking over at the dice table. "How many games do you want me to play?"

"Just one, you'll be playing for Safia; I want you to show her what I taught you about games of chance."

"Alright, I shall try to win," said Ricardo as he extended his hand to Safia, "If you would follow me then."

Safia took Ricardo's hand and allowed him to escort her to the front of the dice table as they waited for their turn. Standing directly next to him as he held her hand, she couldn't help but notice how big he was compared to her. Her hands seemed small by comparison. He had wavy hair and by her standards, he was an attractive man. *And he doesn't mind Amanda having control over him. I wonder why.* After a few more rolls, they moved into place.

"Okay, just place your pendant into the slot and hand

me the dice."

Safia did as instructed, placing the pendant into the slot, watching it glow a set of random colors.

"Okay, a minimum bet of seven hundred points has been made," and the man at the table turned towards Safia. "Would you like to raise?"

"Ah, no. Seven hundred is fine."

"Okay, seven hundred it is. Here are your dice," said the man as he handed the dice to Safia.

She took them in her hand, feeling them between her fingers. They felt heavy in her palms as she felt a bit of dread down in the bottom of her stomach as they rolled across her fingers. *Well, I did want to know how to get the points.* She then turned to Ricardo and placed the dice in his hand. "Here you go."

Ricardo placed his hands over Safia's while looking her in the eyes. "I shall try my best, Miss Safia."

Safia smiled and nodded back.

Ricardo then took the dice and turned towards the table. After shaking them a few times, he thrust his hand forward, opening his palms as the dice flew ahead, bouncing across the green-carpeted pit.

To Safia the world seemed to slow down. She could feel the breath leave her lips as she watched the small white cubes bounce off the side of the pit before falling over and landing on three.

"Okay, place your bets. Who here thinks this man can repeat the number, or will he crap out?" asked the game host at the head of the table.

"I think he's going to crap out," said a man ahead of them as he placed his pendant down into the slot, tapping a red button beside it.

"Any other takers?" asked the host of the game, looking over the table. "No? Okay then." They then pulled out a long stick with a flat piece on the end and stretched it forward, pulling the dice back towards them. He then reached down, grabbing them, handing them back to Safia. "Okay, roll again."

Safia took the dice from the host. Now, they felt even heavier than they did before. She took a deep breath, closed her eyes, turned, and held the dice back out towards Ricardo.

Ricardo took them, rattling them around in his hand, and once again flung his wrist, releasing his hand, and the dice went barreling across the pit, bouncing several times before striking the wall. The first dice dropped on a six while the other dice twirled on its axis with the glimmer of another six spinning through Safia's eyes. The second dice finally stopped its teasing spin and dropped, landing on six as Safia bit her lip only to watch the moment the dice tilted over on its side with a two landing face up.

Oh my goodness. I don't think I'm cut out for this. "Doesn't two sixes mean I lose?" asked Safia to the host.

"Indeed, it does, but it seems your gentleman roller here has a fair amount of luck on his side," said the host before turning back to the guests at the table. "Okay, now who here wishes to place a bet as to the odds of our gentlemen roller securing victory or accepting defeat?" Suddenly, five more participants plopped down their pendants and clicked the button on the side. "Okay, that's four against and one in favor." The host once again reached his stick forward, raking the dice back, and placed them in Safia's hand. "I wish you luck," he said with a smile.

Again, the weight of the dice seemed to weigh much more in her fingers, feeling heavier than before. *Please, just get this over with. Am I going to be able to eat tomorrow or not?*

He shook the dice in his hand before flinging his hand over the pit, sending the dice rolling forward again.

Safia could hear the impact of the dice as they hit the pit. Each bounce seemed to match the thumping of her chest as the dice toppled forward. They struck the green wall of the pit once again and collided with each other, the first dice landing on two, and the last die fell over, landing with a single dot facing upward at the crowd.

"And the roller wins," said the host with a clap of the hands and to the moans from the patrons. All except the one who had bet on their win. "The winning pot is thirty-five hundred points split between our two winners."

Wait, thirty-five divided by two. How much is that? Seventeen hundred? No wait, seventeen fifty. That means I have thirty-five hundred now? No, that's not right, seven hundred was my own, so that's twenty-eight hundred. I think. Yes. Wow, that's almost three months of my debt on just one game? Safia turned to Ricardo with eyes wide. "Thank you, thank you so much."

"I'm not sure I'm the one you should be thanking," said Ricardo with a nod towards Amanda, who was smiling back at them.

"Thank you for bringing me here," said Safia, walking back to Amanda, grabbing her hand. "Thank you so much. This helps me more than you know."

"You can always keep playing if you're feeling lucky."

Safia turned back to the table before walking back and grabbing her pendant from the slot and coming back to Amanda, "I don't think I want to push my luck."

"So, you're more of a 'take the money and run type of girl,'" said Amanda with a smile. "Well, don't worry about it. But don't forget you owe me two favors now."

"I won't," said Safia, calming herself down. "But you still haven't told me what you want from me."

"I'm still figuring that out, but I think I'm getting an idea. Come on, then. If you're done here, I can show you the rest of the area."

"Okay."

"Good, but first, Ricardo, come here for a moment," said Amanda, as Ricardo walked over to her. She pulled on Ricardo's collar, making him lean down as she whispered something in his ear.

"Okay, I will see if I can arrange it," said Ricardo.

"You're a capable man. I know you will find a way to convince her," said Amanda as she turned back to see Safia looking at her curiously.

"What was that about?" asked Safia, watching Ricardo walk back through the curtains to the lounge area.

"A secret that may prove useful, depending on how the night goes. We are in the den of the beasts here. It's wise to have multiple bets going at once," she said, wrapping her hands around Safia's.

"Ricardo can place bets for you?"

"Of course, all discarded can place bets in their owners' name. That's why we have to be selective. A vindictive discarded can utterly bankrupt their owner, leaving them both destitute.

"I... I guess that makes sense."

"Now, come along, I wish to enjoy the fruits of this night a little longer."

The two made their way forward as Safia placed her pendant back around her neck, as she watched people gambling at all types of game tables. The atmosphere was somewhat loud as students at many of the tables cheered in joy or whaled in despair after losing. The room really did feel as if it was a casino, with its dark environment being lit up with random colors from dim lights along the wall.

"Did you know that Ricardo was going to win?"

"Of course, I did. What I didn't know was if you would offer your trust to me and allow me to do so. And I must admit, I'm flattered that you entrusted me with your limited number of points."

"How did you know he would win?" *She seems so sure of everything. There has to be a reason she's like this. A trick or something that I'm not understanding.*

"A question I may answer later. But for now, you should just enjoy the sights," said Amanda as she waved her hands around as they moved forward. The girls gazed over at the games the students were playing. Some tables had cards, others had roulette, while one table even had a cube game where people were slowly pulling out small blocks, trying to see who could make the structure fall.

"Are they betting on everything here?" asked Safia, gazing around at the dozens of games the patrons were all playing.

"Is that so odd? You can bet on damn near anything here," said Amanda, looking ahead and shaking her head with a frown on her face. "Just be sure you learn to control yourself, or you'll end up like that poor bastard there." She nodded ahead of them.

Safia's vision followed Amanda's nod to see a disheveled-looking man come around the bar's corner, looking dead-eyed. His shirt was unbuttoned, and hair was a mess. Safia watched as he gritted his teeth with a scowl on his face, his pendant clutched tightly in his hand.

"What's wrong with him?" asked Safia.

"He looks like a poor fool who didn't know the capacity of his bets. It happens from time to time. Humility or self-control are lessons this school will teach you quite fast."

"What are you two looking at?" snapped the man as he came forward, catching them staring at him.

"Now, is that any way to speak to two ladies?" asked Amanda, as the man stepped past them.

"What's that?" asked the man as he turned around, his eyes filled with anger. "Well, I'm sorry, bitches. I'm in a decently bad mood right now. But seeing as you're ladies and all. How about you ladies both suck on my cock to cheer me up a bit?"

Safia and Amanda both grimaced at the man's vulgarity.

"Tell you what," said Amanda, letting go of Safia's arm and stepping forward towards the man. "I am a woman, and you're right. I sometimes do feel the need to please a man. So how about I please you with fifty thousand points? Would that make a big strong man such as yourself feel better?"

"What? What are you on about?" asked the man snarling his lip down at Amanda.

"It's just a fun game for you to play. It's very simple. All you have to do is walk up and rip off the shirts of three men. You do that, and you win fifty thousand points. Unless you think you're not man enough."

"If this is some type of trick, you can just piss off. I'm not in the mood for this bull—"

"Oh, is that not enough? Well, how about this, Mr. Manly Man," said Amanda, taking off her star-shaped pendant and holding it up in the air above her head. "Excuse me. Excuse me, ladies and gentlemen of the evening." She spoke loudly so that her voice disrupted the normal flow of the environment around her. So much so that the patrons at their nearby tables stopped their games and focused on what was happening.

Oh no. I don't think I'm going to like what happens next. Safia looked around nervously at the people as they began to stare at them. *How do I always get myself into these situations?*

"Thank you for your attention," said Amanda as she smiled out at the crowd. "Tonight we are having an impromptu public challenge for your amusement. One that I'm sure will be the talk of the campus come morning." After getting the proper amount of attention from her audience. She pressed on her pendant, making it click. "I, Amanda Chastain, would like to wager the man in front of me fifty thousand points that if he can rip the shirt off Jeffery Hines—"

"What? Don't drag me into this crazy-ass bet of yours," said one of the men at the card's table.

Amanda smirked and continued, "Jericho Andrews, and Ricardo Reigns. That if he can do this within the next hour, I'll let him fuck me for as long as he wants, whenever and wherever he wants for the rest of this week."

The crowd cheered at Amanda's last statement and the men around began shouting encouragement at the man in front of them, riling him up.

"Wooo come on, Gabe, you gonna turn down that bet?" asked a man at the roulette table.

"Dude, I'd rip the shirt off of God for a bet like that," said a man at the card table. "You gonna let this go?"

"Gabriel Howard," spoke the man's pendant as it began flashing red on his shirt pocket. "You have been identified as the recipient of Amanda Chastain's wager. You must accept or refuse the wager, or you will forfeit the right to wager for a month and lose twenty-five thousand points as a penalty."

Gabriel stared down at Amanda, his teeth showing through his lips as he snarled.

Amanda stared back up at him with a grin stretched across her lips. "What now? Are you afraid of both points and pussy?"

"Fuck him," said a man's voice in the crowd. "Let me take that bet."

"Dude, what are you doing?" said another man. "Just rip their shirts—"

"Shut up," shouted Gabriel to the crowd. "It's my damn bet. You all stay out of it." He then turned back to Amanda with a sinister grin on his lips that sent a chill down Safia's spine. "I hope you're ready, bitch. I'll accept your little bet, and when I'm done, I'm gonna strip you down and have the whole school watch what I do to you."

"Oh, is that a promise? Because I do so get tired of hot-aired men who keep writing checks their dicks can't cash."

Gabriel raised his pendant in front of Amanda with a grin on his face and squeezed it till it clicked, "I, Gabriel Howard accept the bet."

"The wager has been accepted," spoke the pendant. "The time limit is one hour."

Gabriel then turned around, "Jeffery, get your ass over here," and made his way towards the cards table.

"Hey, get away, you crazy bastard," said Jeffery as he

stood up from the table, trying to place a chair between himself and Gabriel. "Get back. Get back, damn you."

"Well, congratulations on finding a way to become the center of attention once again, Amanda," said a blonde-haired woman in a pink flowery dress that split down her legs revealing her thighs and pink high heels. "You were always the eccentric type with your bets."

"I'm happy to entertain you, Miranda," said Amanda, turning to greet the woman. "Perhaps you will find a way to repay the favor one day. I have missed your company since you moved on."

Miranda smiled, "Oh you always were the most delicious flirt. But why bet when he has nothing to offer? I can't imagine you need another fifty thousand points." She then turned to Safia. "And who is this beautiful woman beside you? I see your taste in fine women is still intact." The woman gave Safia look up and down, giving a suggestive bit of her lip.

Is everyone obsessed with sex here? Thought Safia as she stared at the woman.

"This charming woman beside me here is my date, Safia. And she is just an acquaintance, nothing more," said Amanda, turning back to Safia with a smirk. "Despite my best attempts to change that."

"Oh, is that so? Well, that is a shame isn't it," said Miranda, extending her hand to Safia. "My name is Miranda, I'm a second year here. Me and Amanda are somewhat acquaintances."

"Hello, I'm Safia Famosa," she said, shaking the woman's hand. "I... ah... I'm a first year here."

"Oh I figured that much, dear," said Miranda , glancing down at the pendant on Safia's neck. "It's quite easy to tell." She then reached to her side, unclipping her own pendant at her side which was in the shape of a small ornate crystal flower. "Don't worry, soon you'll be able to design your own."

Even Safia had to admit it was beautiful. The way the

jewel in the center sparkled in the light reflecting off of the crystal flower petals around it, it looked like a piece of art.

"It's very pretty. How long did it take to make?"

"Around a week for the art boys to whip up. I paid a decent amount of points to have it designed just how I wanted it, but I'd say the results speak for themselves. But I must ask—"

"Just gimme your damn shirt," came a voice over the crowd, interrupting their conversation as the girls turned to see Gabriel wrenching the chair from the man's hands. "Stay still, dammit."

"I'm not giving you anything. I'll call them, I will. So just stay... ahhh!" screamed Jeffery as Gabriel caught hold of his shirt and slung him down on the floor and began ripping at his clothes. It didn't take long before Gabriel had the man bare-chested on the floor as he raised his shirt into the air to the cheers of the crowd. He then pointed the torn clothing in his hand back at Amanda, who was still smiling at him.

"That's one, bitch," the man yelled. "I'm gonna have you begging me to stop when I'm done with you."

Amanda just waved at Gabriel and blew him a kiss as he threw the torn clothing back down on the head of the bare-chested Jeffery and walked off.

"Goodness, you do know how to rile people up, don't you, Amanda," said Miranda, shaking her head disapprovingly at the display. "It's one of your talents I suppose."

"Perhaps, but I just feel it's better to be proactive than to just stand by and wonder what if. Surely there are many missed opportunities in life simply because one chose to be indifferent to a situation rather than make a decision," said Amanda, looking at head. But it seemed as if she wasn't looking at the same display of ridiculousness that Safia had just seen. "He really is much like a version of a knock-off Dario. I wonder if the term 'bitch' is just a part of their upbringing."

To Safia, she began to realize that even though they

stood right next to one another and would spend this night walking hand-in-hand. The world that each of them saw was vastly different.

"Well, if you will excuse us, Miranda. I wish to continue to entertain my date tonight."

"Oh yes, please go ahead. You've already given me and everyone else here a fair bit of entertainment," said Miranda as she turned and began walking back to one of the tables. "You two enjoy the rest of your night."

As Amanda turned and began leading Safia through the room, Safia turned to her. "Why did you do that? What if he—"

Amanda raised a finger, pressing it to Safia's lips. She then placed her pendant before her own lips and clicked on the jewel. "I would like to send a message to Ricardo Reigns."

"Please send your message when ready," spoke the pendant.

Amanda clicked the jewel of the pendant again. "Oh, Ricardo, honey. I just bet some fellow named Gabriel that if he were able to rip the shirt from your body, that he could do all kinds of sexual things to me. Now you know I don't care whom I lay with, but I thought that you might. So, I just wanted to give you a heads up." She then tapped the pendant again and turned towards Safia. "Okay then, shall I continue showing you around?"

"Why did you antagonize him like that? You did the same thing with Dario."

"I told you. Sometimes this school has a way of putting people in their place. Other times, I just have to do it."

"But... But what if he does take Ricardo's shirt?"

"Then, I guess, I belong to him for a time then," said Amanda with her gray eyes that seemed to not care at all about the bet.

I don't understand the people here. How could she just make that bet? How come she acts like she doesn't even care?

"What's wrong, Safia? You aren't speaking?"

"What am I supposed to say after what you just did?"

"I didn't realize it would upset you so much. It's my body. I mean, I understand Ricardo, but why you?"

"Because you're a girl, that's why?"

"We're both women. What? Haven't you had sex before?"

"Yes, but it was with someone I liked. Not someone like him."

"Does it matter who? Sex is just sex. You have it when you feel horny."

Safia just stared at Amanda, who smiled back at her as if everything were just a matter of fact to her. *There's something wrong with all of this. Who acts like this?* She then thought back to Killian's words under the tree earlier that day. *No, that can't be right. She's weird, but she's not crazy.* Safia continued to look down at Amanda. *Is she?*

"Come on, Miss Safia, there's still a few more rooms I wish to show you," said Amanda as she linked her arms in Safia's again.

"Ah, sure, okay," said Safia as she allowed Amanda to escort her, still confused by what was happening. *What the hell have I gotten myself into?* She thought as they went deeper into the lounge area.

"Are you okay, Safia?" asked Amanda, as they continued walking.

"I'm fine. It's just… it just seems a bit extreme for you to make that bet."

"Oh, that. You don't need to worry about that so much. You've seen the way my Ricardo is built, haven't you? I think that was you that day at the fountain. Now, can you really imagine that Gabriel fellow man-handling my Ricardo?"

"No, I guess not," said Safia after thinking about it.

"You poor baby. If that has got you riled up, then we may need to stop here," said Amanda as she watched a man come through the curtains, holding his arm as if in pain. "Because the games of this school can go way beyond simple betting at card tables."

"What do you mean?" asked Safia as the man passed by them, as if in a hurry.

"I expect if you want a taste of what this school is truly like, then you can look through those curtains. They are probably strapping down another set," said Amanda, closing her eyes and shaking her head. "But I do warn you. It's not for the faint of heart."

Safia looked down at Amanda, expecting her to explain, but all the woman did was shrug her shoulders and walk over to a chair at the bar.

"Go on, have a peek inside," said Amanda, as she took a seat and ordered a drink for herself. "I'll just wait out here till you've had enough."

Safia tilted her head at Amanda, but curiosity got the better of her as she stepped inside the curtain into a black room with a few people standing around talking. Ahead of them was a small stage; on which sat two chairs facing each other, with a small podium between them.

"Hello, ladies and gentlemen," said a man with two gentlemen behind him, stepping out of a door leading to a room in the back. He smiled at the crowd while wearing a black two-piece suit with a red bow tie around his neck. Walking up onto the stage with the two chairs, he then stood in front of the podium. In his hand he held a glass bowl that had some type of liquid inside, along with a brush. "Tonight we are given a special treat. It seems we have a discarded battle to witness."

"Oh, now isn't this getting exciting? Who is it?" asked one of the men standing in front.

"Some poor bastards lost all their points. I wonder who they lost them to," said a woman with a smile on her face.

"Well, there's no need to keep you all in suspense," said the man as he turned around. "Come on out, you two."

Soon, a man and a woman wearing their regular student outfits came out of the back and stood beside him.

"These two here, Miss Felanie Gales and Mr. Beliv Bovash, have both lost all their points and gone into the negative while betting The Husband. And instead of being expelled from school, they both have decided to become discarded. But The Husband doesn't like the idea of keeping discarded and instead has thought of a wonderful addition to the game." The man turned around.

The Husband? What kind of name is that?

"So let us get started," said the man as he grabbed the bowl with the brush and walked over to the woman. He then dipped the brush into the liquid in the bowl before removing it and slowly glossing it over on the back of the woman's hand. Then once again on the woman's wrist and twice up her arm. Each time, slowly stroking the brush, letting it graze over her skin as the woman clenched her teeth with closed eyes as he did so. The way her shoulders rubbed against the back of the chair, all jittery, seemed to tell the tale of how afraid she was.

What are they going to do to her? What is that stuff?

"If you gentlemen, would be so kind," said the host as the two men who came in with him walked over to the woman and began using tape on her wrists and ankles to tie her to the chair. The sound of them stretching the tape echoed throughout the enclosed room, even over the voices of the small gathering in front of them.

"Oh, what's happening?" asked a woman at the back of the crowd. "I'm excited. It's been so long since The Husband has done anything."

"And now, for the gentleman," said the host as he walked over, sliding the brush over the arm of the man in the chair, slowly repeating the same process he had performed on the woman. He was then followed by the two men, who proceeded to tape the man's hands and legs to the chair as he placed the bowl back on the podium, stepping towards the crowd. "Now some of you might be wondering what tonight's game is and why our contestants are strapped down to chairs. Well, you see that liquid that was spread over their arms is a reactive agent, harmless if left alone, but when it is given a playmate, it causes a nasty reaction."

"What type of reaction?" asked someone in the crowd.

One of the men walked up to the host, handing him a bowl of white powder that also housed two brushes.

"Now, I'll not bother you with the scientific details," said the host, showing the bowl of white powder to the crowd. "I don't know much about all that sciencey stuff myself. But when this lye powder comes into contact with that liquid. It slowly starts a chemical burning reaction. It makes your skin feel as if it's on fire, and causes an extreme amount of pain, I've been told."

What? Wait, are they going to burn them?

"You all saw that several swaps of the brush were placed along their arms. Now, lye will be placed on each swap every twenty-five seconds until one of our contestants either verbally gives up, screams at the top of their lungs, or passes out from the pain. The one to hold out the longest wins and will be granted ten thousand points and the loser as their very own discarded, to shape and mold to their liking.

Ten thousand? She looked between the two sitting in their chairs, tied down. *But the price... this is too much.*

"Well, now, I heard something special was happening, but this seems like a mess," said a familiar voice.

Safia looked up in a daze next to her to see Jericho beside her, looking ahead at the stage.

"They... is this normal? They just treat people like this?"

"Normal? No, not normal," said Jericho with a shrug. "But not unheard of either. And they aren't treating people like that. Those two have every right to pack up and leave the school. But instead they choose to do this, to stay here."

Safia turned back to the stage, her eyes darting between the host and the two in the chair, full of anxiety. The two men each grabbed pieces of leather and walked over to each, placing the pieces into the man's and woman's mouths.

"A little something for you both to bite down on, to help endure the pain," said the host with a smile.

Is he... are they all enjoying this? Thought Safia as she turned to Jericho, hoping he had some answers. But his face was emotionless. There was no smile, but there also was no shock or repulsion. He seemed to be watching what was about to happen the same way someone would watch an evening sunset. As Safia looked at him, Killian's words once again came back into her mind. And as the lights of the room moved to the stage, shadows changed and crept over, covering half of Jericho's face from her in the dimly lit room.

"So, let's not keep this suspense going any longer," said the host, as one of the two men wheeled out a large drum of water and plopped it down at the side of the stage. The host then turned towards the two men. "Now, if you gentlemen would put on your gloves, I doubt you want to suffer the same fate that these two have chosen to endure."

The two men both pulled out a set of blue gloves from behind them, sliding them on as one man grabbed the lye bowl and placed two brushes inside it. Running their brushes over the lye, each one stepped over, standing by the man and woman.

"I guess the show starts now," said Jericho as he looked ahead to the stage.

"Okay, gentlemen," said the host, with his hands raised in the air. "Please, start."

Both men took the brushes and rubbed the lye over the wrists of the man and the woman at the same time and then stepped back, placing the brushes back into the lye bowl.

Safia watched along with the crowd as the two strapped down in their chairs waited for what was coming. It only took a few seconds before she could see the two begin to squirm in their seats. And that was just enough time for the two men to both walk back with the brushes and once again brush the lye over the skin of their wrists, which seemed as if the pain was now truly setting in. Both began shaking, their chairs rattling as they wormed inside of them. She could see the chairs had been bolted to the stage so they wouldn't tip over. But that didn't stop the sound of the metal bolts clanking against its rivets as they squirmed.

This is insane, thought Safia, looking around. *Someone has to stop this, right?*

The crowd cheered the two on as the shaking of their chairs grew louder. The man began moaning as the veins in his neck began to show. His jaw extended and his teeth ground on the leather in his mouth.

"Hang in there, fella. I have a thousand points riding on you," said one of the spectators with his fist raised in the air.

How could someone bet on this? Thought Safia as she looked back up to Jericho, whose face still showed the same disconnect from the situation as before. It felt to her as if they were both watching two different things. Where she saw a horrible maiming, he looked as if he was staring over a dewy meadow.

"Okay, add another line of lye," said the host.

His voice snapped Safia out of her trance as she turned back to the stage to see the woman strapped down to the chair, staring intently right at her. Her eyes were wide as tears ran down her face and mucus dripped out of her nose. Safia could clearly see the braces on the woman's teeth as she bore them down onto the leather strap between them. Her head was twitching back and forth as she continued to stare at Safia. Her gaze never once wavering as they applied another round of lye. This time to her lower arm.

Both the man and the woman rattled on in their chairs with murmurs and moans escaping from their lips, along with saliva that dripped down their chins. But the woman and Safia kept staring into each other's eyes. Until, finally, the sounds of screaming broke through the cheers as the leather strap dropped from the man's mouth onto his lap.

"And we have a winner," shouted the host, and then Safia saw the two men pull out needles and injected them into the necks of the two and quickly began cutting at the tape that bonded them. Once free, they lifted them up and dragged them over to the drum of water, submerging their arms inside of it.

"Fuck, there goes another thousand points," said a man in the group of spectators as he placed his hand on his head, gripping at his hair.

"Too bad, Peter. Seems you bet on the wrong horse," said the woman next to him.

"How was I supposed to know he'd wimp out so fast? They must have cheated or something. There's no way that girl should have lasted that long."

"You don't value women highly enough, it seems. Any woman here knew who was going to win before it started," said a woman with a hearty laugh.

"Oh, the hell you did."

"I guess that's the end of the show. Did you bet on the woman?" asked Jericho, looking down at Safia.

"What?" asked Safia turning back to Jericho, "No, I didn't, I mean—"

"Really? Then why'd you help her?"

"Help her? I didn't help her."

"She was staring at you the whole time, and you were staring at her. You gave her something to focus on during the pain. I don't expect she would have lasted as long as she did without that."

"She what? I did? I mean... I thought she was looking at me," said Safia, blinking her eyes and shaking her head. "How do you know she wasn't looking at you? It could..." Safia, for the first time, really noticed Jericho. He was standing before her, shirtless. "What? What happened to your clothes?"

Jericho looked over his own body. "Oh, this. Some crazy fool came into the lounge shouting how he was going to rip the shirt off my body. And I didn't feel like fighting him, so I just gave it to him."

"But... I mean..." Safia's words got caught in her throat. She couldn't even think of what to say. She just stared at Jericho, the shadows still partly covering half of his face.

"Come on. The show's over. Let's go get you something to drink," said Jericho as he placed his hand on Safia's waist, escorting her back out through the curtain, into the light of the lounge where Amanda was still sitting on her stool near the door with a drink in her hand.

"Oh! You're back. After I heard the scream, I half expected you to come out of there screaming yourself. But surprisingly, you seem okay. Your eyes are a little watery, though. But I imagine having a half-naked Jericho helped distract you from that showing." Amanda ran her eyes over Jericho's body. "You do have a nice physique, Jericho. Not as nice as Ricardo, but still, you should be proud. All that manual labor you put yourself through building your little trinkets around campus has been paying off, I see." Amanda grabbed a drink from the counter, handing it to Safia, "Drink dear, it'll help calm the nerves."

Safia gladly accepted the drink with both hands, taking the glass to her lips. The taste of lemon and a hint of alcohol was as pleasant a feeling as she could ask for after what she had just witnessed.

"I am a man of the people, after all," said Jericho with a smile.

"Of that I have no doubt. A man to serve the people," said Amanda, placing a bare finger on Jericho's belly button and slowly bringing it up to his chest, stopping her finger just beneath his chin. "But after your service is done, what will you demand from the people in exchange?"

"Survival is all I seek."

"Ah, the most noblest goal of the self-interested. Sadly, one not allocated to all of us," said Amanda, looking back at the curtains. "But we do the best with the hand we're dealt."
286

She then removed herself from her seat. "I do thank you for keeping my date company during that harrowing experience. Unfortunately, I never had the stomach for torture porn." She stepped to the side, locking her arm once again with Safia. "But you seem to have no problem with it."

"A different tolerance for the traumatic, I guess," said Jericho with a smile.

"Oh, I'm sure there's more to it than that. But let's leave this conversation for another time. I wish to continue to show my date around and get her blood going once again."

"Then, I shall leave you two ladies to your adventure of game night," said Jericho as he playfully bowed and turned around, walking away.

Safia watched her shirtless friend walk back off through the lounge before she snapped back to reality and turned to Amanda. "Wait, Jericho. That guy... he took his shirt. What about—"

"Oh my, are you still worried about me? Even after what you just saw in there. You really are a sweet girl, aren't you?" asked Amanda as she took the empty glass from Safia, placing it back on the bar. Turning around, she patted Safia on the hand, then led her back through the gaming lounge.

Safia began to view everyone sitting down at the tables in a new light now. Their smiling faces were just masks that hid intentions she couldn't even begin to fathom.

"Is everyone here like this?"

"Like what?"

"Like that," repeated Safia, turning back to the curtain where the chemically burned couple were surely still passed out.

"You mean insane, morally depraved, masochistic gambling addicts?"

"I... Ah... I didn't mean that you were. I mean, how can they enjoy it so much?"

"Because I assume that's the kind of people this school targets. It's not as if you're seeing the best humanity has to offer here. In fact, an argument can be made that it's probably the opposite."

"But you aren't like that, or Hashmi."

"Am I not? Is she not? Everyone has a secret or two, even Miss Hashmi. And as for myself, there aren't many people on this campus who have more points than I do. How do you think I've amassed such a total? Through my charming personality?"

"But… you don't act like… well, like you enjoy it. And you tried to protect Mallory, that girl that Dario was harassing. Doesn't that kinda make you a good person?"

Amanda laughed. "Oh my, you are entertaining. So, are you under the impression that I am a degenerate gambler with a sense of decency? You might want to take another look around dear Safia and ask yourself why they invited you to this school. For if they've invited the wolves to play, then they have most certainly invited the sheep to lay."

Why are they all here? Why even come to a school like this? Why am I even in a school like this? But if I didn't, would papa be alive? I wonder what everyone is doing at home. I wonder what David is doing. I miss everyone back home.

"But I can see that this does weigh heavy on you. Let's continue our walk to help calm your nerves," said Amanda as they walked through the curtains of another room where people were sitting down on soft futons and listening to music while smoking from pipes. Small amounts of smoke floated up towards the ceiling of the room as they passed.

The other students here were laughing and smiling in their seats. In front of them sat small tubs of water that illuminated in the color of an emerald green. And poking out of the water top sat a weird vase-looking apparatus with two tubes coming out of it. The people on the sofa were inhaling from the pipe and blowing out a greenish smoke in the air, laughing with each other.

"What are those things?"

"We call them downers. Usually, those that have lost too

many points come here to try and relax. I think someone in our science classes made them for points, but that was way before I joined this school. They seem to serve their purpose, though. Would you like to try?"

"Ah, no thanks," said Safia as she waved a bit of smoke away with her hand. She could smell the scent coming from the devices. It smelled of lavender and something else that she couldn't place.

"Shame, they can be quite helpful, even if you just stand around. And to my knowledge, they aren't habit-forming. Tell me, Miss Safia, how old are you?"

"Me? I'm eighteen. Why? Isn't everyone here around my age?"

"Just curious."

"And how old are you?"

"Twenty. The wonderful age before I'm thrust out into a cold, harsh world," said Amanda, leaning down, grabbing hold of one of the tubes, and taking a small breath.

"When you leave this school, what about Ricardo? Do you see yourselves having a relationship outside of this place?"

"You know," said Amanda, blowing out the smoke and dropping the tub back on the tray above the water. "I've never really thought about that. I suppose he would be a good enough partner for me. The man is loyal, and he does encourage me to spend time with other women. So, I suppose he would be an ideal mate. What about you, is there sweet love and babies in your future?"

"I guess, I mean, one day, it would be nice to have children. But not anytime soon, I think David would be a good father."

"Oh, wow. You already know the father's name. You're certainly farther along than I am then."

"Ahh... well." Safia blinked. *Why did I just say that?* She blinked again and felt her eyes starting to water.

"Well, let us continue forward. There are still a few more

rooms for us to explore at tonight's games. I imagine there's even more fun to be had," said Amanda as they slowly made their way through the smoke-filled room.

On the way, Safia saw a dark hallway that led to a back room.

"What's down there?" asked Safia, pointing in its direction.

"Oh, that leads down to the private rooms, usually meant for secret games or where someone falls asleep away from the action for a while. Would you like to see one?"

"No, it's okay. I was just curious, is all."

"Oh, come on, just admit when you want something. It'll make life far less complicated; I assure you," said Amanda, shaking her head and turning Safia towards the dark corridor. "Now come along, you curious cat. Let's go and satisfy that curiosity."

Amanda escorted Safia down the dark corridor. Inside there were no lights in the walkway itself, but instead the lighting came from the rooms they would pass as they made their way deeper into the darkness. The rooms adjacent to it were circular, with red pillowy couches that fit perfectly along its sphere-shaped walls.

Safia couldn't help but glance out the side of her eye at each room as they passed. Some rooms had couples flirting, looking for a secluded space. Others had people eating what appeared to be some type of foreign food, and some just had people sleeping because they were tired. One room they passed surprised Safia as she caught one boy kissing on another boy's chest, as he removed his shirt. One of the boys caught her glance and smiled back at her.

"Well, aren't they active," said Amanda with a smile as she pulled Safia along.

The rest of the rooms were mostly empty, waiting for their future occupants to arrive. They continued farther down until, finally, they could see the end of the corridor, but out of a room ahead of them came a melody, like someone was humming. The melody gave off an unsettling atmosphere to the dark corridor, which slowed the two girls as they stepped forward.

"Who's there providing us with that little melody?" asked Amanda, her voice carrying off the walls.

There was a moment of silence as the humming stopped before another voice was heard.

"And here I thought I had gotten enough away from everyone to enjoy some quiet time alone," said a soft yet familiar voice. There was another pause of silence. "Well, don't be shy. You spoiled my moment, so at least come and show yourselves to me."

Amanda looked at Safia and shrugged. "It is an adventure for you, after all."

The two girls stepped forward towards the end of the corridor and to their right was a single open room, where inside, sitting on a couch, was Champ Champ with her husband, asleep on her lap with his eyes closed. For once, she was wearing a typical school uniform as well as her sleeping husband. Safia noticed that their brown uniforms' accent was black instead of the standard colors she'd seen around campus.

"Well, this is a surprise. Miss Famosa, please come in. And who is that with you? Why, if it isn't Amanda Chastain. You come in as well. It's been so long since we've spoken."

The two girls stepped into the dimly lit room.

"Now tell me, to what random occurrence do I owe this pleasure?" asked Champ Champ as she stroked the hair of her husband. "But do be delicate with your voice; I'd prefer not to wake him."

"I was just giving Miss Safia here a tour of game night. We just so happened to find our way here, is all," said Amanda, stepping more into the room. "I didn't expect to—" Amanda's words paused as she turned to the side with wide eyes. "Oh my, they certainly are active. Aren't they?"

Safia's eyes followed Amanda's attention as she saw a

man and a woman behind glass having sex, their bodies embracing, intermingling as they seemed to moan in the pleasure of each other. Safia took a breath and realized that the people behind the glass were the same couple that had walked naked through the lounge together. Now they were enveloped in their passions for the display of the headmistress and her 'off in dreamland' husband.

"Oh my. Was this the rest of the bet that they lost?" asked Amanda as she leaned down close to the glass, trying to inspect the couple behind it.

"This was indeed the second part of the bet. The first was to be a jolly stroll nude through our gambling garden," said Champ Champ as the man forced his mate against the glass, ravishing her from behind, the side of her face and breasts pressing against the glass. "Oh my, he is a passionate one, isn't he?"

Amanda slid her finger down against the glass where the woman's breasts were pressed against the cheer sheet. "Can they see us?"

"Of course they can. Where would the fun be if they couldn't? I had planned to rouse my husband for the occasion, but I think I'll just let him rest. You two, on the other hand, are welcome to stay and watch if you like. A show like this should be enjoyed with one's friends."

Safia's attention was enveloped in the couple's rapture as the woman's breath created a fog out on the glass. For a small moment she looked over at Safia and smiled before the man turned her around, taking her from the front, pressing her back against the glass. He then kissed her neck before opening his eyes and smiling at the women in the room, placing his hands on the glass, grinding into his partner as he stared intently at them.

"You know," said Amanda, pressing her hand back on the glass where the man's hand was, staring back into his eyes. "I can't tell who's on display here. Them or us."

"Why can't it be both? I've heard that you enjoy a bit of

girl play. Would you and Miss Famosa like to join in as well?"

"What?" asked Safia, snapping back to reality.

"Oh, that sounds like fun!" said Amanda, turning back around, pressing her back against the window with folded arms, looking back at Champ Champ. "But my sexual time is promised to Ricardo, or whoever that was, if he's able to win the bet." Amanda looked up at the single light of the room. "But I'm guessing that it's already been over an hour, it seems he's lost."

"Amanda Chastain has been awarded fifty thousand points," spoke her pendant as it flashed red.

"Speak of the Devil."

"Offering yourself up as a sex toy? And people say that I'm reckless with my bets," said Champ Champ.

"Well, you are the one with The Husband, after all," said Amanda as she looked down at the man with his head on Champ Champ's lap. "How is that working out for you? You've been married almost two years now."

"Humm," moaned Champ Champ as she leaned down, kissing her husband on the forehead. "It has its ups and downs like any relationship. But a little toil and turmoil are part of any healthy relationship, I suppose."

"Well, since we're talking about up and downs, what's your sex life like? Surely with such a small stature, it can't be the most comfortable thing with that oversized man of yours."

Champ Champ looked at Amanda with a smirk on her face, "Oh, are we betting on this information?"

"No. Given the moment we're in, I'd like to think of this as just girl talk between friends. I, myself, am five-three. How tall are you, Safia?"

"Me, ahh, I'm five-six."

"See, now we're all sharing. Join in, Miss Headmistress. Don't leave your friends out in the cold."

"I'm four-eleven, but I guess one could tell that by just looking. And if you must know, my husband has been very gentle with me. Although sometimes, I'd prefer it if he were a little rougher. Perhaps, after more time together, I can get him to be a little more aggressive during our couplings." Champ Champ tilted her head at Amanda. "And what of you Amanda, how does that toy of yours, Ricardo, play with you at night? Since we're sharing our intimate stories."

"Oh, much the same as the two behind me here, I suppose," said Amanda, lifting a thumb back up at the glass behind her as the couple continued to enjoy each other for their entertainment. "Although, he squeezes my breasts a little too hard. So, don't feel too bad, little Champ Champ. You may be smaller than I am in size, but at least your breasts seem to be bigger than mine. So, God compensates in different ways." Amanda then turned to Safia, looking down at her breasts through her revealing outfit. "Although sometimes God can be a bit unfair when handing out his gifts."

"Agreed," said Champ Champ, also looking at Safia's chest. "Perhaps, it's more to do with that heritage of hers. African and Latin blood has been known to create wonderful specimens of beauty. They often pride themselves on their curves. I believe they even have a song from the past that praises big butts. It was supposedly from a man that could not lie."

Safia self-consciously brought her coat down over her chest in an effort to shield herself from their eyes.

"Come now, Miss Safia. We've shared with you our intimate details. I do believe it's fair that we ask from you the same as what we've shared. Now, tell us. I do remember hearing the story of you and the meat truck when we had you vetted, so no use playing the virgin card here."

"Meat truck?" asked Amanda, giving Safia a curious look.

"Is… is he really asleep?" asked Safia, looking down at The Husband and ignoring Amanda's sudden interest.

"Dead to the world," said Champ Champ. "When he's

like this, it takes quite a lot to rouse him."

"And you promise not to laugh?"

"Oh, please, Miss Safia. Between my small stature and my husband's six-three height, which I'm sure brings into question any pedophilic tendencies he may have. And Amanda's questionable A-sexual or Bi-sexual nature, of which, I'm not even sure she knows the answer to anymore. What could there possibly be to laugh about? Trust and believe that you and your meat truck fetish are safe amongst us."

There was a rumble against the glass as the couple redoubled their efforts.

"And that glass is soundproof," said Amanda, "So no worries there."

"So come, Safia, share with the group."

Safia took a moment to herself before she looked into the faces of the ladies and took a deep breath. *Okay, it doesn't look like I'm going to escape this, so here goes. It's not like there's nothing to be ashamed over. It's just... well...* "I like sexual dominance."

Another small moment of silence passed as the girl processed what they heard. "What do you mean?" asked Champ Champ. "You mean you like to be spanked. I hardly think that's such a—"

"No, it's more about being in control. Even with my boyfriend, ex-boyfriend. The one in the meat truck. I get off on forcing myself on him to the point where he can't resist me. Especially when he's tired and can't fight back. The less power he has, I feel, the more power I have. I want to tie him down and force his dick to get hard and ride him until he begs me to stop. That's one of the few ways I feel powerful."

"A true dominatrix then," said Champ Champ with pursed lips. "While something I haven't dabbled in myself, it is something I have witnessed. Tell me, have you ever tried the whip and chains stuff like they show in those movies?"

"No. I want to try those things, but I haven't yet. There was this on time, but I think I went to far and caused us too break up."

"I'm fairly curious as to what 'a bit too far' means to you. But I won't pry anymore since if that's the reason you lost a lover, it might open up old wounds."

"Thank you."

"But, other than that, don't you feel better sharing that with us, getting that proverbial weight off your chest? Tell me, have you also shared this information with that roommate of yours? What's her name? The Muslim girl, Margaretto, I think."

"What? No? You can't tell her," said Safia quickly, her voice in a panic.

"Relax, Miss Safia. You're amongst kinky freaky friends here," said Champ Champ, trying to reassure Safia. "Your secret is safe with us. Well, safe with me anyway. I think you've just given Amanda a few ideas, and given her passion for both males and females, you might not be safe yourself."

"Don't worry about me. I know how to behave myself," said Amanda with a smirk. "Although, I may ask you to give me a few pointers, as some things I might like to try out with Ricardo."

"And it's not such a crazy secret, really," said Champ Champ as she stroked her husband's hair. "I mean, look where we are. We're discussing this topic while a woman and her discarded plow each other behind Amanda's back. Surely, this conversation is in the presence of the right company."

Amanda turned around to see the woman laying down on top of the man breathing heavily and kissing his chest. "Oh, look, they're done. Perhaps I should have given them more of my attention."

"At this point, I don't think they much care," said Champ Champ, leaning forward, looking at the two behind the glass. "And I have enjoyed our little conversation. Rarely do

I get to speak so openly with girls without some type of bet on the line. It has been a refreshing experience."

"Does that mean we're friends now? I'm touched."

Champ Champ giggled, "Hardly. Perhaps if Miss Safia can survive this next year and a half, then perhaps we shall be friends. But for you and I, Amanda, I'm afraid friendship is something that you and I shall never have."

"Still haven't forgiven me?"

"Some wounds were never meant to heal, I suppose."

A moment of awkward silence hung in the air between the two women as they stared at each other.

"Well, I guess that's enough girl talk for now, and the night is coming to a close for me," said Amanda as she walked back over to Safia, locking arms with her once again. "Come along, Miss Safia. The night has one final surprise in store. We can leave the head mistress here to bask in the afterglow of her entertainment."

"I shall see you both back above ground then. Do enjoy the rest of your evening," said Champ Champ as Safia and Amanda left the room and headed back down the dark corridor.

"Well, that was certainly a fun time," said Amanda, with a smile on her face. "And we got to learn a bit more about each other. So, what do you say we head back upstairs? I think the night is pretty much over now."

"Okay, thank you for showing me everything."

"You're welcome, although one has to wonder how that sweet side of yours hides a dominatrix inside. Tell me, does it only get turned on when you're around men?"

Safia pursed her lips, trying not to think about the uncomfortable question as they made their way back through the smoke-filled room. Everyone was still on their pillowy seats, huffing from their devices. Safia rubbed at her eyes again, trying to blink away the small amount of smoke as it stung at her eyes. Through the curtains and up past the gambling room, they went until they were finally at the steps that would lead them back outside.

"Tall ladies first," said Amanda, as she stepped to the side with her hands on the rail.

Safia smiled. "I'm not that tall. Perhaps you are just short."

"Perhaps I am, but I think that's a judgment only the tall can make."

Safia made her way up the steps, back into the cabin. The door to the outside was open, and as she stepped up, she saw a man lying against the wall, asleep. She stopped at the top step. Blinking, she looked closer to see it was the man from below. The one who made the bet to rip off Jericho's shirt. He now had a black eye, a busted lip, and his clothing had been ripped apart.

"What happened?"

"What do you mean?" asked Amanda as she made her way up behind Safia. "Oh, my," she said, looking at the battered man. "Poor Gabriel certainly has been put through the ringer, hasn't he? Even if he did win the bet, I doubt he'd have been in any shape to claim his prize."

"What happened to him?"

"Have you forgotten already? This man was supposed to rip the shirt off three people. Can you remember who?"

Safia thought back to her time in the game lounge. "Jericho, and some other guy, and." Her eyes went wide as she looked around the cabin, but didn't see anyone else.

"It seems my Ricardo protected his maiden's virtue. How sweet of him," said Amanda as she finished making her way up the steps. "Come on. I think my hero is waiting for us outside." Amanda walked out of the door, looking around. "Ricardo, are you out here?"

"I'm here," said Ricardo's voice from outside the shack. "You really are a handful, sending that guy after me like that."

"Well, technically, he was after me. You were just a proxy."

"Do you intend to keep causing me trouble?" asked Ricardo as he wrapped his arms around Amanda.

"I do. Now shush and kiss me. This has been a wonderful night and I don't want the sight of that ugly man to ruin it."

Safia slowly stepped outside into the night air to see Amanda with her arms wrapped around Ricardo's neck, with her lips pressed against his.

"Oh, she came out," said Amanda. "Now tell me, Ricardo, were you able to secure everything?"

"I did," said Ricardo, turning toward the side of the shed. "Addison, are you ready?"

"Yeah, I'm ready. Let's get this over with," said Addison as she came around the corner, holding her violin.

"And here I always thought the violin was for the refined and the modest. But you seem to be anything but," said Amanda, looking over at Addison.

"Yeah, well, my father also thought the same. He had me learn this shit, thinking it'd make me a prim and proper lady. It didn't take him long before he realized he fucked up. But he made me stick it out. So here I am, and as long as you're paying, I'll be your little violin bitch tonight."

"One truly has to wonder how so much vulgarity can come out of such a pretty face."

Addison pointed the bow of her violin at Amanda. "If you want me to prance around this place like you do, then you ain't paying me enough for that."

"Well, there's something to be said for the direct and to the point type of people. I guess, I can't fault her for that," said Amanda, walking over to Safia. "Okay, it's time for you to pay back those favors."

Safia looked over at Addison and then around her environment. There was nothing here. Just the lake and the grass. "What do you want me to do?"

"Just come alone with me, is all," said Amanda, reaching out her hand.

Safia allowed the woman to guide her down towards the

lake. The wet grass tickled at the spaces between her shoes, sliding against her ankles as they got closer to the water. Safia could see the calm waters that held the reflection of a million stars that shone above their heads.

"It's beautiful. Is this what you wanted to show me?"

"It's part of it," said Amanda as she walked Safia down along the pier. "But for the next part, you might want to remove your shoes."

"Why?" asked Safia as they reached the edge of the pier, overlooking the starlit lake.

"This lake actually has a trick to it," said Amanda as she leaned over, lifted her leg, and began removing her footwear. "But not many here know about it since it only happens at night." She then placed her foot down in the water.

Safia could only stare as Amanda took a step down onto the lake, then slowly another step, her feet creating ripples in the star reflected waters.

"Would you care to join me," said Amanda as she turned around with her hands spread out. "All you have to do is believe."

Safia glanced over the water once more before she slid her feet out of her shoes. She then took a deep breath, closing her eyes, stepping to the end of the pier. Slowly, she dipped her right toe into the water, feeling a cool sensation wrap itself around the back of her foot, sending a shiver up her spine. But inside that coldness, she felt it; something solid just beneath. She released her hesitation, stepping down with both feet to the surface of the lake.

"This is beautiful," said Safia with her arms outstretched as she playfully made her way towards Amanda, water flowing between her toes and splashing at the base of her ankles as she did so.

"I'm happy to see you're finally enjoying yourself," said Amanda as she took Safia's hand, escorting her to the middle of the lake. "I've always wanted to dance amongst the twilight, and this seems to be a perfect chance." Amanda nodded to Ricardo, who was on the lake's bank, watching them with Addison at his side.

"Why are... oh," said Safia as she began to hear the sounds of the violin playing from across the water. A soothing melody that whispered in her ears.

"Would you care to dance?"

"And this is the second favor, then?"

"It is."

"Then, how can I refuse after you treated me to such a night?" asked Safia as she stepped closer to Amanda, grabbing her hand.

"You can't," said Amanda as she also stepped towards Safia, placing her hand over her hips as they began to sway, their feet gliding across the water as they moved in step to each other. And there, in the darkness, illuminated by the moon and stars above, the two began to dance on a sea of stars.

"All of this is probably the most beautiful thing I've ever been a part of. Can I ask why you picked me for tonight? I think you could have had anyone else as your partner if you wanted."

"What's that?" asked Amanda with a smile as they swayed. "You no longer enjoy my company now that you've found the secret for me making my points?"

"No, it's not that. It's just everyone here just seems to live by their own rules. Wait, about before, how did you know Ricardo would win the dice roll?"

"Oh, yes, that. It's because I had Ricardo switch the dice after you gave them to him."

"You what?"

"A bit of the sleight of hand. I must admit Ricardo has gotten quite good at it."

"But... what if they find out?"

"Who's going to tell? Certainly not I, and I imagine not you. Only a fool would admit to cheating at a game unless they have something else to gain." Amanda tightened her arms around Safia's waist, pulling her nearer as they moved together. The sound of flowing water between their feet. "No, sweet Safia, our secret is just between you, me, Ricardo over there, and the stars around us."

Safia sighed, "Thank you, but even though we're standing here, this probably isn't the proper time to tell you that I'm not exactly into girls," said Safia as she allowed Amanda to place her head against her breast and then continue to sway to the music. "Wait, aren't you supposed to lead the dance?"

"You're taller than me, and for once, I'd like it if someone else took the lead for a time. Being in charge has left me wearier than I'd like to admit," said Amanda, breathing in deep and keeping her hands wrapped around Safia's waist. "Tell me, Safia, do you regret coming here?"

"I don't think I have a right to regret that anymore," said Safia as she looked up at the stars. "For better or worse, this place has changed my life. Or should I say it saved it?"

"Saved your life? It sounds like you have some secrets of your own."

Why did I just say that? Safia blinked, confused at what she was saying. "I... ahh, I mean..."

"Don't worry. We all have our secrets here. You don't have to tell me anything if you don't want to."

"Thank you. It's just... it's private. You know."

"Oh, trust me, I'm well aware. This school is filled with secrets. And not just that of the students. A campus in the middle of nowhere, gathering people from all over the world. There has to be a reason behind it. And bringing up the next generation of trust fund kids isn't their whole plan."

"What do you mean?"

"Remember when you noticed those cameras downstairs? Always watching, always looking. And then there's that weird chip implanted in our backs. It makes you wonder who's really behind those cameras."

"If that's the case, should you be talking about it like that? They could be listening."

Amanda laughed. "Oh, I'm sure they are. But this place has been around long before I got here and will be here long after I'm gone. I'll play their little game as long as it means I get what I want."

"Why are you here? What do you want? It's okay if you don't want to tell me. I was just curious, is all."

Amanda stopped dancing and stood looking up into Safia's eyes. "Kiss Me."

"What?"

"It's the final favor I want from you. I want you to kiss me under the stars as we stand here at this moment."

Safia looked down at Amanda. She could see the reflection of the stars in her eyes as she gazed back up at her.

I guess I can pretend she's a shorter version of David, thought Safia as she raised her hands, placing them at the sides of Amanda's face. "Close your eyes."

"But I want—"

"Close your eyes," said Safia in an authoritative tone. "You said you wanted me to take the lead. Now close your eyes."

Amanda frowned, but did as instructed and closed her eyes.

Safia began to stroke the side of Amanda's face, allowing her fingers to gently rub under her eyes and over to her ears. Then over to the top of her temples, grazing over the strands that had come loose from her tied back hair. She felt Amanda begin to tremble a bit in her arms. Whether it was from nervousness or anticipation, she didn't know. But it didn't matter. She was receiving the desired effect.

"Wha... What are you—" asked Amanda with a nervous chuckle before Safia placed her finger over her lips to silence her.

"Shush," said Safia as she teased her index finger across the top of Amanda's lips, feeling her breath flow across her skin as she exhaled. "I'm remembering you. You said before that you didn't want to be forgotten. So, I'm taking my time at this moment to see you. To see your short brown hair, your sharp cheekbones," Safia leaned down, kissing Amanda below her cheek. "The small brown mark beneath your right ear." She moved her lips over to Amanda's neck, kissing her once again exactly where the mark was, and brought her lips up to nibble just slightly on her earlobe, which caused Amanda to gasp and clench her.

"Humm," moaned Amanda as she tried to control her body from shaking.

"You are beautiful, Amanda, and I will forever remember you."

"Thank you," said Amanda as a tear escaped from her eye, only for Safia to catch it on her thumb before sliding it away.

Safia then slid that same thumb down to Amanda's chin and further down to her jacket and undid the one button holding it together. Sliding her hand inside around Amanda's waist, she pulled her into her so that she could feel the warmth of their bodies beneath the thin fabric between them. And it was here that Safia could truly feel the trembling that Amanda was trying to hold back as their bodies pressed against one another.

Then Safia lowered her head so that her lips just barely pressed against Amanda's. Just enough so that she could feel the ridges of their skin, teasing what was to come but not giving it to her.

Amanda's body unconsciously tried to push her face forward, desiring the intimacy.

As Safia pulled back, still teasing the shorter woman with what her body was craving until Amanda was on her toes, her lips trembling, and her breath quickening.

Only then did Safia allow satisfaction to come as she sunk her lips onto Amanda's with such passionate force that drove her bare feet back down into the cold water as their lips pressed hard against one another. Amanda took a deep breath of satisfaction as the kiss filled her world and her need in an explosion of passion and pleasure.

And there, the two shared a kiss surrounded by the stars above and the stars below that rippled through the bodies as well as the water beneath them. A moment that felt as if it would last forever, but passed in an instant as Safia slowly pulled her lips away from Amanda's and stared down into her now watery gray eyes.

"Was that the kiss you wanted?" asked Safia with a loving smile on her face.

Amanda's breath shuttered as she tried to regain her composure. "I... I think... you would make a wonderful dominatrix. I don't think I'll ever kiss a woman like that again."

Safia rubbed the side of Amanda's face. "So, what now?"

"Now," said Amanda, taking another deep breath and stepping back from Safia composing herself, then grabbing her hand. "Now, our night is over. Come on, let's head back," she said as the violinist stopped her melody. They made their way to the pier and onto the grass, grabbing their shoes on the way.

"Did you enjoy yourself?" asked Ricardo with a smile.

"I did," said Amanda, walking over and grabbing Ricardo's hand and turning back for Safia. "Safia dear, I thank you for a wonderful night. But now, seeing as it has ended, Ricardo and I here have some urgent business to attend to."

"We do?" asked Ricardo, looking puzzled.

"Yes, we very much do. Please, see yourself safely back home," said Amanda as she quickly turned and walked back off toward the school, dragging Ricardo along with her.

"Wow," said Addison, walking up behind Safia, "I think she's in heat."

Safia frowned back at Addison.

"What? I didn't even curse that time."

Safia shook her head. "I'm feeling tired. I'll head back now too."

"Can't blame you there. I'm surprised you're even awake now after taking a puff from the smoke room."

"The what?"

"The smoke room. I saw you and Amanda go inside. You know the room with the tubs of water where people were smoking from the pipes."

"But I didn't smoke from the pipes."

"But you were in that room, right? All it takes is a minute or two in there, and you'll start to feel it. Most people can barely stay in there a half an hour before they're passed out."

Safia blinked, trying to think back. *Wait, is that why I told them about David? I mean, that's not why I kissed Amanda, is it? No, I wasn't in there that long, and I was paying her back. Yeah, I'm not high or anything.*

"What? You mean you didn't know? Even Amanda knew. She's probably just used to it more than you. Even your eyes are all puffy. How could you not... didn't you feel anything? Wow, you're a dummy."

Safia frowned at Addison again. "I... I need to go for a walk."

"Yeah, that'll probably help clear your head a bit."

Safia began to walk off towards the dorm.

"Hey, don't forget your shoes."

She turned back, picked up her shoes, and made her way towards the walkways. Walking through the campus, the coolness of the concrete against her bare feet provided her with the stimulation to keep herself focused on the path ahead. *Am I high? I don't think I'm high. Maybe I'm tired. But that's normal. I mean, it's nighttime. Why wouldn't I be tired? Yeah, I'm fine. I kissed her because she gave me points. How many points was it? Two? Four? I don't even remember. I'm too tired.* She glanced down to her side in an attempt to reach into her bag for her tablet device, only to realize that the objects in her hand were her shoes and not her school bag. *Okay, yeah. I probably should just head back and lie down.* She then turned towards Yennefer house. *Hashmi is probably going to—.*

"Stop, let me go. I said I'm sorry," said a voice as two shadowy figures approached out of the darkness ahead of her.

"You keep costing me points. Every time, every damn time. Fucking useless, bitch." And then came a slapping sound through the night air.

Safia suddenly dropped her shoes from her hands and found her pace quickening, and her anger growing as she recognized the voice from the shadows. It didn't take her long following the sound of their argument before she saw the face of Dario standing over Mallory, who was hunched over on the ground, covering her face.

"Hey, stop that," said Safia as she made her way towards them, stepping between Mallory and Dario. "Leave her alone," she said, with her hands outstretched, blocking Dario from putting his hands on Mallory again.

"Who the hell are you?"

"Leave her alone."

"Get out of the way. She belongs to me."

"Not anymore, you're going to leave her alone," said Safia, noticing Dario's weary eyes.

"Or what, what are you going to do? Nothing, because this ain't your business."

Safia was silent.

"Exactly, so just move out of the way and go back to wherever you came from," said Dario before looking over Safia in her dress. "Unless you wanna take her place. Never had me a black bitch before."

Safia grit her teeth, looking around, seeing one of the walkway lamps nearby, and closed her eyes.

Dario pursed his lips, nodding his head. "So come on, you wanna be my little toy for the night? You do that, and I'll loan her out to you for a week."

"Dario, stop," said Mallory, still rubbing her cheek. "Look, Miss, it's fine, really. I struck him first. So, it's my fault.."

"You shut up," yelled Safia, turning her head back around to Mallory. "You don't get a say in this. So just stay down there."

"Woah," said Dario laughing. "This one's got some fire, but you're right. She needs to be told what to do. Otherwise, she's just useless and a bunch of bad luck." Dario placed his finger on Safia's chin. "But you, I might enjoy actually telling you what to do."

Safia exhaled and looked at Dario with narrowed eyes. "And you'll give me what I want?"

He brought his finger down into the side of her dress and pulled it slightly away from her chest, looking down at Safia's breast. "Depends on what you want and what you're willing to do to get it. Wanna make a trade? A night with you for a week with her."

Safia felt the stinging feeling of the adhesive that she placed on her breast beforehand as it was peeled away. "A night with me?" She asked as a smile crept over her lips. "Are you sure that's enough for you?" She reached towards her chest, opening up her coat so Dario could get a better look at the revealing outfit Amanda had given her.

"Now that's what I like, a woman willing to work for what she wants. At least I'll get more out of you than the useless trash behind you," said Dario as he stepped forward, placing his hands firmly on Safia's waist, slowly moving it up through the fabric till he cupped her breast in his hand.

Safia felt disgusted as Dario's hand moved over her body, but kept a seductive grin on her face. "I suppose a trade like that can be made, but what If I want her for more than a week? What are we going to do then?"

"Oh, well, I might be willing to extend our arrangement if you're willing to be a good girl and do what I tell you," said

Dario, as he squeezed her breast.

Safia gasped and smiled. "Oh aren't you an aggressive boy," she said as she leaned back shyly, placing her hand behind her back. "Are you going to teach me how to be a good girl?"

Dario reached into his back pocket and pulled out his pendant. "All deals are final. One night with me, and the bitch is yours for a week." He then let go of her breast and wrapped his arm around her waist, pulling Safia into him. "Oh, I'm going to teach more than you can imagine."

"Then show me how you're going to make me behave," said Safia, grabbing at the pendant at her neck and lifting it above her head. "Or do you think I'm too much for you to play with?"

"Oh, you smart bitch," said Dario with a smile, before grabbing the back of Safia's hair tightly so she couldn't move and pulling her to him, aggressively planting his lips on hers. The two kissed; Safia tasting the slight flavor of alcohol before turning her face to the left and biting down hard on Dario's bottom lip, hard enough that it drew blood.

"Argh," growled Dario as he struggled to push Safia off of him as she wrapped her hand around his neck. But using more of his strength, he got her off of him as she smiled back at him. "You, bitch," said Dario as he raised his hands to his lip and then to his eyes, seeing the blood.

"What's wrong, Dario? Not enough? I thought you were going to make me behave."

Dario's eyes went wide with rage as he drew his hand back with his pendant and swung forward, slapping Safia so hard that it sent her tumbling off the concrete walkway down to the grass beside Mallory.

"You're going to pay for that."

Safia's world went white as she felt the pain from Dario's blow.

"Dario stop!" shouted Mallory.

Safia placed her hand on Mallory's shoulder for stability

before turning back to Dario with a smile. "No, it's you who's going to pay now, Dario." She blinked through the pain in her cheek and saw she still had her pendant in her hand. She apparently gripped it so hard when she fell that the edges pierced the skin of her hand, drawing blood. She clicked the pendant, making it flash red. "Help, I'm being attacked. Someone is trying to hurt me."

"Report of an attack filed, physical trauma detected on Safia Famosa," spoke the pedant. "Who is attacking you? Repeat who is attacking you."

Dario's face went white. "You bitch, you set me up."

"I repeat. Who is attacking you? There are two signals near you. Dario Burrows and Mallory Polana. Is it one of them?"

"I did no such thing," said Safia, spitting blood from her lip onto the ground. "But if you send Mallory back home, then I promise the next day your ass will be sent home right along with her."

Dario laughed. "You've still got no proof, and I'm bleeding the same as you. Who's to say you didn't assault me?"

Safia pointed down a little away from them. "That streetlamp has a camera in there, and I bet it got a nice view of you slapping two poor girls down to the ground. She won't report you, but I damn sure will. And the way you just grabbed me and forced yourself on me. How are you going to explain that, little dick, Dario?"

"We're sending someone to your location now," spoke the pendant.

"You like betting? Then, make your fuckin bet. You think they won't expel your ass the moment they look at that footage?"

Dario looked up to the streetlight and saw one of its cameras looking down at him.

"You won't get in trouble if I don't report it, right?" asked Safia with a smile across her face, as she rubbed the side of her lip with the back of her hand. "Well, fuck off and leave us alone. Otherwise, go home and explain to mommy and daddy why their bitch ass son got expelled for beating up on two girls. I'm sure that'll go over well."

Dario stared down at the two girls on the ground beneath him. "Go on, keep her. I was done with her ass, anyway. But you, I'm not done with you. If you think you can just fuck with me and get away with it. I'm going to show you what happens to those who cross me." He then turned and ran off into the shadowy night of the campus, appearing in and out of view as he passed more of the streetlights in the distance.

Safia then looked over at Mallory, who was staring at her. "Are you okay?"

"Why... why did you do that? You don't even know me."

"I did it because he's an ass."

"Miss Famosa, Miss Famosa," came a voice, shouting her name into the darkness. "Safia Famosa, are you there?"

"I'm here," yelled Safia into the shadows as three men appeared. Two of the men, she didn't recognize, were heading towards her, one having her shoes in his hand and the other man she recognized as Derrick, from when she was first brought to the school. He was still wearing his usual suit, although this time, he seemed a little out of breath.

"Are you okay? Do you know who did this?" asked Derrick, kneeling beside the two women. The other man placed her shoes beside her as he began to look around the area.

"No, it's fine," said Safia, reaching out her hand. "Can you help me up?"

"Of course," said Derrick, grabbing her arms, pulling her up, and noticing the streetlamp nearby. "If you give us permission, we can have a look at the tapes and..."

"No, it's fine," said Safia, standing up. The impact from Dario's blow making her feet feel shaky under her. "It's... it's taken care of now."

"What? Are you sure?"

"Yes, it's been taken care of. I think."

"Okay, if you say so. What about you?" asked Derrick, looking over to Mallory as the two other men helped her up. "Do you wish to report what happened?"

"Ah, no," said Mallory, looking down at the ground. "Everything is fine now. I... I should be heading back."

"No, you're coming with me," said Safia, "I didn't get the shit slapped out of me, so you could just start all this back up again tomorrow."

"What? But... but I can't just not... And I didn't ask for you—"

"Derrick," said Safia, turning her back to Mallory. "I think I will ask you to look at those tapes after all."

"No!" shouted Mallory, but calmed her voice when the men turned to stare at her. "I mean, you're right. I'll do as you say."

"Well, then," said Safia, pulling her short coat together, covering her revealing outfit. "Thank you, Derrick. You helped us out a lot, but if you will excuse me. My new friend Miss Mallory and I should be heading in for the night."

"Right, I guess as long as you're okay," said Derrick, looking around into the darkness. "Would you like one of us to accompany you to your dorm?"

"No, it's okay. I doubt anything else will happen tonight." *I mean, what else could happen tonight?*

"One thousand points have been deducted from your account," spoke the pendant in Safia's hand as it flashed red.

Of course it has, thought Safia with a sigh as she stepped her bare feet back onto the cold walkway, extending her hand to Mallory. "Let's go, new friend. We're heading home."

Mallory looked around as the three men stared at her, then stepped back on the walkway, grabbing Safia's hand. "Yes, ma'am."

The two women walked off into the darkness, heading toward Yennefer house. It didn't take them long until they were at the steps and upstairs, standing before Safia's door room.

"Hashmi, are you awake?" asked Safia with a knock.

"Oh, you're back," came Hashmi's voice from inside the room.

Safia opened the door to see Hashmi lying in bed with a book in her hand, her long hair draped over her shoulder. "I've brought company. Mind if she comes in for a while?"

"Sure, it's a girl, right? Then that's—," Hashmi gasped, hopping out of bed in her pajamas after seeing Safia's face and the dirt on the side of her coat. "What happened?"

Safia stood to the side, pulling in Mallory by the arm. She looked just as worse off as Safia as she also had dirt on the side of her face and clothing.

"Who... what happened to both of you? You're covered in dirt and your lip is bleeding," said Hashmi, looking over the two. "Who is she?"

"She was Dario's discarded, now she's my discarded. Her name's Mallory."

"But... what... Dario?" muttered Hashmi, trying to understand what was happening.

"Mallory, grab my bathing items from the closet. We're going to go wash up."

"Ah... yes, ma'am," said Mallory as she stepped into the room.

"I'm going to have Mallory stay with us from now on."

"From now on?" asked Hashmi, looking around the room. "Where's she going to sleep? There's only two beds?"

"On the floor, by my bed," said Safia, looking over at Mallory. "It's on the top shelf, the one in the blue tub. Yes, that's it."

"The floor? Doesn't she have her own room?" asked Hashmi, looking over at the girl and noticing the yellow of her uniform. "Is that even allowed? I mean, isn't she from another house?"

"Mallory, the washroom is down the hall. Go down there and wait for me," said Safia, standing aside from the door for her to pass.

"Yes, ma'am," said Mallory as she walked between Safia and Hashmi out of the door and down the hallway.

When Mallory had left, Safia closed the door behind her. Then Slumping her shoulders, she fell back against the wall.

"Safia, are you okay?" asked Hashmi as she knelt, catching her friend in her arms.

"No, this night has been too much. Apparently, I'm on some type of drugs, or I was on them. I don't know anymore. And I got the taste of blood and that damn Dario in my mouth. And, on top of all that, I got myself even more responsibility than I need, and now I have to take care of Mallory."

"Taste of Dario? What? I mean, why is she here? What happened?"

"Too damned much," said Safia, looking up at her friend. "Hashmi, I'll explain everything tomorrow. But for tonight, can you just play along?"

"Play along? Play along with what?"

Safia stabilized herself on her feet and took a deep breath. "Just let her stay with us for a while. I'll find a way out of this."

Hashmi looked at the blood on the side of Safia's lip and closed her eyes for a second, nodding her head. "And you're going to explain this to me tomorrow?"

"I will."

"Fine, I'll wait till tomorrow. And she can stay here for tonight."

Safia wrapped her arms around Hashmi. "Thank you." She then straightened up, taking another deep breath trying to stop her hands from shaking. "Do I look okay?

"No! Not at all. You look an absolute mess."

"Then, let's hope she doesn't notice," said Safia before she turned around, and opened up the door out into the hallway, making her way down to the washroom.

CHAPTER 14

Early the next morning, Safia lay in bed half-asleep. Against her back, she felt something warm and comforting. As her senses slowly came to her, an arm wrapped slowly around her waist. Their hands roamed under her pajama top, rubbing the skin just beneath her breasts. She smiled, turning over, snuggling against them. Soon, she felt the welcoming embrace of her lips pressing against his. A soft, warm, and passionate kiss that reminded her of David.

Wait! David?

Safia opened her eyes to see Mallory looking back at her in her bed. Her eyes went wide as Mallory once again pressed her hand under her clothing, sliding her hand up her top and over her breast as her finger brushed across her nipple. Panicking, Safia pushed herself away, but she was on the wrong side of the bed and went falling to the floor.

"Miss Safia, are you okay?" asked Mallory as she leaned over the bed, looking down at Safia with a panicked voice.

Safia grabbed the back of her head in pain. "Am I okay? What do you think you were doing?"

"I was making you feel better. Isn't that what you want?"

"What I want? What are you talking about?" she said as she rubbed the back of her head, squinting, trying to stop the tears from coming. Slowly she raised herself to look at Mallory, who was looking back at her with genuine confusion.

"Yes, I mean. Isn't this why you did what you did? That's why you took me from Dario."

"What?"

Mallory slipped out of bed, and Safia realized she was topless. "I don't mind, I mean. I just don't want you to send me back. And you're already a lot nicer to me than Dario was." Mallory stepped closer, and Safia stepped back till she bumped against Hashmi's bed. Turning around, she realized Hashmi was gone. She quickly looked around the room. But only she and Mallory were there.

"Your friend, Hashmi, went to the bath." Mallory stepped closer to Safia. "It's okay, Miss Safia, I don't mind."

"Well, I do mind. Just stop… stop for one moment."

Mallory stood still, just staring back at Safia with a puzzled look, as if she didn't understand what was going on.

"We need to have a talk. So, put your top back on."

"Ah, okay," agreed Mallory as she walked over to a chair and put on a pajama top to cover herself, and Safia slowly found herself regaining control of the moment.

"First…" said Safia. "Why do you think I'd try to send you back to Dario? I won't do that."

"What? No, not Dario. I thought you got me away from him so that you could send me home."

"No, I'm not going to send you home. Wait! Why don't you wanna go home?"

Mallory looked down at the floor. "It's my step-father, he—"

Suddenly, the door opened up, and Hashmi entered the room and saw the girls talking.

"Sorry, am I interrupting something?"

Quickly, Mallory turned around, trying not to look at Hashmi.

"No, I was just talking to Mallory about last night."

"Hey, you still haven't told me everything about last night. You promised you were going to tell me about all of this."

"I will. Everything just got so confusing, is all," said Safia, turning back to Mallory and grimacing at the sight of the bruise on the side of her face where Dario had slapped her. Instinctively she touched the side of her own face where Dario had hit her. As she also ran her fingers over her lips, she could feel the cut. But was thankful, the taste of blood was no longer present in her mouth, but she could feel the fresh scab on her bottom lip.

Hell of a lot more pain than when I used to fight with Yago when we were little.

"So, have you decided what you plan to do with her?" asked Hashmi as she walked over into the room and over to her closet, putting her items on the top shelf.

Mallory turned back to Safia with fear and desperations clearly showing in her eyes, and her lips began to tremble.

"What do you mean?"

"I mean, she's wearing your pajamas. You said you wanted her to stay with us for so—"

"Oh... ah... Yeah, I want Mallory to stay with us for a while if you don't mind."

"Sure, it's kinda fun having a girl's sleep over. My mom never used to let me have them. So, I think having anoth-er girl around would be fun," said Hashmi as Mallory's shoulder slumped as she sighed in relief.

Why are you so afraid to go home? You said something about your stepfather, Safia wondered to herself, meaning to ask her later when they were in private.

Shaking the thought from her mind, she then reached over the counter, grabbing her glass tablet. Her fingers pressed on the screen. It loaded, showing her the classes she had for the week. Moving her finger across the screen, she tapped on her picture to pull up points.

Eighteen Hundred Points, so that's almost two months. I should be able to squeak by for a while. I just need to do well on my tests and help out with more of Jericho's projects. And If I only make safe bets, I… I should be okay, thought Safia as she placed the tablet to her chest and took a breath. *I can deal with this. I know I can.* She then took another glance over at Mallory, who she noticed was also sneaking a peek at her. *Although, I'm not too sure I can deal with her.*

A little while later, all three girls were up and getting ready for classes.

"Mallory, sit down," said Safia, pulling out a chair. "Hashmi, can you put makeup on her to cover the bruises on her face?"

"No, it's okay. I can do it myself," said Mallory, looking down at the floor. "I'm used to it."

Safia walked over and placed her hand on Mallory's chin, lifting her face. "I know you can do it, but I want Hashmi to do it." She then looked back up at Hashmi, who was putting on one of her long skirts out of her closet. "Can you?"

"Yes, I can, if you want," said Hashmi as she pulled out her makeup kit. She stepped over to Mallory and began putting a bit of foundation on her bruises, rubbing it across the darkened area of Mallory's face.

"Good, and as for clothing, you can just wear this today, and we'll go and get some of your other clothes later." Safia reached into her closet, pulling out one of her extra outfits, placing it beside Mallory.

"Miss Safia, can I ask you a question?"

"Sure, what is it?" *Don't say anything about what just happened; please don't say anything about what just happened.*

"Why are you doing all this for me? I mean, you got hit because of me."

Hashmi looked up at Safia with a face that said she too wanted answers to Mallory's questions.

"There are a few reasons. But the main reason is I hate Dario. I even think Hashmi feels the same on that decision."

"That guy is certainly not a good man," said Hashmi.

"But outside of that, let's just say I have my reasons for why I'm helping you. I just need you to follow along, and I'll take care of everything, okay? And don't worry about what happened. Let's just start over."

"That's not what... no... Yes, ma'am."

Isn't she older than me? Why is she calling me ma'am? I'll figure that out later. Other things that need to be taken care of first. "Good. When you're done, we'll get dressed and head to breakfast."

"What about you?" asked Hashmi, looking up at Safia. "Just because your skin's a little darker doesn't mean I can't see the bruises on your face."

"No, I want mine to show. If we run into Dario, I want him to get a good look at what he did."

"I don't think he's the type for self-reflection and shame."

"Maybe not, but it'll be a reminder that I stood up to him and will do it again."

The girls got dressed with Mallory wearing a set of Safia's clothing, then they all headed downstairs and out of the dorm. It wasn't long before they reached the school cafeteria, where people were getting scanned in. Once again, that guy in the mushroom-shaped chef hat was at the door. He waved a metal wand over Hashmi's badge, making it turn red.

"I, Margaretto Hashmi, am allowing the food-service fee to be deducted from my account." Soon Hashmi's badge changed color with acceptance.

"I, Safia Famosa, am allowing the food service fee to be deducted from my account," said Safia, and soon her badge flashed the color of acceptance.

"I... ah," said Mallory, "I'm not allowed to have points. Dario would always have to pay for mine."

"I figured as much," said Safia, turning towards the boy in the chef's hat. "How do I pay for her to come with us?"

"That's Dario's discarded, right? Shouldn't he be here?"

"She was his discarded. Now, she's mine. So how do I pay?"

"Oh, well, if he's transferred ownership of her over to you, then just say that you wish to pay for her, and it'll work."

"Mallory, what's your last name?"

"Polana."

Safia tapped on her pendant, "I, Safia Famosa, wish to pay for Mallory Polana's food service fee."

After a few seconds, the pendant spoke. "You are not recognized as the caretaker of Mallory Polana. You are prohibited from purchasing anything on her account."

"Sorry then," said the man in the chef's hat. "Rules are rules."

"What do I do now? I have to eat something," said Mallory, looking over at Safia nervously.

"Give us a moment, please," said Safia to the boy, before turning back to Hashmi. "You go in and grab us a table. We'll be in soon."

"Okay, if you're sure," said Hashmi, not understanding, but going inside anyway.

"That's fine. Just click the badge and say you wish to pay for it once you get it settled," said the boy in the chef's hat.

Safia then grabbed Mallory by the hand and headed off the walkway down onto the grass, walking a distance away from the crowd that was starting to get annoyed as they waited.

"What are we gonna do?" asked Mallory.

"Just going to send a message, is all. What's Dario's last name?"

"Burrows, Dario Burrows."

Safia tapped on the pendant, making it click. "I would like to send a message to Dario Burrows."

"Go ahead with the message," spoke the pendant.

"Dario, honey, Champ Champ started asking me all kinds of questions about how I got these marks on my face. I told her they were bite marks from my lover, Dario Burrows. And now she's asking for permission to view some tapes because she wants to make sure I am telling the truth about these marks on me. Oh, also, I can't feed our baby Mallory. She needs her monthly food budget. So, since you like to be in charge so much, and I know you don't want to be put on child support, I figured now would be a good time to ask for full custody. So, tell me, honey, will I be able to feed Mallory, or am I going to allow Champ Champ to see how I got these bruises on my face?" Safia then clicked on the pendant and closed her eyes, waiting.

"You're not going to tell them what happened, are you?" asked Mallory, looking nervously at Safia. "If they send him home, then they'll send me home too."

Safia looked at Mallory, but didn't say a word. She just closed her eyes again and folded her arms in front of her chest.

"You've received a message from Dario," spoke the pendant.

Safia clicked the pendant.

"You better keep your word, bitch," came Dario's voice in a whisper so low she could barely hear it. "Because I swear if you don't and I'm expelled, I will find the people you love, and by the time I'm done, you and that bitch, Mallory, will wish you'd never been born."

Another few seconds passed before Safia's pendant started changing colors again. She clicked it.

"Caretaker privileges of Mallory Polana have been

transferred over to Safia Famosa," spoke the pendant as it flashed its colors.

Safia took a deep breath and exhaled. "Okay, let's try that one more time." She clicked on her pendant. "I, Safia Famosa, wish to pay for Mallory Polana's food service fee."

"Service fee accepted for Mallory Polana," spoke the pendant.

"Good," said Safia, turning toward Mallory, who was staring back up at her. "What?"

"You're scary when you get mad."

Safia reached up to her face, rubbing at her furrowed brows. *Am I mad? Thinking about that bastard Dario, of course I am. Who wouldn't be?* Safia sighed, "Yeah, well, you're not the only one who thinks so." She turned back around, grabbing Mallory by the hand, making her way over to the man in the chef's hat. "Sorry about that. I had to clear up a misunderstanding. Could we try again, please?"

The man in the chef's hat shrugged his shoulders and waved his wand over Mallory's badge. Instantly, Safia's badge turned red.

"Three hundred points for the food service fee of Mallory Polana has already been charged."

"Okay, it says you're good to go. Head on in."

"See? All done. Now let's go get us something to eat," said Safia as they both headed inside to see Hashmi sitting down at a table with her tray waiting on them. She gave them a smile as they both entered, and after getting their food, they both sat down and had their breakfast before class.

"Aren't you both going to class?" asked Mallory as she looked over at a large clock on the wall.

"Our class doesn't start for another hour. But if yours starts soon, you can go ahead, and we'll meet up later."

"Oh... ah... okay," said Mallory, standing up from the table with her tray. She then stared down at Safia.

"What's wrong?" asked Safia, noticing her staring at her.

"Your tray. Should I empty it for you?"

"No, I'm not done with it. Just go on to class," said Safia in an authoritative tone, as she waved her hand in dismissal. "But, this evening, bring a change of clothes over to our dorm. You're going to be staying with us for a while."

"Yes, ma'am," said Mallory, nervously looking at Hashmi before wandering off.

Safia watched Mallory empty her tray and leave the cafeteria before turning back around and planting her face down into her arms on the table.

"Ahhh! This is exhausting," mumbled Safia.

"You're like a mother ordering her child around," said Hashmi with a chuckle.

"Well, I'm happy someone finds this funny because I sure don't."

"Come on, spill it. You said you'd explain what happened. How did you wind up with a discarded? The last time I saw you, you were off with that Ricardo boy, and the next thing I know, you're coming back with her. What in the world happened last night at that party?"

"I told you before that she belonged to that asshole Dario, right?"

"Yeah, but how did she end up with you?"

"The idiot slapped her, and riding that high of beating women, he slapped me in front of one of the school cameras. According to Abigail, that assault was enough to get his ass expelled."

"So that's where you both got those bruises from. But I don't understand; why not just let him get expelled?"

"Because she would have gotten expelled, too. And for some reason, she's terrified of going back home. So, in order for me to keep my silence, I traded to get Mallory away from him."

"And all of this happened at game night?"

"No, this was after."

"Then, what happened at game night?"

Safia thought back to all the events of that night and told Hashmi about the nude couple, their sex behind the glass, the drug-filled air, the gambling and the torture, although she left out the kiss with Amanda on top of the lake and just shook her head.

"They really burned their arms over a bet?"

"Yep, they lost some bet with The Husband, and that was the price," said Safia, shaking her head. "Too damn much happened, half of it I wish I could forget. This place is damned crazy."

"What are you going to do now? I don't mind her staying with us," said Hashmi with a solemn look on her face. "We'll treat her better than that stupid Dario at least."

"We?" asked Safia, looking at Hashmi with the hint of a smile across her lips.

"Well, of course, if she's going to be staying with us. I mean, we're practically best friends already. Didn't you see me doing her make-up this morning? We're already bonding."

"I don't think I could ask for a better roommate," said Safia with a chuckle.

"I might need to make another prayer mat, however. I only brought two."

"What, you're going to try and convert her already?"

"No, but a few extra prayers together couldn't hurt," said Hashmi with a smile as she pointed her finger at Safia's face and bruised lip. "I mean, looking at how beat-up you are, and the situation you're in now, I'd think having Allah on your side would be a good thing, wouldn't you?"

"Oh ha-ha," said Safia, looking at Hashmi's giggling face. "Come on, let's go to class. I imagine that Allah doesn't like the idea of us being late either."

"I'm not sure, but father always told me that we should value our time," said Hashmi as they both stood up from the table and left the cafeteria, making their way over to the school.

In the morning sun, she saw some other students in her class heading inside the building in the distance, including Jericho and Addison. She was about to call out to them when she spotted Killian over to the side of the school beside where they had their orientation. He was looking around the area suspiciously before he headed inside.

Safia kept walking towards the school, but right before the steps, she turned to Hashmi. "You go on inside. I want to check something."

"Oh, no, you don't. I know that look now. You're about to do something stupid and get in more trouble."

Safia looked at her friend with a face of confusion. "What? No, I'm..." She saw Hashmi purse her lips, not even beginning to entertain what she was about to say. "Okay, fine, maybe I am." Safia sighed. "I admit it, I'm a dummy. Are you happy now?"

"Good, the first step to recovering is admitting you have a problem," said Hashmi with a smirk as she looked over towards where Killian went. "Now, let's go see what he's up to."

"What? Didn't you just admit that what I was about to do was stupid?"

"Yes, what you were about to do was stupid, because you were going to do it alone. But now you have me, so that makes it very smart."

Safia narrowed her eyes at her friend and pressed her lips together hard, trying to think of a response. But finding no words, she shook her head again and turned around, going over to the small building beside the school, with Hashmi trailing behind her. Once there, they heard two people talking but couldn't make out all the words. They snuck around the side to the window, where they could hear clearer.

"Things do seem to be going well for you, Killian. You're so close to your goal," said the voice of Champ Champ.

"No thanks to your meddling. If not for that, I would

have been done months ago.”

“What do you mean, Killian? I have always played by the rules.”

“Yeah, your rules. Whatever those may be.”

“Everyone here gets the same treatment. You should understand that better than most.”

“Please, peddle that trash to the first-years. I’ve been here long enough to know how the game is played. Or do you want to make a bet on it?”

“As tempting as that is, I’m afraid I’d only be aiding you on your goal.”

“So, you admit to trying to stand in my way.”

“There are no rules that say I can’t help or hinder someone in their progression.”

“And, of course, you choose to hinder.”

“I do.”

“I’m not that far away in points, little Iris. I just need a little bit longer. Even you should know that I’m going to win.”

“It’s true. There’s probably nothing left I can do. You seem to have won like you always do.”

“Then, why stand in my way, anyway? What have I ever done to you?”

“Because I’m not my grandfather, and I never liked the idea of you owning poor Abigail. My only failing is being so shortsighted that I didn’t look more into you before I offered you the wager. But I’m afraid even if I had known of your condition, I wouldn’t have understood the length you were willing to go to satisfy that need of yours.”

“And yet, you still stand in my way.”

“Much as you’re compelled to think you don’t have a choice, then I’m afraid I am much the same.”

“Think? I don’t think anything. You don’t know how deep inside this goes. And if you think your wanting to help compares anything to what I feel, then you’re not as smart as you think you are. Even your sleepy husband, after our little talk, has chosen to leave me alone.

"It's seven years, Killian. seven years you'll have that girl on your leash. And who's to say you won't feel compelled to force her to do something even you might regret?"

"Is this bringing up bad memories about that husband of yours? Don't pretend you're such a saint. I was there, and I saw what you did to him. You're no better than I am."

"It started out that way with my leash, but at least mine has grown on me. I fail to see yours working out the same."

"Maybe, maybe not. All that matters now is that you can no longer do anything to stop me."

Safia and Hashmi heard the sound of footsteps and the door opening and closing. Then, after a moment of silence, came the voice of Champ Champ.

"Miss Safia Famosa and Margaretto Hashmi, I know you're out there on the left side of the building. Why don't you get out of the morning sun and come in here and have a talk with me since you seem so interested in my conversations?"

Safia and Hashmi looked at each other before standing up nervously, walking around the building, and into the front door. Inside, they saw Champ Champ sitting down in one of the chairs.

"Well, come on. Don't be shy. Come over here."

"How did you know we were out there?" asked Hashmi.

Champ Champ raised a tablet from her dress that showed a map of the surrounding area, and inside the building were three dots.

"You've still got those chips in your bodies, and I'm the headmaster of this school. It's my job to know where all my students are. And speaking of my students, it seems you've picked up another one." Champ Champ clapped her hand together with a smile. "Bravo getting Mallory away from that bastard Dario." She waved a finger at Safia, "Blackmailing him with physical and sexual assault that sure is enough to get him expelled on the spot had you chosen to report it."

327

"I was going to ask if I could let her go, or if not, then give her to Amanda."

"Unfortunately, no. A long while ago, there was an incident where a student was transferred back and forth like that for a group's enjoyment. He ended up taking his own life, and as such, in cases of discarded, we allow only one transfer of privileges through the lifetime of their studies here. And since you seem to have just done that, I'm afraid that means you're stuck with her."

"But it's so unfair. Is any of this even legal? I mean, the thing with Dario. What about the police?"

Champ Champ just stared at Safia for a moment? "Miss Safia, where do you think we are?"

"What?"

"You seem to think normal rules apply here. And if so, which rules. Which country do you think we are in?" asked Champ Champ as she waved her hands around. "The only rules that matter here are the ones we set. If you continue to think about your old world's rules. You're going to be in serious trouble when you really compete for points next year."

"What happens next year?" asked Hashmi, looking confused.

"It's... it's complicated."

"But on the topic of points, then that shouldn't be much of a worry for you in terms of your discarded. All points that are accumulated by a discarded are instantly transferred over to their caretaker. That includes tests and acts of campus maintenance. These incentives ensure that the discarded keep following the rules and going to class."

"Well, that's good news at least," said Safia, taking in a deep breath and looking up at the ceiling. "At least, now, I can focus on my own point problem?"

"Okay, enough of that," said Hashmi, folding her arms in front of her. "Are you ever going to tell me what's going on with you? Why did you just suddenly feel the need to start gambling when you said you were going to avoid it?"

Safia looked down at Champ Champ.

"Don't look at me. It's your secret to share. I'm only the deal maker."

"Fine, I guess telling you can't hurt anything."

"That, I disagree with," said Champ Champ, interrupting. "I have seen information destroy people. And oftentimes, it's both parties, not just the recipient. The only real secret is the one you keep to yourself."

"I wouldn't try to hurt Safia," said Hashmi with anger in her voice..

"It's fine. She knows enough to figure it out without me having to tell her directly."

"I do?"

"You know that situation Abigail is in?"

"Yeah, I remember you telling me about that."

"Well, I'm in the same situation."

"What? How?" asked Hashmi, but before Safia could answer, her eyes went wide. "Your father?"

"See, you already figured it out."

"But... how many?"

"Not as many as Abigail, but it's enough. And it's going to get worse next semester."

"I won't tell anyone. You know that, right?"

"I know. I trust you."

"Maybe not, but trust isn't the issue," said Champ Champ, shaking her head. "What if someone overheard you talking about it? And found a way to use it against her. Are you prepared to take that responsibility for the sake of your own curiosity?"

Safia turned towards her friend. "Hashmi, you still want to know the rest?"

Hashmi looked back and forth between Safia and Champ Champ and closed her eyes. "No, it's probably best that I don't know the rest. That was enough. Especially if it could be used against you. It means a lot just knowing that you were willing to tell me if I had wanted."

"Thank you, Hash—" Suddenly, Safia saw something move from a nearby window on the other side. She ran over to it, only to see the back end of someone with blonde hair and a red accent in her uniform disappear around the school.

"Who was that?" asked Hashmi, as Safia came back over to them.

"I don't know," said Safia, turning back to Champ Champ. "You knew they were out there. That's why you said that."

Champ Champ tapped her tablet in her hand. "As I said, it's my job to know where all my students are."

"And you're not going to tell me who that was, are you?"

"Now, what would be the fun in that? You'll have to figure that part out on your own. It's all part of the game."

"Then, can you tell me this, does Dario have a powerful family or something? Can he really find my family and hurt them?"

"Yes, although he would never do such a thing as long as he wanted the benefits and connections of this school. We don't deal with our members attacking one another without just cause."

"I guess he's not just hot air then."

"Why didn't you just warn us about the person at the window?" asked Hashmi, looking frustrated. "Instead of almost letting me expose Safia's secret?"

"Because, at the end of the day, it's your choice. All I did was offer advice. What you do with it is up to you. It was your choice to expose yourselves, especially considering the actions you both had just taken. You should have assumed that perhaps someone would overhear you, just as you overheard me and Killian. I, myself, am only allowed to interfere with the students so much before I overstep my bounds."

Hashmi turned back to Safia, "I'm sorry. From now on, keep whatever it is that's going on with you to yourself."
330

Safia thought back to when they made the arrangement, how she was asked to enter a secure location and then made to climb all those steps. *Did she already plan to make me that bet? Is that why she had me meet up there?* Safia just stared down at the small woman as she sat up from her seat.

"What's wrong, is there something else you wish to ask?"

"No, it's just. This... this place, this whole school. Why does it even exist? Does someone out there just enjoy playing with people's lives?"

"Oh Miss Safia, if you only knew. You seem to think a school like this is singular."

"What? What do you mean?"

"I mean, there are other schools, Miss Safia. At least three others that I know of. Oh sure, they vary on things such as their purpose and goals. But somewhere in other remote regions of the world, sits three other schools much like this one, where students compete against one another. And with far more brutal endings than our little discarded system here. One of them even believes in magic, I think."

"Magic?" asked Hashmi, "You mean like the people on the telly who pull rabbits out of their hats."

"Exactly," said Champ Champ, shaking her head. "So with that foolishness in comparison, I happen to think we're fairly tame."

Safia's mind raced with the thoughts of other places like this one. *She said far more brutal ends. So, a place where people kill each other? What is all of this?*

"Well, I guess I'm done for the day," said Champ Champ as she headed for the door, throwing up her hand in dismissal. "Take care of that new discarded of yours. Between her home life and dealing with Dario for the past six months, I think she's deserved a bit of a break for a while."

Home life? thought Safia. But before she could ask another question, Champ Champ was out of the door. And when the door closed, both Safia and Hashmi stood looking at each other for a moment before someone spoke.

"Safia, even though I'm not sure what's going on, I am sure that if you continue to play whatever game they are playing, you're going to get caught up in something bad."

"I'm already caught up in something bad. But it's not like I can just quit," said Safia, sitting down in a chair and dropping her head into her hands, rubbing at her face. "Even if I wanted to go home, I couldn't. If I quit, Mallory would also be expelled, and my family is expecting me to..."

"What?" asked Hashmi, looking at Safia's face as the words paused in her throat. "What's wrong?"

"My father, he should have come home today. I need to call and ask how he's doing," said Safia, standing back up to her feet. "Will you take notes in the first part of class today? I'll be back soon."

"Okay, sure. I'll do that. You go ahead and call your family," said Hashmi as they both left out of the auditorium together, back out into the morning sun.

"Thanks, Hashmi," said Safia as she headed towards the communication house. "I'll be back soon." And as Hashmi headed over to the school, Safia walked off, heading across the campus.

It didn't take long before she was at the door to the communication house. After tapping the pendant around her neck and waiting for entry, she couldn't help but notice the trees that Jericho had planted were now growing bigger. Even the one that looked to be dead was now sectioned off inside a pot that sat atop the ground. Its leaves were slowly falling off and being replaced by new growth. As Safia continued to stare at the small tree, the door to the communication building opened, and out stepped Derrick, still in his suit.

"Hello, again, Miss Safia. I'm happy to see you safe and sound."

"Hey, Derrick. I would like to speak with my parents again. Can I do that?"

"Of course," said Derrick, turning to the side and

allowing Safia to pass. "Your father, he was to be released from the hospital today, if I am correct. I expected you to show up in the coming days."

"You knew?"

"It is our job to look after the safety of our students. Remember, we were the ones who came to inform you of his shooting. It would be terribly remiss of us if we didn't keep track of his recovery, especially since it was one of our alumni that performed the surgery."

They both walked down the hallway until they reached the room with the phones and entered.

"Please, take booth number two."

Safia walked over to the booth, sitting down with Derrick taking a seat beside her to monitor her call. Placing her finger inside the rotary phone, she twisted her finger, and once again, the clicking of the phone ran through her ears over and over until, finally, she heard the sound of ringing. It was a soothing sound she hadn't even realized she missed, but it soon ended and was replaced by another familiar voice that already knew she had missed so much.

"Hello," said the voice of Hector Famosa.

"Papa, hey... It's so great to hear your voice again.."

"Hey, it's my girl. How's my baby doing? Are you okay?"

"Me? What about you? I was so worried and... and..." Safia started to fumble her words as her eyes began to sting. Slowly, the rotary phone before her started to get blurry as the tears began to drop from her eyes unwillingly as she began sniffling to try to hold back her emotions.

"Hey, hey, I'm fine, okay. Remember, your Papa's a strong guy. Ain't no robbers going to take me down, and them doctors did a good job setting me back right. They even had some fancy pants doctor from Germany come and fix me up."

Safia tried to control her breathing. "I... I'm just..."

"Come on, us Famosa's are strong. Now tell me, who's my big girl?"

Safia took a deep breath and then tried to regain control of herself. "I am."

"That's right, you are. Now tell your old man how's school going? You making any new friends down there?"

"Yes, Papa. I met this girl named Hashmi. She's my roommate."

"When you come home for the summer, you should bring her."

Instantly Safia felt a ping of pain in her chest as she looked back at Derrick, who shook his head. "Yes Papa, I... I'll try to do that." *But I'm not allowed to go home until graduation.* She thought to herself as she tightened her grip around the phone. "What about Mama and Yago? Are they okay?" she asked, wiping the last of the tears from her eyes.

"Oh them, they're fine. Your mother's handling the customers downstairs and Yago's in his room. Oh, hey, you wanna speak to David?"

"David..." said Safia as her grip loosened on the phone. "He's there?"

"Yeah, he's here. The boy's been back here for a month, came back a week after I got shot and has been helping Yago. He's on the sofa, asleep in front of me."

"But... but isn't he supposed to be in school?"

"He said he took care of it, and he's doing those online classes things now. But he's supposed to be headed back soon, I think. Now that they've let me go from the hospital. You want me to wake him. Hey! David, wake up. Safia's on the phone."

"No, it's okay. If he's sleeping, just let him sleep."

"You sure?"

"Yes, Papa, I'm sure,"

"You know, Safia, I was kinda against you dating this white boy at first, you know. But he ain't that bad. You know, coming back here to help after I got shot and all. That takes good character, shows he cares about the family, and not just himself. That's surprising coming from a white kid, you know. Must be something wrong with his brain?"

"Papa, stop talking like that," said Safia with a smile on her face, remembering how brazen her father could be.

"I'm just saying that, you know, you could have done worse."

"I know, Papa," said Safia, nodding her head, "But what about—"

"Hey, there's your brother. Hey Yago, come over here and say hello to your sister."

There was a small moment of pause before Safia heard a click and then sounds of the phone being passed from one hand to the other.

"Hello, Safia, you there?" asked Yago.

"Hey, Yago. How are you? Is everything going okay?"

"I'm fine here, just getting ready for Christmas break from school. What about you? You still enjoying college life?"

"I'm not sure enjoying is the right word for this place. But I've survived so far. Tell me, Yago, is Papa really okay? Did everything really go well?"

"Yeah, he's fine. They got him in a wheelchair for a while, though, since it's painful for him to walk. But the doctors said he should be up and walking in about a month. Until then, they got him taking it easy. Although, he refuses to take his pain pills."

"I ain't taking them pills. I've been through worse than this back in Cuba," came Hector's voice in the background. "I don't need 'em."

"But other than him being stubborn, he's fine," said Yago. "So, are you coming home for Christmas break?"

"What? Ahh. No, I don't think so. A lot has happened at school, and I need to take care of you a few things." Safia felt the tears stinging her eyes once again.

"That's a shame."

"Hey, Yago. Are you sure everything's okay?"

"Huh? Yeah, everything's fine."

"What about Ma? How is she handling things after everything that happened with Papa? He said she was downstairs in the restaurant."

"Yeah, she's working hard to keep everything going. I think it helps her keep her mind off of things. She's been running around back and forth while I take care of dad."

"Oh, okay, that's good. You guys take care of him, and I promise I'll be home as soon as I can. I'm late for class now, so I have to go. I just wanted to hear your voices and make sure Papa was okay."

"Is there anything you want me to tell David when he wakes up?"

"Just… just tell him I miss him, okay," said Safia, shaking her head and closing her eyes.

"Alright, talk to you next time, Safia."

"Bye, Yago," said Safia, hanging up the phone and turning towards Derrick. "I'm done now. Thank you for letting me speak to my family."

"You're quite welcome, Miss Safia. I'm happy to hear that your father is okay and doing well."

"Yeah, me too. Can you let me out now? I still need to make it in time for Miss Abigail's class."

"Of course, follow me," said Derrick, escorting Safia out of the room and back into the hallway, towards the door. "Are you okay, Miss Safia?"

"What… what do you mean?"

"Your face and lip were bleeding the last time I saw you. And I still see traces of the bruise on your cheek. Are you certain you don't wish to have us investigate that for you?"

"No, I'm fine. Really. Besides, it's not as bad as it looks. I'm a tough girl."

"I believe you," he said as the door opened and he led her back outside. "Well, if you ever change your mind. Please, feel free to contact me."

"Thank you. And if it ever happens again, I will call you," said Safia, stepping outside. "Thanks for the help." She
336

watched the door close with Derrick behind it and turned back around, heading back off to class. All the while, she couldn't help the feeling that something was wrong.

It didn't take long for what Champ Champ said to make sense to Safia. A few days after the test, Mallory's points were added to her point total. Along with those, a few bets that she felt were safe and helping Jericho around the campus, Safia found that she could easily cover her and Mallory's food as well as her monthly thousand point cost for her father's surgery.

CHAPTER 15

The season had changed, and the girls soon realized that wherever they were, it was a region of the world that received a fair amount of snow during the cold months. Mallory stood by the window, looking out at the snow that covered the campus.

"It really is pretty outside. If I were back at home, I'd never see this."

"I can't imagine Florida getting much snow," said Safia, flipping through her tablet and clicking on Mallory's picture. Moving her finger over to the image of a clothing hanger, an assortment of winter clothing images appeared on the screen. "Do you know what type of clothing you want? Like gloves, hats, that sort of thing."

"Oh, anything is fine, Miss Safia."

She's still calling me Miss Safia. "No, you come over here and help me pick out what you want. These are your clothes. I just have to buy them. We can't all be like Hashmi over there, who's dressed for any occasion."

"At least my clothing saves me points," said Hashmi with a smile as she pointed at them. "Now, look at you two over there. It's cold outside and not a thing to wear. Let's see you wearing those knee-high skirts now," she said, nodding to the snow-covered window.

"Hashmi," said Mallory, "What is the UK like?"

"What do you mean?" asked Hashmi, rubbing her eyes. "It's a place like any other."

"I mean, what is it like? In the movies, it always shows up like it's raining. And everything's all gray."

Hashmi looked to the ceiling. "Well, it rains a lot, but it's not like we're drowning in gray skies over there. Maybe only half the year, it looks like it's gonna rain. The rest is pretty pleasant. Why? Didn't you say you're from Florida? What's that like where you live? Do people really ride on the backs of those alligators? I see that on the internet sometimes," said Hashmi with a giggle.

"Sometimes they do, yes."

"What, really?"

"They have competitions to see who can ride on the back of the gators the longest before they flip off."

Hashmi just stared at Mallory for a long moment before looking at Safia, who just shrugged her shoulders. "Wait, are you being serious?"

"Yeah, they do it every summer back at home."

"Excuse me, but I must know. How does someone ride an alligator? Don't they have sharp teeth and such?"

"Oh, yeah, but they tape their mouths closed before they hop on their backs. But most of the alligators are ridden by their owners. There's no real danger of anything happening."

"Owners? The people there keep alligators as pets?"

Safia couldn't help herself but start laughing as Hashmi's face continued to twist the more questions she asked. "Just stop, Hashmi. I think you're going to hurt yourself if you ask any more about it. Mostly everyone else in the US just accepts that Florida is in a parallel universe." Safia lifted up her tablet. "Mallory, come back over here and pick out the jacket you want."

"Okay," said Mallory as she turned around, smiling, and began poking at the tablet.

"Careful, said Safia. If I take my hands off of it, the screen goes black. It only works as long as I hold it."

"Oh, sorry."

"Mallory. How old are you?" asked Safia.

"I'm sixteen."

"Sixteen? But... then you should be in the tenth or eleventh grade. What are you doing here?"

"I'm really good at taking tests. So, I skipped some grades. Why? How old are you two?"

"I just turned eighteen, last month," said Safia.

"What? But you didn't tell me. I would have got you something, or made something," said Mallory, frowning at Safia.

Well, at least she's a nice girl, I guess, thought Safia, looking at the brown-haired girl's face.

"What about sisters and brothers, any siblings back at home?" asked Safia.

"I have an older sister. We don't really get along the way her and my step-father do."

"What about boyfriends, then? Ever had one before?" asked Hashmi. "Or did you step-father run them away?"

"No, I don't like boys that much."

We're changing this subject, thought Safia as she felt Mallory squeeze her fingers. "It's still impressive for you to be in college at sixteen. You didn't want to stay in school with your friends?"

"I did, but… it's just." Mallory looked down at the floor. "I didn't wanna be at home anymore."

Once again, Safia felt Mallory squeeze her finger, but this time she squeezed her hand back. *I'm probably going to have to ask about it. But maybe when we're alone. It'll probably be easier to talk if it's just us.*

"But to be here at sixteen is impressive," said Hashmi. "When is your birthday?"

"In two months. Then, how old are you, Hashmi?"

"I'm eighteen also, but my birthday is coming up, so apparently, I'm a little older than Safia."

"So, I'm the youngest one here?"

"And the shortest," added Hashmi, picking up a book.

Safia wrapped her arms around Mallory, trying to provide the girl more comfort. "Now, now, no picking on our junior, Hashmi. We have to set a good example."

"That's not fair," said Mallory, "I've been here a year longer than both of you."

"Yeah, but that was a year under Dario," said Hashmi. "And I imagine a year under that snake is a year akin to hell. How did you wind up under him, anyway?"

Instantly, the depression returned to Mallory's face after Hashmi brought up Dario, and Safia felt the younger girl's shoulder slump in her arms as she dropped her head.

And there it is. She's gone back inside of herself again. "Hey, now," said Safia, squeezing her arms tightly around Mallory's waist and placing her face on her shoulders. "We can talk about that later. It seems our clothing has arrived." She waved her tablet in front of Mallory. "Can you go get our clothing from down-stairs? It says that they left it at the front door."

"Ah… yes ma'am… Miss Safia," said Mallory as she stepped out of Safia's embrace and headed out, closing the door behind her.

"I guess, I asked too soon," said Hashmi with a sigh.

"Yeah, she still gets like that when we bring his name up. I had hoped that talking about it might make her feel better. But I don't know if it hurts too much to talk about or if she just can't open up to us yet."

"And who knows what he had her doing while she was with him."

"I saw how he treated her at the fountain. I have a good idea how he treated her," said Safia, shaking her head. "But I think it's best we wait. She'll tell us when she's ready. I'd hate to run her off when she's finally started opening up to us."

"What now? She can't just hide behind you every time she runs into him on campus."

"I honestly don't know. She's—"

The door opened, and Mallory appeared in the door with a huge box in her arms.

"I... have it, Miss... Safia. I... just... have to."

Safia jumped off the bed to the floor, rushing to the door. "Oh, for goodness' sake. If it was that big, just ask one of the boys to help you."

The girls helped Mallory squeeze the box into the door. Opening it, they began trying on their winter clothing. Safia put on a long-hemmed dress with a small brown pleated pattern that had a purplish streak that flowed down from the collar to the base of the dress. Underneath, she wore a set of fleece stockings that went down into a cozy set of light purple boots.

"I'm amazed that they always have the right size of clothing," said Safia, twisting in the dress after trying it on. "I don't even have to pick the clothing size. It just shows up and it fits."

Mallory slid out of her pajamas and stepped into her outfit. While it had the same small, pleated pattern as Safia's, it didn't have her house colors down the side. Instead, the bottom of her dress, as well as the end of her long sleeves,

342

had a rim of light crimson. The dress stopped slightly below the knees; underneath were wool stockings that came up to the ankles and went down into her brown wedge shoes. The dress had several buttons on the back that Mallory struggled to reach.

"Oh, turn around," said Safia, losing her patience at watching Mallory flail her arms behind her back, trying to button up her dress. "Now, hold still." Playfully slapping Mallory's hand away, Safia proceeded to button up her dress for her.

Hashmi wore her usual attire but pulled out a form-fitted woolen dress coat from her closet that buttoned up in the front.

"Okay then. Shall we head out?" asked Safia, finishing up on the buttons on Mallory's coat. "It seems everyone else is enjoying the snow. So, I don't want to miss out on the fun."

The girls all headed downstairs and out of Yennefer House, stepping into a world of white. As far as they could see, the frost covered the campus grounds as if a blanket of powder had come down around them.

"This is my first time seeing snow that isn't on the television," said Mallory, stepping down off the walkway. Her feet instantly sank into the snow with a crunchy squish sound, causing her to lose her balance and fall on her butt with an "Oof."

Safia laughed, watching Mallory fall and walked over to help her up, "You gotta be care—" but she misjudged where the walkway ended and where the snow began. And instead of the hard walkway, her foot caught soft white powder as she stumbled, falling face forward into the snow.

Hashmi doubled over, grabbing her waist in laughter. "Oh, goodness. Like Mother, like daughter, you two are hilarious."

Safia rolled over with snow half stuck to her face, frowning at Hashmi. She then turned to Mallory, who was wiping the snow from her sleeves. "Well then, my supposed daughter, shall we have Auntie Hashmi join us?"

"What?" asked Hashmi, just shortly before she was pelted with tiny snowballs, which forced her to run and hide behind a nearby lamppost. "Stop that. Both of you are children."

Mallory and Safia laughed as they lifted up from the snow, brushing themselves off.

"I guess we should head off to breakfast for some warm food now," said Safia. On the way, they spotted Jericho and Nasir amongst a group of similar students who were playing football in the snow. To the side was a group of ladies cheering them on and betting on the outcome of their activities.

"Don't they seem to be having fun?" asked Safia, walking over to spectate.

"But isn't it too cold to be out here playing in the snow?" asked Mallory, looking confused at the boys.

"Really? Back in the UK, the boys often played in the snow like this."

"Same in Minnesota. It can snow for around four months off and on at home."

"I think I'll stick to my Florida weather then. My body isn't used to cold weather like this."

"Well, look over there," said Safia, pointing over to a small female wearing a Victorian winter coat that had fur on the hem, neckline, and wrists. Covering her hair was an overly large square-shaped fur hat that drooped over her head. The fur parts were so big that they seemed to be consuming her. Safia shook her head. "At this point, I just have to wonder where she gets these outfits. They sure aren't in the school catalog."

"Is that Champ Champ?" asked Hashmi, squinting her eyes.

"It's hard to tell since she's swallowed up by whatever that is that she's wearing, but it's her. Oh, and she's spotted us."

Champ Champ waddled her way over to them in the

snow, appearing a bit out of breath as she came within speaking distance.

"Hello there… ladies. Are you… enjoying the weather?"

"Yes we are, but I'm more concerned about you," said Hashmi, looking down at the woman. "You seem as if you're about to tumble over in that getup."

"Yes, well… This is more of my husband's teasings. He finds the most annoying things for me to stroll around in. This one has been particularly difficult to master."

"You must love him very much to put up with whatever that is," said Hashmi, pointing to Champ Champ's outfit.

"Love? I'm not sure you can call our relationship love. It's probably more akin to the relationship between Mallory and Miss Safia. But perhaps a little bit more erotic. That is, unless Miss Safia prefers the company of women, then perhaps it is what you are thinking."

"What? No? I'm not having Mallory do stuff like that."

"Then I suppose that's a welcome change from your last caretaker, then, isn't it, Miss Mallory?"

"That's not… I mean… yes, ma'am," said Mallory, dropping her head.

I guess that answers that question, then. Did Champ Champ already have talks with her about it?

"Are you sure you don't prefer the company of women, Miss Safia? I mean, Mallory is such a lovely girl. And if that night on the lake means anything, I say you seemed up for the idea."

Safia's eyes widened.

"What happened at the lake?" asked Hashmi.

"Nothing," said Safia as she grabbed Champ Champ's fluffy wrists and dragged her off through the snow, away from the girls. Her small legs struggled to keep up as they stomped the snow beneath.

"Goodness, Miss Safia. Slow down, I'm about to fall."

"How do you know about that?" asked Safia, turning around after they had gotten a reasonable distance away from Mallory and Hashmi. "Do you have your little cameras everywhere?"

"There's nothing to be ashamed of. All sexuality is endorsed here as long as it is consensual. And Mallory is the submissive type to male or female."

"Wait, she's what? How do you know that?"

"Because she once participated in one of our glass exhibits with one of our female alumni. I think you remember the last exhibit we had."

Safia's mind began to whirl as she thought about the couple behind the glass, her mind replacing the man with Mallory. "Wait, stop. Are you being serious?"

"Why would I lie?" asked Champ Champ, looking up at Safia and tilting her head in confusion.

"Then, why tell me that? Don't you have rules about exposing unnecessary stuff about students?"

"Safia, I think you've forgotten your relationship with Miss Mallory. Discarded are not allowed to keep secrets from their caretakers. This information is already yours, you just have to ask her about it."

"What do you mean?"

"Do you ever use that tablet of yours properly? It has a wealth of information inside of it. Including all the bets you've been involved in as well as all the bets that any of your discarded has been involved in. This includes before they became yours."

Safia blinked, staring back at Mallory. "*Wait, that means every bet she made with Dario, or is that every bet involving her?*"

"Oh, it seems you might be understanding things better now. Knowledge is power here, Miss Safia. I would encourage you to seek it out and use it. I promise you that everyone else here is."

"I don't want power over Mallory."

"Even if she enjoys you having power over her?"

Safia frowned, looking back at Mallory, who was starting

to build a snowman with Hashmi.

"Don't pretend you haven't noticed her nature. We calculated your intelligence before we ever decided to bring you here. And it was shown that your perceptiveness is one of your strong points."

Safia sighed and started rubbing her eyes in frustration. "All of this is just too much. What am I even supposed to do with her? She just does everything I say. I'm trying not to take advantage of her, but all she says is, 'Yes Ma`am, I'll do it, Miss Safia. Yes, Miss Safia. Should I wash your back, Miss Safia?'"

"Well, that last one, I didn't know about."

She frowned at Champ Champ,

"Just accept who she is and keep letting her get you the points you need. You can't tell me she hasn't made your monthly quota easier to acquire. If she likes to look up to you as her knight in shining armor, then let her. What's the harm? I swear that girl could probably use a hero right now."

"So, I should just keep using her, then?"

"We all use each other, dear. My husband uses me for his enjoyment. You used this school to save your father, and Mallory is most certainly using you for some type of stability in her life. It's not that we use people; it's what we use them for that matters."

"Fine. Then, you tell me. What am I supposed to do with her? I don't want to end up just being another Dario to her."

"Oh no, I'm not allowed to tell you what to do with your discarded. That's your decision to make. But," said Champ Champ, raising a finger. "If I may be allowed to make a suggestion."

"I'm listening."

"Get her to open up to you. Remember, she's not allowed to keep secrets from you. So if you ask, she will answer. Just try not to do it out here in this snow. Sometimes, the best healing will be in the form of manipulation."

Safia looked down at Champ Champ with narrowed eyes.

"And are you allowed to keep secrets from your husband?"

"No," said Champ Champ in a quick response.

"Then, between the clothing and the secrets, what's the difference between you being involved in this terrible discarded system?"

"Not much, except that it was my husband that was the broken one, and it took a long time for me to fix him. And I expect you will have quite the journey ahead of you if you wish to fix what's broken on that girl," said Champ Champ, turning back around to see Mallory and Hashmi finishing their snowman and stomping back through the snow towards them. "Hey, you should have let me join in. We can use some rocks for his eyes."

Safia watched Champ Champ make her way back over to Mallory and Hashmi. *Everybody has gone crazy, or maybe it's always been crazy, and I'm just realizing it.*

"Watch out," screamed a voice on the field.

Safia turned to the side only to see a male figure barreling through the snow towards her and above him a spiraling brown object floating in the air, also headed directly at her. She instinctively drew her hands over her head to protect herself. But there was no impact, only a hard slapping sound. She slowly opened her eyes to see Jericho standing before her, holding a football.

"Woo, I got here just in time. The last thing we need is you heading off to the doctor's office." He turned around and threw the football back to the boys on the field before turning back to Safia. "How've you been, Safia? Still enjoying our wonderful college experience?"

"No, unfortunately, I am not. And being tackled to the ground by you would have made it even worse."

"Wow, that's a sour mood you're in," said Jericho, raising his hands, showing he was unarmed.

Safia noticed the tone of her voice. "No, I'm sorry. I didn't mean it like that. I'm... I just have a lot on my mind, is all."

"Does that mean you want me to tackle you to the ground?" asked Jericho, looking around suspiciously. "I mean, it's not my style, especially in front of so many people. You really are a bold woman."

Safia shook her head with a giggle despite herself.

"Now there's that lovely smile I've grown accustomed to seeing. Not that gloomy face you just had on."

"Oh, shut up. What are you and your group of followers doing out here, anyway? Aren't you supposed to be building a monument to the Gods or something around the campus, like usual?"

"I am building something. Friendships that will hopefully last a lifetime, and after the game, we're all going to build a snow house."

"A snow house? What does that even mean?"

"It's a little house made of snow. We'll use water to harden it into ice, and people should be able to walk through it like a tunnel."

"Of course, they can. You're always making something."

"A man needs to stay busy. I just got permission from Champ Champ over there. Can I look forward to your participation?"

"Well. I'm always looking for another opportunity to make points."

"If that's the case, and seeing as you've started betting. How about you betting on me to score a touchdown?"

Safia looked over at the rest of the boys on the opposing team and how big they seemed, "Can you do it?"

"I have faith in myself. I'm the man who supports the whole campus with my work. You just watch." .

"Okay," said Safia, as she began walking over to the crowd of cheering girls. "Let's see what you've got." And as Jericho ran back to the field, Safia went over and tapped on her pendant, placing bets with the other giggling girls on Jericho's performance before turning around to watch.

The man with the ball on the ground squatted, throwing

the football behind him to another man, then took a few steps back, handing the ball to Jericho, who ran forward with it. He jumped over a boy who had fallen on the ground as the snow flew around him and then dodged another man with a fancy spin maneuver. He then turned to his left only to be tackled by two large boys and slammed down on the snowy ground hard as they climbed off of him. He laid in the snow for a moment as Safia walked over with Nasir, as they both leaned over, looking down at him.

"That looked like it hurt," said Nasir, shaking his head.

"It did, but not as much as my pride at this moment."

"Well, it doesn't seem to have hurt your adoring fans over there," said Nasir, nodding over to the girls who were still looking over at them.

"Yeah, it seems I'm still okay in their eyes," said Jericho as he sat up in the snow, still clutching the football in his hand and shaking his head.

"I'll be back. I need to ask Hashmi something," said Nasir, leaving Jericho and Safia alone.

"I do hope I didn't cost you too many of your points, Miss Safia. I'll pay you back if you like. I can buy you a coat or something."

"No need, I bet against you."

"What?"

"My father and my brother forced me to watch football with them when I was younger, and there was no way you were going to make it past those two truck-like guys there. You would have been better off trying to play wide-receiver rather than running back."

"Oh, ye of little faith."

"And this little faith won me fifteen hundred points from your foolish female admirers over there."

"Are you saying you're not my admirer?"

"I already have enough problems, and I'd rather not add fawning over you to that list. But I do appreciate the points you get me with all of your projects. Please continue to invite me on those."

"What a heartless woman."

Safia laughed. "Better to be heartless than foolish, especially in this school."

"I can't argue with that," said Jericho, reaching his arm up. "Give me a hand, please."

Safia helped him up and began brushing the snow out of his hair. "You really are the hopeless type, aren't you?"

"Am I? Does that mean you want to take care of me?"

"I take that back, perhaps you're just hopeful," said Safia shaking her head, but in truth she was enjoying this flirty banner with Jericho. He was starting to grow on her.

"A man needs to have hopes and dreams. I could make you a part of them if you wish."

"Hey! You done flirting over there?" asked one of the boys from their makeshift game. "How 'bout we get this game back going?"

"Alright!" yelled Jericho back to the group before turning back to Safia. "I guess I should go, but we can continue our talk later."

"Maybe, but have fun with your game. I have to take off, anyway. Try not to get flattened again," said Safia with a smile. Then she turned around and walked back over to Hashmi and Mallory, who were both chatting with Nasir. "Where'd our pocket-sized headmaster run off to?"

"She said she had something to do, so she left," said Mallory, still fiddling with the snowman.

"You aren't going to join back into the game, Nasir?"

"I prefer to watch. I think it's already cold enough without me working up a sweat out here."

"Finally, someone who understands," said Mallory, still rubbing at her shoulders.

"Well, let's go and get something to eat before class then, preferably something warm."

"Okay, I'm here," said Addison, as she walked up wearing a pleated winter goat with yellow accents and a brown wool hat. "It's fucking cold. I hope you're happy dragging me out here."

"Addison!" said Safia, surprised to see the woman just appeared as she walked over and stood by Nasir?

"Oh, well, if it isn't the Trojan, her puppy, and the hypocrite."

Hashmi narrowed her eyes at Addison. "I see you're still as vulgar as ever. Shouldn't you be off chasing children somewhere?"

"Ah, just as soon as you find a cliff to throw yourself off of."

"Ladies please," said Nasir, with his hands up. "There's no need to fight."

"Try telling her that," said Hashmi. "All she does is antagonize people. Why are you even here?"

"I don't want to be out in this boring cold either, but my needy boyfriend asked me to pay him a visit," said Addison as she leaned over, rubbing Nasir on the chin and giving him a kiss.

Instantly, Safia's and Hashmi's eyes both went wide.

"Wait, you two are dating?" asked Safia, blinking to make sure she wasn't imagining things.

"Yes, I believe I mentioned I had a girlfriend."

"But Addison, really?"

"Yeah, so? And what's wrong with me dating Nasir, Trojan girl?"

"Nothing, I mean. I thought... well... you made fun of Hashmi for being a Muslim."

"What?" asked Addison, placing her hands on her hips. "No, I made fun of little miss uppity for being a self-righteous hypocrite. Why would I make fun of her for being a Muslim when my boyfriend is one?"

"Wait, are you a Muslim?" asked Safia, curiosity getting the better of her.

"What? Of course she isn't," said Hashmi in response. "Nasir, is this the type of woman you wish to be with?"

"I admit Addison can be a bit abrasive. But she's a good person after you get to know her." Nasir furrowed his eyes at Addison. "Although, it would be nice if she would temper that impulsive nature of hers."

"Oh, shut it. We started dating because of my impulsive nature. Or do you not remember us staying late and…"

"Ahem," coughed Nasir, "Be that as it may, we are a couple and have been so for some time now."

"Nasir, surely you don't think your parents will approve of this."

"Probably not, but is that not the reason we are attending this school; to secure a future of independence away from such bindings."

Safia noticed Hashmi's voice beginning to sound more and more desperate as she spoke.

"Why are you so hell-bent on trying to break us up?" asked Addison, standing in front of Hashmi. "Honestly, this has nothing to do with you, little Miss Hypocrite. So why don't you just go back and stay out of our business?"

"Why, you insufferable woman? I have had enough—"

Safia quickly grabbed hold of Hashmi by the arm and started dragging her away with Mallory trailing behind them. "Let's go, Hashmi, we're leaving."

"Yeah, take her away," yelled Addison, with Nasir holding on to her. "Go on and find someone else's life to ruin." Addison yelled after the girls.

Safia and Mallory escorted Hashmi back onto the winding walkways towards the school.

"I swear, Addison is the only person I've seen who can get under your skin like that."

"That woman is impossible to tolerate. What does Nasir even see in her?"

"Well, they do say opposites attract. Maybe that's true for them too."

"And what if they have a child? Does Nasir think his family will accept a child with that type of woman? I swear men are all the same."

I see where she's coming from. But there's no way I'm stepping into this mess. "It's okay, Hashmi. Come on, let's go get that food we talked about and forget about them," said Safia as she pushed Hashmi forward trying to comfort her friend.

Around an hour later, Safia was in class with Hashmi as Abigail walked back and forth with a textbook in front of the students.

"Can anyone tell me why governments place sanctions and trade embargoes on other countries?"

"Isn't that what they do when other countries perform like war crimes or something?" asked one of the boys in the class.

"That's correct, but why do they do it?"

"So, it's not because of war crimes?" asked another girl in class.

"In a way, yes. But it's not the root cause. There are two main reasons why this is done," said Abigail, as she paced in front of the class. "One is because they wish to place economic pressure on a country, essentially starving them out of trade goods, structural support, or food supplies. Now the reason it's done is because the sanctioning country is trying to impose its influence. Have you ever noticed how trade is very rarely interrupted between the major world powers? Instead, it's often enforced on weaker second or third world countries."

"That can't be because America and Russia are friends. So why?" asked a boy in the back.

"It's because the first world countries already have enough military power to destroy the world a dozen times over. So, the odds of a third world war that doesn't destroy the planet are small. Instead, the first world countries play a different type of game called espionage."

"So, what other reason would a country have to make these sanctions then?"

"Because of public perception. This is especially true in America or any other country that operates on a voting democracy. Standing out of the crowd and voicing your opinions on atrocities worldwide is one of the mainstays that political figures use to stay in office. Wars of questionable origins have been started solely for certain world figures to stay in office longer than their allotted time. It may sound selfish, but inherently wars are very selfish. It's one side trying to take control of something. Either physical or mental. But it's when—"

The bell signaling the end of class rang, and the students all lifted from their seats.

"Okay, more homework before you go," said Abigail as the class groaned at her words. "I'm going to need five pages from each of you on how you would handle sanctions from a major first-world country if you were an impoverished third-world nation. Make up your own realistic scenarios on what the sanctions are for and how you would handle them. Be as descriptive as possible."

"That's too much work."

"I'm sure you think so, but it's my job to prepare you for life outside of here. And if you go into the world market, questions like these will become common."

Safia and Hashmi grabbed their things, walking out of class together.

"I'm going to head off back to the room and study," said Hashmi. "What about you, are you coming?"

"Mallory has science, so I'll probably just wait in the library and try to get ahead of the homework, I guess."

"Don't you have that little tablet? Why not just download the book on there like your textbooks?"

"Staring at this screen for too long hurts my eyes. I'd rather hold the book in my hand if I can. Plus, flipping through the pages feels a lot more satisfying than just swiping up and down."

"Alright then," said Hashmi, turning to go. "I'll see you back at the dorm."

"Hey, Hashmi."

"Yes?"

"Thank you."

"For what?" asked Hashmi.

"Just for being you, I'm not sure how I would have gotten through this place without you."

"I think the same can be said for the both of us," said Hashmi with a smile.

"Now, head-on. I'll meet up with you later," said Safia before turning around and walking off.

She then started walking out of the building into the snow, headed towards the left library. Making her way over, she noticed that the snow-covered buildings on the campus seemed like something out of a fairytale. Tall concrete arches and spires arose from the white frost covered rooftops.

Who would be the princess in each of these castles?

After a moment of standing in the snow, gazing over the campus, Safia made her way over to the library. On the way, she saw Amanda walking beside Killian as they were standing over on the snow, looking at the school.

"Oh, Safia, could you help us?" asked Amanda.

"Sure... I guess. What do you need?" replied Safia suspiciously, as she walked over to them.

"We seem to be at a loss on what type of events we should be having for the winter games. If you would be so kind as to provide us with some suggestions. We've walked around all morning asking the students but haven't quite narrowed it down."

"I don't understand. What are the winter games?"

"Well, for you, freshmen, it's your first game night of the year. For us, it's a way to unwind before we all have our mid-term tests. Think of it as a game night in the snow. Whereas below, you saw a multitude of different games and types of play. Well, we wish to recreate that feeling above ground at the end of the month."

"Oh, ahh, well, in Minnesota, hockey is popular during the winter, and earlier, the boys were playing football. That might be something?"

"I, myself, also thought about football," said Killian, "But seeing as the event takes place at night, that might not be a visually appealing thing to watch. Especially when you consider the large space needed."

"What about ice skating then?" asked Safia, thinking about what Mallory had told her earlier. "That's more of a spectacle sport. You can have it out on the lake since it's probably pretty frozen over now."

"I wonder how many here actually know how to ice skate," said Killian.

"It's not a bad suggestion," said Amanda, looking towards Killian. "Depending on how many people show up, that could just become the highlight event of the night. We might ask Jericho to search for participants, as he seems to have a knack for finding talented people."

"We can even get judges if enough people join," said Killian, rubbing his chin. "That would solve the betting part. Have people play the odds on whom they think will place in what positions. I'm pretty sure we can use lighting fixtures to shine a light on them at the lake. Perhaps, a portable power supply."

"Good job, Miss Safia. It seems you've got him going," said Amanda with a laugh.

"I did?"

"I can probably get Jericho to make some bleachers for the fans," said Killian to himself as he began to pace back and forth in the snow. "Oh, and a trading post, maybe even charge an attendance fee."

"Yeah, there's no use talking to him now. Better to just

let him work his way through this. Tell me, Miss Safia, how have things been for you? We haven't had much time to talk since you gave me that wonderful night on the lake. I've heard that you've taken up a greater interest in joining us in our debauchery here. So how has the gambling life been treating you?"

"I only gamble enough to make sure that Mallory and I are taken care of."

"Oh, that's right. You also have a discarded now since you took Dario's little toy. Congratulations on succeeding where I failed. If I may ask, how did you pull off such a feat? Goodness knows I tried hard enough to get her away from that bastard."

"Ah, I'm not sure I'm allowed to say."

"Oh, some secret bet then? Well, either way, good job. You're only a freshman and managed to grab a discarded for yourself. I do hope you're treating her properly. I imagine that poor girls' suffered enough for two lifetimes under Dario's uninformed oppression."

Safia looked over at Killian, who was still pacing back and forth away from them before she leaned down and whispered to Amanda. "Is it possible to make a discarded have sex with you?"

"What?" asked Amanda as her eyes went wide before she narrowed them with a smile on her face. "Well, Miss Safia Famosa, I didn't know your hobbies went that far. However, I'm a bit offended that you didn't try to have me join you in bed that night. But given your passion for being a dominatrix, perhaps you're getting off on the power you have over her. But be careful. I'd hate to see you become the female version of Dario."

"What? No? I would never do that to her. It's just, she never wants to talk about her time with Dario. And I was just curious if he could make her do that."

"Oh, I see. Well, shame on you for giving me hope that the fantasy of you and I being together could happen. But as for your question, yes. If I so choose, I could order Ricardo to come and pleasure me in my bed. Threatening him with the risk of expulsion and so forth. And given how deftly afraid that girl seems to be of going home. Then, just as a guess. I would assume he has done so."

"What about ordering them to have sex with someone else? Is that possible?"

"I imagine so. It's not unheard of. But circumstances are different for everyone. For example, could you imagine if I ordered Ricardo to suck another man's cock? The poor boy would be off on a plane back home that same night, and they would probably never find my body. But Ricardo has no fear of going home. Your discarded, on the other hand, she might submit to such an order. It just depends on what a person is willing to do to stay here, and how evil a person who owns them wants to be." Amanda waved her hand. "But you do realize you could just order her to reveal these things to you? But, then again, I guess you're not the type to give such an order, are you?"

"No, I'm not," replied Safia assuredly.

"Then, your options are limited, I'm afraid," said Amanda, reaching up and patting Safia on the cheek. "Such a sweet girl. Try not to have that need of yours to help others end up being your downfall. This school's nature is to break delicate things. Goodness, you really are beautiful in this snow."

"I think I can do it," said Killian, walking back over to them and noticing Amanda's hand on Safia's cheek. "Oh, am I interrupting something?"

"No," said Amanda, removing her hand. "Just trying to imagine some wish fulfillment. Now, tell me, what have you figured out?"

"I think I have an idea for the winter games. It can be the main attraction if enough people know how to skate professionally, even if it's only a small amount. If we ask for the lumber now, we should be able to build everything we need before the end of the month and still have time to set up a few games as side attractions."

"Well then, I'm happy to hear you have it all figured out. I imagine the school will give you a hefty point reward for leading this operation."

Safia looked over at Killian after the mention of points. *He wants to buy Abigail. And Champ Champ said there was nothing she could do to stop him. I wonder how many points he has left before he's done.*

"Thank you for your suggestion, Miss Safia," said Killian, with a smile on his face. "I will inform the school that the skating event was your idea, and if it becomes as popular as I think it will, then I'm sure they will reward you with a hefty point sum as well. The winter games are a large event at this school."

"Oh, thank you. I could always use more points." *He would be a nice guy if it weren't for his obsession with Abigail. Why can't you put your attention back on someone who actually likes you? Do you even know that the people around the campus call you the stalker?*

"Well, come along, Killian, you can explain this plan to me in more detail while we go and find Jericho and get him started right away," said Amanda, linking her arms around Killian's. "Ricardo isn't here now, so I'm going to commandeer your services to escort me around in preparation for our winter wonderland." Amanda then dragged Killian away while waving back. "Take care, Miss Safia. I really hope to talk with you again."

She really is a forceful person. She might have more in common with Champ Champ than she'd like to admit. Safia watched the two walk off before she herself stepped back on to the walkway and made her way over to the library. Making her way up the steps, she opened the door, and once again, the air of the building rushed out, hitting her in the face as the smell of old books danced in her nose.

Okay, so I needed books on third-world nations, I think.

Now, where would they be? thought Safia as she began making her way through the numerous shelves of books. *Am I even in the right library?* Ahead of her, she noticed the familiar dreadlocks of Austin as he passed by her aisle. In his hand, she could see some type of weird metal object.

"Austin," called out Safia. *He might know where a book on third-world nations might be.* But he must not have heard her as he continued on his way. Safia stepped forward, trying to catch him, but as she entered the walkway she saw him turn into another book aisle.

"Austin," she called again, but he gave no answer. With a frown on her face Safia increased her pace and followed behind him. She saw him take another turn and took a few skips to catch up. But after turning the final corner to catch up to him, she was met with a dead end. Another shelf of books against the wall stood in front of her, with no sign of Austin.

But... where did he go? Safia glanced around, confused. *I'm not crazy. That was him.* She reached forward, removing two books from the shelf, and peered forward between the opened space. Inside was just a concrete wall, as one would expect. *Maybe I was... No. I saw him. I know I did. There's something strange here.* She started peering around again, looking at the books around her and up against the walls. It didn't take her long before she found it; another one of those black orbs up against the ceiling, looking down at her. *There's something here. I know it. This school and its damned secret*s.

"I don't have time for this," muttered Safia to herself, as she shook her head and took a deep breath. "I've got other..." A book caught Safia's eye. '*The history of trade throughout the world.*' Safia placed the other two books back on the shelf and reached out, grabbing the one that caught her eye. Let them have their stupid games. *I've got my own problems to worry about.* She then made her way through the aisles and took a seat at one of the tables ahead of her. *But does that mean that Austin is involved with whatever they have going on here? Or maybe they're using him like they're using me. Agrh. It's frustrating.*

"Well, if it isn't the water dancer," said an obnoxious voice.

Safia looked up from her book to see Addison walking over with a pink book in her hand. *Not now. Why are you here? Go bother someone else.*

"What are you doing here?" asked Addison, pulling out a chair and plopping down beside Safia.

"I'm studying for a paper I'm supposed to write," said Safia, holding up her book for Addison to see. "Why are you here? Aren't you supposed to be back out there with Nasir, annoying people, or something?"

"I've got to do some research of my own," said Addison, holding up her pink book. Across the cover were the words. *'So, your man likes to be spanked.'*

"What the hell kind of book is that?"

"The fun kind. I'm sure it's far more fun than what you've got."

Safia shook her head. "I'll leave you to it then."

"Hey, don't be like that. I came over for us to share some girl talk."

"What? But you don't even like me."

"That's true. You seemed like a no fun, stick in the mud, goody-two-shoes type of girl," said Addison as she stretched her arms out, leaning her back against the chair. "But you somehow managed to steal Dario's little puppy, and you got Amanda pretty hot and bothered, so I figured you might be fun to stick around with."

"Addison."

"Humm?"

"I honestly have no idea what Nasir sees in you."

Addison smiled. "Is it what he sees in me, or how he feels in me?"

"Wow, you're a horrible person."

"I'm glad you finally noticed, but don't worry about me. I'm able to keep myself in good company since almost everyone here is a horrible person in one way or another. Especially that little hypocrite friend of yours."

"What is your problem with Hashmi, anyway? Why do you keep pushing her like that?"

"I simply hate stuck-up people; thinking they're so high and mighty, like everyone's supposed to listen to them. So, I'll drag 'em down with me before I ever listen to them peddling their shit over me."

"Hashmi isn't like that. You two would get along with each other if you tried."

"Yeah, well, unless Miss Uppity apologizes to me, that ain't never gonna happen. And I think she feels she's just a little too good for that."

Safia shook her head, but had no response.

"See, even you got nothing to say to that."

"That's because you're both stubborn."

"Can't deny that. Better to be a cocky piece of trash than a submissive, walked-over fool."

"So, where are the boys now anyway, still beating the mess out of each other in football?" Safia asked, trying to change the subject.

"Nah, someone came and got Jericho. That underwater platform broke because of all the ice. So, I guess, you and Amanda's little love spot is gone now till they fix it."

"It's not our love spot, and why get Jericho for that?"

"Because he's practically the Mr. Fix It for this campus. Speaking of which, has he fixed you yet?"

"What do you mean?"

"I'm asking if you've fucked him yet?"

"What?" Safia blurted out loud in the library, causing a few other studying students to glance up from their textbooks.

"Oh, please, don't *what* me. I've seen how you look at him. You're dating, aren't you?"

"No, we're just friends."

"So, you telling me friends can't fuck? Seems like a waste of a good friend."

Safia just stared at Addison for a long moment. Then suddenly, her pendant glowed red.

"Mallory Polana would like to know your location. Do you accept?" asked the pendant.

"Oh, and there's the puppy now," said Addison, clapping her hands. "Come on, invite her over. I wanna see her lick your boots."

"Do you act like that out of hatred, or were you just born a bitch?"

"Why can't it be a little of both?"

Safia frowned, tapping her pendant. "I accept, give her my location." She then turned back to Addison. "If you're going to stay here, then you're going to behave and not try to rile up Mallory like you do Hashmi. She's been through enough."

"My, aren't we protective of our little toy?" asked Addison, before catching Safia staring daggers at her. "Fine, fine, I'll behave. I guess actually studying can't be so bad."

A few minutes later, Mallory appeared and walked over to the table.

"Hello, Miss Safia. Oh, I didn't know you had company."

"Hi, my name's Addison. We met earlier. I'm Nasir's girlfriend. Don't mind me. Safia and I were just talking about our past boyfriends. What about you? You ever fell in love with a boy and wanted to throw him in front of a bus after he cheated on you?"

"I… ah…" Mallory just stared at Addison for a moment.

"Don't mind Addison; she suffers from some type of mental issues. Just have a seat."

"Okay," said Mallory, taking a seat at the table.

"What are you studying? You're a second-year so I'm not sure I can help much."

"Oh, no, it's nothing hard. We're just going over the

campus and dividing the structures into categories."

"Oh, yeah," said Addison. "You got that too, huh. Miss Froyal and her stupid building class."

"Building class?" Safia looked confused. "Why is that even a thing?"

Mallory shrugged. "Don't know, but together there's about eighty-something structures on campus. I think. As long as we don't count trees and stuff. But this also includes the stuff Mr. Jericho has built, like when he made the gazebo."

"Okay," said Safia, throwing up her hands. "I'll try, but I'm not sure what help I'll be."

They all began to study and go over their notes for the next hour, with Addison even chipping in and correcting Safia on any mistakes they were making.

"Ah! What a pain this is," said Addison as she rubbed at her eyes. "So damn boring."

"Well, you lasted longer than I thought you would. I had figured you would run away as soon as we started."

"Just because I can do the work doesn't mean I like doing the work," said Addison, scratching at her head. "You, puppy girl, you actually like being discarded? The way you keep looking at Miss goody-two-shoes over here makes me wonder."

"What do you mean? Miss Safia treats me nice."

"Yeah, and so do most owners with their dogs. I've never understood this whole discarded thing."

"There are plenty of discarded on campus," said Mallory, shaking her head, "Even Amanda has three men as discarded."

Three? She has three?

"Yeah, well, I'm pretty sure she's fucking one of them. So, he has a reason to stick around." Addison's eyes went wide as she looked between the two girls, and she lowered her voice, dropping her head low to the table. "Is that the way of it? Are you two bumping pussies at night?"

Mallory's lips pursed as her face went red.

"Holy shit, you like your little owner. Ha! just wait till Amanda hears of this," she turned to Safia, "And after you rejected her that night. So, spill it, what's your type? You get off on having power over her or something?"

"No, stop that? Miss Safia and I haven't done anything yet."

Yet? thought Safia, her eyes twitching as she tried not to show her surprise.

"Yet," repeated Addison with a smile as she bit her lip in joy, "But that means you want to, doesn't it."

Mallory tried to stand from the table, but Addison quickly reached over, grabbing at her wrists, holding on to her.

"Oh no, don't run away," said Addison, with eyes wide with crazy excitement. "Not yet. This is just too much fun. Now, don't make too much noise. You don't wanna cause trouble for the one who takes responsibility for you, now do you?"

Mallory's face began to twist with embarrassment as she looked over at Safia, who was rubbing the side of her head.

"Sit down, Mallory," said Safia.

"Miss Safia, I'm—"

"Sit down, Mallory," said Safia in a harsher tone.

"Oh, I like that anger in your voice," said Addison.

Mallory sat back down at the table with her head down, being quiet.

Safia took a breath. "It's okay, Mallory. I already know that you have feelings for me." *That's a lie. How was I supposed to know you liked me? You're so damned timid, and I just thought you were the quiet type. You kissed me, but I wasn't even sure what was happening. I thought you were just doing it so I wouldn't send you home. Wait? Or did I kiss you? Argh, I was half asleep. I thought you were David.*

"You do?" asked Mallory.

366

"Of course, I do." *Great, now I'm lying to her.* "And Addison, leave her alone. She hasn't done anything to you, so stop trying to embarrass her."

"Who's embarrassing her?" asked Addison before turning back to Mallory, the smirk still on her face. "What's there to be ashamed about with her little girl crush," said Addison. "Your owner here's already been going around kissing other girls."

"She what?"

Oh no, "Addison, stop."

"Yeah, I was there watching her and Amanda smooching out by the lake. They even paid me to play that damned violin for them while they were in each other's arms." Addison turned her face to look at Safia, "You like kissing girls, except for the one you own that actually likes you? Now that's just a weird fetish to have."

"And you're a pain in the ass," said Safia.

"I prefer cock, but if you wanna have a go at me? I'm game if you are. We can even throw your little pet in there to spice things up."

"Do you even think about things before you say them?"

"What for? It'd just slow down my fun. Oh, and speaking of which, there looks to be even more fun out the window. Look," said Addison, pointing her finger.

Safia turned to see Abigail outside the window, under a tree, talking to Killian in the snow.

"Now there's a bit of fun. That bastard Killian is apparently close to buying his darling bride."

"You know about that?" asked Safia, turning back around to Addison.

"Ahh, and here I was hoping it would be a surprise, and I could tease you with the information. Way to spoil my fun."

"What do you mean? What's happening?" asked Mallory, looking between the two girls.

"Oh, so she doesn't know. You wanna tell her, or should I?"

Safia shook her head.

"Well, little puppy, Lady Abigail is about to be in the same situation that you were in with Dario. And I promise ain't nobody coming to save her like Safia did for you. Killian's on a whole other level of genius. Even that little headmistress tried to slow it down by kindly suggesting that no one on campus bet him. But you know how some people think they're all high and mighty. They tried to bet Killian anyway, and he'd knock 'em off so hard that people on campus don't even bet him anymore. He's like a walking *Do Not Bet* sign."

"So that's why Dario was always scared to bet him," said Mallory as her face showed her mind working her way through her thoughts.

"Yeah, it's common knowledge. But it makes me wonder just how many points he has. Because even I don't know what the price tag on a teacher here would be."

"You really think he's as bad as Dario?" muttered Mallory softly under her lips.

Safia turned to see Mallory staring out of the window, her gaze seeming as if she was looking off to a distant planet. *I guess if we're going to talk about it, now would be as good a time as any.* "Addison, can you—" said Safia, turning her head to the obnoxious girl only to feel Addison's lips press against hers.

"Hey, what—" said Mallory.

What the hell? thought Safia as she tried to pull herself back, but Addison pushed herself forward, grabbing hold of her wrists and holding them down to her sides. *Dammit, why is she so strong?*

Addison breathed deeply for a long moment before letting Safia go, pulling away from her and standing up from her seat.

"Woo. So that's what it feels like," said Addison, wiping her thumb across her lips.

"What the hell is wrong with you?" asked Safia, wiping

her hand across her lips as the hint of lemon danced across her tongue.

"I wanted to see what it felt like to kiss a girl, and you were close by."

"And you never thought to fucking ask first?"

"Oh, please, Safia, do I seem like the type to ask for anything?" asked Addison, as she turned to Mallory. "And you're not really missing out on much. I prefer a hard cock over soft lips any day. But I guess it just depends on what you're into."

"Just go away," said Safia, who was still trying to wipe off the taste of Addison from her lips. *Why does she taste like lemons?*

"Oh, I see how things are. You take my first girl on girl kiss and then you toss me to the wayside," said Addison with a pouty face before turning to Mallory with a smile. "Be careful, puppy. This one's a heartbreaker."

"Shut up, and just leave," said Safia.

"I'm going," said Addison as she began to walk off. "You two enjoy yourselves."

"Ma`am, please," said one of the students in charge who was nearby. "This is a library. Keep your voice down."

"Oh, fuck off. I'm going."

"Miss Safia, are you alright?"

"Yeah, I'm fine." *I'm more angry that I missed the chance to talk to you about Dario than I am over that damned kiss.* She turned back to see that Abigail and Killian had moved on from whatever conversation they were having under the tree. *And, of course, they're gone.* Safia sighed, "Okay, let's go. We can head back. I suddenly feel like I want to brush my teeth."

CHAPTER 16

The night of the winter games had come, and Hashmi, Mallory, and Safia arrived at the gate down by the lake. Inside, they could see the efforts of all their labors bearing fruit. An assortment of colorful tents were spread throughout the area. Decorated ropes went through each structure as the supports were nailed into the ground.

Ahead of the girls was a small house that looked to be made entirely out of snow. It even had the design of windows chiseled out on its walls. There was a tunnel inside of it that led to the opening of the event.

Safia glanced around the man made cave as they walked

inside. There were colorful lights that hung from the roof of the tunnel, giving the area around them a mixture of the shades of blue, green, and red that shined off the walls.

"I can't believe you did all this with Jericho after we left," said Hashmi.

"I didn't. I mean, we just gathered the snow. It was him and Killian who managed all this. But it's still better than I though it would be. I thought it would be just a giant snowball."

"That's what I would have thought also."

"It's one hundred points to enter," said a man as they made it through the tunnel and appeared on the other side. Safia noticed it was the same boy who wore the chef's hat in front of the school eatery.

"And here I thought it'd be free since we helped build it."

"Technically, it will be," said the man as he looked over the festival. "But you won't be reimbursed for the points until after the night is over. We charge everyone to be sure that no one lies about their contribution to the event. I think Jericho has already allocated the point percentage that everyone will receive when the event is over."

"Okay, then I'll be paying for two. Myself and Mallory here."

"Yes, ma'am. That's two hundred points. Just click your badge and wave it over the podium."

Safia did as the man asked, and as her badge turned red, she was allowed into the winter festival, and with Hashmi following suit. The event was as lively as Jericho said it would be, with people scattered throughout the grounds all dressed in their prospective dorm's winter clothing. Above their heads were light bulbs of varying colors that hung from strings, casting down a rainbow of colors around the snow-packed ground. In the air, the smell of food floated around them as Safia saw several grills spread throughout the area. Some even had their little makeshift stalls.

"Ribs here, Ribs here fifty points," screamed one of the

nearby merchants as the girls made their way through the event.

"Oh, they even have cotton candy," said Mallory, as she focused on one of the stalls that had a rotating machine to create the sweet spinning yarn.

"You want some?" asked Safia.

"Yes, please. I haven't had this stuff since I was like five."

"Okay, then, how much?" Safia asked, after walking over to the stall.

"Fifty points, Ma`am."

"The same as the ribs? That's odd."

"All the food here costs fifty points. Most of us serving the food are from Marigold house. So, we all just decided to share the profit."

"Isn't that your old house, Mallory?"

"Yes, but I never really stayed there. Mostly, I was with… well… with Dario."

Safia clicked her badge, sliding it across a small plate with the school sigil on it, and grabbed a cotton candy stick, handing it to Mallory. *What am I, her mother?* "Well, come on, let's go see what else all our hard work built."

The girls made their way down to the lake, where they could still see Jericho and Killian fiddling with some wires.

"Let's go see what the boys are up to," said Safia. Over beyond the fence, she could see the shanty house where she went to the previous game night. Now, it was closed off again, with two large boards nailed across the entrance. Snow had covered the rooftop and it stood high in front of the door.

Turning back around, she noticed that circling the lake was an assortment of black poles sticking out of the ground. Atop each one in a cylinder were huge lights that were pointed towards the lake.

"Well, hello there," said Jericho as he handed a set of cables off to Killian, who took them over to a large machine on wheels.

"How much did all this cost?" asked Safia, looking around the area. "I mean, all we did was help build some tents and a part of the bleachers around the lake together. But now, it looks like a little town."

"Thank Killian for that. My plan was a lot more modest than this. But he's the one who had the idea of the grand spectacle," said Jericho as he trotted through the snow to the sounds of rumbling from the large machine. After a few flickers in the dim light, all the black poles around the lake started to light up, each one shining a different color down onto the frozen lake. The colors then began to rotate around the lake before converging on the center in a beautiful rainbow snowflake pattern.

"Wow, that's even more impressive than I'd thought it'd be," said Jericho as he turned toward Killian, who was over by the large machine, which apparently was some type of generator.

"How are you doing that?" asked Mallory as she stared out over the lake, watching as the colors once again broke apart and began rotating.

"That's all, Killian," said Jericho as he turned toward the man. "Hey, Killian, stop playing with your new toy and come over here and explain all this stuff to your adoring fans."

The light show stopped as Killian turned off the generator and made his way over to the group.

"Oh, sorry, I need to learn how this thing works before the skating event."

"You still have a few hours until then. You should at least enjoy the festival. After all, you're the one who paid for it."

"I must admit that even I'm curious about how much all of this would cost," said Hashmi, as she turned around looking over the lake and all the tents up above. "Surely, the school didn't just hand over all this equipment."

"A little over two hundred twenty thousand points."

"Two hundred twenty ? How many points do you have?"

asked Mallory.

Killian laughed. "Well, that's a secret, but I can promise you that I now have two hundred twenty thousand less than what I had before."

"Don't feel bad for Killian and his points. He's going to make a lot more than that after tonight."

"How?" asked Safia.

"Well, obviously, I didn't have enough points to make this happen. So, instead, all the points we make tonight, minus the builder fee for you guys, will be handed off to this bastard in the middle of next month. Don't let his sob point story fool you. He's already figured out what he will make. While it's my name on the event, he'll be the one reaping all the rewards at the end of the night." Jericho slapped Killian on the back. "Tell us, Mr. Moneybags, there should be enough of a sample size for you to guess how much you'll be bringing home. So share with the group on how much you're gonna make."

"Well, let's see," said Killian as he looked up the hill. "If people keep gathering like this for the next few hours or so and let's say that every four out of five people here will each spend around three to five hundred points in the gambling tents, plus the cost of admission, then add to that your average big point spender. I guess it should average out to around five hundred thousand points if you include my organizing fee from the school, but that might fluctuate either direction by about twenty thousand points. It's really a percentage of everything that happens tonight."

"Wow," said Jericho as he clapped his hands together. "Either way, by the end of tonight, you will have gained a lot more than what you spent to make this place. What do you plan to do with all those points? You gonna try to have the school named after you? You can probably do it with as much as you're gonna have."

"No, there's only one thing that I want," said Killian as he stared up at the few stars that were poking through the cloudy night sky. "And I'm almost there."

"Almost? What the hell could cost more than five hundred thousand points?"

Abigail, he's gonna use the points to buy the years she has left. Jericho, you dummy. You've just given him everything he needs!

This time, Killian slapped Jericho on the back. "Now, that's another secret. But don't worry, Jericho, I won't forget what you've done for me. If tonight goes right, you would have saved me three months off my plan. When I leave this school, you'll always have a friend in me."

"I appreciate that. It's good to have people in high places that call you their friend."

While watching the two men laughing joyfully, Safia couldn't help but feel a tightening in her stomach. *There's nothing I can do, is there? She* glanced back over at Mallory, who had stepped a few feet away and was staring off into the sky, looking up at the stars. Her long hair being lifted into the air by a slight breeze that nipped at Safia's face, making her squint. *It's not the same thing. It's only by luck that I was able to help Mallory. There's nothing I can do to stop him. Five hundred thousand? Even the number is absurd.*

"Okay, you bastard," said Jericho, clapping his hands together. "You can go on back to your light show. I'll try to entertain the ladies here until everything is ready."

"Ladies, I hope you enjoy your night here," said Killian. And after a smile, he walked away, back over to the generator with neither a second glance at them. He turned to the machine and pressed a button and with a rumble it started back up again and the light show returned to the crystal ice over the lake. He never even looked back at the ice. His eyes focused purely on the screen ahead of him. Not a smile or a frown, just focusing on his task.

He smiles when he's around people, but as soon as his back turns he doesn't seem like the same person. I wonder what he's thinking about when he's not around people.

"So," said Jericho with a knowing smile. "What's the plan for you girls tonight? Meeting up with a secret admirer to have him profess his love under a snow-covered mountain top?"

"Funny," said Safia, focusing her attention back on Jericho. "But there are no mountains to climb."

"You sure about that?" asked Jericho, pointing behind them as he walked ahead.

Safia turned around to see over in the distance an impressively large amount of snow near the edge of the camp area that stood higher than the tents. While off in the darkness a bit, after focusing on it, she could see its absurd size when compared to the setting ahead of it. At its peak she could see the shadowed images of people as some went running and sliding down the side.

"Wow," said Mallory, "It's so tall. How long did that take?"

Safia smiled back at Jericho. "Why did they even make that? Is it even possible to charge people just to climb that thing?"

"No, not really. People just are drawn to it and the moment we finished and cleared out this area, they just attacked it and started climbing up its sides. But we figured we could just put up a warning sign and let the curiosity of the mass public lead them to their snowy mountain top. Also, it's kinda cool to know that I had a hand in building my own little Mount Everest," said Jericho as he watched a couple go sliding down the side of it. "You girls should have a go at it. I've named it Jericho's mountain."

"Of course you've named it after yourself," said Safia, shaking her head as she watched another couple go down the side of the mountain. "Don't you think it's a bit arrogant to name it after yourself?"

"Hey, it's brand marketing. I need my name to become synonymous with fun around here."

"And what if someone hurts themselves on the way

down?"

"Then I'll rename it Killian's mountain. People are already terrified to bet him, anyway. And his name has the word *Kill* in it. So, I think it fits."

"What a wonderful friend you are," said Hashmi with a giggle.

"I'm happy you think so. I want everyone to call me a friend, so I try to help out as much as possible," said Jericho, as he stood behind Safia, placing his hands on her shoulders. "Look, Safia still even has the necklace I gave her. I'd say that's proof of our strong bond. And I do remember you saying something about professing one's love on a snow-covered mountain top. That was you who just said that."

"Are you sure? That sounds like something you would say." He smiled. "Either way, the rope part is still true."

"You mean the small piece of dirty rope that I had to wash because it was staining my clothes? Oh yes, that certainly is a bond, that I had to use a lot of soap to get out."

"But you're still wearing it," said Jericho as he wrapped his arms around Safia's waist, holding her close to him. "That shows how much you value me. Or maybe there's more to our relationship and you want to take a trip going down on Jericho's mountain with me while making kissy faces."

"Oh, shut up," said Safia as she felt Jericho's arms tighten around her waist. She smiled as she embraced the extra warmth that his closeness provided her.

"Well, don't you two look comfortable like that," said Hashmi with folded arms. "You making me feel as if I'm intruding on you—"

"Oh, shit!" screamed a man's voice ahead of them. They all looked up to see a man lose his balance at the top of the snowy mountain and go tumbling down the wrong side, crashing into a nearby pole. Quickly, a few other students rushed to his side.

"Jericho's mountain is closed, and Killian's Mountain is open for business," said Jericho with a chuckle as he released Safia and stepped forward, peering into the crowd that had just gathered around the man. He shook his head with that same stupid grin on his face. "Boy, I'm happy I didn't make a sign or anything."

Safia just turned to him, shaking her head. "Aren't you going to go and check on him?"

"Yeah, I guess that would make sense. They don't know that it's Killian's mountain yet. I better go over there and make sure they can't blame me for this. Well, if you ladies will excuse me. I'll go make sure he's not dead. If so, I'll probably need to hide the body until the night is over," said Jericho as he headed over. "You girls, enjoy yourselves. I'll see you at the skating competition."

"You certainly have interesting friends, Safia," laughed Hashmi.

"Me? Why me, you've helped him too."

"No, I've helped you and Nasir, and by proxy, I've helped him. And Mallory just helps out in general. So, she only qualifies as your friend. And neither of us were the one looking all comfy with his hands around our waist."

"Well, gee, thanks. But I'm not sure Jericho even knows what a real friend is."

"Why's that? He seems to get along with everyone well enough," said Mallory.

"It's..." Safia thought back to game night and the look on Jericho's face. "It's nothing. Let's go and enjoy ourselves."

"You won't be taking a ride down Jericho's mountain then?" asked Hashmi with a smirk.

"Oh, you're just all kinds of sassy tonight."

The girls went on their way and started playing the games of the night. There were several colorful events, along with silly carnival music that played throughout the area as they walked along.

"Oh, that looks like fun. Let's play that!" blurted out

Mallory as she pointed her finger towards a stall with a bucket that was draped in purple and pink cloth that hung down in an arch.

Inside the stall stood a man, who gave them a smile as they approached.

"You lovely ladies looking to have a go?" asked the man.

"So what do we have to do to win?" asked Safia, pointing forward to a pyramid of cups that were stacked on top of one another. "Just knock down the cups?"

"Correct," said the man as he came forward, grabbing the bucket and placing three snow balls inside and sitting it back on the counter in front of them. "So what do you say? Care to show me some girl power? Or are you three princesses too fragile to knock down a few plastic cups?"

Safia frowned, "You trying to goad us into playing."

"That's correct," said the man with a sly smile as he leaned forward, placing his elbows on the counter. "Is it working?"

"I'll show you who's weak," huffed Mallory as she grabbed the bucket and turned back towards Safia. "Come on Miss Safia, let's show him."

Wow! She's actually aggressive about something, thought Safia as she saw the determination on Mallory's face. *I guess it couldn't hurt,and it's good to see her excited.*

"I'd like to have a go as well," said Hashmi with a step forward towards Mallory, who held the bucket.

"What? Hashmi is actually going to join in on a game?" Safia said with genuine surprise.

"Well, technically, this isn't gambling as much as it's paying for entertainment. Plus, I want to try and win one of the items they have up there." She pointed up towards some prizes and stuffed animals hanging on hooks above the game.

"I guess that settles it," said Safia as she stepped forward, removing her school pendant from her neck, grasping it in her palm. "Are there any special rules that we should know?

Knowing this school, they'd probably try to make us play blindfolded."

"Now that's an unfair assumption. Everything here is on the up and up. I promise. Just slide your pendant over the plate. It'll take fifty points away from your account and you'll get three snowballs. Throw 'em however you like, but you must knock down everything in one hit. If not, then the cups will be reset. If you knock them down on your first try, then you get a grand prize."

Safia was up first. Swiping her badge across the plate she received the small blue bucket from Mallory and stepped up. Grabbing one of the three balls, she launched it at the plastic cups. It struck the center cup, which sent the three cups on top flying, but left the three at the bottom. "Damn." She tried again but got the same result; each time, leaving cups standing.

"Well, that's hardly fair. How am I supposed to knock down nine cups with only one attempt?"

"You need power," said the man as he flexed his arm. "You girls sure you don't want to wait for your boyfriends to show up and try to win it for you? They might stand a better chance."

"You certainly are an annoying stall worker, aren't you?" asked Hashmi with a frown.

The man grinned. "Gotta turn up the sexism to make you keep playing. And I'm very good at my job."

"So it would seem," said Hashmi, not amused by the man's antics.

"I'm next," said Mallory, as Safia shook her head and swiped her pendant. She grabbed her snowballs, launching them wildly one at a time. Her last attempt missed the cups completely, going wild, and striking the man running the game in the face.

"Ahh," yelped the man, falling back on the ground with snow caked to the side of his face and in his hair.

"Oh, sorry," said Mallory, looking over the counter as

Safia and Hashmi giggled.

"I think that last one might have been intentional," said Hashmi as she walked up to the stall. "Are you okay? It looks like that girl power was a little bit too much for you."

The man frowned back up at Mallory before sighing, wiping the snow from his face, and standing back up to his feet. "Yeah, yeah. Maybe I did deserve a bit of that."

Hashmi swiped her badge, and waited for the stall worker to place another set of snowballs on the counter. After doing so, he quickly decided to stand a bit farther away from the cups this time around. "Okay, let's see what I got." The first throw went wild and missed completely. The second struck hard and sent the cups flying, but left two. And the third took out the bottom right cup, which caused the two above to fall but still left three cups standing. "Dang it, not even close. It's a lot harder than it looks." Hashmi gave a quick glance over to the stall worker.

"Hey, don't look at me like that. I didn't say nothing this time."

"Can I try again?" asked Mallory.

"Sure, just try not to hit the worker again. They're might be some secret penalty involved with it," said Safia, swiping her badge over the plate and then turning back to Hashmi.

"Well, that's only one of the games," said Hashmi. "There are still plenty others to try since we're here. Perhaps some that are actually winnable. What do you want to try next?"

"Depends on what... look at this girl," said Safia, turning back to see Mallory with an oversized snowball held up in both her hands. She placed it over her head, squatted, and with a little effort, pushed up, lobbing the giant snowball in an arch through the air. It landed with a crash of white powder, obliterating all the cups.

"Ha! Take that, you stupid cups."

"Where'd you even get that thing?"

"Huh? I packed all the snowballs together and threw it that way."

"What? Can you even do that?"

"He never said I couldn't, and he said that we could throw it however we liked. We just had to throw one at a time. Well, that was my one throw and it was my first throw, so we get the grand prize."

Safia turned toward the stall worker, who had either a look of disbelief or disgust on his face. She really couldn't tell.

"Well, she's not wrong. I did say that," said the stall worker as he shrugged. "Fine, pick out whatever you want. It's my fault for not being specific enough, I guess."

"Yay!" shouted Mallory. "Which one did you want, Hashmi?"

"Me? You're going to let me pick?"

"Yeah, you said you wanted something right. I really don't care. I just wanted to play."

"Wow, thank you! Can I have the small tablet there as the grand prize?"

"Here ya go," said the man, handing Hashmi the tablet.

"I'm a little jealous," said Safia, "I had to pay eight hundred points for mine, and Mallory wins one for you in a snow game."

"Don't be. It took me almost six months, and I only got one because Mallory was so kind. But later on, you have to show me how to use it."

"Alright then. But right now, let's go see what else there is to play."

The three girls went off exploring the rest of the campsite, and continued to stop at the stalls, playing a multitude of simple party games, such as bowling, barrel catching, and ping pong.

"You know, I'm starting to think either we're just bad at this or Mallory is some type of secret genius," said Safia, turning back behind her to see Mallory holding a bundle of prizes in her arms.

"You can have them if you want," said Mallory as she

struggled to keep a grip on all her winnings.

"And deprive you of the joy of marching around with all of that. No, I think I'll let you suffer from your success."

"That's so mean."

"I already have three items. I can't carry any more of your winnings. Are you like a servant of carnival affairs?"

"My father used to work at the fair. He used to play games with me and make me figure 'em out."

"Come on, Hashmi. I don't think she can win anymore. Let's go take a seat down by the lake. It looks like they're starting the skating show, anyway. That way, we can let little miss I-Win-Too-Much take a load off."

The girls made their way down and stepped up onto the bleachers, taking a seat at the edge, near the walkway, watching as a few skaters practiced on the lake.

"Hello again, ladies," said Jericho, walking up wearing a hat with colored lights on his head. "Wow, it looks like someone's really cleaned up. Look at all that junk."

"It's your event and even you're calling it junk."

"One man's trash is another person's treasure."

Safia shook her head and thrust a thumb at Mallory. "Apparently, our Mallory here is the carnival queen. But what are you wearing on your head?"

"What, this? It's a party hat. It's supposed to draw attention and make me seem like a fun guy so that people will like me."

"What is your obsession with making friends?"

"Friends are good to have. They can come in handy when you're in trouble."

"Are you in trouble?"

"Not yet," said Jericho, turning towards the skaters practicing on the ice. "But Killian's lake might have something else to say about that."

"Killian's lake?"

"Yeah, after that mountain debacle, I figured it'd be best to be safe rather than sorry. Someone might fall through the ice or something."

"Wow, you're horrible," said Safia, holding in a laugh. "Some kinda friend you are."

"Don't worry, I won't name it Safia's lake or anything."

"How nice of you."

"I have that planned for the knife-throwing contest."

"Oh, get out of here," said Safia, playfully swinging her arm at Jericho, who nimbly stepped back, dodging her swipe.

"Farewell, ladies. I hope you enjoy the show."

Safia watched Jericho and his shiny hat wander off towards a booth. Glancing around, she saw more people down below make their way around the lake, taking their seats in the stands. Over to the far left of the last stand, she could see Killian over at a small booth with another man. He seemed to be teaching him how to work the lighting system as they began doing a few test runs with the colorful lights over the lake.

"I wonder how many people they managed to wrangle in to participate in this event," said Hashmi, looking over the crowd for contestants.

"Aren't a lot of people here from rich homes? I think a lot of 'em probably know how to skate? My Ma used to take me to our mall, where they had an ice ring in the center of it. That's where I learned."

"So... you're an ice-skating, alligator riding, carnival queen? Is there anything you can't do?"

"Hey, I never rode the gators. We only watched."

"I'm not sure that makes it any less amazing."

"Ladies and Gentlemen of Apex Academy," said Jericho's voice over a speaker system. The sound of his voice echoing over the crowd, causing them all to look around the snow filled night. "Welcome to the Winter Wonderland event. I hope you all have been enjoying yourselves at the games tonight and please keep in mind that we are in no way responsible for any personal injury that you suffer tonight."

Wow, he really is an idiot.

"Killian's mountain is free to all. Try climbing it at your own risk."

The girls giggled, while Safia shook her head.

"But for all of you here tonight for the skating competition, the betting will go like this. You will watch all ten participants. And at the end of the competition, you can wager five hundred points on who you think will come in first place. The points will then be added to a pool, and whoever amongst you votes first place correctly will get fifty percent of the pool. The people whose vote gets second place will be awarded thirty percent of the pool, and the people whose vote gets third place will be awarded twenty percent of the pool. And to all the rest of you, you get to watch performances tonight by some truly amazing, I hope, skaters. So I suggest you all watch carefully because there are big points to be won."

"He sure is a people pleaser," said Safia as the crowd cheered around them.

"Everyone does seem excited," said Mallory as they watched as the first contestant came out onto the ice. "Oh, it's a guy."

A boy came out dressed in a brown and orange suspenders set with an orange cape.

"Our first contestant, Vigalor Dresputin, will show off his skills," said Jericho's voice as the man made his way towards the center of the lake as the strobe lights followed him onto the ice.

"Oh, he's wearing the house colors," said Mallory. "I wonder if the dorm gets a special prize for having the winning skater."

They all watched as the boy began to go into his routine, his blades sliding along the ice, with the cascading lights of colors following him as he made his way around the frozen lake's surface. As he began to navigate the ice, a soft melody flowed over the crowd from some nearby speakers that went along to highlight the boy's movements.

"Wow, they really did go all out for this," said Mallory as she stared down at the entertainment.

But Safia's attention was focused on Killian, who was walking back over through the crowd. *But wasn't he supposed to be...* Safia turned back to see the light following the skater. *I guess he just needed to set everything up.* She watched Killian stroll over to Jericho's booth and then watched both men leave together, making their way back up the hill towards the festival's tents and game booths.

Where are they going? Shouldn't they be watching the event? Unless something else... Safia quickly turned to the other girls. "Hey, Hashmi, Mallory, I'll be right back," she said as she made her way down the stands back towards the ground. She didn't try to hide herself and instead just made her way back up the hill, catching Jericho, patting Killian on the back and sending him off. Jericho then turned around and headed back down the hill, smiling when he saw Safia and giving a friendly wave.

"Well, hello again. Not staying for the show."

"Just going for a walk. Where's Killian going?"

"Oh, well, apparently some idiot finally decided to challenge Killian to a bet. I would go and watch this massacre myself, but I have to finish hosting the skating competition."

"Do you know who it is?"

"Yeah, apparently, it's Dario. The guy you took Mallory from. If you ask me, he really is an idiot. First, he loses his discarded to you, and now he challenges Killian to a bet. That man sure is a glutton for punishment."

Safia looked up the hill, watching as Killian went inside of one of the tents. "So you really think he'll win?"

"Who? Killian? Of course he will. I've never seen him lose. I'd sooner bet against the sun rising in the morning before I'd bet against him."

"Is he really so good that everyone is afraid to bet him?"

"I thought it was silly at first myself, but the man simply doesn't lose. It'd be something else if he was cheating. Cheating I can understand, but Killian is just driven." Jericho tapped his own head playfully. "The way his mind works is just different from us mere mortals and our petty problems."

"Can I go watch? I'd like to see what everyone is so afraid of."

"Sure. It's not like it's a private bet or anything." Jericho rubbed his chin. "I guess watching Dario get his ass kicked would be a pleasurable sight for you, considering the history you two have."

"Yeah, something like that."

"Well, don't let me slow you down. Dario's entitled ass whooping will be starting soon, I guess. You might as well hurry up and grab a seat before more people show up. There's already a few people in there, apparently, and..." said Jericho, narrowing his eyes at Safia. "Wait? You're not planning on doing something stupid, are you?"

"What? What do you mean?"

"I know how you got Mallory. Remember, Dario, along with a lot of others, think of me as their friend. He told me how he lost Mallory to you. And I get it, Dario's a jackass, but Killian has a one-track mind, and you have this knack for getting yourself involved in stuff that doesn't concern you."

"What?" asked Safia, her tone beginning to grow harsher. "Do you even know what Killian plans to do with those points?"

"Yeah, he's going to buy that teacher Abigail."

"You knew?"

"I knew, and I said nothing because I can't do anything about it. She made the choice that put her in that position, like he is making his."

"So, you're saying you don't care if he just takes Abigail," said Safia pointing her finger up towards the tent.

"Oh, he will get her. Either tonight or maybe a month or two down the line. But that woman belongs to him. Even she knows it. I'm sure you've noticed how she acts around him. She's just waiting for when her times up. But it's not like Killian is a Dario of some kind of campus dictator. Who knows, maybe she'll even start to like him."

"How can you just say that? Don't you care at all—"

Jericho turned his attention back to the lake as the lights began to dim. "Shit, the music is slowing down. I'll need to get back soon. I can't let the people down. That'd be bad for my reputation."

"Jericho!" yelled Safia. "Can you stop thinking about yourself for one second? Don't you care what happens to Abigail. Do you understand what that means?"

Jericho turned his attention back to Safia as he began to scratch his head. "I think you're the one who doesn't understand Safia. This isn't a fight you can win. Maybe if you were here a year ago, you could have done something, but it's too late now. Killian has devoted his life to the sole purpose of getting that woman. This whole school could burn down, and he'd still be out here trying to get points. It's best to just let some things go. Even if you win, he'd never bet enough points to jeopardize himself not getting Miss Abigail, so at best, you'd be buying her another month or two."

"Are you done now?" asked Safia, the anger in her voice clearly audible.

"Hey, don't get mad at me. I'm just trying to warn someone who I think of as a friend."

"And if you think like that, then I'm not sure we can be friends."

Jericho's face went still as he stared at Safia for a moment. Looking down into her almond eyes, he then shrugged his shoulders and shook his head. "Well, go on, hero. Can't say I didn't try to warn you." He stepped to the side and bowed his head, gesturing uphill towards the tents, "Your destruction awaits, my lady."

Safia narrowed her eyes at Jericho before turning away from him in disgust, making her way toward the tent where she saw Killian enter. Suddenly, the chill of the night seemed to finally set into her bones, and for the first time tonight, she noticed her own breath in front of her face. She stood outside of the tent as the cold wind picked up its pace, lifting her hair off her shoulders. It caused the flaps of the colorful tents to make a popping sound as they swung back and forth in the breeze. And for the first time tonight, Safia felt a chill go up her spine. Grabbing at her arms for warmth, she looked around the illuminated area, watching the people go about their enjoyment of festivities.

"Come on. It wasn't that bad," said a boy walking with a girl hand in hand.

"You've lost five hundred points and didn't even win. How is that not bad," said the girl as she shook her head.

"It's not about winning. It's about the fun. And it was fun, wasn't it?"

"Will it be fun tomorrow when I have to try and make it all back?"

Safia watched the couple bicker as they headed off through the grounds before the flutter of a crystal floated down before her, catching her eye. She blinked and looked up into the night to see the coming of thousands of snowflakes appearing against the blackness, floating their way down. She stared at the sight for only a moment in a daze as she felt the water crystals land on her cheek before she was taken out of the moment by the cheers of the crowd inside the tent. Brought back to reality, she turned back towards the tent and stepped forward. Inside, there were lanterns hanging from poles and at the center was a single table where Dario was sitting with three other men, but she didn't see Killian.

"Hello, Miss Safia," said Killian from behind her as he placed a hand on her shoulder. "Have you also come to watch?"

"What?" she asked, surprised by his sudden appearance. "Ah… yes, Jericho said you were going to play a game."

"Indeed, I am, but only after they've finished here with their current round."

Dario and the three people around him all had a marker, along with a set of index cards in front of them. And in the center of the table was a little scoreboard with the number eleven hundred on a small screen. One person stood at the side of the podium, calling out questions.

"How does this game work?"

"Oh, it's actually quite simple. They wanted to make a game where everyone has a chance of winning. So they made a list of the questions that teachers here would use for tests, or give out as homework and compiled them all together. I believe there's over five hundred. And each contestant writes down the answer they think is correct on the card. For every one you get right, your total points owed stays at the hundred level that it is at. But for everyone you get wrong, it costs you double the points into the pot. You can see the number it's up to on the screen at the center of the table."

Safia watched as the four men raised their hands, but only Dario and another man at the table celebrated.

"Ha, take that, you bastards."

"Okay, I'm out. I need to at least be able to eat tomor-row," said one of the men at the table.

"I guess that's my cue," said Killian as he stepped ahead of Safia through the small crowd.

"So who's next?" asked Dario, looking around. "Oh, so the guest of honor has arrived. I've been waiting for you. Let's see what everyone's so afraid of."

"What, you invited Killian?" said one of the men at the table, as Killian took the seat of the man who had just left. "Nah, Dario, I'm out. I at least wanna feel like I can win."

Safia listened to the crowd's murmurs as Killian sat at the table. All were conversations that reinforced the notion that no one wanted to bet him. But Killian sat there with the same smile he had always shown her, placing his hands on the table as he began playing with the cards that were left by the man before him.

"Yeah, Dario. I'll let you deal with this one. There's a reason why no one on campus wants to make a bet with him. I ain't in for just giving my points away."

The two other men at the table pulled their pendants off the tablet, stood up, and walked away.

"Cowards," said Dario, leaning back in his chair. "You were going to lose to me, anyway. What's one loss over another?"

Killian smiled. "Well, this might have been my shortest game ever. I sat down and won, and I didn't even get to play. Unless you wish to go one on one, but I'm not sure how much fun that would be for the people watching here."

"You're damn right I'm going to play. I didn't get everything I have by running away like those fools. I know how to win," said Dario, looking around the crowd. "Well, are all of you cowards? I know somebody has the guts to jump in."

The crowd continued to mutter to themselves, but no one came to the table. Some tried to pressure others into joining the game before them, but no one amongst them took a step forward.

"What? Seriously, no one has the balls to even attempt to bet? People, he's not the gambling boogie man. And this whole game is just based on basic knowledge. What? Did all of you skip class all year?"

The crowd parted as Safia found herself coming through and standing at the table, placing her hand on one of the chairs. She looked across the table to see Killian raise a brow at her, but when she turned to Dario, she saw that he had a huge smile across his face.

God, I hate you and that dumb grin on your face. Why do people like you even exist? Just a waste of space.

"Well, if it isn't my favorite little bitch blackmailer. I've been looking for a way to get back what you took from me."

"She wasn't yours to begin with," said Safia with a scowl on her face. "And you didn't get nearly what you deserve."

"That so? Well, we'll see about that. You sit your ass down at this table and you're gonna end up being mine. And I promise to do a whole lot more to you than I did to little Miss Daddy Issues."

Safia snatched the chair out from under the table and took a seat.

"Oh," said Dario, wiggling his fingers at her. "Seems I pissed her off. Well, come on, ask the first question. I'm looking forward to making this one cry."

"Wait," said Killian with a hand raised. "She's a first-year."

"Yeah, so?"

"So... we should restrict the questions to first-year questions. We'd have an advantage if we included second-year questions."

"So what? She sat down at the table and I'm supposed to play nice because she's stupid."

"No, you're supposed to play nice because it's in the rules. All bets must be completely fair, or else the bet becomes void. We can bet all night and win a million points. But if she claims it's unfair, and the system decides it is, then we've just wasted our time."

Dario grit his teeth before flicking his wrist in Killian's direction. "Fine, let's play with baby rules. I'll beat you both either way."

"Okay," said Killian, turning to the man at the podium. "Please, remove all second-year questions from the deck. Keep specifically just the questions for the first six months of a first year's semester."

"Yes, sir."

"I assume this is satisfactory, Miss Safia?"

"It's fine. And thank you."

"No problem. Remember, you can always leave the table at any time. The table will only take the points you have agreed to bet. If you feel it's too much, just remove your pendant from the table before the start of the next round."

Safia nodded her head, as all three participants placed their pendants on the table; each one turning red at the start of the game. *He's still acting nice. But you can't fool me. I remember you in that library and I know what you're after. You aren't going to trick me.*

"Okay," said the host of the game from behind his podium, as he looked down at his tablet. "The first question is what is the number one reason why a first world country would go into war with a third world country?"

Can I do this? Can I even win against these two? Wait, don't think about this now. Just answer the question. I remember this. I went to the library for it. Ah, what was it again?

Safia reached forward on the table and grabbed a marker, popping the top off. Instantly the smell of the chemicals inside washed across her nose as she scribbled her answer on the index card.

"Everyone ready?" asked the host. "Okay, the starting bid is one hundred points and will double each round until someone loses or quits the game. At that point, the person with the highest number of points will take that number of points from both the losing players. Now, if everyone consents to the rules, then flip over your cards, and the game will begin."

The people all muttered to each other as they all flipped over their cards.

"Okay, so Safia and Killian both have won. And Dario has the wrong answer."

"That means Dario will put two hundred into the pot to continue, while Safia and Killian will only contribute one hundred."

I lost a hundred points even though I won? Wait, no, that's not right. I won fifty points with Killian, and Dario lost one hundred points... I think.

"Do you all agree to another round?"

They all nodded.

"Okay, then. According to the school, what is the purpose of power?"

Wait? Power? I know this... I think. I'm pretty sure it has something to do with control. Dammit, what was it? Financial control? Economic control? She looked at Killian and Dario, already writing their answers on their cards. *Dammit, I should have paid more attention. But so much has happened. Ahh, I'll try financial control.*

Once again, they all wrote their answers and held them face down until they were told to reveal their answers.

"Dario and Killian have the correct answer, and will stay the same. Safia has the wrong answer. Her total has now gone up to two hundred points."

Dammit, so I lost two hundred? No, that's not right. I won fifty before and lost a hundred. I really just lost fifty. Safia looked around the table at the two men. *Are we supposed to keep this up in our heads? Is that how they play?* Killian caught her looking at him and smiled back at her, nodding his head. *Should I just get up and leave now? I don't think... No; I don't have to win. I just need to stop him from winning as much. That'll buy Abigail some time.*

Another round of questions, then another, and then a few more. Time flew by until it got to the point where Safia began to wonder how long she had been at the table. One moment they were all so close, and now Dario was up to eight hundred per round, and Safia was up to six hundred, while Killian was still at the entry fee of one hundred points.

"It's been an hour, gentlemen and lady. Would you like some refreshments?"

"I'll have a lemonade, please."

"Alcohol, something strong."

"And for the lady?"

"A water, thank you."

"You know, I'm looking at mine and the woman's points, and then I look over at yours. It makes me wonder if you ain't cheating, somehow," said Dario as the man brought his liquor, placing it down on the table along with a shot class.

"I get that a lot, but I'm very proud of the fact that I never cheat. Although I suspect you have at least three times now.

"What?"

He has?

"Your associate over there has been making funny hand signals since we started playing. But I guess his knowledge is limited since he hasn't been able to provide you with all the accurate information you need," said Killian to the gasps of the crowd as they all turned and started looking amongst themselves. "Really, one must commend Miss Safia for still being ahead of you. Although I must wonder if you would not be doing better if you had chosen not to listen to your associate, as he does seem rather unintelligent."

"Hey, fuck you. I ain't stupid," said a man in the crowd as onlookers all quickly turned in his direction.

"And thus, my point is proven."

"You still can't prove that I've cheated."

"That's correct. I have no intention of stopping you. I will simply beat you no matter what you do."

"You are a high and mighty fucker; I'll give you that. You think you're better than everyone here?"

Killian sighed, "No, sadly, I'm jealous of all of you."

"What do you mean by that?" asked Safia.

"Well, since tonight will probably be my last night betting, why not indulge you both a bit while we enjoy our break? I suffer from an addiction that I have spent the last ten years learning to control, where I can't help myself but to pursue the object of my interest."

"Welcome to the club. It's called gambling. Everyone here either has an addiction to it, or will have one by the time they leave. That doesn't make you special. It makes you just as depressed as the rest of us."

"Oh, I can assure you, I don't have a gambling addiction. I hate gambling. I think it's a waste of time. What I have is more complicated than that."

"Is that a joke? An addiction is an addiction. What's so special about yours?"

"I wish it were. You don't know this because you're a second year and Miss Safia is a first. But I originally came here as an art student, where I could spend days locked up with my paintings, obsessing over the color pallets and sketch designs. A perfectly harmless way to spend my life and put my condition to some good use. Then, one day, someone showed up after class and began talking to me about my art. It was harmless at first, I thought, because I'd never liked anyone before. But before I knew it, the target of my compulsion had shifted from my wonderful art to something new; a caring and remarkable woman."

"You mean to tell me that you have some crazy type of OCD, and that you're doing all this, collecting all these points, to impress some girl? That's insane."

"I agree. By your standards, that would be insane. But for someone who's spent their entire life this way, it's my normal."

"But that doesn't mean you can just do what you want," said Safia, her fists clenched on the table. "What if she doesn't like you or hates you?"

"And by that exchange, what if I hate her? My compulsion doesn't care about what I like or dislike. It chooses what it wants to focus on, and I simply follow."

"But... but it's not right. That's just called being a stalker."

"I admire your idealism, but there are many things in this world that are, 'not right'. Some would say that the control you have over Mallory isn't right."

"It's not right. I would let her go if I could."

"But you can't, and neither can I. What is the difference between the situation you find yourself stuck in and mine? We both are being compelled to do something we honestly do not want to do. But instead, we find ourselves doing it anyway."

Safia was quiet as she tried to think of an answer.

"Oh, well, look at that," said Dario with a smile. "The bitch has gotten all hypocritical. Ha, at least something good came out of tonight."

"I have a question for you, Miss Safia. If you drop a pencil from six feet high down onto a perfectly flat concrete surface, do you know the odds that it will land straight up on the eraser, perfectly vertical?"

"What? Why would I—"

"I do. For me, the number was one out of one million eight hundred seventy-four thousand five hundred and ninety-one. Doing that test took me a little over two years, or eight hundred and forty-four days. Two years of my life wasted, because I couldn't control myself and I felt that I needed to know the answer to such a pointless question. Now tell me, Mrs. Safia, can you imagine the time and energy I put into this school in order to achieve my goal here?"

"I call bullshit," said Dario, tapping his hand on the cards. "You're just saying this to fuck with us. There is no way anyone is that obsessive and not locked away somewhere getting dosed up to their eyeballs on medication."

"Dario, you've lost a total of six thousand nine hundred and fifty points while Miss Safia has lost a total of four thousand one hundred points. Together, you both have more than given me enough points to walk away with what I need. For what reason would I have to lie?"

Have I really already lost four thousand points?

"You bastard, you've been keeping up with our points. How do you even keep all those numbers in your head?"

"That's what my compulsion is, Dario. It takes everything away from me. Food, sleep, none of it matters. All you do is focus on what you want to know. I remember whatever I think will get me what I want. I even know the number of breaths you've taken since I've sat down at this table."

"Woo," said Dario, shaking his head. "That's a whole

new level of crazy. Makes sense why everyone's been calling you a monster. But I'm not afraid to play the game a little longer. I'll count it as a victory if I can just get you to lose at least once."

"If that's the case, then let's disperse with the questionnaire cards. I'm certain I know everything they could possibly ask. Instead, let's make it interesting and show you how far it goes. As an alternative for these cards, let's have people from the crowd ask us anything about the campus. The buy-in will be one thousand points per question."

"I'm game, but who's going to pick the person in the crowd?"

"You and Miss Safia can, since I brought it up. I imagine it'd be unfair for me to pick someone. And if at any point where I answer a question, and you think it's wrong, you can counter. Oh, and if you're right and I'm wrong, then you'll win ten thousand points from me."

"You're that confident you'll win, huh?"

"It's not confidence. It's just I doubt anyone has observed as much about this campus as I have. As long as it's information that can be gained here as common knowledge, then I'm fairly sure of my chances."

"Alright, not like I ain't never lost points before, and I want to see more of this freak show?"

"And you, Miss Safia?"

Safia looked at Killian while he was speaking and noticed that not once did he smile. Instead, he seemed tired. Like everything was pointless. "I guess so. I can go a little longer." *Just one time, If I can win just once, then I can give Abigail some time. Killian said he has what he needs, but I bet if he loses another ten thousand, he won't.*

"Okay then, who goes first?"

"I'll go. You," said Dario, pointing to someone in the small crowd. "The bastard in the red shirt with that cotton candy. Ask us a question about the campus. Something hard."

398

"Ahh... okay," said the boy in the crowd. "What is the difference between the tallest point in the school and the second tallest? No, wait. That's too easy, the fourth tallest?"

"Seventy-eight feet. That would be the school spire as the first and the top of the right library as the fourth because it sits down a hill when compared to the left library, even though they both are identical to each other."

"How the hell are we even supposed to look up all these crazy trivia facts, anyway."

"Ah, I can," said their host, as he pulled out a tablet of his own and began flicking and tapping the screen. "Or, at least, I think I can. All the information should be in the school records. Okay, here it is. And he's right. The difference between the first and the fourth seems to be exactly seventy-eight feet with second and third place being two service antennas near the outside of campus."

"Let me see that shit," said Dario, standing up to peer at the man's screen. He then gazed down at Killian and shook his head. "You gotta be kidding me."

"Satisfied, Mr. Burrows?"

"Yeah. Satisfied to know that you got some real fucking problems," said Dario in disgust as he turned to Safia. "You, blackmailer, ask your damn question."

I just lost a thousand points. "Oh, ah... yeah." *I should stop. This is getting out of hand.* Safia began looking around the room and saw Mallory staring directly at her with a look of worry on her face. *Wait... no, I can win once. I think.* Safia pointed to Mallory. "We talked about this campus earlier, Mallory. What was the question we were trying to figure out?"

"Hey, you can't just bring your bitch friends into this. Pick someone else."

Safia pointed at Killian. "He said, 'Someone in the crowd.' And, besides, you apparently had someone in the crowd trying to help you. I don't see a difference between the two. At least, maybe he can answer the question we've been wondering about this morning."

Kilian laughed. "She has a point. You did have one of your associates in the crowd earlier. So I suppose turnabout is fair play."

"Yeah, well, I ain't admitting to shit," said Dario, as he waved his hand. "Fine, go ahead. Let's keep this freak show going."

"Go on, Mallory, ask the question."

"Oh, right? We were trying to figure out how many structures this campus has in total. You know, like buildings and stuff."

Killian rubbed at his chin. "If it's just man-made structures, then, at this moment, the total should be eighty-six."

"Then, I say it's eighty-five," said Safia.

"Oh! And what makes you say that, Miss Safia? Although I do welcome being wrong for once."

"The lake, doesn't it have a platform under it that allows you to walk on it."

"That, it does."

"Did you add that to your list of things?"

"I did."

"The ice broke it this morning, did you know that?"

"No, I didn't," said Killian with a smile. "If that's true, then, congratulations. It seems I'm out ten thousand points and back to square one."

"Now, there's some lucky insider information shit," said Dario, looking up at the host. "Well, is she right?"

The man flicked the tablet looking for the answers, "One moment, it's not easy narrowing down the searches like... okay, yes it seems she's... wait, it's updating... No, it says the total is still eighty-six."

"What?" asked Safia, "So the platform didn't break?"

"No, it is indeed broken, as you said, but a new building has been erected in that time."

"What building?"

"One second, I'm trying to find out." He stared at his

tablet a little longer, moving his finger over the screen. "Ah… apparently, it's the snow house or tunnel thing outside of the fence, before you enter."

"A snow tunnel? Don't get me wrong, I'm happy the bitch lost. But are we really counting buildings made of snow in this?"

"Ah… It's still updating… It says that the building has wooden structural supports that were put in place by Jericho Andrews."

Dario started laughing and banging his hand on the table. "What? That building bastard actually started to build a real house inside his snow house."

I lost? Of course I lost. I'm not some type of professional gambler. She looked over at Killian, who was staring at her again. Dario was still laughing about Jericho's snow house. *These two are just so casual about losing thousands of points. But a thousand points to them means nothing. How many points do I even have left? I don't even know anymore.*

"Do, you agree, Miss Safia?"

"What?" asked Safia, the host's voice snapping her out of her internal thoughts.

"Oh, sure I—"

"I'm done," said Killian.

"What?" asked Dario. "What do you mean, you're done? I ain't won nothing yet?"

"I'm afraid that if I were to continue, I would be forced to suffer an unwanted burden."

"A what? Speak English. What do you mean, burden?"

Killian stood up from the desk. "Dario, if you wish to continue our game, I will have to come back later. I'm afraid I still have work to do down by the lake."

"You're running away when things are about to get good?"

"A man has his responsibilities, after all. I'd expect you to understand that, given your family ties. I gave my word to Jericho that I would assist him. I don't suppose you're telling me to break my word, are you?"

Dario narrowed his eyes at Killian. "Alright, you bastard, fine. But this game of ours will continue. I ain't satisfied yet. You ain't as all-knowing as you think you are."

"I appreciate your understanding," said Killian as he walked over to Safia, placing a hand on her shoulder. "A moment of your time, Miss Safia."

"What? Why?"

Killian smiled and leaned down, picking up her pendant and whispered, "Follow me if you wish for your points to remain a secret?"

Safia's eyes opened wide as she blinked, staring back at Killian, who was holding her pendant in his hand.

"I think Mr. Jericho made you this rope for your pendant, correct? Come, let's see if we can't find you something more suitable," said Killian as he walked out of the tent holding her pendant. Safia followed behind, opening the tent flaps and once again stepping out into a world of white. The snowfall had increased as more flakes blew past her. The ground was completely white now.

She squinted for a moment and caught sight of Killian walking away towards the wooden fence they had erected around the event grounds, and quickened her pace to catch up to him.

"Hey, wait."

Killian ignored her words as he continued his steps in the snow.

"Stop," Safia yelled out.

Killian finally stopped, resting his hands on the fence before brushing off some snow from atop of the wooden post.

"You know, the snow really is one of nature's marvels," said Killian, reaching out his hand and allowing some of the snowflakes to land on his skin.

"What?" asked Safia as she stopped a few away from Killian, his back turned to her.

"The snowflakes. Each one singular onto itself, beauty only found one." Killian turned around to face Safia still with his arm out as the snowflakes landed on his skin and instantly melted away. "But the moment you try to grasp it. You lose it."

"Why... why did you call me out here?"

"A moment of inspiration is lost," said Killian with a sigh as he leaned back against the wooden fence post. "Because Miss Safia, you were about to become my discarded, and to be quite honest, I'd rather not be forced to deal with you."

"What, how... you don't know that."

Killian tossed Safia back her pendant and tapped his own. "I challenge Safia Famosa to a wager that if she can prove to have over five hundred points left, then she will win ten thousand points from me."

Safia caught her pendant, the cold metal of it stinging her hands, even in the winter weather as it began to glow red and spoke, "Do you accept the challenge? Failure to answer will result in a deduction of five thousand points, and you will be forbidden from any wagers for a month."

"Do you even have five hundred points left? The way your eyes are moving tells me you don't even know yourself. But go ahead, prove me wrong. All you have to do is ask your pendant how many points you have. And if it's over five hundred, then you win ten thousand. That sounds like an easy thing for you to do if I'm wrong."

Safia clutched the pendant in her hand before bringing it up to her lips and spoke. "No. I refuse the bet," and let her arm drop to her side.

"I could have exposed you in front of Dario and that whole crowd, but then everyone would have come after you trying to either get you expelled or get you under their control. Or just played another round and kept you for myself. So, tell me. Why go this far? When we were under the tree together, you said you had no interest in betting. What changed?"

Safia was silent.

"You want me to go back in there and expose your..." Killian's attention shifted for a moment. "Oh... oh wait... so that's what it was," he said as he began to stare over at the side of a tent. "I understand now. It's because of Abigail, isn't it? Because you managed to get Miss Mallory away from Dario, you thought to do the same to me. That's what that little outburst in there was all about." He rubbed at his chin. "Yes, that does make sense."

"What you're doing to her..." said Safia, lifting her head and looking Killian in the eyes. "It's not right."

"I agree, it's not. But it's still what I'm going to do. But is what I am and what you are any different. You also have your Miss Mallory. I don't think much—"

"That's not the same. I... I wasn't thinking straight and... and... I wanted to save her from Dario."

"Save her?" Killian stared at Safia for a moment. "Yes, I guess that is certainly a way to think of it. Tell me. Do you think of yourself as a hero then?" Killian gestured around the darkness. "To save all the discarded of this campus."

"What? No."

"Why not? Surely you've seen more discarded around this campus. Why single out my situation?"

Safia thought back to the instances she had seen around the campus. The nude display at game night. *Why didn't I check back on them? Or the people who were burned?* "That still doesn't make what you're doing right?"

"Does it not? You saved Miss Mallory. Who's to say I'm not saving Abigail?"

"What?" said Safia, her face twisted in confusion. "How can you say that? She doesn't want you?"

"And who's to say she won't change her mind. You see, Miss Safia, Abigail is already a discarded under the control of this horrible school. I am merely transferring ownership of her from the school to myself. In fact, I think we are in a similar situation since you did the same with Miss Mallory."

"That's not the same," said Safia in protest. "I'm not—"

"Is it not? Are you going to stand here and say that Mallory was agreeable to the idea of you when you first took possession of her?"

"That... I mean... I'm not taking advantage of her."

"And I haven't done anything to Abigail at this moment. You just assume I will. Why? But I do suppose if you see yourself as the hero, then I guess it's just easier to cast me as the villain." Killian smirked, shaking his head as he took a step forward. "It's true what they say. One side of the coin most certainly can't see the other. Tell me, which one of us would be heads or trails in this situation?"

"But I... I heard you in the library? You... you said you wouldn't let anyone one else have her?"

"And I believe you threatened Miss Mallory with expulsion if she didn't immediately follow you home after that altercation with Dario."

"What?" Safia thought back to that night and remembered that she had indeed done such a thing. "How do you... That's not... I did that to protect her."

"Perhaps you did. But I still don't see the difference between the two of us. We both did what we did because we felt compelled to do so. But there is one glaring thing that separates us. You did what you did out of a choice, while I on the other hand never had one."

"You're just saying this to make yourself feel better about what you're doing to Abigail."

"I guess that is one way way for you to compare our situations and still see yourself as the hero." Killian took another set of steps forward, his feet mushing the snow beneath until he stood in front of Safia, looking down at her. "Well, in that case, I shall play my part and thank you and Dario both for ensuring that I will obtain my goal as soon as this school relinquishes the funds from this event to me."

Safia started back up at him defiantly. *I'm not wrong? Am*

I? I can't be. I know what he is doing is wrong. I'm not the same as him. I'm not.

Killian twisted his lips after looking down at Safia and closed his eyes, taking in a deep breath. "Yes, you certainly would have been a handful, had I tried to make you my discarded. But forget about tonight. Our drama will play itself out, I'm sure. What about tomorrow? You're so worried about my relationship with Abigail. What about yours with that Mallory girl that you took from Dario? You're standing here with less than five hundred points, probably, and you have to feed that girl starting tomorrow along with yourself. That's six hundred points. Where's that going to come from?"

Once again, Safia was silent.

"Of course, you didn't think that far ahead, did you? So in trying to save one person, you've ruined another person's life. You do know that if you can't feed yourself then they are going to expel you and any discarded that you have, right?"

"Why do you even care? You won. All you care about is yourself and what you want."

"If you really believe that, then you're a far worse idiot than I took you for. And that Mallory girl over there would have been better off with Dario."

At realization of Killian's words, Safia turned around to see Mallory and Hashmi peeking their heads out from behind a tent.

"Go on, Miss Safia. Explain to Miss Mallory who's the one responsible for sending her back home to her abusive step-father. And then go to sleep tonight and try telling yourself that I'm the one who's a monster," said Killian as he placed a hand on Safia's shoulder and leaned in close to her ear. "Well, go on hero. Now go over there to tell her what you've done. Then try going to bed tonight convincing yourself that I'm the side of the coin still casted as the villain."

Killian's words cut deep as Safia bit her into her own

lip, reinjuring the wound from the night where she paid the price to acquire Mallory. Suddenly, she felt a pain in her chest as the rush of emotion hit her. Safia couldn't tell whether this new pain was from the reopening of the old wound on her lip or the sting Killian's words. But it didn't matter as the result came in the form of her eyes starting to water as she looked into Mallory's face and couldn't handle it as she turned, trying to walk away, heading out of the winter wonderland campgrounds and back towards the school's main area.

But it didn't take long before Mallory and Hashmi came after her, and soon caught up.

"It's not true, is it, Miss Safia? Are you really out of points?"

Safia couldn't even bring herself to look at Mallory as she just kept walking forward in silence; her head downward and face turned away; the night feeling colder with each step as she clenched her fists.

"But everything's going to be okay, right? I mean, you have a plan. I mean, tomorrow's the first of the month, and we gotta pay for the food and all."

"Just let it go, Mallory. I think she feels bad enough right now."

"Bad enough? We won't be able to eat tomorrow, and they'll send us home if they think we can't feed ourselves!"

"And I'm sure Safia knows that. Just give her some time. I'm sure there must be something we can do."

Mallory looked between both Safia and Hashmi before she began to shake and rub at her shoulders as all three girls silently made their way through the winding concrete path, back towards Yennefer house with the snowfall cascading down all around them.

CHAPTER 17

Later that night, the girls sat in their room watching as the clock ticked towards midnight.

"There has to be something we can do," said Mallory.

"I've been trying to think of anything," said Safia, "But I don't have the points anymore."

"But I don't want to go back home. I don't want to go back to that," said Mallory, the sound of her voice trembling as tears began to roll down her cheeks. She was huddled on the floor, her back against Safia's bed and her arms wrapped around her ankles.

Safia bit down on her lip as she looked at Mallory on the

floor beneath her. *I'm so stupid. Why did I do that? Even if I had won, he still would have eventually gotten the damn points. And because of this, I'm gonna be stuck in the same position as Abigail, and Mallory gets sent back to that bastard father of hers. Argh, I'm such a fucking idiot.* "Mallory, I'm so sorry."

Mallory didn't say anything or even look up at Safia. She just sat quietly on the floor. A gesture that hurt Safia even more. Just knowing that the girl who had praised her just a few hours ago couldn't even look at her now.

Safia placed her hands on her head. *Come on, come on. Think, think. There has to be...* Safia looked up at Hashmi.

"Hashmi, you think if I became discarded, then whoever got me would have to take care of Mallory too?"

"I... I don't know. I mean, I guess so," said Hashmi as her eyes went wide with understanding. "Wait... You can't mean me. I don't even have a thousand points to begin with. And then there's the food cost tomorrow. That's nineteen hundred points."

"No, not you," said Safia, taking a deep breath before tapping her pendant.

Around half an hour later, Safia was out walking along the spiraling concrete walkway. The lamps highlighted the paths, glowing dim light as the cold breeze blew through her hair. As she made her way forward, she could see the final light being shut off downhill towards the lake as the tents that stood above the ground slowly faded back into the darkness.

Making her way further through the campus, she stopped at the gazebo she had helped make months earlier. Inside, someone was waiting for her. They wore a huge brown coat with red accents as they sat on the bench, sheltering themselves from the cold. A light inside flickered on and off, as if providing a signal. Safia took a deep breath and made her way over, stepping into the gazebo and stood before the person she needed to help her.

"Hey, Jericho."

"I was surprised when I got the message saying you wanted my location," he said as he extended his hand. "Please, take a seat, Miss Safia. I've already wiped the snow away."

Safia took a seat in front of Jericho, "I guess you're wondering why I asked you out here."

"Oh, I have a few ideas, but before we start, can you tell me what time it is?"

Safia tilted her head at Jericho, but pulled out her tablet and placed her hand on the screen. "It's eleven thirty-two."

"Thank you. So, please, Miss Safia, inform me as to why you invited me out here in the middle of the night. After our last encounter, I find it hard to believe that you suddenly have had a change of heart as to how you feel about me. The look you gave me as you walked away sent chills down my spine. Unless you're planning a surprise confession, in which case—"

"I want you to make me your discarded."

A moment of silence passed between the two, with only the sound of the wind being heard between them.

"Well, that's certainly an idea," said Jericho as he rubbed his chin. "Certainly not the confession I was speaking of." Jericho tilted his head, taking a closer look at Safia with squinted eyes as he began to rub his hands together for warmth. "Why? I somehow doubt you're the kind of girl that enjoys someone having that kind of power over you."

Safia sighed. "I made a deal with the school, that I'd pay them one thousand points a month if they saved my father's life. And in about thirty minutes they will take the points and if it's not there, then—"

"Then you'll become the school's property, and that poor Mallory girl will be sent home to her sexually abusive step-father," said Jericho, finishing her sentence for her.
410

"How... how did you know that?" asked Safia, looking at him with eyes wide.

"I told you before that am a friend to a lot of people, Safia, and that includes Dario. One night while drinking, he just so happened to let it slip why Miss Mallory was so deftly afraid of going home. The knowledge that he used to torture that poor girl until you came along. And now, because of you, that same girl is about to be sent back home to the same thing she tolerated Dario's abuse to try and avoid." Jericho shook his head with a chuckle. "The irony of it all is comical if you think about it."

"This isn't funny, Mallory is—"

"Your responsibility," said Jericho, cutting her off while holding up his finger. "A responsibility you're trying to dump on me because of your mistake. A mistake that I tried to warn you not to make."

Safia closed her eyes and shook her head. "Yes, you're right. I'm sorry." She lowered her head. "Will you please help me?"

"Well, you being timid certainly isn't something I ever expected to see."

"What do you want from me?" Safia snapped back. "Just say it. You always want something." Even though it was snowing all around her, Safia felt hot inside as the anger inside of her grew.

"That's true, but right now. I want you to tell me what time it is."

"What?"

"The time, Miss Safia. What time is it?"

Safia looked down at her tablet again. "It's eleven forty. What? Are you planning to make me wait just before midnight to torture me?" *I can't believe I thought you were different. I can't believe I thought... I... I hate myself. I hate all of this.*

"What, me? No, I take no pleasure in torture. But I do have a plan. And as to your problem. I'm afraid I won't be able to take both of you as my discarded.”

“What? Why? I know you have the points.” *I can't give up. There's no one else I can go to. It's too late to try and contact Amanda. It has to be—*

“Oh, you're right, I do have the points. But discarded can only be transferred once. It's a hard rule on the discarded system, and I'm afraid Mallory lost her chance at another owner the moment you took her off Dario's hands. If I were to make you my discarded now, Mallory would be immediately expelled and sent home. And I don't think either of us wants that.”

Safia's mind went back to when Champ Champ told her the same thing. “Ah, how could I forget that?” She buried her face in her hands. “I'm such an idiot.”

“Indeed, you are,” said Jericho, leaning forward, placing a hand on Safia's shoulder. “But, what if I could offer you a way out? A way where you could stay Mallory's caretaker and still be allowed to attend the school as you normally would.”

Safia looked up into Jericho's face. The despair of the moment abated for only a second by his words, until she looked into Jericho's face. The way he looked at her was as if he was looking at one of his plants or the gazebo they were in. Like an object to be used. But Safia latched on to the hope he was giving her, nonetheless.

“What, how?” *I'll do whatever it takes. I can't be the reason Mallory is sent back home.*

“I've arranged for you to receive a certain influx of points in the next few minutes. That's why I've had you look at the time.”

“But… I thought you weren't allowed to give points.”

“You're not. But don't worry. I assure you, what I've done is perfectly within the rules of the school's system.”

“But why… why would you do that?”

“Why, indeed? But, for now, I need to know if you will accept my offer.”

Safia's hand began to shake nervously. "And what do you want in return?"

"I merely want you to be my friend. At first, I thought of you as just some high-minded idiot. And yes, you are that, but I watched that video of how you took Mallory away from Dario. And I realized that under that pretty face is a person who could make something of themselves. And I'd like a person like that to be my friend."

"A friend that listens to what you say and does what you tell them to do," said Safia, narrowing her eyes at him as her hands clenched the fabric at her knees.

"Well, you rejected my last offer of friendship. But come now, does it even matter at this point," said Jericho, as he placed his hand up over half his face, while staring at Safia. The light on the side casting shadows down on him where only his one eye could be seen. He grinned wide, so much that she could see the fangs under his lips. He did indeed look insidious to her. "You were willing to be my discarded, Safia. Surely this is the lesser of two evils, no matter the outcome. And be certain that the outcome will be you and Miss Mallory continuing to stay together here."

There really is something wrong with him. There's something wrong with everyone here.

"Tik-Tok, Miss Safia."

"I accept, whatever it is. I accept." *It's too late for me to change my mind now. I've already decided that I would do what I needed to do before I came out here. I shouldn't be second guessing myself. Not now. Not after everything that's happened.*

Jericho lifted his hand from his face, pulling his hair back over his head as he resumed the happy-go-lucky friendly face that she was accustomed to seeing. "I'm happy to hear that. I'd hate to see you distraught because your friend Mallory was forced to leave. Now, you both can continue to be at school together."

"Yes, because I'm sure you care so much about us."

"Oh, but I do. And, by that, I mean that I care about me.

And having you think of me as a friend, I think it will be very good for me. But don't worry, I'm not some sex-crazed fiend or anything. Your womanhood will be free from my assault, I promise you. Sex tends to make men short-sighted. So, I prefer to pleasure myself. It provides clarity to the mind."

"How nice of you," said Safia, a scowl of disgust crossing her face.

"Isn't it? I'm practically a monk, a sexless monk. I think that makes me a religious man. Oh, which reminds me, what time is it?"

Safia placed her finger on her tablet again. "It's eleven forty fi—"

Safia's badge flashed red and spoke. "Safia Famosa and Dario Burrows have been awarded a refund of ten thousand points each after Killian Jones admitted to cheating on their last game. As such, the refund has been doubled from the amount initially lost."

"Oh, he lost twenty thousand points. That must hurt," said Jericho with a grin. "Congrats on winning over ten thousand points, Miss Safia. You have earned it."

"What? Why? What happened?" asked Safia, confused as she looked around the gazebo into the darkness of the night, then turned back to Jericho, who sat in front of her with a smug grin on his face. "How?"

"I merely offered him what he wanted most in the world."

"But... Why would he..." Safia's mind went whirling around in her head as she tried to think of what was going on.

"Miss Abigail really is a sweet woman. When I informed her of your situation, after your tragic loss to Killian, she went straight to him and begged him to give the points back, and in exchange she would become his a few days earlier. And that Killian, the love-sick puppy that he is, after waiting two years for his prize, agreed in an instant. After which, I just had them wait until the proper time before he told a little lie about cheating on that last bet. So now everything's all right in the world."

"Is it?" asked Safia, placing her hands over her face and taking in a deep breath of the cold air. "Everything's all messed up. And now, he has Abigail."

"An outcome he would have had anyway, whether you interfered or not. You can't save the world, Safia. At best, all you can do is protect yourself."

"And I'm just supposed to believe everything's okay now?" she said as water began to mount at the edges of her eyes; her voice cracking with emotion.

"Of course," said Jericho, still with a smile on his face as he clapped his hands together. "Killian gets the love of his life. Granted, her love for him is questionable at best. But fifty-fifty isn't bad. Think of it as an arranged marriage. Who knows, maybe she'll grow to love him. And Miss Mallory gets to stay here at school instead of going home and getting exploited by her stepfather. And then, there's me."

"What about you? Why even do all this?"

"I told you, I wanted you to think of me as your friend, Miss Safia Famosa. A true friendship that will last a lifetime. Because, if it doesn't." he pointed his finger up at the light in the gazebo.

Safia looked up, following his gesture, and focused. Behind the light, she could see one of the little black orbs that housed the school's security system.

"This whole fairytale ending would all come crashing down if the school ever had a reason to check those tapes."

Safia looked back down at Jericho's smiling face and felt the heat of disgust inside of herself. It mixed in with hatred for him and herself then filled throughout her body. She then reached up, sniffling, rubbing at her eyes and refusing to allow herself to cry in front of this man. "So, friend." She spoke with as much venom in her voice as she could. "What do you want from me now that you have everything you want?"

"I want you to have a happy-go-lucky school life, Miss Safia. Graduate with as many points as you can and go on to become a big influencer in this world. And then use that influence to help me, when the time comes. Because you're a smart girl, Miss Safia, smarter than I'm sure you even realize. And I'm going to have you use those smarts to ensure that I live a wonderful life."

"You really only care about yourself, don't you? Is this what you think being a friend to someone means? Just using and taking advantage of them?"

Jericho chuckled. "Oh, I don't think you've been paying attention, Miss Safia. I have always said that I wanted everyone to be my friend. But I never once said that I would be theirs."

He really is the worst.

"Come, stand with me," He and Safia then both stood up, and he reached forward, placing his hand on the pendant around her neck, stepping closer, he tightened his grip around the pendant which made Safia take a step closer to him as he placed his hand under her chin, forcing her to look up at him.

"Now what do you want?" *I'm just so sick of all of this.*

"Remember that conversation we had about sharing a kiss underneath this gazebo. I'd say that I've earned it now, wouldn't you?"

"What? But you said you didn't care about sex," said Safia, starting to feel nervous about being out in the cold alone with him.

"I don't. But I need to keep my word."

"And you think it's okay to just kiss your friends when you want to?"

"Only the special ones," said Jericho as his grip tightened even more on the pendant's rope around her neck. It now felt like a leash that he could use to control her. And suddenly the Gazebo that they had built together started to feel as if she were in a cage. "And I'd say our relationship just became very special." He looked down at Safia, the smirk still on his face.

"Just do it... I'm just so—" and before she could finish her sentence, she felt Jericho's lips against hers. The warm feeling of his skin, it contrasted with the cold snowy weather around them. She began to hate herself as she couldn't help but kiss him back, as if her body was responding on its own. She squeezed her eyelids, balled her fingers into fists, trying not to cry.

Stupid, stupid. Why am I like this? Why do I like him? He's just as rotten as everyone else, she thought, as images of his smiling face from all the times they'd talked before came into her mind.

Jericho released the rope around her neck as she stepped back, away from him.

"Thank you, Miss Safia."

"Sa... satisfied now?" asked Safia, wiping her lips with the back of her hand. The heat behind her eyes began to sting at the corner as she stared daggers back at Jericho..

"I am. That was quite the experience. And memorable," he said as he looked around the Gazebo. "To have my first kiss inside of something that I built. I hope that you will help me build a lot more."

"You're lying."

"Am I?" asked Jericho, tilting his head. "Can you name any other time I've lied to you?"

"Fine. What am I supposed to do now?"

"Now, you go on, Miss Safia. We have our agreement settled, and I'm sure there's someone else you might want to speak with. There's no use standing out here in the cold talking to me any longer. And I'm sure she's waiting for you, now."

Waiting for me? "Who?"

"You know who," said Jericho, pointing to his temple, "Think about it."

Safia shook her head but placed her hand to her neck,

feeling the threads of the rope that Jericho had given her months ago as a sign of their supposed friendship. She let her fingers glide down the small rope before clicking the pendant once more.

A few seconds later, Safia walked out of the gazebo and back through the campus until she reached the front doors to one of the libraries, where Abigail stood waiting for her.

"Hello, Miss Safia. I'm glad you're okay. Did we make it in time?"

"I'm sorry," were the only words Safia managed to utter.

Abigail just smiled as she looked off into the darkness of the campus. "It's fine. At most, I gave up two weeks to give you your life back and save Miss Mallory. I'd say that's more than a fair trade. And perhaps life with Killian won't be so bad. He's actually the one who insisted I come out here and meet you. I was actually afraid to."

"What? Why?"

"I didn't know how I'd react. But he said I needed to do it so that I could have closure. And so here I am? He was actually boasting about you; saying how no one had stood up to him like that in so long. I think he likes you."

"I'm sorry."

"And there you go, apologizing again. It's fine, Miss Safia. It's not like I'm going anywhere, I'll still be a teacher here. Although I guess, I'll have a new last name. But my sister will live a happy life. And I'll still get to live most of mine. Just missing a small part of it, is all. A part I would have lost anyway, apparently after hearing what a rousing success tonight's event was. The total points he managed to collect from tonight were over seven hundred thousand. Did you know that?"

"He had said it'd be something crazy like that."

"So even if you would've won, it wouldn't have mattered. The school will be releasing the points to him sooner or later."

Safia slumped her shoulders. That acknowledgment

hurt Safia even more to hear it from Abigail's lips.

Abigail stepped forward and wrapped her arms around Safia. "You can't save everyone, dear. My future was already made the moment I saved my sister's life. But yours, you still have time to fix yours."

"What... what am I supposed to do?" asked Safia with tears in her eyes, as she began to shake in Abigail's arms.

"Fight... fight, honey. Fight as hard as you can... Fight harder than I could."

And the two women stood there in the cold night, holding one another and finding strength and warmth in each other's arms as the snow continued to fall and the wind whispered around them. Then, once again, Safia's pendant turned red between them.

"One thousand points have been deducted from your account."

CHAPTER 18

The next morning, Safia was in her pajamas, watching the sun come up. Beside her lay Mallory, asleep. She had come back into the dorm to find her discarded asleep in her bed and Hashmi up, waiting for her return. She awoke Mallory for only a moment to tell them that everything was going to be okay and after giving her the assurance she needed, allowed Mallory to fall back asleep. Hashmi, while skeptical, accepted Safia's words and said she would wait till morning to speak on it. Safia then crawled in bed beside Mallory, comforting the girl until she fell back asleep, but Safia herself didn't get much sleep as the previous night's happenings continued to plague her mind clear through till the morning.

Now, she sat up on the bed with her back against the wall. In her lap sat her tablet, and now written across its screen in bold green coloring was the number total of nine thousand one hundred and fifty points. She took a moment to close her eyes and embrace this number before glancing around the room at the sleeping faces of Hashmi and Mallory.

They were so happy when I told them that I found a way for us to stay. But I couldn't even tell them how I got the points. How could I be so stupid? That thought ran through her mind the whole night while Hashmi and Mallory slept. All of yesterday's experiences replayed in her mind over and over. Every mistake she made, the look on Mallory"s face when she thought she was going back home, it replayed in her mind. And the more it replayed, the angrier she became, until it felt like she was going to explode. She was mad at Killian, furious with Jericho, but most of all, just disgusted with herself.

On the other side of the room, she heard the sound of shuffling and a yawn, before Hashmi popped her head up, squinting in the early morning light.

"Good morning, Sa… Are you okay?" asked Hashmi with concern in her voice as she stared at Safia.

"I'm fine. Why?" asked Safia with a voice more groggy and soft than she had expected.

"Your face, you look like you haven't slept at all."

"What? No, I've just been thinking about… you know, about everything really.. Don't worry about me."

Hashmi climbed out of the bed, reaching into a cabinet drawer and pulling out a mirror, then handing it to Safia, "Look?"

Safia reluctantly took the mirror, taking a look at her reflection as Mallory stirred from sleep. Her eyes were red and puffy as the dark shadows beneath them showed the lack of rest and unease she had suffered.. *I don't even care.* "It's fine." She laid the mirror down beside her. "It's fine. I'm fine."

Then slowly Safia felt a pair of arms wrap themselves around her waist as Mallory's head creeped up behind her, resting her head on Safia's shoulders. "I knew you could do it. Thank you so much, Miss Safia."

With her discarded's words stabbing at Safia's heart, she reached down, grabbing ahold of Mallory's hand for reassurance that she had done the right thing and began to rub her thumb across the girl's hand.

"I'm just happy everything worked out," said Safia, with slumped shoulders.

"Is something wrong? You, you don't seem to be happy at all? Is everything not okay now?"

"No, it's fine. I... I'm probably still just tired, is all?"

"Miss Safia, you've done so much for me. Is it so wrong that I ask you to trust in me when something is bothering you?"

Safia sighed. "It's just... just that... I'm sorry for being selfish during game night. I should have thought about you before I did what I did. I should have remembered that I'm not the only one who suffers when I make a mistake. I know what I did was stupid, especially since you've been trying too hard not to go back home. I... I don't want to be the reason you're forced to go back. Safia felt Mallory's arms tighten around her waist at the mention of going back home.

"But it's fine now, right? Everythings—"

"I'm sorry that I put you through that. All I had to do was walk away and enjoy the night like everyone else. Instead, I almost messed your life up." Safia blurted on as she squeezed her hands on Mallory's, her words just continuing to leave her mouth as if they had a will of their own.

"Miss Safia, stop. It's okay. You fixed it," assured Mallory.

"Did I?"

"You said that Mr. Jericho got us to stay and all he wanted

in return is for you to be his friend."

No, I couldn't say it then, but I'll say it now. If I hide it now, I'll be making the same mistake again. "Look, Mallory, I'm not sure the word 'friend' means to him the same thing it means to us."

"What?" asked Mallory, looking confused." Then, what does it mean?"

"I honestly don't know. He wasn't very clear. But he wants me to graduate on time, that's for sure. But I don't know what he wants in the meantime. The only thing I'm sure of is that I have to do whatever he says or I'll be expelled."

"What?" asked Hashmi, "But I thought you didn't become his discarded."

"I'm not. At least not how this school thinks of it. But he can probably have me expelled if he wanted. So for now it looks like I'll just have to do as he says."

"Do you... do you think he's like Dario?"

"No... I don't think so. He's... he's self centered, but he's nothing like Dario. I think he... he seems to only care about himself."

"And you think that's not like Dario?" asked Hashmi with a raised brow. "They sound similar to me."

"It's hard to describe. He wants something. I... I just don't have a clue what he really wants from me or why he did what he did? Because he didn't have to, especially after I told him off earlier."

"Maybe he just wants to help but doesn't want to admit it. I've heard that some guys are like that," said Mallory innocently.

Despite her feelings, Mallory's words actually brought a smile to Safia's lips. "I doubt that's all there is to it, but it's a nice thought to have. Either way, I'm sure it's going to be something crazy and not just building more of those damn gazebos."

"Then we will work through it together," said Hashmi.

"I will try to help out however I can. I'm sure we can find a way out of this mess if given enough time to think on it."

"Thanks Hashmi. I wanted to tell you all before about, well... all of it. But all I've done is just end up overthinking everything."

"Yeah, well, all that thinking is making you look like you haven't slept in years."

"Margaretto Hashmi, you have a message from Harmony Davis."

Safia looked confused. "Harmony?"

"We made up last night after you left the stands. And she wants to try and spend time together now," said Hashmi as she reached over, grabbing her pendant and giving it a tap..

"Hey, Hammy," came Harmony's voice from the pendant. "Ah... I'm just calling to check on you and ask if you... Ah... wanted to get lunch today. Just call me back if you want to. If not... then that's fine too."

"I'm surprised you two made up."

"Allah teaches us to forgive. I simply wish to follow suit."

"Does that include Addison as well?"

Hashmi grimaced a moment before she gazed out of the window."That may take a bit more time, but anything is possible... Maybe."

"Who's Hammy?" asked Mallory.

"That's the nickname she has thrust on me," sighed Hashmi. "Ever since she caught me singing that day, she has insisted on calling me that. She views us as a duo called Hammy and Harmony."

Safia smiled at the nickname. "My brother does the same. He's been calling me Saffy ever since we were little. But ours started because he could never pronounce Safia correctly. So he just started calling me Saffy, and he's been doing it ever..." Safia's eyes went wide as her words froze in her mouth.

"Safia?" said Hashmi, with a worried tone in her voice. "What's wrong?"

"He's been…" Safia reached down and grabbed Mallory's hands, freeing herself from her embrace as she slid off the bed, standing in the middle of the room.

"Safia, what's wrong?" repeated Hashmi. "You look like you've seen a ghost."

"It's not… it's," said Safia as the room seemed to start spinning as her mind went off into different directions. Before she even knew what she was doing, she walked over to her closet, grabbing her coat. "I… I'll be back. There's something I need to do." Slipping on her shoes, grabbing her school pendant, and putting her coat on over her pajamas, she hurried out of the door, leaving Hashmi and Mallory looking at each other bewildered.

Safia made her way downstairs and out of the building into the snow, foregoing the usual path of the twisting turns of the spiraling walkway. She sprinted across the snow until once again; she was standing outside of the doors of the communication building with the school's pendant clutched in her hand. She could see her breath escape from her mouth as she clicked on the pendant and brought it up to her lips.

"I… I would like to speak with my family, please."

After a minute or so of standing out in the cold, the doors to the communication room opened once more and out stepped Derrick in his usual three-piece suit.

"Miss Safia, is everything okay? Why are you dressed like that?"

"Hey, I know I look weird, but can I please speak with my family?"

"Of course, it must be important for you to show up dressed like that. Please come inside out of the cold and I'll escort you to a booth," said Derrick, turning around and heading inside, with Safia following behind him. "Is everything okay?"

"I'm not sure," said Safia as they entered the room with the booths. "That's what I want to call and find out."

"I see. Well, you're free to use number five. It's been assigned for you to speak with your family."

Safia walked past all the other empty booths and sat down at number five, as instructed. She placed her hand into the rotary dial and after pulling back; she began to hear the clicking as the phone dialed her family's number. Soon after repeating the process a few times, she heard the sound of ringing, followed by the sound of someone picking up the phone.

"Hello," said Yago, followed by a clicking sound.

"Hey, how's everything going?"

"Oh, hey, Safia, how's everything at that school?"

"It's fine, but Yago, I have something to ask you."

"Sure. Is everything okay?"

"Yeah, everything is fine," said Safia, glancing over at Derrick, who was listening to the call, but fiddling with his tablet. "Hey, Yago, did David tell you that after we graduate, we're going to get married?"

"Huh, no, I didn't know that. But congratulations, I guess."

"Thank you. Now Momma only has to worry about you. One day, you gotta get yourself a girlfriend."

"Maybe one day, but I'm fine just working now. I'll be graduating soon and don't have time to worry about that stuff."

"Yago,"

"Hmmm."

"You're wrong."

"Huh, what do you mean? How am I..."

"You've had a girlfriend for over a year before I came to this school."

There was a moment of silence as Safia turned to Derrick, who was now staring right at her.

"Who is this?" asked Safia, with hatred in her voice, as she stood up from the seat, knocking over the stool in the process. "You have Yago's voice, but you're not my brother.

Who am I speaking to?" There was another long moment of silence as Safia gripped the phone tightly in her hand. "Who is this?" Another moment of silence on the phone before Safia finally lost her patience. "I'm done with your damned games. Answer me."

"Well done, Miss Safia," said a soft femine voice over the phone. "You're only the second person to ever figure out this part of the game."

"Game? This isn't—" Safia shook her head. "I'm done. You hear me? All of this, this whole school is just one big lie. And I'm done; done with all of it."

"No, Miss Safia, I'm afraid you are nowhere near done. We saved your father, so we're going to expect you to keep up your end of the deal. That's what you agreed to."

"You say that, but how do I know that's not another lie? When I call home, how do I know that I'm even talking to my family? Was my father even hurt? You could have made that whole thing up."

There was a moment of silence on the phone.

"Answer me!"

"I guess since you've come this far. I suppose a bit of proof is in order. Congratulations, Miss Safia. We will be sending you home for a week."

"What?" asked Safia, taken aback by the response as she stared down at the phone.

"You wanted proof that we did what we said we did, right? Well, consider this a prize for figuring out half the puzzle. Derrick, are you listening?"

"Yes, Madam,"

Madam? That wasn't Champ Champ's voice. Who am I talking to?

"Please ensure that Miss Safia is sedated and sent back home, safe and sound. I suspect allowing her to have a week at home should suffice as a decent reward for her troubles."

"Yes, Madam," said Derrick, standing up, then stepping towards Safia, placing his hand on Safia's shoulder. "Come with me and we'll—"

"Wait, please," said Safia, stepping back away from Derrick, stretching the cord of the phone as far as it would go. "Not yet, I… I… can't leave Mallory. If I'm gone, she won't be able to do anything."

There was another long pause as Derrick stood there, staring at her.

"Derrick," said the voice. "We're also allowing Miss Safia to escort two roommates home with her. Both Margaretto Hashmi and Mallory Polana, if they decide to join her."

"You are very generous, madam."

"Aren't I," said the woman with a chuckle. "It's always good to reward hard work. So, I think we can be a little generous here, especially since we allowed the other one who figured it out to marry our little head-mistress."

"That was a surprise, when you allowed it to happen?"

"He won the bet, and we had to honor it?"

"Speaking of which," said Derrick, turning his attention back towards Safia. "Are you satisfied with your prize, or do you wish to gamble it or make another bet?"

"I'm… satisfied. I know you'd find some way to screw me over if I didn't take it."

"You seem to have such little faith in us here," said the woman on the phone.

"Faith is earned, and I won't believe another word out of your mouths until I see my father."

"Then it seems we have a deal?"

"Yes, but only if my father is okay and you aren't making this up."

"Derrick." spoke the voice.

"Yes, madam?"

"Let Miss Safia pass and go back to her dorm and inform their friends that they will be taking a trip. I imagine they will be very excited. Since no one has ever left this school before it was their time."

Derrick stepped aside, exposing a path to the exit.

"You're free to go, Miss Safia."

"Oh, and Miss Safia," said the woman's voice over the phone. "I shouldn't have to tell you to keep what you discovered here a secret. Or I simply might not be able to promise that you and your little friends the safety and security of a life without interference."

"Your interference."

"I'm glad we understand each other. Enjoy your week back at home, Safia Famosa, because when you return, then the game will continue," said the woman, and just like that, the call ended. The only thing left behind was the dial tone that drummed in Safia's ear.

"Congratulations, Miss Safia, for figuring out this part of the game," said Derrick, as he walked back to the door, waiting for her to follow.

Safia stared back at Derrick before looking back at the phone in her hand. The dial tone was still sounding off, drumming over and over. She frowned down at it before dropping the head piece in disgust. "Who was that? Why even pretend to be my family."

"It wasn't pretending," said Derrick, as he rubbed at his chin. "You did indeed talk to your family. Just with a bit of manipulation on both ends."

"But why?"

"Why indeed, Miss Safia. Very few things at this school are what they appear to be."

Safia shook her head, exhaustion and frustration finally consuming her. *I'm just so done with all of this.* "When can I go home?"

"Whenever you decide you're ready. Of course we would need to make the proper preparations to get you all ready for—"

"I won't be sedated again."

"You will," said Derrick with assurance. "I'm afraid there's no choice on that matter. While we will accommodate some of your desires, there are certain things that are not negotiable. And risking the exposure of this school's location is one of those things."

"And if I refuse?"

"You have won, Miss Safia. Do not taint this victory by overplaying your hand. I imagine Mallory and Hashmi both would find it terribly uncomfortable to find themselves expelled because of your actions."

"Is that all you people know how to do is threaten others."

"On the contrary; what you see as a threat, we see as protection. Now come along," said Derrick as he turned and walked out of the door, back into the hallway with Safia reluctantly following behind him.

Safia bit her lip as she made her way back through the tiled room into the hallway, where the main doors opened and she stepped back outside into the morning light. She then turned around to see Derrick staring at her.

"What? What now?"

"Don't look so distraught by your situation, Miss Safia. I assure you that you are in very good one."

"You say that like it matters one bit. You and whoever that was are the ones controlling all of this. So it's not like I can really do anything, is there?"

Derrick stepped back with a smile as the doors began to close on him. "Well, there is that old saying after all."

"And what's that?"

"The house always wins."

CHAPTER 19

A week later, Safia awoke at the airport inside the cabin of a plane. Her body felt sluggish as she opened her eyes, trying to focus through the stream of bright light shining in through the cabin's windows. She moaned as control of her body returned to her from what must have been the hours that she was out. Clenching her teeth she focused ahead as she struggled to lift herself from her seat only to notice that in front of her sat a man whose face seemed familiar to her. He sat calm in the seat with a book in his hand as he flipped over a page.

"Wha... Where am..."

"Oh, you're awake," said the man as he closed his book and leaned forward. "Welcome back to the land of the living, Miss Safia. Your friends should be coming around soon."

"Wha... friends?" murmured Safia as she sat up in the seat, supporting herself with her arms. She then nervously looked around the cabin, noticing Hashmi and Mallory in the seats adjacent to her and the man ahead of her. Safia blinked, trying to remember as the past day's events flooded back into her mind. Remembering the school and the events that lead to her coming home, she turned back to the man, looking confused. She had seen him before, but her mind was still in a daze.

"Have you already forgotten me? I guess I don't really make much of an impression on people."

Suddenly, Safia's mind flashed back to the diner with her father, "You're... you're the one who got me into the school, the one who was sitting down with Mr. Alvarez."

"Indeed, I am. My name is James Adams, and it's a pleasure to meet you again."

"Why are you... Am I... am I home?"

"Why, I'm here to pick you up. And yes, you are home. Well at the airport at least. Your family is waiting to see you. We couldn't ask your father to come since he's still in his recovery. So, I offered my assistance to him, in that I would come to receive you and deliver you safely into his arms." He then turned to Hashmi and Mallory, who were beginning to stir from their slumber. "Although, I'm sure he's going to be surprised to be receiving so many guests."

"Why?"

"Hummm?"

"Why me? Why did you ever pick me for that damned school?"

"Oh, that. In truth, they were recruiting Yago. By the way, he should be on his way to the school at this very moment."

"What?" asked Safia, sitting up in her seat. *Those bastards, they didn't. Dammit, Yago why... wait. He shouldn't have graduated yet. How... stupid Yago. Don't you already know the type of place that is?*

"It seems he's managed to graduate half a year early. I think he meant for it to be a surprise. I had to rush to get everything cleared for him. Your brother is apparently quite exceptional. Wait, did you not enjoy your time at the school?"

Wait? Does he not know about the school? "No, I mean, it was really hard, is all. So many classes and tests," said Safia as she rubbed the side of her face in frustration. *I need to be careful what I say.* She looked around the cabin of the plane again, this time looking for any of those small black orbs that she noticed around the campus but couldn't find any. *I know they're listening. There's no way they aren't.*

"Ha! Welcome to the real world, my dear. I promise it's going to be much harder after graduation."

"Mr. Adams, have you ever been to the school?" asked Safia, turning her attention back to the man in front of her.

"Me? Goodness no. They just hire me to recruit people. But it was surprising when they asked for me to replace people like they did with you."

But Yago knew about the school. If this man didn't tell him about the school, then who did? Was it Mr. Alvarez?

Hashmi and Mallory continued to worm around in their seats.

"Oh, they're finally waking up. I swear, I tried to shake you girls and call you names, but you were just dead to the world. The pilot just said to let you all rest because of the jet lag."

Pilot? Safia lifted herself up on the seat, turning around and staring towards the cockpit of the plane. But while the door was open and she could see part of the control terminal, she didn't see anyone in the pilot's seat. *I didn't see the pilot last time either. It... it was just Addison in the stewardess's outfit.* She then turned back to Mr. Adams. "You said you met the pilot. Was it the same pilot as before?"

Mr. Adams looked at Safia confused. "Yeah, I don't know any other pilots the school has had. He's been the pilot for as long as I've worked for them. Why? Is something wrong?"

"What? No? *So it's a man. Either way, that means that someone here knows exactly where that school is and how to get to it.* "I just wanted to thank him. Usually we clap our hands after a landing, so I thought it would be a good thing to thank the pilot since it's only us here."

"Oh, well, I'll inform him that you would like to meet him next time. Maybe you all can have a chat before take off on your next flight."

"I'd appreciate that." *Maybe I can find something out from him. But I still need to find a way to not be put asleep when I go back.*"

Soon, all three girls were fully awake with Mr. Adams. He then escorted them through the airport and over to a car that he had waiting. They all engaged in small talk about their classes with Mr. Adams as Mallory and Hashmi just gazed out of the window, with Safia pointing out any interesting things they'd happened to ask about on their way into the city. Soon the familiar concrete and dirty air of the city filled Safia's lungs. The smell provided her with a final sense of realness and comfort that she realized she hadn't felt since she first left for the Academy.

"After talking it over with your father, Safia, I've arranged for you girls to have a hotel room for your stay here. I hope you enjoy yourselves," said Mr. Adams, hanging up his phone as they approached her family's restaurant.

Safia got out of the car to see her mother and father waiting for her through the restaurant's window. They both came out of the bar with smiles on their faces. She felt a ping in her chest as she watched her father walking out with a crutch.

"There's my baby," said Mr. Famosa as he hobbled his

way forward and wrapped his arms around his daughter. "You know you just missed your brother. He was going to surprise you, but I guess he's the one who's going to be surprised when he gets there and finds you've come home."

"Papa, are you okay? Does it hurt?"

"Ah, look at my baby worrying over her papa. But don't worry about me. In just a little while, I'll be as good as new. If you wanna feel sorry for someone, feel sorry for the guy who tried to rob me. Because I messed him up good. Coming into my home and trying to take what he wants. That bastard got what he deserved! I'll tell you that."

"Your father likes to tell the story about how he protected his family and restaurant from the lone gunman," said Safia's mother, kissing her husband.

"That's because I did. But enough about me. What about you? You leave for school all nervous and shaky, and then you come back with your girlfriends? Well, go on. Introduce them to your mother and me."

"Oh, sorry," said Safia, turning around to her friends. "This is Hashmi and Mallory."

"Hello," said Mallory with a smile.

"Hello, sir, I'm pleased to meet you," said Hashmi.

"Oh, she's one of them Muslim girls with the hats. Well, don't worry. We got them here too."

"Papa!" shouted Safia in embarrassment.

"It's alright. Your father seems to be quite the lively character."

"Oh, and she speaks all proper too," said Mr. Famosa. "Well, I would invite you girls into our home, but it's already getting late. I just wanted to see my baby when she got here. I would let you all stay the night here, but your mother said you should get a hotel."

"We're not going to have the girls sleeping on the floor. We don't have enough room for them," said Safia's mother. "And besides, David's getting everything straight at the hotel now. You girls can head over there for the night."

"Nonsense. One of them can take Yago's room. He ain't here to use it. And the other one could just sleep in the bed with Safia. They're girls, after all."

"I wouldn't mind that," said Mallory in an anxious tone that made Safia turn back to look at her. "I mean, hotels are expensive and all. You might need to save some money."

"It's okay. We still have a little more saved up from my insurance plan."

"Apparently, your father was part of some type of Apex Life insurance policy, and they've been helping us out since he's got out of the hospital."

"Apex Life insurance?"

"Yeah, apparently it's part of the insurance I had when I insured the restaurant. The man said it covered burglary, theft, and all kinds of stuff. Your brother and David have been handling most of the day-to-day stuff now, though."

"Wait, you said, David's still here?" asked Safia.

"Huh, oh yeah. He's still doing them online classes so that he can help us out," said Mr. Famosa, shaking his head. "The boy should just go back already, I'm fine now."

"You should be happy that he's been around so much," said Mrs. Famosa. "He and Yago kept everything going when you were out."

"Yeah, but it feels weird having that white boy watching me all the time. All that, 'Can I get you some water, Mr. Famosa? Can I help you down the stairs, Mr. Famosa?' I get it. You and Safia are all lovey-dovey. Damn boy, should just start calling me Pa," said Hector, looking towards his daughter. "Safia, just hurry up and marry him and get him out of my house."

"Papa, stop," said Safia as she noticed the smirk on Hashmi's face.

"What? What did I say? It's not like we don't know it. That white boy is looking after a Cuban and an African. Something's wrong with his head. You know, we even tried to put him in the kitchen, but he never used the right spices.

Everything just tasted like dirt. He was gonna run us out of business."

"Hector! Stop that! You're embarrassing the girl," said Safia's mother with a smile. "Come on. I'm sure they're tired after their trip here. Let's let them go get their sleep, and we can see them tomorrow."

"Alright, you girls have fun," said Hector as he hugged his daughter once more, kissing Safia on her forehead. "I'll see you tomorrow, honey."

"Okay, papa."

The girls said their goodbyes to Mr. and Mrs. Famosa and allowed Mr. Adams to escort them to the hotel. When they arrived, they discovered it was fancier than they had expected.

"I'll take your keys, sir," said the valet as they approached and stepped out of the car.

"My father paid for this?"

"Well, your father thinks he paid for a simple hotel about two miles from here. But I contacted David earlier and asked him to make reservations at a more respectable establishment. The school insisted that you were treated properly while you were home."

"This place is all types of fancy," said Mallory as she watched the people walk by in their expensive-looking clothing. "That one even has a dog in her purse."

"Come on then, let's go and get you checked in," said Mr. Adams, leading them inside.

The hotel was spotless, with its marble pillars, velvet furniture, and a large red carpet that led up to the front desk.

"Hello, I think I have a reservation."

"Yes, sir, and what name would it be under?"

"Ahh, under my name. James Adams."

"Yes, your rooms are ready, here's your key card, the unoccupied one is three fifteen. You can leave your bags here, and they will be brought up to your rooms shortly."

"Thank you," said Mr. Adams, taking the key and handing it to Safia. "Well, you girls enjoy your night. I'll be heading back now. Safia, I'll call up to your room tomorrow and take you back to your family."

"Yes, sir, thank you," said Safia as the girls all said their goodbyes to Mr. Adams, dropping their bags off at the front desk as a man shuffled them into a cart. They then took the elevator to their room, where Safia walked down the hall and swiped the key card at the door. Inside, the room was just as beautiful as the rest of the hotel. Soft cream carpet floors that lead up to two large beds with satin sheets. And on each of their sides sat colorful flowers in large vases. The girls walked in with Mallory going over and jumping on one of the beds.

"Oh, it feels so soft," said Mallory, bouncing on the sheets and looking over the room. "I wonder how much it costs to even stay here."

"Probably, more than my family makes in a week," said Safia, closing the door and walking in, placing her back against the wall, "Judging from the people we saw walking in and out of here."

"You don't seem happy to be home, Safia," said Hashmi. "I thought you would be more excited to see that your father was okay."

"I am. I needed to make sure he was okay. But it's just…"

"It has something to do with us being here, doesn't it?"

Safia bit her lip, looking at Hashmi.

"I understand if you can't tell us. But it doesn't take a genius to notice that something happened. One minute you run out of the door in your pajamas, then an hour later you tell us that we will be able to leave the campus and visit your home. I don't know what type of situation you've gotten yourself in. But it must be big to get all three of us off campus."

"I've been wondering about that too," said Mallory, sitting up on the bed. "But I've been too afraid to ask."

"If I could, I promise I would tell you both everything," said Safia, looking up at the ceiling, "But this... this I'm not allowed to share with anyone. I'll lose everything. And not just me, but both of you, too. And I won't put you both at risk any more than I already have."

"Fine," said Hashmi, shaking her head and walking over to Safia, placing a hand on her shoulder. "I've messed up already by asking you to expose your secret to me. I won't make that mistake again. I trust you, Safia."

"Thank you," said Safia, placing her hand on top of Hashmi's.

"But have you decided what you're going to do when we go back? You said we only have a week here and I doubt they will just let you go. Because I'm sure whatever you did to get us here will have a lot of people looking at you when we get back, if they find out."

"Honestly, I've been trying to—"

"Hey, what are these?" asked Mallory as she opened up a cabinet near the bed.

"What's what?" asked Safia as both she and Hashmi turned to look.

"There's little baggies in here with our names on them."

"What?" asked Safia as she came over to look with Hashmi. And indeed, inside the cabinet were three bags with tags that had their names written on them.

"I wonder who left these," said Hashmi, grabbing the bag with her name on it and looking at Safia.

"Don't look at me," said Safia, raising her hands in defense, "I was never told about this."

"Let's find out what's inside then," said Mallory as she sat back on the bed and opened up the bag. "Oh... it's so cute," she said, pulling out a large red and white panda bear. "I wonder who sent it. You think it was the school?"

"I guess it could be, but why?" asked Hashmi as she sat down with her own bag, reaching inside, and pulling out a large brown teddy bear with a white belly. "Well, it certainly is cute. Although, I have no idea why we have them. What did you get, Safia?"

Safia opened her bag, reached in, and pulled out a large rubber inflatable alligator. "What in the world? What is this?"

"That certainly doesn't match. I was guessing it'd be a polar bear or something," said Hashmi as Safia handed her the inflatable gator.

"Well, I'm from Florida. Maybe it was meant for me," said Mallory, looking at the rubber gator with a smile on its face.

"But it has Safia's name on it," said Mallory, squeezing the rubbery gator, causing an odd stretching sound. "You think they made a mistake?" she said, turning to Safia, who was looking in the bag. "Did you get anything else?"

"Huh," said Safia, looking down into her bag. "Oh... no, nothing else. What about you two?"

"Nothing."

"No, just the teddy bear."

"I'm going to ask the front desk if they know who put these in our room," said Safia as she walked towards the door. "I'll be right back."

"Okay," said Mallory and Hashmi.

Safia exited their room, closing the door with the bag in her hand. Walking down the hall, she reached into the bag and pulled out a pair of pink handcuffs and a key card. *Don't think about the school. Don't think about Yago. I'll talk to him when I get back. My father is safe. That's all that matters. I have one week at home and I plan to enjoy it.* She continued down the hall, stopping at door three twenty-two. Swiping the card, she opened the door, stepping inside. Closing it behind her, she walked past the bathroom, stopping at the corner, resting her shoulder against the wall.

"A rubber alligator, really?"

"Well, I figured the other girls would need something to keep them company tonight," said David, sitting on the bed.

"And who's going to keep me company?"

"Come over here and let's find out."

"And what about these," said Safia, raising her hand, letting the fluffy, pink handcuffs dangle on her finger.

"Sometimes, the company you keep can be rough."

Safia shook her head with a giggle on her lips. *God, he's a corny idiot. But I guess he's my corny idiot.* Taking a look down at David with that familiar grin on his face with his soft eyes that had always watched her. The memories of him comforting her began to come back to her, and she could feel all her worries wash away. *Whatever. The rest of the world can wait till tomorrow. But tonight, I need this.* Safia smirked, walking over to the bed, and leaned over, giving David a kiss. "You know, after everything I've been through. I think I deserve a bit of rough company."

David wrapped his arms around Safia's waist, dragging her down to the bed on top of him. Their lips playfully teased each other as they savored the moment.

"Was college really that hard on you?"

"It was awful. More than I could ever explain," said Safia, as she embraced the feeling of David's hand over her thigh, pressing against her clothing. "Lucky for me, I have you here to make me feel better."

David raised his hand and began caressing Safia's face. He embraced her soft brown skin, drinking in her dark eyes as they focused on her in the dim lighting of a nearby lamp shade. Allowing his thumb to gently slide over the corner of her lips, he placed his hand on her ass.

"That's funny. And here I could have sworn it was me, who was the lucky one."

445

THANK YOU

for enrolling in APEX ACADEMY. The current semester has ended and winter break has arrived. Please look forward to returning, when classes resume for the next year.

If you enjoyed this story and are interested in more novels from this author. Please visit:
www.TeddyBaire.com
for more info.

This book is part of my 10 book project. My bucketlist goal is to write 10 novels in different genres. I hope that some of them are an entertaining read for you.

www.ingramcontent.com/pod-product-compliance
Lightning Source LLC
Chambersburg PA
CBHW050848210726
48290CB00004B/1130